WYOMING

A NOVEL

RICHARD G. TUTTLE

Cat's Paw Publishing, Inc.
P.O. Box 385
Spring House, PA 19477

Cat's Paw Publishing will be happy to assist you in bringing the author of this work to your live event. Please contact us at our email address set forth above.

Print ISBN: 978-1-09835-972-0
eBook ISBN: 978-1-09835-973-7

Printed in the United States of America on SFI Certified paper.

First Edition

For Lucie

PART I

CHAPTER 1

Coolidge, Wyoming, is not a picturesque place – like most towns in the American High Plains, it's for living in, not for postcards – but it's simple and clean. Like Denver, it's mostly rolling prairie when you look east, and mountains when you look west. You don't have to look very far west; the Bighorn Mountains begin, in earnest, three miles west of town. The sun reflects off the peaks in the west before it begins to warm front porches in Coolidge.

With a population of about 2,800, Coolidge ranks 29th in population among Wyoming's cities and towns. A little smaller than Kemmerer, where J.C. Penney Company was founded, and a little bigger than Glenrock. There's a public library, eight small churches, three bank branches, an Ace Hardware store, four bars, and six places where you can get a bite to eat, none of them fancy. The supermarket is an Albertson's. There are no stoplights. Kids play mostly unsupervised in the playgrounds, and in fifty fields and lots around town – which is not a reproach to the rest of the country, it's just the way it is.

Like many towns in Wyoming, there are no outskirts to speak of. The streets end, and empty prairie begins. Wild is always trying to get in. Mule deer, in groups of five or six, wander through everyone's front and back yards, and in September, they eat a lot of fallen crabapples. The fawns study the humans who pass by.

Coolidge straddles U.S. Route 14, about eight miles west of Interstate 90, and about eighteen miles west of Sheridan. Sheridan, population 18,000, is Wyoming's sixth largest city. It's where you go for anything you can't find in Coolidge. The Montana state line is nine miles north of the center of Coolidge; the quickest way to get there is to go to the Interstate and turn left. Wyoming

Highway 343 heading north will also work, but it's slower, and usually full of farm machinery.

The town has an elementary school, a middle school, and a high school, all grouped together, and all in the town itself. None has more than a hundred and sixty students. There is no police force in Coolidge, just the Sheridan County Sheriff, or, in a pinch, the Wyoming Highway Patrol. There is a Mayor and five town council members, which is more government than most residents of Coolidge believe they need, until the weekly trash collection is late.

The town was not named for Silent Cal Coolidge, 30th President of the United States. According to old records that are available for examination, but not circulation, at the library, Coolidge was named for Sherman Coolidge, an Episcopal priest who proselytized the Arapaho in the nineteenth century. Father Coolidge was Arapaho himself, so in a sense, Coolidge, Wyoming, is a little like Geronimo, Oklahoma, or Cochise, Arizona. Seattle, Washington, for that matter.

Like a thousand small towns in Pennsylvania, Ohio, or Indiana, Coolidge has no reason to be. There is no key industry, no large employer, no railroad or highway junction. If Coolidge was once a trailhead for bringing logs out of the Bighorns, no one alive remembers that to be the case. The town exists because the people there enjoy what they have. By and large, the people who are there stay put, and some people, like Patrick Flaherty, come to Coolidge and don't leave.

CHAPTER 2

Patrick Flaherty was making his way across an alfalfa field, toward the dry grass. A few Prairie Blazing Stars were still blooming, up as far as the tree line. He was feeling the upward pitch of the ground as he walked over a rise, but he was used to it. At six foot one, and 175 pounds, Patrick was lean and in good shape. He had dark hair which was usually a little long – he cut it himself -- and Irish-blue eyes. He was 29 years old and one hundred and seventy five years removed from County Galway.

It was early September, and he knew the antelope would be alert. Their eyesight is good, and they would be watching for hunters. Patrick had drawn a good lottery number, and was carrying an "All Antelope" resident hunting license for Antelope Area 109 in the pocket of his hunting vest. Bagging an antelope would mean two things: meat for a few days, and protein that he could grind into an additive for his chicken feed. He unlimbered his rifle -- a Winchester Model 1873 -- and found a depression in the grass near where he'd seen a small herd for the past four or five days. He settled in the grass, checking automatically for rattlers, and waited.

The Model 1873 had been in almost continuous production for a century and a half, and his was new when his dad gave it to him for his high school graduation. The rifle, a lever-action carbine, was chambered in .38/.357, which meant that it fired pistol ammunition. The idea, back in 1873, was that a cowboy would be better-served by the Winchester Repeating Arms Company if he could carry just one kind of cartridge for his rifle and his six-shooter. That still made sense to Patrick. He was able to use .357 ammunition for larger game, and .38 Special for turkeys and any small game that had sufficiently poor judgment to be standing still when he came within fifty yards. Another advantage was that the .38 Special and .357 Magnum are relatively inexpensive loads, and Patrick's friends would often toss him a box, just because. And his dad would always make sure that he put six or eight boxes under the Christmas tree every year, back in Colorado.

Patrick left the field three hours later carrying a smallish doe. With every step, there were ten grasshoppers swirling around his calves. The ground was firm. He didn't have far to move the carcass -- Patrick's home was about a mile away on Hamm's Hill, near Water Creek, Allen's Pond, and the lower slope of Big Pine Mountain. Water Creek was a translation of two Shoshone words meaning "water" and "creek." To Patrick's knowledge, the Shoshone were not unusually prone to redundancy; perhaps something had been lost in the translation. The stream flowed across the boundary of the Bighorn National Forest into Wyoming state lands and private lands, through Allen's Pond, and into the Tongue River.

Back in his cabin, Patrick added wood to the fire in the stove. He went outside to the deer hoist, and cleaned the antelope for a good part of the afternoon. He had learned to clean animals by trial and error, and had no idea whether there were simpler ways than the ones he used. But cleaning game was not a major part of his day or week, and he saw no need to become more efficient.

He'd been in his cabin for about six and a half years. He and his friend Stanley had discovered it, dilapidated and overgrown, during a hunting trip. Patrick decided, virtually on the spot, that he was going to fix it up and move in, and in the years since he had gradually made it more livable.

Equally important, he learned how to keep himself alive. He couldn't reasonably live by hunting alone: antelope, rabbit and pheasant weren't enough. He acquired his first few Nubian goats and Orpington chickens as gifts from neighbors. There was always an animal that didn't get along with the rest, so his neighbors were happy to help. Mrs. Vogel gave him most of the chickens, and Eric Dormer gave him five goats. Orpingtons were ideal because they liked cold weather, and were good for both eggs and eating. His chickens free-ranged for the most part, as did the goats. Patrick built a goat pen out of wire fencing he got from a friend, Harry Detmer. He found that his goats would follow him onto the hill to scavenge, but wanted to be back in the pen when he went back inside. Patrick locked his goats in the goat house and his hens in the henhouse when he went into town, and while he slept, to protect them from coyotes and cougars.

Patrick didn't have a paying job. To the extent he needed to buy things, he took it from the $100 a month his parents sent him, in cash. Clothes, boots, and shoes were available almost for free at the Salvation Army Thrift Store in Sheridan, and Patrick made sure to ask to ride along whenever someone was driving over. While he was in Sheridan, toiletries, kitchen utensils and household items were available at the Dollar Tree. He could brush his teeth, shave, and bathe for twenty dollars a year, and buy kitchen gadgets and household tools for another twenty.

Thursday afternoon had turned into Thursday evening. Patrick was tired, and he began to get ready for bed at 9:30. He had to do some driving for Harry at noon on Friday, and of course there would be Happy Hour at Cousin Clem's at 5:00. But he was really thinking more about Saturday.

CHAPTER 3

Ray Bando, Ray Tillson, Toby Ernst and Patrick Flaherty were sitting at one of the back booths in The 14 Diner on Saturday morning. Ainslee Abbott, Ray Bando's girlfriend, was waiting on them, which meant that Ray and Ainslee had to finish their argument from Thursday night before Ainslee would take their order. But they did, finally, and she did, finally. Ray, Ray and Toby ordered big breakfasts. Patrick ordered just an English muffin.

Patrick, Ray, Ray and Toby were Four Toe Joe. When Ray, Ray and Toby played country rock on Friday nights at Cousin Clem's, they played as Three Toe Joe -- Ray Bando on lead guitar, Ray Tillson on bass, and Toby on drums. Patrick played rhythm guitar when they were Four Toe Joe. There were a lot of reasons that Four Toe Joe became Three Toe Joe on Fridays. First, the stage at Cousin Clem's could only fit three musicians. Second, Patrick knew more songs than anyone else, so he could do a solo gig at Cousin Clem's from 5:00 to 7:00. Third, Patrick could man the sound board later in the night, while the other three were playing. And fourth, they had all the equipment they needed, for the time being.

The fourth reason – equipment – was the subject of that morning's discussion. The issue was whether to buy a bigger PA head. They'd been using a 300-watt powered mixer for a couple of years, and they didn't *need* a bigger head, strictly speaking. But, as Ray Tillson pointed out, why wouldn't you *want* one?

Their discussion was animated. The 14 was full, however, so nobody really noticed the sound from their booth. The 14 was always full on Saturday mornings. It sat on the north side of U.S. Route 14, smack in the middle of Coolidge, and their Western omelets were famous from Sheridan to Lovell, and halfway up to Billings. They even put "Famous Western Omelet" on the sign out front. Mindy was in her usual spot behind the front counter, directing traffic.

"It's good to have a backup PA, anyway," said Ray Tillson, "and we can always turn the power down on the new one when we're in a smaller room." Ainslee came over with their food, and they passed plates to where they were supposed to go. She was wearing jeans with little diamond studs on the back pockets, which were a nice touch, given how hard her job was.

"I just think we need lighting more," said Toby. "We look half dead most of the time, and I think it affects how we're perceived."

"Perceived?" said Ray Bando. "Dude, are you fucking with me?"

"The other thing we're going to need to do at some point is upgrade the mics and mic stands," said Patrick.

"Three more gigs and we'll have enough to do *something*," said Ray Tillson. Ray was calculating one quarter shares from the gig money for the next three Saturday engagements for Four Toe Joe. The way it worked, Ray, Ray and Toby would take a share, and then Patrick's share was re-contributed to the pot, and saved for new equipment. Toby kept the accumulating cash in an old cigar box on his dresser at home. On average, all four of them played together about one or two times a month, mostly private parties or barbeques. They had tried for a couple of years to get Patrick to accept the cash, but he wouldn't, so they gave up.

"What time are we due at the field?" asked Toby. He directed the question to Patrick, who played shortstop on their softball team.

"Noon, I think," replied Patrick. That particular Saturday, September 12, was the day of the 12th annual Montana vs. Colorado Softball Classic. The Montana vs. Colorado Softball Classic was the reason that Patrick had been looking forward to Saturday for most of the week. In the spring, there was a six-team league in Coolidge, with the rosters all formed from a common draft. The fall game, however, pitted players from the north side of Route 14 against players from the south side of Route 14. The game used to be called the "North-South Classic," but there were accusations that the North was bringing down ringers from Montana, and the South, it was claimed, responded by bringing in ringers from as far away as Colorado. Patrick and Toby both played for

"Montana," and had T-shirts from the past five or six years to prove it. There was a guy across the room, Ed or Ted or Ned, they weren't sure, wearing an old "Colorado" T-shirt.

"I'll pick you up at ten of," said Toby.

The discussion turned back to music, and then to the Broncos. Patrick sort of wished he were hunting, but Montana vs. Colorado was a priority. Ainslee came with the bill, and Ray, Ray and Toby tossed in. Patrick reached for his wallet. "Pat, we've got it. English muffins don't count."

As they filed out of The 14, Patrick bumped into his old girlfriend, Doreen Parsons. He said, "See you guys later," to the other three, and turned back to talk to her. She looked happy; he hadn't seen her in a couple of months. She was dating someone from Ranchester she'd met online, and she filled him in on some of the details.

As they parted, Patrick was struck by a thought. After this kind of chance encounter, and if he were just like everybody else, they'd talk on the phone, or text, and figure out a time to sit down for coffee and catch up. But Patrick didn't have a phone. So it was like, "Take care of yourself," and "Yeah, take care," kisses on the cheek, and that was it.

Patrick headed back up toward his place. He had enjoyed bumping into Doreen, and he was glad there were no hard feelings. When Patrick cared about somebody, he didn't really stop. The breakup wasn't fun, but there was no reason to carry bad feelings around afterwards. Patrick had an hour to gather some firewood before he'd have to get ready for softball.

CHAPTER 4

The game was anticlimactic. Montana took a 6-0 lead after the first inning, and Colorado, despite some guys hitting the ball hard and far, kept ruining their rallies with pop-ups and strike-outs. In the fourth inning, Montana added another three runs. Colorado finally scored in the bottom of the fourth, but the score was 9-2 at the end of the inning.

During the fifth inning, a player from Montana and a player from Colorado started shoving each other after a collision at second base. The umpire, Mr. Paul, told them to cut it out, and they did. Patrick and Toby weren't really sure whether "Paul" was Mr. Paul's first name or last. He was 94 years old, and it seemed impertinent to ask him directly. Mr. Paul lived with his daughter and her husband on Buffalo Street, and once played Triple-A ball for the Buffalo Bisons – they of Buffalo, New York, not Buffalo, Wyoming.

Because it was September, and because the 40-man roster rule was therefore in effect, there was a lot of substitution in the final four innings. Colorado caught up a little, but the final score was 13-7, Montana. The post-game picnic lasted until sundown. Mr. Paul told baseball stories, and everyone talked about people who once lived in Coolidge, but who had since died. Mark Grable told the story, that never got old, about how he once finished in the top ten in calf roping at the Wyo Rodeo. The grill chef, Clem Labrecque, did not have any trouble getting people to eat the Angus burgers (in Wyoming, most cattle, and most beef, is Angus), and, unlike last year, the beer held out pretty much to the end. Patrick Flaherty had to leave a little early to get to Saturday evening Mass, because he knew he was going to be in the mountains on Sunday.

CHAPTER 5

Patrick climbed up the shallow ravine formed by Water Creek. It was early Sunday morning, and he was about two miles northwest of home. The thermometer outside his kitchen area showed 39 degrees when he got up, and would rise to 82 by afternoon. Wyoming in September, in the mountains. Water from the previous night's light rain splashed off the scrub oak onto his clothes, and he was wetter than he would have liked. The stream was noisy, carrying the run-off.

He smelled the carcass before he saw it; the white-tail fawn was scattered in pieces by the stream, with her forelegs, neck and head facing downhill. Her eyes had a frightened look. Or maybe Patrick was projecting. As he reached the carcass, he saw very fresh bear tracks beside the stream, with a set of prints heading back into deeper wood. He wondered if he had interrupted a meal – he involuntarily palmed the bear spray canister on his hip, and squeezed his rifle a little tighter.

Patrick had seen bears occasionally, from a distance, but he had never been confronted by one. If a confrontation happened, the catechism was to face the bear – don't turn and run, or she'd chase you – and back up slowly, yelling. If she charged, bear spray carried for twenty-five feet, and continued for five seconds before the can was empty. Of course, you would probably miss, or the wind could be against you and the spray would come back onto you. After five seconds, at any rate, the bear is chewing on your arm. Your rifle is a discarded metal rod under her foot. Patrick feared bears because he knew that, if he encountered a startled one, a lot had to go right, and nothing was allowed to go wrong, in five seconds.

Crossing the stream to put some distance between himself and the bear, Patrick continued his climb, wondering whether the smell of large animal blood and meat suggested to other mammals, "not a good place to be right now." If so, he was going to have to range farther to find game. There were two big lazy buzzards overhead – let them fight with the bear.

As was the case through most of the Bighorn National Forest, the trees on the side of the big hill were almost entirely conifers. There were plenty of hardwood trees down by Water Creek and the Tongue River, but they didn't climb the mountain. There were clearings on most hills, and game animals wandered in and out of the trees. That meant that the edge of a clearing was often an ideal hide. When he reached one of the clearings on Big Pine Mountain, Patrick spotted a big turkey enjoying the sunshine, fifty yards away. It was an easy shot, but turkey season wouldn't begin for a couple of weeks. No success, and no meat, that morning.

Walking back down toward his cabin, he looked out from the side of the mountain. The rolling, grass-covered hills to the east continued forever. He never tired of the view, and considered himself very lucky to live where he lived.

CHAPTER 6

Father David Hernandez was standing by Mavis D'Antonio's desk at the Rectory in St. Ann's Roman Catholic Church, on Baxter Street in Coolidge. It was Monday morning.

"I don't understand why they won't run the ball," he said. "Third and two and they're throwing twenty yards downfield. You have to expect to lose if you play that way."

Mavis was unimpressed, and said so. "According to the analyst guy, that was a check-down. He didn't set out to throw long."

"They call it Monday-morning quarterbacking for a reason," he said, "but you're doing it backwards. You're Monday-morning defending them, instead of Monday-morning knocking them. Admit it, it was a terrible call. They should have run the ball."

"The Broncos are going to be fine," she said. "The talent is there. I don't know why everybody thinks an 0-2 start is the end of the world."

She stared at him calmly with a "you must be standing at my desk for a reason" look.

"I just got an email from the Diocese approving the LGBT hospitality event," he said, shifting gears. "Lots of work to do in three weeks if we want to be ready."

Mavis rolled her eyes. As Father Dan had learned over the course of ten years, and Father Michael for eight years before that, when Mavis had an opinion, she shared it. Her value as a Parish Administrator was that she charmed everyone and feared no one, including, especially, priests. She called them

"Necessary Nuisances," to their faces and behind their backs. She saw that they had been sent to Coolidge from faraway places to civilize the heathens, and she had no patience for the civilizing process. She straightened them out quickly, and the Diocese knew it needed her where she was. Father Dave had only been at St. Ann's for two years, but like a young Second Lieutenant, he knew who the Master Sergeant was, and he knew when to listen and when to speak.

"We're going to be spending tons of hours for an event that may draw three people, if we're lucky," Mavis said. "I know we're allowed to welcome gay parishioners. But we have to pretend to tell them they have to be celibate. And then they have to pretend they're being celibate. And if all that happens, they can take communion. If we really wanted to be helpful, we'd send them across the street to the Presbyterians. They'd all make Deacon in a week."

"Matthew Shepard died in Wyoming in 1998," said Father Dave, "and I don't think attitudes have budged a millimeter since that day. I think we need to . . ."

"Please don't start again with the cowboy-bashing, Father. Wyomingites don't talk about their sex lives, and you have no idea how many gay people there are in Coolidge. I certainly have no idea, and I grew up here. And they filmed 'Brokeback Mountain' in Wyoming, so there's that."

"No they didn't," he said.

"Look, I know this was probably a big issue in New York at St. Joseph's, or St. John's or whatever the name of your seminary was. I don't mean to be harsh, I really don't, but it seems we may be doing all this because you're lonely. I think you're tired of feeling like the only gay person on the planet."

"You're exactly right," he said. "I *am* doing it because I'm lonely. And so is every other gay person in Sheridan County, male and female. I would like to meet some of them. And I expect they'd like to meet me." When young David Hernandez got stubborn, it always reminded his mother of her father, his grandfather, still living in Puerto Rico. Don't budge an inch, cariño.

Mavis's expression softened. "OK, Father. You're right. We'll get the promotional materials together."

"Do Presbyterians have Deacons?" asked Father Dave.

"I don't know," replied Mavis. "I was on a roll."

“I have a window in my office that won’t close all the way,” said Father Dave. “What’s Patrick’s schedule this week?”

“He’ll be here tomorrow,” replied Mavis, “he’s fixing the shelves in the storage closet, and doing some other things. I expect he’ll be able to get to your window by next week, if we ask.”

“That would be good. Can we talk to him again about paying him some money? I think even a few bucks would be helpful to him.”

“I can try,” replied Mavis, “but he has said ‘no’ at least five times. Give him a discount on an indulgence, he’ll be happy.”

Father Dave laughed. For all of her sharp edges, Mavis was nice to have around.

CHAPTER 7

In September, morning clouds in the Bighorn Mountains rarely last till midday. Patrick was a little surprised that he was still carving his way through mist at 11:00 a.m., only about half a mile from home, near where Water Creek met the Tongue River. A few larger trees had begun to turn color, but the smaller vegetation was still green. He reached a circular clearing he knew well, mostly rocks. He waited with his shotgun for a rabbit.

A large branch cracked loudly off to his left. Something – he was guessing a set of antlers – was pushing through the brush toward the clearing. The sound was about 150 feet away. He was waiting for a deer to stick its nose out of the vegetation. Nothing moved.

Patrick realized that he was upwind from the noise, and he expected that whatever had caused the sound could smell him. The stillness lasted for most of a minute, animal and human both waiting for the other to move first. Finally, Patrick saw a shape moving through the brush at the edge of the clearing, heading away from him. Still thinking deer, he saw black fur, four feet above the ground. He felt a surge of adrenaline, realizing the shape he saw had to have been a black bear.

Twice in a week.

CHAPTER 8

It was Friday night at 8:00. Every seat at Cousin Clem's was filled, people were two-deep at the bar, and conversations were shouted. Maybe a hundred people. Two-and-a-half percent of the population of Coolidge, by Pat's math, although he knew he wasn't accounting for people who might have come in from inner- and outer-ring suburbs. But there weren't any – suburbs, that is -- so he stuck with his original calculation.

Clem's sound system behind the bar was playing country music, but it was drowned out by all the people. On average, the people at Clem's were happier on Friday than they were on Wednesday or Thursday. Work was done for the week.

The bar was big and L-shaped. There were fifteen seats running down the long side, and four seats around the corner to the right, as you were facing. There was a small stage set in the back wall, so that the patron in the last seat at the toe of the "L," could swivel all the way around, look a little left, and enjoy the best seat in the house, five feet from the show. Three Toe Joe was setting up, and Patrick had finished his solo set an hour before. There was a 20 x 20 dance floor out in front of the stage, and tables at the back of the dance floor. In the corner across the room from the stage there was a pinball machine, a video poker game, and a dart board.

The entrance to Clem's was in the middle of the wall facing the bar. There was an outside door and then an inside door, with an alcove-y kind of thing between the doors to keep the weather out. There were a couple of rows of tables between the door and the bar. The bathrooms were all the way to the left as you came in, and the door to the kitchen was between the bathrooms and the end of the bar. The kitchen served burgers, hot sausages on rolls, chicken Caesar wraps, chicken fingers, Buffalo wings, French fries, basic sandwiches, a soup of the day, and pie and ice cream for dessert.

Two bartenders, Clem and Syrena, worked the weekend crowd. If they started to get behind, Claire, Clem's wife and co-owner, would come out of the kitchen and help pour drinks. Olivia and Edie made the food. The names and identities of the two servers working the tables varied, but they were always teenaged daughters or sons of regulars. There was one dishwasher – Silent Al, who smoked Kools outside on his break, in any weather. Patrick was carrying something out back for Claire one night, when he stumbled over Al's ankles. They started talking, and Al surprised Patrick with some observations about east-Asian art. Patrick wasn't surprised that Al knew about east-Asian art. He was surprised that Al had said anything at all. Al, like Pat, was single and lived alone. He had been stationed in Okinawa in the 70's.

The four seats on the short side of the "L" were referred to collectively as the "dais." On an ordinary night, the dais held only First Cousins, patrons who had been with Clem since the day he opened thirty years ago. Cousins who had been flagged and ejected were referred to, of course, as "First-Cousins-once-removed," or "First-Cousins-twice-removed." Clem's was not Chicago, and the First Cousins weren't jerkoffs. If you were new to the bar and you sat in one of their seats, you'd get an earful of stories everyone else had heard a million times, but they wouldn't ask you to move.

Second Cousins were long-time regulars who sat on the long side of the bar. Pat had only been coming to Clem's for seven years, but he considered himself a Second Cousin.

This was a mid-September Friday, the 18th. Patrick picked up his conversation with Harry where it had left off the day before, each shouting in the other's ear to get over the sound of the music.

"Fuck if I know why the Broncos didn't draft a cover corner. They're getting killed deep." Harry Detmer, standing by Patrick's stool to make his point, was upset about the defense in the first two games.

"They had other needs," replied Patrick. "I'm more concerned about the D-line. They're not generating any pressure, and you're gonna get hurt deep when you give 'em all day to throw."

Their conversation would still be going on tomorrow. In eastern Wyoming, the "home" teams for professional football, as determined by the live feeds provided by the networks, are Denver in the AFC and (usually) Minnesota in the NFC. But there are as many Green Bay, Dallas, and Seattle fans as there are Vikings or Broncos fans, and no strict lines. Coolidge is different – only the Broncos matter in Coolidge. On an average Sunday, the town might as well sit in the parking lot of Mile High Stadium in Denver (no one calls it Empower Field).

Clem clicked wooden nickels onto the bar in front of Harry and Patrick. "Frog," he said. Frog Adderly was a First Cousin who had bought a round for all of the First and Second Cousins. "Thanks Frog," said everybody. The wooden nickel signified the recipient's impending entitlement to a drink of his or her choice. The other bars in Coolidge used an upside-down shot glass to signify the same thing, but Clem had learned to use wooden nickels in Montreal, and he stuck with his system. Frog had no special reason to buy a round. He was looking at his friends around him, and was moved to the gesture. He owned one of the town's two gas stations, the Cenex, and he could afford it. Every one of the First Cousins, and many of the Second Cousins, would buy a round that evening, because they wanted to, and because they could afford it. The wooden nickels accumulated quickly, even for somebody who was drinking fast.

After he finished the beer that Frog had bought, Patrick headed over to the stage and helped Three Toe Joe finish setting up. Patrick ran the sound check at 8:45, making sure that the vocals and guitars were balanced. They didn't usually mic the drums in Clem's, because the room wasn't big enough to call for it. Toby made himself heard without amplification. Patrick plugged Ray Tillson's iPhone into the sound board, so that they'd have recorded music before they started and during their breaks.

Looking around at ten minutes of nine, Patrick noticed that the Girls were out in force – no AWOL's. When the band started, they would form their circle on the dance floor, eight women in all, all facing inward. Ranging in age from 25 to 41, and in height from 5'0" to 6'0", they would move to Three Toe Joe's standard opening number, "Pour Some Sugar on Me" by Def Leopard. Toby Ernst, the drummer, sang the lead vocal, which would be the only lead vocal he would sing all night. "Sing" in a loose sense. He was able to shout it, which was why the song fit his voice. Their second song was usually "Put Some Drive in Your Country," by Travis Tritt.

The Girls used to call themselves the "Wonder Women," but a consensus ultimately formed within the group that they were going out on Friday nights to be with the girls, not with the "Women" – too formal -- and the new group identifier evolved. They were aware that their circle discouraged requests from any male in the room to ask one of them to dance. But Friday at Clem's was their group time. They looked forward to it all week, and they took charge of the bar while that circle lasted, typically less than an hour, till the band's first break. One would have thought – or at least Patrick would have thought – that the symbiotic dependence between the Girls and the band would have resulted in one or two relationships between individual Girls and band members. Strangely, only one or two Girls had ever known one or two Joes in the Biblical sense, and only very late in the evening after other options had been exhausted. The fact is, Ray, Ray and Toby were playing music on a Friday night because their social skills were notably weak – hiding behind drums or a guitar is easier than making conversation, and the higher-status males in the room were throwing darts, not singing. And besides, Ray Bando and Ainslee had been together for almost a year at that point, and Ray was loyal.

Patrick, at the sound board, actually had a better relationship with the Girls than did any of the other three. After the circle dancing was done, they would come to talk to him at the sound board in ones and twos, yelling over the music. He didn't know it, but he was the subject of frequent conversations among the Girls, and most had considered the "what ifs." They thought Patrick was hot, but he was also different, and they liked that. He would ask for a dance every once in a while, which they liked even more. But for well-known reasons, he had never bought drinks for any of them -- which they didn't like.

Occasionally, the Girls would go on road trips to Sheridan, Billings, Buffalo, or even once to Casper. On those occasions, they would refer to themselves as the Coolidge Girls, because they were proud of their town. The trips made for great stories. Like the one when Andi McIntyre, their acknowledged Queen Bee, threw her drink on a bouncer in Billings, with the owner standing right there, because the bouncer called her a bitch. Such was the force of Andi's personality that she persuaded the owner to tell the bouncer to apologize, and the Coolidge Girls were allowed to stay. Andi had once asked

Patrick out, despite the difference in their ages (she was 38 at the time, and he was 27). But Patrick was going out with Doreen, and had to say no. Andi never took it personally, and continued to ensure that Patrick was viewed with high approval among her group.

What was really fun about the Girls, finally, and what everybody acknowledged, was that they danced the roof off the place. Every one of them could stone-cold move, and they lit Clem's up like a Spanish fiesta.

CHAPTER 9

When 5:00 Saturday Mass was finished, Patrick eased slowly across the little parking lot to the Parish Hall for the Hospitality Supper. A short line had already formed for food; Mavis, Marie and Betty were behind the long table, spooning and cooing and ooing. It was all women in front of their table as well, everyone in her sixties or seventies. Old friends doing what old friends liked to do.

He stood in the doorway to the Multi-Purpose Room; Father Dave came up on his left. "Hi, Pat," he said. "Where are you watching the game tomorrow?"

This was a loaded question, and Patrick took his time answering. On two occasions in the past two years, he'd accepted invitations to watch the Broncos in the Rectory with Father Dave and Father Dan. He liked them both, and both understood the game -- but it just wasn't the same.

At Cousin Clem's, thirty or forty people were yelling at the three televisions, spilling beer and shots, eating, laughing. There were cigarettes and cigars in the parking lot during TV timeouts and halftime, and Clem passed around plates of fifty cent wings, mostly neglecting to charge for them. The party continued into the evening when the Broncos won, and usually ended abruptly when they lost.

Father Dave and Father Dan, on the other hand, talked quietly during the game, and listened carefully to what the play-by-play and color guys had to say. "Have another beer, Pat," they'd say, but would hardly touch their own. Patrick liked to hear Father Dave's memories of New York Giants games he went to as a kid. And he listened to Father Dan's much more distant memories of football in Bozeman, Montana – Father Dan, now 75, was parish priest at St. Mary's in Bozeman for ten years – with polite interest. That was about it; there was nothing else to say. People speculated, mostly incorrectly, that Patrick led a solitary life; but Father Dave and Father Dan, my God, what a lonely existence.

"No plans yet, Father," replied Patrick, finally.

"Then why don't you come over to the Rectory? Dan and I will be watching, and we invited Mavis and Martina as well." This was hopeful, Patrick thought. Martina rarely spoke, but Mavis always, always made him laugh. "OK, Father, see you at 2:00?"

"Done deal."

A parishioner tapped Father Dave on the shoulder. Making a little 'excuse me' face to Patrick, Father Dave turned to greet her.

Patrick joined the food line, and picked up a thick paper plate and some plastic silverware. There were trays of chicken piccata, pork chops, and beef patties in a sauce, Kaiser roll optional. There was manicotti with cheese, for vegetarians and for the occasional Catholic Lady for whom it was always Friday, 1958, or Lent. Salad, vegetables, and desserts were a few steps farther along.

"Patrick!" cried Betty. "Have some of this chicken piccata. Gloria made it."

Patrick loved chicken piccata. His mom used to make it. "Absolutely, load me up," he said. "Is there any ketchup to go with the burgers?"

"Sure, it's down on the small table at the end," she said. "Let me know if it needs a refill, not sure we checked it first."

"Hi, Pat," said Marie. "How are your parents?"

Marie was eighty-three years old. She looked sixty-five, and laughed like she was fifteen. For Marie, as Patrick came to understand some years ago, all the world was parents and children. She was animated by the knowledge that everyone was, at the very least, once a child, and everyone had, or once had, parents. Patrick might have dismissed her insight as trite, but he reminded himself, as often as he could, that you take wisdom where you find it.

"My parents are both good, Marie, thanks for asking. I haven't talked to them for a couple of weeks, but last time I called, they said to say hi to you." Patrick hesitated. "I guess I told you that last week."

"You did," replied Marie, with a smile.

Patrick smiled back. "I think the rule is, any 'hi' can be repeated as often as necessary. So hi again from Dina and Ed."

"Aw Pat, that's sweet. I think that's the rule – 'hi's' don't wear out."

Patrick's parents had only met Marie a couple of times. But when Pat talked to them on the phone, he often asked them, to ask him, to say hello to her, for them. Dina and Ed understood Catholic parish hall food lines.

Mavis was next. "Hi Ugly," she said. "So do you want a pork chop? Make up your damn mind already."

"Yes, please. Father Dave said you might be coming over to the Rectory for the game tomorrow."

"True, and I'm bringing Martina with me. Her boyfriend has National Guard duty this weekend, so she's kind of loose-endy."

Patrick liked Martina. She was about twenty-two, and smiled easily, but talked less than any adult human being Patrick had ever known, with the exception, of course, of Silent Al. She worked in IT for Paul Madden's food distribution company.

"Can I finish painting the back office this week?" asked Patrick.

"I'm going to have to find something for Father Dan to do while you're working," Mavis replied. "If you want to come over on Tuesday, I can send him to Sheridan for the daily Mass at St. Joseph's – they always need someone to do it on Tuesday -- and then I can send him to the office supply store."

"That'll work," said Pat. "If I need the afternoon, can you send him to play golf?"

"Depends on his back. But at worst, I can find another errand. We always need something."

"OK, cool." Pat took his plate to the veggie table and loaded up. He put some chocolate brownies on a smaller plate and balanced his way to a table – sat down, bounced back up for some iced tea, and then back down. He was sitting with Tony Paige – the only other Clem's regular who came to Saturday Mass and Hospitality Suppers – and with Paul Madden, who had done the readings tonight. Paul sold frozen foods to restaurants and caterers all over northeastern Wyoming. He was a good guy, albeit cynical about a lot of stuff.

As the meal was winding up, the ladies began to gather back at the serving tables. Pat heard his name several times. He rose and crossed the room.

"Patrick, don't let me hear you're not taking my pork chops," said Emma Train. "There's three left over, and *I'm* not going to eat them. What would I do with them, I'm fat enough already." Andrea Porter insisted that the burgers – at least four were left -- were not going to eat themselves. Gloria Antonelli was already placing the last two chicken piccatas into Styrofoam, with an imploring look in Patrick's direction. Mavis was packing up the left-over vegetables. Patrick rarely accepted all of the leftovers, but he usually left with a full knapsack of food.

There were only about 75 people at Saturday evening Mass in any given week. Overwhelmingly female, and overwhelmingly 65 and older. At least 40 came across the parking lot for the Hospitality Supper. And, not surprisingly, a few parishioners who usually came to Mass on Sunday also came over for the Hospitality Supper on Saturday night. And there was always food enough for an army, because food is love. How was it possible, Patrick always wondered, that these kind people could feel that *he* was doing *them* a favor when he took home a lot of the food that was left?

In many ways, the Hospitality Supper on Saturday night was the most important hour of Patrick's week. He needed the calories, the vegetables, the variety, the flavors, and the people. He ate almost 3,000 calories while he was there, and he left with 4,000 more in his knapsack – in total, more than a third of what he would eat during the week. It was a nice night, and the walk home to his cabin was pleasant. There was no Four Toe Joe gig that weekend, so Patrick turned in early.

CHAPTER 10

The Broncos and the Chiefs were tied 14-14 at halftime. Father Dan went outside for a cigar, and everyone else opted to join him in the sunshine. Mavis opened a beer, and she and Martina stood with Patrick on the porch.

"Most people complain about Christmas showing up in the stores before Thanksgiving," said Mavis. "I wish I had that luxury. I need to start worrying about Christmas in September." She took a sip of Coors Light.

Martina turned to Patrick. "I've been hearing this since I was six," she said. She didn't elaborate.

"What do you need to worry about this far out?" asked Patrick.

"Decorating the church," said Mavis. "Every year we need to test a few hundred lights, dust off garland and wreaths. I have to put in orders for poinsettias. We use a lot of holly. Nobody likes plastic, so we use as much natural green as we can."

"I have a huge patch of holly out by my place," said Patrick. "The bushy kind, not the trees."

"It sounds like you're probably talking about Winter Red Winterberry," said Mavis.

"Holly. I don't know about Winterberry. Could you use it?"

"I'd love to look at it, at least," said Mavis. "Can we give you a lift home after the game, and see what's growing?"

"Sure," said Patrick. "I also know where there's some dwarf mistletoe. Easy to find. But it's a parasite, and kills trees. I don't know why it's so popular."

"Yeah, we can pass on that," said Mavis. "Great for office Christmas parties, but we try not to encourage random kissing at Mass. Although come to think of it, we probably should. Attendance would probably improve."

"Second half is starting," said Father Dave.

It was a good game, and Patrick was surprised at the level of sophistication of the group in the Rectory. Their football knowledge was at least as high as the crowd at Cousin Clem's, with less noise. Patrick was reminded, as well, of how informed Mavis was about football, generally. Her late husband had played linebacker for the University of Wyoming Cowboys while they were both students there. 'Poke Pride. She had had good instruction.

After a see-saw second half, the Broncos scored on a late drive to win by three. The line had been Broncos, minus two, in Denver. Patrick imagined some happy faces at Cousin Clem's.

CHAPTER 11

At 5:00, Father Dan headed back to his room for a nap, Father Dave went to call his mother, and Mavis, Martina and Patrick loaded into Mavis's Explorer for a trip over to Patrick's cabin. They turned northwest off of Route 14 onto a small, thinly-paved artery – "Side Road," according to the road sign. Side Road crossed the Tongue River – a thirty-foot wide creek, really – over a small bridge. It continued for a mile or so up to Allen's Pond, climbing slightly. The path to Patrick's cabin was on their right, near where Side Road ended.

"Follow me, ladies," Patrick said, as they stepped down from the SUV. They climbed the path for about two hundred yards.

Mavis was impressed when they reached the cabin. A lot had been done since her last visit a couple or three years before. Martina had never been to see the cabin, so Mavis explained a little bit. "Patrick discovered this place seven or eight years ago, while he was hunting with a friend. We all just found out about a year ago – maybe two, Patrick when was it? – that this cabin is sited on Parish land. We own two-hundred and fifty acres up here, through a charitable trust, that we really had no idea about. Father Dan didn't know it was Parish land. When we checked with Father Michael, who was literally on his death bed at the time, he said he had a vague recollection about it. I didn't know, because there's no tax bills – it was apparently exempt."

"Did you ever find the deed?" asked Patrick.

"We never found the original," she replied. "But the County Clerk had a record of the original conveyance from the church to the trust back in 1921 or 1922, with metes and bounds. And there was a map of the parcel in one of the documents. So we know it's ours. Everybody in town had sort of assumed it was state land, because no one was living on it."

"Is it one room?" Martina asked Patrick.

"Yeah. It's about thirty-by-twenty, so I probably could have created a couple of rooms. I just never saw the need." He rarely invited visitors inside, but he could see they were waiting for an invitation. "Would you like to come in for a minute?"

As they stepped in the front door, Mavis and Martina were surprised. They expected dorm room provincial – what they saw, instead, was clean, orderly, and well-lit. A double bed was in the far left corner; a large wood stove was straight across from the entrance; and a refrigerator was to the right of the stove. There was a sink with a hand pump on the back wall to the right of the refrigerator, and to its right, in the corner, was a screen partially concealing a white toilet. An old-fashioned galvanized bath tub was next to the toilet, on the right wall. There were chairs and an eating table to the right of the front door, and some more comfortable chairs, a guitar, fishing tackle, and two long guns to the left. In the middle of the left hand wall was a large sheet of thick, transparent plastic, that covered a dark area that looked like storage.

"Wow," said Mavis, "you've been busy."

Patrick nodded. "I've always got something I need to do."

Martina pointed to the stove. "That's beautiful, where'd it come from?"

The stove was, in fact, in miraculous shape. It had a big firebox, a broad stove-top, and an intact metal chimney up to and through the roof. Its legs were set in cement footers that extended through the floor into the ground.

"It actually didn't come from anywhere – it was here," replied Patrick. "The original cabin was built around the stove; the legs of the stove are all footed. I'm guessing a long line of scavengers over the years gave up on the idea of taking the stove out of its moorings – it was too heavy to move. So they just left it."

Patrick took a small pot from the stove-top and walked it over to the water pump at the sink. He pumped the handle a few times and filled the pot with water. "Where does the water come from?" asked Mavis.

"It's a line from a pool in the creek," said Patrick. He turned back to the stove, blew on the embers, and added a few small logs from a pile near the stove. "I'm having some carrots with dinner – I like to cook 'em."

Mavis glanced behind the screen in the back right corner. "Did you have to install a septic tank?" asked Mavis.

Martina rolled her eyes. "Nosy enough, are we Mom?" she said.

"Don't need it," replied Patrick. "I bought a portable composting toilet with my last paycheck, years ago. Those are allowed, without a permit, under Wyoming DEQ rules. It's worked great."

Mavis looked at the flooring, which was a mixture of tiles and rolls, all in some form of vinyl. One of the vinyl panels said, "To Gymnasium," with an arrow. Apparently, a school had been renovated. Glancing up, Mavis noticed the plastic sheet to the left of Patrick's bed. "Remind me, what's behind the plastic?"

"That's my henhouse and the goat house," said Patrick. Then to Martina: "They need protection from the cold and from predators, and I couldn't think of a good way to heat the enclosure without installing a gas generator. I have a 12 volt system, but it isn't enough. So I built their houses back-to-back, with the end of each house aligned with half of the old window opening. Then I tightly covered the entire window opening with plastic." He gestured toward the sheeting, framing it in the air. "The plastic allows heat transfer from my living area, but keeps the air in the coops out of the cabin. In the winter, I'll warm two buckets of rocks on the stove, and I put one in the middle of each house. The heat moving through the plastic, combined with the rocks, keeps the animal houses above freezing during the winter. I use a little 12 volt heater if I need to supplement."

"I don't see how you can keep yourself alive, and have any time left over for St. Ann's, or for Cousin Clem's," said Mavis. "It looks like you must be working all the time."

"You'd be surprised," said Patrick. "I have time for a life in town. The biggest challenge, believe it or not, is gathering firewood. I'm doing that every day of the year, because I have a fire every day of the year. I feed the animals every day, and every day I milk the goats and collect eggs. I only go hunting three days a week, if that, and I only fish two or three times a month."

"How much milk do you get from the goats?" asked Mavis.

"Nubians are big producers," he said. "I get five or six quarts a day from each of the two females, for ten months a year each. I drink a lot. I can't use all of it, so I spread the extra on my vegetables. They like the calcium. I spend a fair amount of time gathering hay for the goats – I use prairie grass, which I roll into small bales. Bobby Bays helps with feed."

"How about eggs?" she asked.

"I'm still experimenting," said Patrick. "I'm not a great chicken farmer, but I'm getting better. Hens need light for fourteen hours a day to continue producing. Some light comes through from my living space, and I have some LED's hooked up to the car batteries, but I don't get as many eggs in the winter. I get one egg per hen, per day, in the summer."

"How do you power the refrigerator?" asked Martina.

"It's 12v DC," said Patrick. "The fridge was expensive as hell – I bought it when I was still working for Marty Brace. It's super well-insulated, and I can fit a lot of meat in it. The freezer's always packed, because in the late winter I need the protein." Patrick pointed to the floor. "It runs off car batteries, under the cabin. They get recharged by the solar panels, the wind turbine, and the water turbine in the creek. I also bought the water turbine while I was working."

"Can you hunt all year?" asked Mavis, who had never hunted.

"Yes and no, mostly no. The only edible game I can hunt all year are jackrabbits. They're good to eat. I can hunt raccoons all year, but I don't like the meat very much – I'll eat it if I have to. You can hunt coyotes year round. If I shoot a coyote to protect the goats, I'll add the meat to other meats for burgers or a meat loaf. I have a hand grinder that my mom gave me for my birthday one year. But all of the best-eating game, you know, deer, antelope, elk, pheasant, grouse, turkey, that kind of thing, there are seasons, mostly pretty short. Everybody from everywhere wants to hunt in Wyoming. Turkey has a fall and a spring season, which is nice. I eat a lot of turkey in the spring."

"Good thing you're not a child," said Mavis. "If you were eight, you'd refuse to eat all that stuff, and you'd starve. Is there a fishing season, or is that year-round?"

"Fly fishing is year-round. But it's hard, and I'm not very good at it. Regulations say you can't use a net. So for me, fish protein is just an occasional change of pace, it doesn't contribute a lot to my diet. It helps more when hunting season is closed."

"I couldn't do it," said Mavis. "I don't know many people who could." She paused and took a last look. "Hope we haven't intruded – let's go look for Winterberry."

The three of them stepped back out the front door, turned right, and strolled around to the back. The animal pen was the first thing they came to, in the side yard. From habit, Patrick grabbed a handful of chicken feed from a bucket hanging on a post, and spread it over the chicken yard, which extended part way up the hill. He pointed up the hill to his vegetable garden, which had grown to 100 feet by 100 feet. "I grow carrots, potatoes, yams, turnips, beets, rutabaga, sweet potatoes – any root vegetables I can think of. They store well – I dug myself a root cellar, up at the corner there."

As they walked, he thought for a moment. "I take that back – not *all* root vegetables. I hate radishes."

They crossed the stream on a little plank bridge and walked through scrub vegetation. Patrick pointed out wildflowers, deer tracks, antler scrapings, gopher holes, an eagle's nest, and a coyote den. And that was through three hundred yards. Mavis was astonished, for the millionth time, at the richness of the place where they lived. Father Dave once said that if the Tongue River Canyon were in Northern New Jersey, it would be the most-visited natural attraction in the world. As it was, you could picnic up there at the end of a five minute car trip from Coolidge, and you'd hardly see anyone for an afternoon.

The pine forest was visible another three hundred yards ahead -- the Bighorn National Forest. They continued to walk. Then, to the left, maybe 50 yards off, Patrick pointed to a copse of small trees, hardwood mixed with pine, still in the area of the stream. "Here we go."

A 60-foot patch of Winter Red Winterberry was growing right near the edge of the trees. There were thousands of bright red berries and the shiny green leaves, and the effect was a little outrageous. Christmas in September.

Mavis ran to the spot. "Wow!" She shook her head in disbelief, and turned to Patrick and Martina, both just catching up. "This is amazing! This will be perfect in so many places."

"Show me the kinds of cuttings you want," said Patrick, "and I'll come up and gather some and bring it over to the church. A little at a time, I can have what you need by the middle of next month."

"Listen to me, Patrick Flaherty," said Mavis, turning to him. "You already do more than enough for us. I'm not going to let you interrupt your keeping yourself alive, for something like this. As the crow flies, we're under a mile from where we parked. If I bring a crew of volunteers with me, and if everyone has a piece of canvas to wrap around some cuttings, it'll be easy to carry out what we need, in one shot."

Patrick shrugged his agreement. She had a point. There were limits, he supposed. "OK, we'll pick a day. I think we could get Alan Barton's ATV up here if we follow the deer track, and we can pile a bunch of cuttings in the back."

As they walked back to Mavis's car in the twilight, they talked about Martina's boyfriend's National Guard assignments, bridges freezing before road surfaces (and different ways to say it on road signs), stores in Sheridan, and tire rotations. When they got to the car, Patrick kissed each on the cheek, and opened Martina's door for her. "Thanks for the lift," he said to both. "It was nice to have a visit." They waved to each other as the car headed back down Side Road.

CHAPTER 12

Patrick was tired. He had just finished a new fence row for his goat pen, and his muscles ached. But Clem's felt like an old comfortable shoe. He was enjoying his beer – a new Black Tooth blend that Clem was getting from the microbrewery in Sheridan.

All hands were on deck that night, which was always good. The First Cousins – Bean, Satch, Frog and Marty – were at the dais.

At least seven Second Cousins were on hand. Anita Boyle was down near the corner, sitting next to Marty. She was a lawyer with a solo practice, single, dark-haired -- with a quick wit and lively eyes. Larry was to the left of Anita. Patrick had known Larry pretty well for six years, but he didn't know his last name and had no idea what he did for a living. Very nice guy though. Next to Larry was Harry Detmer, a general contractor with a pretty wife and four well-behaved kids. He spent too much time in Clem's, but so did everyone else. Patrick was next to Harry. On Patrick's left was Eric Dormer, who owned a ranch out Route 14 toward Ranchester. Eric could probably have bought and sold everyone in the bar, but you wouldn't know it. Jeannie Conwell was next to Eric. Jeannie was a flirt, a tease, a muse, a siren and a confidant. She ran a real estate office during the day, and dressed to party at night. A tall redhead, she looked younger than her thirty-six years, and her smile lit up the room. She was utterly unobtainable, of course, but was loved nevertheless. Three over on Patrick's left was Pete Banner. Pete was a carpenter and painter, and the Mayor of Coolidge. So he took endless abuse from everyone.

Farther to Patrick's left were a married couple, Brenda and Eddie. They were five years old when Billy Joel wrote his song about them. Once, when he was visiting his parents in Colorado, Patrick met a Jack and Dianne. He knew that he only remembered their names because of the Mellencamp song. That made him wonder whether there were a Molly and Desmond somewhere, and whether they ever took their barrow to the marketplace.

Beyond Brenda and Eddie were Zeke and Manny, brothers and contractors. Zeke was an electrician and carpenter, Manny was a painter, plumber and HVAC guy. Very few tradesmen in Coolidge practiced only one trade.

The conversation at that moment was about oddities. Marty Brace was a big man with a big voice, wild salt and pepper hair, a goatee, and a permanent astonishment about life's surprises. He staked the goal post: "Name the only two states where you can't pump your own gas. Ten bucks to the winner or winners, if you get it. No cheating with phones. And I need to hear both."

"New Jersey," said Anita, who grew up in New Jersey.

"Right," said Marty, "that's one. What's the other one?"

Blank looks.

"Oregon," said Marty. "My kid could've had the answer on his phone before I finished the question."

"You said 'no phones,' goddammit," somebody grumbled.

"OK, here's another one," said Marty, "same ten bucks. What are the only two states or provinces in the U.S. or Canada where the only stores allowed to sell hard liquor are owned by the government?"

"Pennsylvania," said Anita.

"Quebec," said Clem.

"Aaargh," cried Marty. "Here's the ten." He put it on the bar. "Bean, buy a round with me." Clem picked up the ten from the bar, another ten from Marty, a twenty from Bean, and some more from Frog and Tony Paige, a/k/a Satchel, a/k/a Satch. Wooden nickels went down in front of every stool.

Time passes quickly at Cousin Clem's, and it was closing time before most of the people there realized it was time to go home.

CHAPTER 13

Patrick was fixing the window in Father Dave's office – shaving some wood off the sash to permit it to move – while Father Dave read his emails. The radio was playing Drake.

As Patrick announced that the window was fixed, Father Dave took a breath and said, "Patrick, I need to ask you for a favor."

"Sure."

"This is a big one," said Father Dave. "Emma Train's grandson Roger has a problem with OxyContin, and she asked me to ask you if you would talk to him."

"Me?" Patrick was surprised. "I don't know Roger that well. I don't know anything about addiction. And you'd be better for that than me. I'm not following. Why me?"

"I've already talked to him, about three months ago," replied Father Dave. "She talked to me about it last May or June. I went over to visit. He hasn't stopped, and Emma's a little desperate. She asked me to ask you to help. She's afraid to ask you directly, and she figured it would improve the chances you'd say 'yes' if I asked you. She knows you coached him in baseball."

"That was for one year of American Legion, Father. That's four years ago now. He's not going to listen to me any differently than he would anyone else."

"Maybe that's the point, Patrick. You'll be one more voice in his ear. He's 21 and lost. He needs to know that people are watching what he's doing to himself. It couldn't hurt."

"I don't want to do this, Father. It's not me to go butting into people's lives. I have enough trouble managing my own. And I couldn't persuade a dog to eat a treat. I hope you understand."

"Oh, I understand," said Father Dave, placidly. "But remember who you're dealing with. You know if you say 'no,' I'm going to bug you to change your mind until your hair falls out. You might as well take your medicine now. Just say 'yes.'"

Patrick knew that resistance was probably futile. But he held out hope. "Maybe. Let me think about it."

"No, that's not the answer I'm looking for. The answer I want is, 'Yes, I'll go see Roger.'"

Patrick smiled. "OK, I'll go see Roger. Remind me why we hired you here. Weren't there any parishes in Mordor that needed a Golum?" And then, "What can you tell me about OxyContin addiction?"

"All kidding aside, I can tell you that you're being sent on a hopeless mission. Roger will stop when he decides to stop, or when it kills him. But the point is to show him he's not alone, and that his grandmother – all of us, for that matter – want him to live. You'll be doing the Lord's work, as the saying goes."

Patrick wasn't happy, but he was persuaded. Father Dave was a piece of work.

CHAPTER 14

"Yo, Patrick! You there, bud?" Patrick heard the shouting while he was cleaning his rifle. It was late Thursday afternoon. Has to be Stanley, he thought. He dropped the cleaning rod, crossed to the front door, and threw it open.

"Stanley!" Patrick charged through the front door and hugged his oldest friend. He didn't know what to say, so he didn't say anything. Finally, he stood back, and asked, "When'd'you get in?"

"Just here for a day," said Stanley. "I want to see my uncle and eat a bacon cheeseburger at The 14. I thought I'd get you to come along." Stanley had been to Coolidge three or four times in the last couple of years, but it wasn't often enough. Patrick missed him. It was Stanley who had invited Patrick to Coolidge seven years ago. Stanley was there because his uncle lived there, and so he had a place to crash. He moved up from Colorado and got a job with Marty Brace's contracting crew. He called Patrick when Marty said he needed extra help. And he said the hunting was good.

Patrick was a year out of college, and sleeping in his parents' spare bedroom in Adams Heights, north of Denver. He said yes to Stanley's offer, and told his parents he was off to Wyoming. He was twenty-three years old, out of work, bored with Colorado. He had fifteen hundred dollars in his pocket. He didn't know much about carpentry or plumbing, but he had time on his hands, and, according to Stanley, Marty *really* needed the help. Patrick took the job, and began to learn how to drive nails and saw boards.

"Come on in." Patrick led the way through the front door. "I'll be ready to go in a minute."

"Cabin looks nice," said Stanley, as he looked over the familiar space. "More like a real house, less like a Quonset hut. Almost like a respectable citizen."

"But it's still a cabin in the woods," replied Patrick. "I'm not gonna bullshit you. I'm isolated up here. And when I'm not busy, there are way too many conversations going on in my head. But I love it. The things I need to do to stay alive are mostly things I can control. And I know my friends – really, the whole town -- would help me if I got sick, or if I had some kind of disaster."

"Yeah, and you don't have a boss," said Stanley. "That's worth $127,500 per year, right there. Maybe $132,750."

"Yup. I don't have a boss."

"You could rent this place for twenty-five hundred bucks a weekend to hunters from Chicago or St. Louis," said Stanley.

"Well, that's the worst idea I ever heard," said Patrick.

"Oh, I forgot to mention," said Stanley, "I called your mom this week. She sends their love. I caught her up on what I've been up to. She told me about her painting."

"Yeah, it's awesome," Patrick replied. "She sells a painting a month, all online." He pointed toward the front wall, by the front door. "That's hers." Dina had oil-painted the Flaherty house in Adams Heights, in early morning sunlight. Patrick choked up when he looked at it, more so with Stanley looking at it too. "Catch me up, how're you doing?" he asked, as he stowed his gun kit. "How's carpentry?"

"Fine, really good. I'm learning a ton, and I'm getting paid to learn. I really like the work." Stanley had been working for a year as an apprentice carpenter in Denver, Local 555. At 28, he expected to be the oldest apprentice in his entering group. As it turned out, 28 was about average. A lot had changed in a generation or so.

"I really hated office work," said Stan. "I thought I was going to like HR, but it turned out all I did was listen to my fellow employees whine all day. I couldn't admit I hated my job worse than they did. And my boss was psychotic. She used to humiliate me just because she could. You know -- you remember how I was when I was working in that job."

"A year ago, you were still doing your apprentice classes. I haven't seen you since they started sending you on construction jobs. I need details, dude."

"We have an hour of daylight left," Stan replied. "Let's head over to The 14, and then to Clem's. I'll fill you in on everything."

As they left the cabin, they turned and looked back for a moment. "You didn't have stucco last time I was up to see you. Brilliant. Howd'you think of it?"

"All the other options were terrible," said Patrick. "I needed to replace the tar paper. Plastic siding, aluminum siding, brick, cedar, none of it made sense. So I found an ASTM recipe for stucco. I've been using the computer at the library when I need to go online. Stucco's nothing but water, sand, cement, and lime. I got the sand from the stream, and the cement and lime were broken bags from around town."

"What's underneath the stucco?" asked Stanley.

"Nothing that complies with any building code -- but there's no code out here. Scrap plywood, a layer of tar paper or Tyvek, and some chicken wire. Whatever was available. Stucco doesn't care what it sits on, as long as it can get a grip."

Stanley had another thought. "Animals all healthy?"

"Yeah, knock wood."

As they were walking down the path toward Side Road, Patrick thought back over the past seven years. "Remember, just after we started the work, when we put in that illegal toilet? We had a couple of very cool parties that fall."

"Speaking of which, is Patty Mumphrey still in town?" asked Stan.

"Yeah, and you'd better hope you don't bump into her," said Patrick.

Stanley rolled his eyes.

CHAPTER 15

Harry Detmer had mentioned to Patrick the night before last, at Clem's, that he had some scraps of good pressure treated lumber on the back lot. It was left over from a job they did on the north end of town. Today was Friday, his normal day for stopping by to see Harry, and to make the run to the dump in Sheridan. He walked over to Harry's place to see how things looked.

Harry's contracting business was probably the biggest in Coolidge – Marty Brace might dispute that, but he disputed everything – and they went through a lot of construction materials. Harry's garage, office and shop were behind his house, on a three-acre lot near the end of Gillette Street, on the far side of town from where Patrick lived. Harry's father founded the business in the 1970's or 1980's, and it had grown to nine employees. They had a carpentry crew, an HVAC/plumbing crew, two electricians, two painters, and an office manager.

It normally took Patrick about a half hour to walk to Harry's shop from his cabin. On a sunny day like this one, the walk was a pleasure.

"Hey Pat, how're you doing?" asked Harry's wife, Jeannette, as he walked up the driveway. She was watering some bushes.

"Not too bad, can't complain. Is Harry in?"

"Yeah, you just caught him; he's getting ready to go back out."

"Thanks." Patrick continued down the driveway to the office, and entered without knocking. The little bell over the door rang, and Harry's office manager, Nancy McDermott, looked up from her desk. "Hi Sweetie. We have a lot to move today."

"No problem," said Patrick. "D'you want me to load up the Silverado? Are the keys in?"

"I think so," she said. "Let me know if they're not there, we'll go searching."

Nancy was 65, and had made the business run for 35 years, starting with Harry's dad, and continuing with Harry. Every Friday, weather permitting, Patrick loaded construction debris into one of the trucks and drove it to the landfill in Sheridan. Nancy would give him a signed check to pay the dumping fee – all Patrick had to do was fill in the amount – and after the run, he would swing by his own cabin, if he had anything to drop off. And then he'd return the truck.

"Yo Pat, perfect timing," said Harry, as he stuck his head out of his office door. Harry looked like a cowboy – just under six feet, thin and gnarly, piercing brown eyes, greyish hair, and a deadpan expression. But an incongruously warm smile, when he wanted to show it. "Mel and Tommy just dropped off some fencing scraps from the job on North Street. Genuine Cyclone. They'll be perfect for your coop. And the pressure-treated is waiting for you."

"Super, I'll take a look."

Harry thought for a moment. "Pat, do you have a second to sit, I need to talk for a minute," he said.

"Sure." Patrick walked into Harry's office and took a seat as Harry sat down behind his desk. The door was open; Harry had no secrets from Nancy.

"Pat, I'm worried that this arrangement isn't fair to you anymore. Your property doesn't need the amount of work it did a couple of years ago. Shit, as far as I can tell, almost every time you come over, you spend two hours loading, driving, and offloading, and you leave with not very much. I know I'm never going to be able to talk you into coming to work for me, but would you at least consider accepting some cash for the work you're doing?"

Patrick hesitated. He wanted to explain his own motivations in a way that would make sense to Harry. "I don't take as much as I used to. But I gotta say -- this back lot is super important to me. Most of the materials that've gone into my animal enclosures in the last three or four years have come from here. You have the Home Depot in Sheridan; I have your back lot."

"I get that," said Harry, "and I'm still happy to help. But you're welcome to anything you need, you know that, as long as it's from slow-moving inventory. Fencing gets old, styles change, and it just doesn't move that fast. On almost all of our fencing jobs, we special order new fencing that the customer selects. When you ask for old fencing, that kind of forces us to decide whether it's worth storing here. It's win-win. And wood, beams, railroad ties -- I mean, we have enough that I'd never miss the little bit that you've taken over the years."

Patrick knew that if Harry was sure he was going to use something, he'd say "no, can't do it." It had happened a couple of times. He thought about how to respond to Harry's generosity.

"The other thing," Patrick continued, " is that the construction debris is a goldmine for me. When you cut a 4 x 8 piece of plywood or drywall, you don't have much use for the 4 x 3 or 4 x 4 piece that's left. But I used your drywall scraps for my interior walls, and your plywood scraps for my roof. Every time you shingle a roof there's leftover asphalt shingles. Since I don't care about color, I was able to shingle my whole roof from your leftovers. And every one of my windows – all five – came from a demolition or window replacement job that you were doing. If I hadn't been over here looking, I wouldn't have found that stuff. Knowing that you're counting on me to make a run to the dump gets me over here to look at what you have."

"That's the thing, Pat, we wouldn't be counting on you, except we know you're going to do it. Nancy gets all happy when it's 'Patrick Day,' because she knows you're going to solve a bunch of problems for her. How often do you stop at Ace Hardware, or deliver something to a crew, while you're supposedly just making a run to the landfill?"

"I'm happy to do that stuff."

"Pat, let me say it one more time, as clear as I can. You can have the stuff, I'm happy you can make use of it. You can have it whether you take the debris to the dump, or not."

"Thank you, Harry, I mean it. As long as I'm taking materials from you, I want to keep making the run to the dump. It's important to me to do that." He looked across the desk. "Are we good?"

Harry gave up. "Absolutely, yeah. I'm glad I caught up with you. It's good we talked."

Patrick rose, gave a smile and a nod to Harry, and a wave to Nancy as he left. He headed out to the debris pile to begin sorting the materials.

Harry came out to Nancy's desk. "I love that boy," he said. "I couldn't live like he does. But I guess he couldn't live like I do."

"He's one of a kind," said Nancy. "If I were going to change anything about him, I would give him some cunning."

"Haven't heard that word in a while," said Harry. "But you're right."

CHAPTER 16

Patrick knocked on the apartment door at 3:00 p.m. on Tuesday, half-hoping that Roger wasn't home. The door opened almost immediately.

"Hey Patrick. What's up?" Roger was wearing a Portland Trailblazers basketball shirt, and a pair of cargo shorts. His hair wasn't combed, and he was barefoot, but he seemed awake and alert. ESPN was on the TV.

"Long story," said Patrick. "Mind if I come in and talk for a few minutes?"

"Sure, come on in. Get you a beer?"

"No, I'm good."

Roger didn't look suspicious or wary. He led Patrick to a battered couch, and then took the chair next to it. Roger knew that Patrick and Emma Train knew each other. Patrick assumed that Roger would put two and two together. The two of them sat.

"Let me guess," said Roger. "My grandmother wants you to talk to me about the Oxy."

"Yeah, that's pretty much it," replied Patrick.

"Tell her thanks."

"That's all?"

"I know she loves me, and I hate that she worries." Roger's shoulders slumped a little bit. "There's no reason for me to make you sit here and try to think of something helpful to say. That's not fair to you. Let me tell you where I am with it, and maybe it'll make my grandmother and you feel better. Or maybe not. We'll see."

"OK."

Roger shifted in his chair and stared at the ceiling for a moment. "I started a year ago. I only take pills, and haven't started to snort or smoke. Been tempted, but haven't. I like Oxy, but I don't want to do it forever."

"Do you have a plan to quit?" asked Patrick.

"Yeah."

"What is it?"

"A new job. I'm landscaping now, but I'm starting work in two weeks as a package sorter with a delivery company down in Sheridan. I'd rather not tell you which one. So I'm going to start my withdrawal next week. I did it once before, and it wasn't as bad for me as it is for most people. It only took me a couple of days, and I didn't feel that sick."

"What are your chances of staying off it long-term?"

"I'm not sure. It's not easy to stop. Hopefully I can stay clean for the first few months on the job, and then get into a program if my health insurance pays for it."

Patrick nodded slowly. "It sounds like you're dealing with it," he said. "I wish I could contribute something intelligent, but I don't have any idea what you're going through." Patrick fidgeted, and looked at the floor.

Roger chuckled. "I hope you understand how I mean it when I tell you you're really bad at this. But, shit, so's everybody else. It's not easy to tell me anything I don't already know. Father Hernandez was probably worse, and it's supposed to be his job. He came to see me back in June, and I'm not sure he'd ever met an addict before. He did his best."

"He always does," said Patrick.

"But the bottom line is that getting addicted was a stupid-ass thing to do, and I need to fix it myself. Nobody who doesn't run a treatment center can really help me."

"I think there's one thing we can do, maybe. I talked to Terry Painter, without mentioning your name. He was able to kick Oxy five or six years ago, and he's got an extra bedroom at his place. He knows what it's like. It would probably be easier to go through it again if you're not staying here, surrounded by stuff that reminds you of your pills. I'll drop by a few times a day. We could have the doctor swing by too."

"Let me think about it," replied Roger.

Patrick laughed quietly. "You sound like me. Why don't you just say yes, and you'll be rid of me for now, and then you can change your mind if you change your mind."

Roger hesitated.

"Just say 'yes,'" repeated Patrick. "You've already decided to stop – *you* did that, nobody talked you into it. There's no reason not to have some help while you're following through on your decision."

"All right, I give up. I'll pack a bag and start Monday. And thank Terry for me."

CHAPTER 17

By 4:45, Patrick had already had a beer, changed the strings on Clem's guitar, tuned it, and adjusted the sound at the mixing board. Three Toe Joe and the Saturday night bands at Cousin Clem's favored "11" for every 10 position knob and slider, so he had to fix, at a minimum, channels 1 and 2.

Patrick was not a born performer. He was very nervous before he sang, and a little nervous while he sang. His voice was accurate – you're born with that, you either have it or you don't – but not rich or resonant. Like a lot of country singers, he let a little Tennessee twang creep into his lyrics, and he did that throat-catchy thing that Garth Brooks perfected. He half-talked lyrics, if he needed to, to avoid having to go above his range. What he did perfectly was sell a song. That's why he had the gig. He could make people listen to the lyrics, and when you play country music, the hooks are in the words. Like Holly Dunn: "Why Wyoming, did you take him from me? He's the only cowboy that I've got, and you got all you need . . ."

Patrick reasoned that the crowd at Clem's understood that jukeboxes, and road houses, and hats and boots were props in a set piece, and, to be effective, the lyrics of a country song didn't need to reflect your life as a CPA candidate in suburban Atlanta. Eighty percent of Patrick's listeners wore Nikes, and not boots, to work and to Clem's, and Clem's road house jukebox was the Amazon Echo behind the bar. Patrick's surmise was that Westerners tend to like country music because it made them feel good. Or something like that. He didn't think about it much, because the whole point of country music was not to think about it too much. Bartender, pour me another glass of forgettin'.

For the 100th time, Patrick considered the Martin D-28 guitar he was about to play. It belonged to Clem. An orchestra in a rosewood and spruce box, with six steel wires strung across it. He had heard somewhere that Martin, Gibson and Fender were all having trouble because kids didn't buy guitars anymore – they layered vocals over a rhythm track and synthesized chords in their phones. Patrick's dad used to say, "I hate change." Patrick always thought he was kidding, but had come to agree with him, at least when it came to music.

"Hi everybody. Welcome to the weekend." Patrick sat on a simple chair in the middle of the small stage, with the D-28 across his lap. The guitar and his vocal mic were plugged into the board, and the mains carried both sounds. No monitor necessary. The volume was set carefully to "loud enough to be heard, but not so loud that people had to shout, and not so low that the conversation would drown out the music." There should have been a setting that did all that, but there wasn't. Patrick set everything to 4, which seemed to work.

He took a sip of the beer that Clem had set on the floor beside his chair, and began to play his first song: "Galway Girl," by Ed Sheeran. Irish music and country music are the same music, just different sets of drinkers. Everybody liked it. Second song: "Tequila" by Dan & Shay. "When I taste tequila, baby I still see 'ya." Third song: Florida Georgia Line, "Cruise." Then, The Band Perry, "If I Die Young." Chris Stapleton, "Tennessee Whiskey."

He took another couple of sips. "Thank you. Thanks, as always, to Clem's for having me. It's great to see everybody. Wyoming is folk." He played "Big Yellow Taxi," by Joni Mitchell. Claire always came out of the kitchen to hear it. "Chicken Fried," by the Zac Brown Band. "I Want to Hold Your Hand," by the Beatles. Then his fix of Kenny Chesney – this week, his acoustic guitar masterpiece, "American Kids." Pick, strum, pick, strum, "Momma and Daddy put their roots right here, 'cause this is where the car broke down . . ." Big hand for that one. Patrick smiled. "The Unforgiven," by Metallica. Very underrated song, very adaptable for solo acoustic. Jeannie, especially, loved it. Patrick wouldn't have figured his local real estate professional for a metal-head.

Patrick ended with Delbert McClinton's "Birmingham Tonight." Better on piano than on guitar, but it worked, and it got a nice round of applause when he wrapped up at 7:00. The room was packed, and while he couldn't say that he "knew it was me they'd been comin' to see," he also knew that a lot of his friends looked forward to his weekly set. He didn't play solo more often, because he didn't want to run out of material, and because he found it stressful. Fun, but stressful. Patrick's life was filled with activities he found non-stressful, only occasionally interrupted by stress-producing things.

Three Toe Joe stepped up to begin their setup, even though they wouldn't be starting till 9:00. Ray and Ray and Toby. Patrick shook a lot of hands and clapped a lot of shoulders on the way around the bar to the kitchen. He had Friends in Low Places, and nothing was more important to him. He walked through the kitchen door, and Claire gave him a hug. "Ah, Joni. Don't ever stop playing that song."

Every Friday, Patrick would sit at the little desk back in the kitchen, and eat a hot cheeseburger with tomatoes, pickles and ketchup. That weekly cheeseburger inevitably took him back to high school in suburban Denver. Flavors he didn't have in his diet now, people he hadn't seen in a long time, music he hadn't heard in a long time. He ate it with a Coke. French fries, with more ketchup.

Claire always took fifteen minutes to talk with him. It was just about the only time they were able to talk during the week. Claire wanted him to get married immediately, and was untroubled by the fact that he was not dating anyone. Nor did she seem concerned that no one would want to marry a cave man hermit. She understood the challenge -- she had a French Canadian expression she loved: "T'es ben colon." Roughly, you're a Troglodyte. But she seemed to feel that any girl would see the positives. She had particularly liked Stacey, because Stacey had seen them.

Patrick finished his burger and fries, and began to walk his plate over to the dishwashing station. "Let me take that," said Claire. "Go be with your friends."

CHAPTER 18

The path from Side Road to his cabin seemed steeper that day. Patrick had finished placing a patio's worth of paving stones in the rear of the Rectory at St. Ann's. It was noontime. As he trudged upward, one of his goats appeared abruptly in front of him, and bleated.

Two things were possible. Either Patrick had failed to secure the back gate of the goat pen, or the goats had figured out a way to jump over, or burrow under, a fence that was designed to defeat both strategies. He wasn't worried; goats want desperately to escape their pens, so that they can find their way back in. But he hadn't had an escape for a while, maybe three years.

Patrick made his way around the cabin to his goat pen, and discovered there had been a third possibility. Ten feet of fencing was crushed flat, and the pen was empty, except for a couple of chickens. As he looked closely at the damage, he saw bear tracks on both sides of the downed fence, with what looked like scuffling goat hooves. And there was some blood.

Various thoughts and possibilities ran through his mind, but, mostly, he needed help and advice. First he had to find what goats and chickens he could, and he needed to rig a temporary repair of the fence. Neither job was easy, and it was 3:30 in the afternoon before he was ready to head down the hill to make some calls. He had found four of his five goats – a male was missing. Making his way back down the path to town, he debated whether to head to Bobby's store, or to Cousin Clem's. As he walked past Frog's gas station, he saw a WGFD vehicle – Wyoming Game and Fish Department – parked in the lot. Its driver was drinking an iced tea and filling out paperwork. A good place to start, and it saved him borrowing a phone.

Patrick waved, and approached the driver's side window. "Hi, I'm Patrick Flaherty, I live up on Hamm's Hill. You have a second?"

"Sure, what's up?" The ranger's badge said "Harmon." She was blond, petite, and looked like she probably enjoyed her job.

"Do you folks have a protocol for reporting nuisance bears?" asked Patrick. "A bear snatched one of my goats today, and ruined my goat pen. I'm worried that he's getting too close, and it's getting dangerous."

"Yeah, we have a unit that specializes in bear removal, if the situation warrants," said Harmon. "Have you seen the bear before?"

"Problem is, I haven't really seen him, or her, at all," said Patrick. "The first evidence I saw was bear tracks around a white-tail fawn carcass a couple of miles up Water Creek. Then I think I might have seen a black bear in the brush, near a clearing about a mile and a half from here. And now this thing today. There are clear bear tracks again today, and some blood, but I wasn't there when he came."

She thought for a second. "I'm really not sure how the bear unit is going to want to handle this one. I'll report it, and they'll probably come out and talk with you. This is a close call, I think. On the one hand, it's a bear getting too close to human habitation, and stealing livestock. On the other hand, he hasn't come into town, and you're pretty isolated. So they may just tell you to be careful and learn to live with him."

"Understood. But I don't want to have to shoot him. If he comes around the goat pen again, I'm going to have to. I need those goats."

"I'm not going to tell you not to do that. But legally, you can only shoot a bear in self-defense, unless it's in-season, and you have to have a bear license. Otherwise, it's hunting without a license."

Patrick had never applied for a bear license. Bear meat was supposed to be very unappetizing.

Ranger Harmon took a sip of tea. "Maybe the U.S. Forest Service would have an idea. The first evidence you saw of this bear – if it was the same one – sounds like it was in the National Forest. You can report it to them and ask if they have any relocation protocols that they follow."

"OK, I can do that."

"Can I run you up to your place?" she asked. "I'd like to take a look at the incursion so that I can describe it accurately when I report it."

"Sure." He went around to the passenger side of her SUV and jumped in. He directed her back up Route 14 to the left turn at Side Road, and up to where the path to his cabin started. They got out and walked up the path, and around the cabin to the goat pen.

Patrick pointed out the bear tracks, and said, "I fixed the fence, sort of."

Harmon nodded once, and then again more vigorously. "It's a male," she said, "a large adult from the looks of the prints."

"How can you tell?" he asked.

"Looking at a hundred sets of prints over the last six years. And working beside the bear unit." She took out her phone and took some close-up pictures.

"Is it common for adult males to start liking people food?" he asked.

"Actually, it's not," she said. "Dumb juvenile males get into the most trouble. A lot like people." She smiled. "But maybe an older adult, maybe sick or lame, would look for easy pickings. Don't know. I'll write this up, and we'll see what we can do. Like I said, I'm not sure how it'll go, but I'll wheedle a little bit if the bear unit people seem reluctant. It's an adult male – that alone is reason for concern, I think."

"OK, thanks," he said. "Do you have a card I can have?"

She reached in her pocket and took out a business card. "My name is Alice Harmon. Call me if you notice any further evidence."

"OK, will do. If you need to reach me, leave a message at Cousin Clem's and I'll call you back."

She looked surprised. "No cell phone?"

"They cost money," he said. "And most of the people I need to talk to live in Coolidge. I can be on their front porch by the time I get a good signal out here."

She smiled again, and they shook hands. Patrick didn't see any rings. As she made her way down the path, he wondered whether she had a boyfriend.

CHAPTER 19

Which made him think about Stacey. Stacey was living in Sheridan now, still working at District 4 – Trooper Stacey Andrews of the Wyoming Highway Patrol. She married a lawyer named Steve three years ago, and was happy. They had a daughter, and another baby on the way.

Stacey and Patrick met one afternoon at The 14 Diner when Stacey was taking a break from her patrol. It was about six months after Patrick arrived in Coolidge. Patrick walked in for some food while he was still working with Marty, and sat two seats away from her at the counter. They were both talking to Mindy, and soon they were talking to each other. He asked for her phone number. The first few dates were hunting and rafting.

It was while he was starting to go out with Stacey that Patrick quit his job and moved into his cabin. She was skeptical, but was as curious as he was, probably, about whether it was even possible to live off the land in Sheridan County. She encouraged the experiment. They thought of new ways to go on cheap dates.

When they spent the night together, it was always at Stacey's apartment on the second floor of Mrs. Cantrell's house in Coolidge. In the morning -- or sometimes later in the day, depending on her shift -- she would commute to the District in Sheridan in her little Toyota Tacoma pickup. Occasionally, she'd bring a cruiser home when she would be headed west along Route 14 for her next shift, and Pat would take her pickup to scavenge construction materials in Coolidge, or at ranches out of town.

Stacey and Patrick were in love, anyone could see it. The challenge was where to go from there.

"I don't see why it wouldn't work," she said one Sunday morning over coffee. "I love my job, the pay is fine, and you wouldn't need to change your life very much. I'd need to live in a regular house – we could build it, and it could be out of town, in the hills. But we can stay near Coolidge, and we can have kids and raise 'em here. I'd be happy to handle the money, and you wouldn't need to worry about it."

He thought for a moment, started to change the subject.

"Focus, Patrick," she said. "Tell me what you're thinking."

He sighed. "I don't know." He paused again. "Stacey, right now, I'm Conan the Barbarian. I'm pulling a livelihood out of the ground and the woods in a hostile place. I'm proud of what I'm doing. I'm not sure I could say the same if I were just Mr. Mom."

She opened her mouth to speak, and closed it slowly. Then: "I wouldn't want you to change. That's the whole idea. You can hunt, you can fish, you can raise goats and chickens, you can keep the house repaired, and keep it warm in the winter. I'll join your church if you'd like, and we can go on dates for free. I'd be *with* you. We'd be doing life together, each with our own jobs to do."

"What I'm worried about is that I wouldn't *need* to hunt, I wouldn't *need* to tend my animals," he said. "It might be true what the salesmen say – they can only sell when the choice is to starve. I don't know whether I could make myself do what I do, if I didn't need to."

She paused, and thought. "You wouldn't know, I think, until you try. Marriage changes everybody some, but it would be up to us to decide whether it would be a little or a lot, and we'd deal with the changes together. Either you'd stay doing what you're doing, or you wouldn't. If you did, that'd be great. And if you didn't, I think that would mean that you weren't meant to live as Conan forever. Maybe a few years will have been enough."

She took a sip of coffee and looked at him. He knew she couldn't read his thoughts. But then, neither could he.

"Can I think about it?" he asked.

She broke it off a year later. "I want to have a family," she said. "I love you, but I need to get going on babies." She moved to Sheridan on a Tuesday day off.

He let her leave, and he knew it was his fault.

He was with Doreen Parsons for the three years after that. When they broke up, it was her fault.

Doreen and Patrick were all white-hot phosphorous for the first year. And then pretty good for the second. And then Pat started escaping to Cousin Clem's during the third. Logistically, it was about the same as it was with Stacey: two or three nights a week at her place, a lot of time in the hills, Pat free to live his own life.

Early on, he knew he needed to clarify. "Do you agree with me that the worst thing you can possibly do before you fall into a relationship is to assume you can change the things you don't like about the other person?" He was testing.

Patrick remembered her words in response: "Absolutely," she said. "My mom tells me that all the time. 'You're not going to change him.'"

The "all the time" should have rung alarm bells for him. Why had Mrs. Parsons felt the need to proffer that advice to her little girl more than once, or twice? He asked himself: Could it have been, Patrick, you idiot, that she had to repeat the advice "all the time" because Doreen repeatedly tried to change the guys she was going out with? Why did it take *you* so long to figure it out?

Patrick's friends thought Doreen probably liked the raw material, and thought she could make something out of it. Patrick worked very hard; he was honest; and he listened to what she had to say. But there was no obvious logical progression from Patrick's raw material to Doreen's "if I can get him to find and hold a job, we'll be fine."

She tried to be subtle. "Why don't you consider," and "you should think about" were her vectors of choice. But her meaning was always, "take this suggestion, or else." Or else, what? She never said. The more Patrick resisted the suggestions – and he was clear with her that he was resisting her suggestions on purpose – the more determined she became. "Or else" she'll keep trying to change you, forever.

It was Doreen's fault. Not malign, but dumb. She had broken Rule 1 – don't assume you can change him.

They had broken up by mutual agreement back in March. They both realized that she would be wearing out her drill bit on solid rock, for five or ten or thirty years to come. Afterwards, he had only good feelings for her, and he didn't blame her for wanting someone different.

CHAPTER 20

"Hello. You have reached the Bighorn National Forest office of the Department of Agriculture's U.S. Forest Service. If you are calling for information about recreation in the Bighorn National Forest, please press 1. If you are calling about camping regulations, and campgrounds, in the Bighorn National Forest, please press 2. If you are calling about fire regulations, please press 3. If you are calling about employment opportunities with the U.S. Forest Service, please press 4. If you are calling to inquire about hunting in the Bighorn National Forest, please hang up and contact the Wyoming Game and Fish Department. If you are calling about any other matter relating to the Bighorn National Forest or the U.S. Forest Service, please wait on the line, and someone will assist you. Please note that we are experiencing unusually long telephone wait times in the summer months. You can also reach us through our website at www.fs.usda.gov/bighorn."

Patrick didn't hear any mention of bears, so he reckoned he would need to stay on the line until someone assisted him. He was in Cousin Clem's at mid-day, and was calling on Bean's cell phone. Bean was in for lunch. He mouthed "I'm on hold" to Bean – not sure why, he could have said it out loud – and stared at the wall behind the bar. Like just about every bar in 21st Century America, Clem's had top shelf liquors on the top shelf; pretty good liquors on the middle shelf; and budget liquors on the bottom shelf. If you asked for just "whiskey," "vodka," "gin," or "rum," they poured from the bottom shelf. If you asked for "bourbon," or "rye," or "sour mash," or "Irish," or anything else that sounded like you knew that there's more than one kind of whiskey in the world, they poured from the middle shelf. And if you named the liquor you wanted, they gave you the liquor you wanted – at $0.50 more per shot if it was on the middle shelf, and at least $1.00 more per shot if it came from the top shelf. Notwithstanding that he hated money, Patrick approved of capitalism, and believed that price signals were enormously effective in ensuring the distribution and availability of scarce, and semi-scarce, goods and services.

Still on hold. From the liquors, Pat's attention drifted to the beer taps. Clem's were at the inside edge of the bar. Other bars had them on the back wall. What were the factors influencing the placement? Was it a bad thing for bartenders to have to turn around and face away from their customers? What about the bar and eating space you sacrificed when you placed them on the inside edge of the bar? Which location was better for cleaning glasses? Which way was better for . . . .

"Forest Service."

"Uh, hi, my name is Patrick Flaherty. Is this the number for calling to report a nuisance bear?"

"Where are you calling from?"

"I'm calling from Coolidge. I have a goat pen here . . ."

"Coolidge isn't in the National Forest. You'll have to call the Wyoming Game and Fish Department."

"I did, I talked to them already . . ."

"You don't need to report it to us. Coolidge is outside the National Forest."

"But WGFD suggested that I ought to call you guys as well, because I live right near the edge of the National Forest, and they think the bear probably lives there. They thought you'd want to know."

"I don't know why they thought we would want to know about an incident that isn't in our jurisdiction. You're going to have to hang up and call them back."

"Sir, the bear took one of my goats, and his tracks were heading straight for the National Forest. I was thinking maybe there have been other sightings, or maybe he's tagged, or maybe you have specialists who can help me keep my livestock safe and out of . . ."

"I don't know how many times I'm going to need to say this – a bear creating a nuisance outside of the preserve is not in our jurisdiction."

"If I see him again, inside the preserve, can I . . ."

"Right now, he's not in our jurisdiction."

"Do you have a special number for bears, or something like that . . ."

"I'm telling you for the last time, I'm not going to take a report from you."

Patrick had been holding his anger in check, but this particular bureaucrat had pushed his last button. He paused. "I was only trying to get some help. Why do you have to be such a dick?" He pushed the "end call" icon on Bean's phone, and handed it back to him.

CHAPTER 21

It was a Tuesday night. Patrick knew a lot of people, but he was aware he didn't always know their stories. Like Larry's. He didn't want to pry, and he was shy about asking for details. So he'd usually wait for someone to start. That night, he was talking with Clem at the bar. Clem was a big guy -- probably 260 pounds, and, at about 6'2", taller than Patrick. He had sandy hair and brown eyes that were always watching the room, with attention rather than suspicion. He was wearing his trademark bowling shirt. For the first time in the seven years Patrick had known him, Clem talked about his childhood in Quebec.

"My grandfather worked on the Canadian National, and was Anglophone, didn't speak much French. He and my grandmother lived down the street. We always heard English at Sunday dinners and holidays, and a lot of other times, even if we didn't speak it a lot. We took it in school. I could always make myself understood in English, and when I moved to Montreal and started working in the restaurant business, my English improved in a hurry."

Patrick pointed back toward the kitchen. "How'd you meet Claire?" Claire was pretty, blonde, and barely five feet tall. She must have been stunning when they met, thirty-five years before – and when it came right down to it, she still was. They had two daughters, both of whom were in graduate school at UW in Laramie.

"We met at a community college in Montreal. We were taking the same restaurant management course. It turns out she was from Lac St. Jean too, but I didn't know her 'dere." With the dropped "th," the slight accent that remained was recognizably Quebecois.

"Did you get married pretty soon after you met?"

"We got engaged: my family name is Labrecque and hers is Laperriere. The Labrecques and Laperrieres all knew people who knew people in the other family, and everybody was invited to a big wedding in Chicoutimi. After 'dat, we got an apartment together in Montreal and started working in expensive restaurants. We saved a little money, took out a big mortgage and bought a fixer-upper brasserie on rue St. Denis, north of Sherbrooke."

"So how did you wind up in Wyoming?" Patrick heard himself asking the question that was posed to anyone who didn't grow up there. It had already been posed fifty times to him in the years he'd been in Coolidge. Wyoming was the smallest state in the Union, by population. It wasn't as if Wyomingites didn't appreciate what they had; but they had surely noticed over time that people were not breaking down the gates to get in. It was therefore a matter of interest when people came and chose to stay.

"Claire's brother was a miner," Clem replied. "He was working at the open-pit asbestos mine in Thetford Mines, back in Quebec. He found out Powder River Coal Company was offering good pay and big bonuses to work at the open coal pit down in Gillette. He settled out here, and eventually married an American girl. We visited as often as we could – we had to ask our parents to look after the brasserie while we visited – and we fell in love with the Bighorn Mountains."

"So, one day we were out here visiting Claire's brother and his wife, and we drove through Coolidge. We saw a 'For Sale' hanging out front 'dere." He pointed over Patrick's shoulder. "It was called the 'Wishing Well' at the time. We came in, had a drink. We were hooked. I was born in Maine, while my dad was working 'dere. I'm a U.S. citizen, so I knew I could buy the place, and stay. As a spouse of a U.S. citizen, Claire was eligible for a Green Card. Wally, he was selling the bar, he rented the business to us for a dollar a month while we were putting together our purchase package. My real name is Clément – it sounds better in French – and so Cousin Clem's was born. Anyway, we sold our brasserie in Montreal for a nice profit, invested it here. We've been here for thirty years. We saved a seat for you."

Patrick smiled and raised his beer. "Thanks." Then, "What happened to Claire's brother?"

"He retired a couple of years ago. Big family, lots of grandkids. Still living near Gillette. We see 'em pretty often."

Clem refilled Patrick's Black Tooth. "You hungry?"

"A little. I don't want to impose," said Patrick.

"It's no trouble, come on." Clem called through the window into the kitchen, "Edie, a cheeseburger and fries, please." Turning back to Patrick, he said, "Let me pour you a shot of Jameson to go with your beer. And I'll have one. Irish is best. I always hated Canadian whiskey."

CHAPTER 22

Bays Feeds sat on Route 14 on the east rim of town. The store and parking lot took up about two acres. Bobby was there every morning at 6:00 to open the doors for ranchers who considered a 6:00 a.m. trip to the feed store a mid-morning break.

At about 7:00 a.m., Patrick drifted in to fetch Millie. Millie was Bobby's German Shorthaired Pointer, and Patrick was her best friend other than Bobby. When Patrick showed up, it was time to head into the fields and chase things, and Millie was circling around her tail in celebration.

That morning, Patrick had seen about 100 white-tails scattered in the alfalfa fields north of town. They gathered in groups of about 20, rather than in one big herd of a hundred. Patrick didn't know why. One big buck per 20 deer? One thing was for sure – they'd all be hiding on the first day of white-tail season, in November.

Patrick headed into the store and found Bobby behind the counter. Bobby was a hard-packed five-foot-eight, with thinning brown hair and a quick smile. He looked like an actuary, until you noticed that he could probably break you in half. "Hi Bobby," said Patrick. "She looks like she's ready to go."

"She knows when it's going to be a Patrick day, somehow, before we're even open. You have that effect on young girls."

"I wish. Grouse season started yesterday, so she's going to have some fun. Borrow your Remington?" In Patrick's view, Bobby's Remington semi-automatic 12 gauge was the ultimate grouse gun, because the fraction of a second you saved not having to pump the slide increased your chances for a second-shot hit by about 80 percent. Patrick's own shotgun was an old 12-gauge Savage pump. It worked, and shot straight, but Bobby's gun was a Cadillac in comparison.

"Sure, let me go find it," said Bobby. He ducked into the back office.

"Hi girl," said Patrick to Millie, scratching under her jaw. "We're gonna have fun today, aren't we, yeah." Patrick checked her for ticks, looked at her teeth and eyes, and squeezed each paw. She was two years old, and in great health. Patrick had been training her as a bird and rabbit dog since she was a puppy.

Bobby returned, placing the shotgun and a box of shells on the front counter. He loved to see his dog happy – she was built to run, not spend all day in a store. When Patrick showed up, he was as glad as she was.

"How long d'you think you'll be out?" asked Bobby.

"She'll try not to show it, but she'll be tired after three hours. So, maybe 10:00, 10:30."

"That works for me. With the heat early this month, I'm only keeping most of my feeds for 120 days, and I've got a bunch of 50 pound bags that are past that – I think four goat pellets and five chicken feed. I also have one broken bag of chicken feed. I can show you which ones they are, and you can drag 'em out." Patrick nodded, and Bobby added, "You're going to need the truck to get 'em back to your place, the keys are in." Bobby and Patrick both knew that, like people food, animal feed was almost always still good to eat after its sell-by date. But it wasn't as salable. Bobby was happy to have Patrick lift the fifty pound bags, and Patrick was happy to have the feed.

"Six bags are four months of chicken feed for my birds," said Patrick. "I should ask Miriam Vogel whether she has any roasters who are getting on her nerves. I'll have enough feed for them, and I can split the meat with her when I get ready to cook 'em." Patrick got his first four Orpingtons from Miriam, as a gift, five years earlier, and some more since. Miriam cared for a flock of more than 50 birds. Orpingtons were good for eggs and meat, and Patrick had been pleased with the way they worked out. Miriam hated to clean chickens, and was happy to have half a bird if she didn't have to pull it apart.

Patrick thought of some news he hadn't shared yet with Bobby. "I had a bear on Thursday. He took one of my goats."

Bobby just nodded; bears were a fact of life around Coolidge.

"Luckily, he took a male, that I was probably going to butcher this fall anyway. So the bear will have at least one more meal than me."

"Keep your spray on you," said Bobby. And then he thought of another subject he'd been forgetting to raise with Patrick. "If I got another pointer, would you be willing to work with a second dog?" he asked.

"Sure!" said Patrick. "I didn't know you were thinking about a second dog."

"I think Millie's lonely. With a little sister, she could transmit all of her neuroses to a younger version of herself. Like we all wish we could do."

"Don't call my girlfriend crazy," said Patrick. "Yeah, I think she could use the company."

"The thing is Pat, I don't want to abuse your good nature. You're the best dog trainer I ever knew, and I want to be fair with you. The feed you're taking is eventually going to the dump if you don't use it. Not only is it zero value to me, but it takes a lot of handling. You solve all those problems for me. And I'll be asking you to spend even more time, because you're going to have to work with the new dog by herself, at least for some of the time. You'll be spending almost double the time."

"I'm happy to do it, Bobby," replied Patrick. And he really was.

Patrick and Millie left through the front door, heading on foot toward prairie. Grouse is very good eating, and Patrick was hoping to come back home carrying a meal or two.

CHAPTER 23

Patrick awoke to terrified bleating from the goat pen, and chickens screeching in the night. Every one of his animals was screaming. His first thought was "human"; his second thought was "bear." He sat up, swung his legs over the side of the bed, and grabbed his Winchester, which was leaning against the wall next to the bed.

A random thought occurred: Why didn't I ever plan for this? And the next: what do I do? He needed more information, and he had no means to acquire it. He couldn't do what his parents would have done in Denver – turn on flood lights at the corners of the house. He couldn't step out the front door, because he had no idea what he was facing.

He grabbed a flashlight from beside his bed and pointed it through the plastic sheet into the goat shelter and chicken coop. Nothing to see but frightened, noisy animals. He doused the light.

Patrick knelt on his bed, in the corner of the cabin farthest from the front door, right knee on his pillow, and left foot planted on his bedcover. He rested his left forearm on his left knee, in a kneeling firing position, and swung the barrel of his rifle between the door and each window. There was enough moonlight coming through the windows that he could see, at least a little. Nothing to do but listen and wait.

There was silence for thirty seconds or so. His front door was solid, in fact massive, a trophy from a house demolition two or three years before. He didn't think the bear would be able to break it down. But: the lever. Why did I use that damn door with the lever, instead of one with a knob like everyone else? The front door burst open before another thought came. The animal was huge, and moving directly into the cabin, toward the refrigerator. He was fifteen feet from Patrick, not looking his way.

Patrick's heart was pounding, and no clear thoughts came. He instinctively growled at the animal, with his finger on the trigger of his rifle. The bear turned to him, surprised. He swiveled his head from Patrick, to the refrigerator, again to Patrick, and to the front door, obviously deciding. Decision made: he had come for food, and he was going to find some. Pat watched over the top of the stove as the bear pawed at the refrigerator with his right foreleg, and tripped the handle with a claw. He inserted his left paw into the gap as the door cracked open, and pulled. The refrigerator swayed. Patrick's antelope meat was front and center, and the bear grabbed a large chunk with his jaws.

By default, Patrick had settled on a strategy – let the bear eat, and shoot him only if he came nearer. Maybe the bear saw himself as an apex predator -- no coyote, lone wolf, or scared human was going to interrupt his meal. Maybe the bear figured that if he left Patrick alone, Patrick would leave him alone. Another piece of antelope meat went down his throat.

The bear rummaged through the refrigerator and ate everything edible. The process took three minutes; the longest three minutes of Patrick's life. When he finished, the bear looked toward Patrick, and then turned toward the front door. Not in a rush. His lack of fear was reassuring, in one sense – if he didn't feel threatened, maybe he had no reason to attack. Live and let live, my brother. The bear slipped into the night.

In another sense, the bear's lack of fear was terrifying. Patrick had to live there, and he knew the bear would be back whenever he wanted an easy meal. Something would have to give.

CHAPTER 24

Patrick and Bobby Bays were climbing up from the junction of Little Goose and Tepee Creeks, hunting for elk. They weren't expecting much. Wyoming's hunting seasons vary by region, and the rules are mindnumbingly complex. The constraints that day were that they couldn't hunt in the National Forest; they were restricted to antlerless elk; and they could only hunt within Region 37. If they had elected to stay near Coolidge, 25 miles away, that would have been in Region 38, and the season hadn't begun yet in Region 38. But hunting was hunting, and you never knew what could happen.

Patrick was telling Bobby about Stanley's psychotic boss. "Did you ever have a boss like that?"

"No, I'd quit." Bobby replied. "I don't like being humiliated for sport. The closest I came to that was in the Army. Drill sergeants. But you knew it was temporary, and you knew they were play-acting a little. I think I could get along with almost any boss as long as I'm not being asked to give up my self-respect."

"Yeah," said Patrick, as he fiddled with his spotting scope.

"I'll give you an example," Bobby continued. "Our tank commander was an E-6 from Michigan." Patrick nodded. Bobby had been a tank gunner with the First Armored Division in Desert Storm, and rarely talked about the experience. "In some ways, a terrible leader," continued Bobby. "He was just a cold fish. When we'd have a great day on the range, or we'd win a ribbon or a tournament, there were no compliments, no thanks, no praise for a job well done. Just nothing. But overall, he was an OK boss, because he had three things going for him. He knew the machine inside and out. He gave really clear orders. And when he criticized you, it was always in private, not in front of the other guys. The result was that we were a good crew, and really tight-knit off duty, except for him. He wasn't real close to any of the other sergeants, either. I still wonder whether the Army made him lonely, or what he felt about any of it."

"Did you start your own business to avoid having a boss?" asked Patrick.

"Oh yeah, that was a big reason," replied Bobby. "I could never go back to being an employee. What's tough, though, is having a business partner. Anybody will tell you, it can be harder than being married. I had a partner earlier on. He wanted to have a fight over every nickel, and I usually just shrugged my shoulders and gave in."

"Do I know him?" asked Patrick.

"Naw, he's in Billings now, still in the feed business. Buying him out wasn't easy. What happened was, we had a couple of bad years in a row, and he wanted to skedaddle. But he wanted a ridiculous amount of money for his share, and he wanted a mortgage on the business to secure the buy-out, shit like that. I finally just stopped talking to him about it."

"How did you manage to end the partnership?"

"Well, I let it fester for a most of a year. He wasn't coming into the store anymore, but was still taking his partnership draw. Finally, I got Anita Boyle involved. I told her, 'Just get me out of this.'" Bobby shook his head at the memory.

"Did your partner have a lawyer?"

"Yeah, most of it was done lawyer-to-lawyer. But I remember this one meeting with lawyers and clients, not long before we signed, where my partner was shouting and waving his arms at Anita for about twenty minutes, and his lawyer just sat there watching. Anita looked at my partner while he was going on and on. She was calm, not saying a word. I never saw anything like it, just ice water in her veins. And finally he stops yelling, and she says – nothing. Just kept looking at him, calm and quiet. She wasn't backing down an inch, but she wasn't giving him anyone to fight with, either. My partner gets frustrated and says, 'Don't you have anything to say?' and Anita says: 'No.' Just like that. Still looking at him. Finally, his lawyer took him outside the room to talk, and when they came back in, they agreed to our final offer. Anita hadn't said a word in response to his rant, but they had figured out they weren't going to move her."

"I can imagine that, that sounds like Anita," said Patrick. "She's tough. I don't know anything about her law practice. What I like about her is, she's sociable. She doesn't talk much about herself, and certainly not much about her job, but she's curious about everything and everybody. She likes people. She holds her own in Clem's."

"Yeah, I like that," said Bobby.

"I've gotten to know her better over the last couple of years," continued Patrick, "and she's starting to remind me of Claudette Colbert, or some other actress you think you'd like to be friends with. And we are; we're friends. I get along with her."

"Claudette Colbert?"

"Yeah. *It Happened One Night*, with Clark Gable. Got an Oscar for Best Picture in, like, 1933 or 1934. You can probably find it online somewhere."

Patrick saw a brown shape moving on the hill across from them, at least a mile away. He zeroed it in with the spotting scope and let out a quiet "Woah." He handed the scope to Bobby and said, pointing: "Take a look just to the left of that big rock outcropping."

Bobby focused the eyepiece. "Damn. He's a big fella," he said. "We'll come back in two weeks when the antlered season starts, see if we can find him."

"Yeah, absolutely," replied Patrick.

"In the meantime, let's spend one more hour looking for his best girlfriend, and if she doesn't show up we'll find an afternoon beer in Sheridan. We can go to the Black Tooth."

"Works for me," said Patrick. They trudged down the hill toward Little Goose Creek, being careful to stay out of the National Forest.

PART II

CHAPTER 25

Whoever had scheduled the meeting for 2:30 on a Thursday had forgotten – or worse, was fully aware – that the Nationals were playing an afternoon game. At least three of the twelve lawyers present – well, actually eleven lawyers and one CPA – had tickets they were not going to be able to use.

Walter Kruminsky, Director of the OTP – the Office of Tax Policy within the Department of the Treasury – was co-chairing the meeting. With him was his deputy director. The IRS sent over its Chief of the Criminal Section. The Deputy Attorney General for Tax Enforcement and Economic Crimes was on hand, as was the DAG for the Criminal Section.

Kruminsky had just been asked to head up the "Section 61 Task Force" to support the administration's "Revenue Enhancement Project." He opened the meeting with some background facts that most, but not all, of the participants understood. "The President has made clear that he's not going to negotiate with two parties in a deadlocked Congress to try to raise taxes. As he said, 'don't try to wrestle with a pig, because you'll get muddy, and the pig likes it.' The President told the Treasury Secretary to close some loopholes in the Treasury regs, and to focus on income that's being under-reported by taxpayers, so that we can raise some revenue without new legislation.

"About ten weeks ago, the Treasury Secretary, my boss, told OTP to come up with a list of about ten regulations that were more generous toward taxpayers than the language of the corresponding sections of the Internal Revenue Code required, and which offered a reasonable prospect of raising revenue once they were modified. We did that. As you know, we identified aspects of carried interest, like-kind exchanges, publicly-traded partnerships, barter transactions, cafeteria plans, life insurance ownership, charitable contributions to racist or non-diverse organizations, definitions of recognition events for trusts and educational endowments, and a couple of other items.

"As of, I would say, four weeks ago, we had eleven amendments to the regs drafted and ready to present to the Secretary. These were all relatively simple, large dollar changes. We know that when we put them out for notice and comment, K Street is going to go crazy, members of Congress are going to scream, and every industry directly affected is going to go nuts. The President says he's willing to take the heat, and he's willing to blame Congress for not acting.

"But the Secretary was emphasizing that all of this is going to take time. The new regs need to be finalized; they won't be effective until next tax year, if we're lucky; and revenues won't pick up until tax collection season almost two years from now. In the meantime, the noise from all the usual suspects to roll back the new regs will continue.

"So, as you know, the Treasury Secretary and the Attorney General were backbenchers in the House together, and they're friends. They were having lunch after a cabinet meeting and talking about all of this. And, as I understand it, the AG says, 'Why not bring some high visibility prosecutions for criminal tax evasion, based on existing statutes and regulations?' As the Secretary described it, they discussed the idea, and it has some obvious advantages. Only two percent of all returns are audited, so almost no one is afraid of an audit anymore. But everyone is afraid of going to jail, and voluntary reporting works when people are afraid to cheat. With criminal prosecutions, no delay would be involved, because theoretically, we could refer some obvious cases of evasion to the Department of Justice, and DOJ could indict very quickly. That could happen before next tax season. And nobody likes tax cheats who get caught, so the administration can publicize the prosecutions and convictions.

"But what should we prosecute?" he asked rhetorically. Kruminsky checked his notes. "In terms of under-reporting, we dusted off a study we did way back in 2005 about where the most cheating was going on. As you'd expect, cash businesses with two sets of books were the biggest source of lost revenue – but restaurant owners have been ignoring the risk of criminal enforcement for decades, and we don't expect them to change now. Capital gains, surprisingly, were way under-reported, because a lot of people have no idea what they paid for a stock they just sold, and were making up favorable numbers. The problem there is that we could nail them for failure to keep records, but we can't prove what they paid for their stock either. Our records are no better than theirs. So we can't prove they're cheating. Taxes due on illegal drug profits were a big part of the total number, but of course nobody is expecting those profits to be reported anytime soon.

"Which brings us to barter transactions. Let me spend a few minutes on that. Under Section 1.61-1 and 2 of the regs, if I'm an architect, and I design your new building in exchange for a year's free rent when it's finished, I have to declare the free rent as revenue for my architectural practice, and you, as my landlord, have to report the value of the architectural services as rent received. Likewise, under Section 61 of the Code, if I landscape your mansion and grounds in exchange for a truckload of topsoil from down below your pool house, I have to report the value of the topsoil as revenue to my business. You get the concept.

"The problem is, nobody, and I mean nobody, ever reports this kind of income. Every small-town lawyer in America is trading collection work for free rent, but Uncle Sam doesn't see a dime of that – either from the lawyer or from the landlord.

He sipped his Poland Spring.

He looked around the table. "So, one of the key areas of under-reporting that this group is going to go after is the barter economy. By and large, the people who are doing the bartering are well off, and they have a lot to lose if they were ever to face prosecution. So a few high profile cases are likely to raise taxpayer awareness of this issue, and are likely to generate some enhanced, voluntarily reported revenue as early as next year.

He checked his notes again. "OK, before we jump into the meat of the agenda, and action items, let me introduce Kevin Paulson to all of the Treasury people here. Kevin is the Deputy Attorney General for Criminal Tax Enforcement, based here in Washington. I've been liaising with Kevin on these issues for a couple of weeks. Kevin speaks tax, but he also speaks cops and robbers, so he's going to talk a little about how criminal enforcement would work in practice. Kevin?"

Paulson adjusted his glasses. "Thanks Walter. OK, under the IRS Tax Examiner's Manual, in the ordinary case, an IRS examiner who spots potential criminality during the review of a return, or during an audit, will direct a report to the IRS Criminal Enforcement Bureau, who will look it over and decide if a formal criminal investigation should be initiated." He nodded at Samuel Prentiss from the IRS, sitting three seats away. "Sam can talk in a little bit about how that internal IRS process works."

"Once the IRS has determined that criminal tax evasion has likely taken place, the chief criminal investigator on the case will contact the local U.S. Attorney's Office to request that the case be taken in front of a grand jury. If the U.S. Attorney agrees that the facts show likely criminal conduct, the U.S. Attorney's Office will open a case file and begin to prepare the case for prosecution."

"So just to be sure that the Treasury folks here understand what I'm talking about, there are 93 United States Attorneys' offices in the country. Each United States Attorney is nominated by the President and confirmed by the Senate, and there is one U.S. Attorney for each federal judicial district."

"Every U.S. Attorney's office employs Assistant United States Attorneys – roughly equivalent to Assistant District Attorneys in a local D.A.'s office, except they work for the federal government – and it's the AUSA's who do the day-in day-out trial work, some civil but mostly criminal."

"In the larger U.S. Attorney's Offices – Southern District of New York, Northern District of Illinois, Central District of California – there are one or more AUSA's who specialize in tax prosecutions, and those lawyers will be assigned all of the criminal referrals from the IRS. But a lot of smaller districts like, say, the District of Idaho, do not have full time tax prosecutors, and if a tax evasion case is complicated, they'll normally ask for help from Washington."

"On the other hand, most districts have at least one AUSA for Economic Crimes, and they can usually handle simple tax cases if they need to."

"All this is by way of background, and you'll see where I'm going in a minute. For criminal tax prosecutions to have the desired effect – encouraging voluntary compliance – we need to bring them at the local level, and in as many federal judicial districts as we can. We need to have local, and hopefully national, press coverage, and local investigators putting the cases together for local grand juries. For that matter, we need to have AUSA's with the right local idioms and accents, so we can take these cases to local trial juries."

"We've already started to put together a consulting team of criminal tax prosecutors, both here in Washington and in U.S. Attorneys' offices around the country, who can be detailed to our projects. Each of them will be assigned to assist with cases in districts where there aren't any experienced tax prosecutors, and they'll work with the Economic Crimes prosecutors in those districts, or, in some cases, regular front line criminal AUSA's."

"Most federal criminal prosecutions are handled by teams anyway, so the local AUSA's will be used to cooperating with teammates. The tax lawyers will work largely on documentary evidence and deciding what proof needs to be offered to get a conviction, and the local prosecutors can handle taking witnesses before the grand jury, examining witnesses at trial, arguing objections, and making opening and closing arguments to the jury.

"That's the strategy. What happens next is that the AG will issue a directive to every one of the 93 U.S. Attorneys to prioritize criminal prosecutions for each of the revenue enhancement subject areas that are amenable to criminal cases. The Commissioner of the IRS will send a similar directive to every IRS-CID area. It's already been decided that barter transactions will be on the list, and will be a part of that directive. Or maybe there will be separate directives for separate subject areas, we're still thinking on that. Our job, as a committee, is, first, to recommend language to include in the directive or directives. Second, we'll need to draft a memo for the Commissioner of the Internal Revenue Service, and the responsible Deputy, instructing regional IRS enforcement offices what to look for to identify prospective cases. And third, we need to designate some of our people, in Justice, Treasury and the IRS, to serve as resources for people out in the field as they have questions in working up the cases.

He turned back to Kruminsky. "Walter, do you want to talk about some of our action items?"

"OK, thanks Kevin," said Kruminsky. "We're going to try to talk this afternoon about prospects for criminal prosecution of at least five different types of underreported income. Since we've already touched on bartering, let's start with that."

Turning to his left, Kruminsky gestured to one of the younger IRS representatives at the table. "Robert Cavelli, you're one of the few people in either Department who has ever prepared a bartering case for trial." Checking his notes: "As I understand it, you worked with IRS counsel to present a civil bartering case to the Tax Court about three years ago, is that right?" Cavelli nodded. "I also understand that the case involved an intentional understatement penalty, so it was a little bit like a criminal case. Can you give us a two-minute summary of what facts need to be proved in a bartering case?"

Cavelli cleared his throat. He had spent eight hours the day before preparing for his two minutes in the spotlight. "Well," he began, "the biggest challenge is that you have to prove that the taxpayer knew he was cheating the government . . ."

CHAPTER 26

Lloyd Grant was hosting Saturday night poker at his house. As was customary, Lloyd Grant, Bart Quigg, Terry Painter, and Toby Ernst were playing Texas Hold 'Em, and Patrick was the permanent dealer. He was the permanent dealer because he didn't have any money, and didn't use money, so he was the perfect solution to the fights that used to break out when the players dealt their own hands. Also as usual, Terry was winning and Lloyd was losing.

Patrick liked poker night because it was his best chance during the week to hang around with people who were pretty much his age. All stunted adolescents, to be sure, but so was he.

Between hands, just after 11:00, talk turned to the subject of Patrick's bear.

"We should get that bear the fuck over here for some attitude adjustment," said Lloyd. "You know, we'll all just kinda beat the shit out of him."

"Nope," said Bart. "Too strenuous. We should invite him over to play cards. We'll take all his money in three hands. He'd be, like, too ashamed to show his face around here again."

"Naw, fuck, I wanna find out about Goldilocks first," said Toby. "I'd ask him, 'Why didn't you and the Missus *eat* that little bitch?'"

"No, no, Patrick'd be like, all serious and shit, '*Do* bears really shit in the woods?" offered Terry. "And the bear would be like all confused and shit, and he'd say, 'Is that a rhetorical question?"

"And Lloyd'd go, 'What's rhetorical?'" said Toby, "And the bear'd just look at him like he's an idiot. Like we do."

"We can get rich," said Toby. "We'll all dress up in bear costumes before he gets here, and then we can take some 'Bears Playing Poker' pictures. That shit would *sell.*"

"Yeah, but *you'd* be so pretty in a bear suit, he'd drag you home to his cave," said Lloyd. "That would be a long winter."

"Like Leo DiCaprio in *The Revenant,*" said Patrick. "But it would go on longer."

"Leo DiCaprio is an asshat," said Lloyd. "I was rooting for the bear."

"That's what I mean," said Bart. "We can convince him we're on his team, and maybe he'll leave Patrick the fuck alone."

"But we gotta start by inviting the bear," said Terry. "Yo, Pat, where do we send the invitation?"

"It's simple," said Lloyd, "we can send it to your cabin. Dude likes hanging out there."

"Yeah, he's 307," said Patrick. "He's not going anywhere."

By 1:00 a.m., Terry had cleaned everybody out. It was $100 table stakes, so nobody went home poor. Patrick walked with Toby as far as Frog's Cenex station, and then stumbled up Side Road to sleep. He was nervous walking up to the cabin with only his bear spray on his belt.

CHAPTER 27

The coffee machine was broken. Special Agent Arthur Bolton slipped out of his office on the third floor of the O'Mahoney Federal Building in Cheyenne, Wyoming, and headed for the Starbucks across the street and around the corner. His Caramel Macchiato would be his second of the day, a Monday. He was thinking about the odd memo that he had received from the Denver Field Office of his agency, the Internal Revenue Service, Criminal Investigation Division.

The memo, originating in Washington and addressed to every IRS-CID Special Agent in Charge, instructed SAC's to instruct their Special Agents to "undertake to develop" potentially prosecutable cases of failure to report bartering income. The memo identified, as its principal example, a landlord who gives free rent to a tenant artist, in exchange for a free painting. Although it was news to Bolton, there was apparently an IRS regulation that required the monetization and reporting of income from bartered exchanges. The memo also mentioned the possibility of ordinary "Section 61" income resulting from what it called "quasi-barter" – namely, the receipt of property, rather than money, in exchange for services. For that practice, it gave the example of a divorce lawyer who handles a car dealer's divorce, in exchange for a free car.

The reason Bolton found the memo odd was that it amounted to an instruction to drop everything else, at least temporarily, and get to work on a barter income case. As he had learned years before, "undertake to develop" was CID-speak for "you will find a case, you will work it up, and you will present it for prosecution, or else you will hear about your failure to do so in your next annual review." Bolton learned about that hidden meaning the hard way, when a similar memo had required the development of at least one oil and gas tax shelter case, and Bolton had failed to follow through with appropriate zeal. No merit raise that year, for sure.

When Bolton got back to the office, he decided to call his boss. Bolton's boss – Dan Price, Special Agent in Charge – worked in Denver. Cheyenne was an IRS-CID Sub-Office, and Bolton was *Acting* Assistant Special Agent in Charge in Cheyenne. There was no plan to make him the ASAC, and no plan to bring in someone else to be the ASAC. There were budget considerations – a real ASAC required payment of an ASAC's salary, GS-13 at a minimum, and Bolton was barely a GS-12.

Almost every time Bolton talked to his boss, it was by video-link between Cheyenne and Denver. Everyone in both offices was likely to be able to hear the conversation. Bolton and SAC Price were friends, but their video conversations were different. Had Bolton been sitting with his boss in person, his first question about the memo would have been, "What the *fuck* is this all about?" On video, the same question was posed in the form, "What other detail can you give me about the memo on barter transactions?"

"What I'm hearing is that this whole thing is a joint venture between IRS-Treasury and the Department of Justice," said Price. "It's all about encouraging voluntary compliance. Problem is, nobody knows about these bartering rules. So the first case or two will be wake-up calls for taxpayers across the CID Western Area, across the whole country, for that matter." What he would have said if they had been in an office together, with the door closed: "I feel sorry for the first unlucky bastard we arrest for this."

"It's just the two of us here in Cheyenne." Bolton was referring to himself and Karl Lawless, the newly-hired Special Agent Trainee, fresh out of the Federal Law Enforcement Training Center in Georgia. "Will the FBI field offices be getting some form of this memo, and can we expect some help from them?"

"I'm discussing exactly that issue this afternoon with their Denver SAC," said Price. "I'll have a better feel for what we can expect after I've talked to her. Certainly, when we get to the point of arresting somebody we'll have Feebie help, but I don't know whether they'll be detailing any agents for investigations. Doubtful. Even if DOJ in Washington tells them to help, if FBI headquarters doesn't push it, it won't happen. And I don't see any reason they'd want to put their fingerprints on this."

Bolton knew he had a challenge. He was not excited about it.

CHAPTER 28

It had been a rough four days. Special Agent Bolton had never handled a bartering case, and he began with the notion that there was likely to be taxable "bartering" wherever there was a transaction between two taxpayers that didn't involve cash. But he was soon disabused of that notion. If Taxpayer A trades a used lawnmower with a fair market value of $150 to Taxpayer B, in exchange for Taxpayer B's used snowblower, also having a fair market value of $150, neither side of the deal makes a profit. If there was no profit, there's no income, and if there's no income, no tax is due. In wasn't the barter itself that gave rise to an income tax obligation.

Bolton went back through all of the case files he had opened within the past five years – all likely involving at least some conduct within the six-year statute of limitations – to determine whether there were hints of barter activity that might have resulted in unreported income. None jumped out at him.

He reviewed audit files that the Civil Division had opened involving lawyers, especially lawyers who handled divorces, hoping to find an example of a lawyer trading services for free rent or a car. No good.

On Wednesday, he followed up on a suggestion one of the revenue agents made, and did some online research on radio stations' trading free commercial airtime for services. That idea was probably the best of the week, because his Bing searches produced a lot of evidence of bartering. He focused primarily on the party dealing with a radio station. Where an electrician fixes a radio station's transmitter in exchange for five 30-second commercials, his deemed income received for services is the "fair market value" of the commercials, say, $500. Because his marginal costs are not going to rise substantially when he does the work, he's $500 ahead of where he would have been. He gets the value of advertising that he might otherwise not have had. And unless he has a sophisticated tax preparer, he's not going to report the $500 in additional bottom-line profit.

But Bolton also saw a problem in investigating the practice. Did radio stations keep records of the free advertising time they gave away? They surely had records of their advertising revenues, but did they have similar records of time given away? And a bigger problem: the radio station charged different rates for different time slots, failed to sell some of its ad time, and probably gave volume discounts. How was he going to prove the "fair market value" of the advertising time allotted to the electrician? It would take him months to put together a case that would stick. He didn't exactly back-burner the idea of radio time for services, but it couldn't be his front-burner project, either.

He looked at the examples in the memo again. It dawned on him, slowly, that it was the little guy who was most likely to avoid taxes by bartering. The little guy can't deduct the value of his own labor. So if Mr. Little Guy landscapes your property for a day in exchange for a used big-screen TV that you were going to sell on eBay for $200, he has received untraceable income. If he had taken a $200 check, and put it in the bank, there would have been a record for Mr. Tax Man to see. Income. But a $200 television for his living room is a win-win. Mr. Little Guy gets a TV out of it, and he doesn't have to pay Mr. Tax Man any tax on the $200 in additional income.

Bolton spent much of Thursday thinking about the rent-for-services problem discussed in the memo from Washington. He checked IRS Publication 525 that addresses the issue. A landlord gives free rent to a residential tenant in exchange for services. His tenant is a starving artist, who for a variety of reasons, is not eligible to deduct any part of her apartment rental as a business expense. No one declares any part of the exchange on any tax return. The landlord receives, say, an oil portrait of his wife, in exchange for a free month's rent worth $1,000. If the landlord had received cash for the rent, his income would have been bumped up by $1,000. When he fails to declare the painting as income, he avoids tax on $1,000. The starving artist, in the meantime, will not declare the free rent as income from her painting work, and she winds up saving tax on $1,000 she would have received if she had sold the painting.

Bartered rent seemed to be a problem more likely to involve a richer taxpayer – somebody rich enough to be a landlord, at least. Maybe landlords were the best place to look. He was looking for mismatches – circumstances in which a taxpayer received valuable property in exchange for services or rental space, without being able to take advantage of a corresponding deduction. Now that he was clear on what he was looking for, Bolton hoped that finding a good case would not be hard.

There was paperwork to do on some pending cases, which took most of Friday morning. Bolton was due to start a week-long vacation that afternoon. He considered postponing it, but he knew he could spend some time working online if he needed to. His plan was to visit Steve and Laurie, his brother and his brother's wife, up in the Bighorn Mountains. Arthur Bolton and his brother Stephen grew up in Casper; Steve was two years older. Both had spent time in the Bighorns with their parents. Steve and Laurie had moved to Lovell, Wyoming, fresh out of UW in Laramie, to work as expedition guides.

Bolton took I-25 North out of Cheyenne toward Casper. He knew Casper well, because it was Wyoming's second largest city, and in his enforcement region. The U.S. District Court for the District of Wyoming conducted a lot of its trials there. He stopped for a bite to eat in Casper, and then continued on I-25 North to Buffalo. In Buffalo, he picked up I-90, which ran almost north-south at that point. He continued on I-90 through Sheridan, and got off on U.S. Route 14 in Ranchester, headed west. Just after Coolidge, he saw a sign that said, "You are now entering the Bighorn National Forest." He always felt better when he saw that sign. Escape.

The weekend – the last weekend in September -- was quiet, which was the way Bolton liked it. Since his divorce three years earlier, he had learned to value silence. During the 25 years he was married, he hadn't experienced much of it. Steve and Laurie usually worked weekends in September, so Arthur was free to sit, and hike, and think. He was more anxious about the bartering project than he wanted to admit – agents will "undertake to develop" cases.

He practiced thinking about bartered exchanges. What if Steve and Laurie gave away their guide services in exchange for gasoline? And then traded the gasoline for food? And suppose they took in a boarder in their empty bedroom in exchange for housecleaning and maintenance services? Is that income? If so, do you value the services at a professional rate? Suppose the homeowners would have done the cleaning or maintenance work themselves, and not paid for it at all, but for the fact that the boarder was there and able to do it?

He had never considered these issues before. But that was his job at the moment.

He remembered, somewhat randomly, the first time he ever encountered HIPPA – the law that guarantees privacy for patient records -- when his mom was in the hospital, and the doctor couldn't tell him anything about her condition. The doctor apologized, and called HIPPA a "solution in search of a problem." It seemed to Bolton that Washington's crack-down on bartering was a solution in search of a problem.

On the other hand, Arthur Bolton believed deeply in what he was doing. People who cheated on their taxes offended his sense of right and wrong. Although he tried not to take it personally, he was offended by the smugness of most of the people he investigated. Most of his defendants seemed to enjoy putting one over on the government, and, almost invariably, they didn't think cheating on their taxes was morally wrong. They were the barbarians at the gate; they wanted to tear it all down. Every case he won, by plea or verdict, was another brick in civilization's wall.

Monday and Tuesday were days off for Steve and Laurie, and, as September faded, Steve and Laurie and Arthur relaxed, drank wine, and grilled steaks and chicken. But Arthur was antsy. On Thursday, he announced that he'd be heading back to Cheyenne on Friday afternoon. His plan was to stay overnight in Sheridan, drive Saturday morning to Cheyenne, and then spend the remainder of the weekend on laundry, food shopping, and responding to work emails. Church on Sunday if he had time, and maybe a quick visit to the office to check his snail mail. He wanted to hit the ground running on Monday.

CHAPTER 29

On his way back to I-90 on Route 14, Bolton noticed the sign for Cousin Clem's. He was hungry, and turned into the lot. He parked his car, stretched, and stepped out into a night that was warm for early October. The parking area was almost full.

When he stepped into the bar, a singer was playing a country song on an acoustic guitar, and there was a pleasant hum in the room. A seat was opening at the middle of the bar just as he reached it, and he settled in. The bartender was wearing a bowling shirt, with the name "Clem" embroidered above the left-hand pocket. Had to be the owner.

"Hi, welcome," said Clem. "What can I get you?"

"A Coors Light draft, please," replied Bolton, placing a twenty on the bar. And then, "Busy night."

"Warm Friday night in early October," replied Clem. "Perfect night to go out to a bar." Clem stepped sideways to the beer taps and filled a pint glass with Coors Light. He stepped back, took Bolton's twenty, made change, and put the change beside the glass.

"Many thanks," said Bolton.

As the singer ended his set, Bolton noticed Clem hand him a beer that he didn't pay cash for, and he headed into the kitchen after saying hello to a few of the customers. He didn't come back out. Bolton paid attention to some other things. He noticed that the bar was no-smoking. Not unusual, of course. But twenty-five years ago, there would have been a war in Wyoming if bars had tried to ban smoking. Now it was routine. Things change. After about ten minutes, the singer came back out, holding his beer and eating a French fry.

Bolton saw four men at the far end of the bar who looked liked regulars. One of the four – the big guy -- was handing Clem at least three twenty-dollar bills. Both were laughing. Bolton looked around some more. Not surprisingly, most of the customers in the bar seemed to know each other.

The bartender moved down the bar and tossed a wooden nickel in front of every seat, including Bolton's. "That's Marty," he said, pointing back to the big guy at the end of the bar. When all the nickels were down, glasses were lifted, and "Thanks, Marty" tumbled across the room.

"Fuck the IRS," said Marty very loudly, shaking his head. He was in speech mode. Bolton was all ears. "Those fuckers just sent me a letter. They say I owe 'em five hundred bucks because somebody sent 'em a 1099 they didn't send me. The fucking computer in the basement of the IRS decides I didn't pay tax. They send me a notice with penalties, interest, self-employment tax, income tax, I don't know what the fuck else. They charge me 500 bucks on $1,200 of revenue. I must be really fucking rich, because they're sending me a bill for 40% of $1,200 I didn't even know about. Happens *every* fucking year." Mumbles of assent.

"What's worse, you have to pay an accountant fifteen hundred bucks to file a business tax return that you don't know is wrong," said a well-dressed woman two seats to Bolton's right, to the bald man on Bolton's immediate right. "And they love to audit real estate businesses. I'm dreading that, if it ever happens."

A short round man next to Marty spoke up. "Fuck this IRS shit. Rich people's problems. I got a problem for you: As the crow flies, what's the first foreign country you'd fly over if you started south from downtown Detroit?"

"Aw, fuck, Bean, the problem with your riddles is that you lie about the real answers." said Marty. "Venezuela, who the fuck cares?"

"No," said the short round man. Bean.

"Cuba?" suggested somebody else.

"No."

"Colombia?"

"No."

More blank looks.

"Canada," said Bean. "Check the map."

"I had an aunt who lived in Windsor," said someone. "I should have gotten that one."

"OK, I've got one," said the well-dressed woman. "U.S. paper currency is printed in two places. Washington, D.C. is one; where is the other?"

"Whoa, Jeannie, are you talking about *now*?" asked Bean.

"Yes, right now."

"San Francisco."

"No."

"Denver," said somebody else.

"No."

"Philadelphia."

"No. Come on guys, we're talking about bills, not coins," said Jeannie.

"Fort Worth, Texas," said Pete Banner.

"Way to go Pete!" said Jeannie, waving him a mock high-five.

"Refund my taxes, you bastard," said Bean to his Mayor. "This town has too much money in the bank if you know an answer like that."

"I would, if you paid any, you prick," said Pete. Even Bean laughed.

"Yo, Patrick, I wasn't sure who was gonna get that one, but I was sure it wasn't gonna be you," shouted Marty down half the length of the bar. The singer had sat down next to Bolton, on his left. Bolton saw the singer look up and smile. Marty continued: "Currency is the stuff the rest of us use to pay for things. You may remember it from your childhood."

"Not ringing any bells," said the singer. "And, unlike your fat ass, I don't have any problems with the IRS. They probably don't know I exist – if not, I'd like to keep it that way. How did you put it – 'Fuck the IRS?'" He raised his glass. "Fuck the IRS," replied Marty and one or two others. Not everybody laughed; it wasn't that funny. Bolton raised his glass, but he didn't drink.

CHAPTER 30

Talk turned to other things. Bolton told the singer that he was headed to the restroom. He left his jacket and a couple of sips of beer in his glass, universal signs that the seat was occupied. As he got to the men's room, he pulled a pen from his pocket and wrote a note. When he came back out, he settled back in next to the singer, and emptied his glass. He pushed it forward, hoping to attract Clem's attention.

While he waited for Clem to come by, Bolton turned to the singer. "Hi, I'm Art Smalls. On my way from Lovell to Cheyenne. Enjoyed the music."

Patrick offered his hand and they shook. "Patrick Flaherty," he said. "Thanks, appreciate it. Do you live in Cheyenne?"

"Yeah, for the last twenty," said Bolton. "I grew up in Casper."

"I grew up near Denver, so whenever I go home I pass through Cheyenne. It seems like a nice town."

"It's a good place to live. State capital, though, so a little too much government for my taste. All my neighbors work for the state."

"Not surprising, I guess, for a state capital," said Patrick.

Bolton caught Clem's attention. "Another Coors Light draft, please. And a round for Patrick."

"Thanks, Art, I appreciate that," said Patrick.

Clem collected the wooden nickel that Marty had paid for from in front of Bolton's seat, in payment for Bolton's second Coors Light draft, and threw the wooden nickel back into the pot. "That's your Coors Light." Then he reached back into the pot, extracted a wooden nickel, and placed it in front of Patrick. "Pat, that's your next one, from this kind gentleman here." Finally, he completed the double-entry bookkeeping by taking the price of Patrick's wooden nickel from Bolton's change pile. "This is Patrick's drink." He could have handed Bolton a Coors Light draft; slid a wooden nickel over to Patrick from in front of Bolton's seat; and taken Bolton's cash for a drink, with no further explanation. But therein lies perdition. As Clem's fifth-grade teacher always said, show your math.

"The weather in Cheyenne is a little bit better than in the north of the state," said Bolton.

"It's gotta be better," said Patrick. "'Cause it can't get any worse than winter in Coolidge."

"I heard somebody say you don't use cash," said Bolton. "Congratulations. I'm trying to get to the point where I only carry a debit card, but it's hard. As soon as I don't have any cash, I need it for something."

"I actually use cash in here," said Patrick. "I don't have a debit card, but just about anywhere in town will take one. You can use yours here if you want."

Bolton patted his pocket. "Good to know. It makes me crazy, though, when I use my debit card, I never really know whether they're going to process it as a Visa transaction, with that freezing thing they do with your checking account, and they make you sign the slip, or whether I'm going to enter my PIN and have it done with."

Patrick had no idea what he was talking about. "Mm-hmm," he said.

"I hope they give you free beer and food when you sing," said Bolton, shifting gears.

"Oh, yeah," said Patrick. "Clem and Claire are great about that."

"What do you do for your day job?" asked Bolton.

For six years, Patrick wrestled with how to respond to the "what do you do for a living" question from people he'd just met. For the first couple of those years, he was tongue-tied. Now that he felt established, he tended to keep his answer simple: "I'm a farmer," he said. "I raise goats and chickens, and grow vegetables."

"Do you sell your eggs, milk and produce here in town, or do you need to go to Sheridan, Casper or Billings?" asked Bolton.

"I don't sell anything I raise," said Patrick. "The milk, eggs and vegetables are what I eat to stay alive. That and wild game. I'm a subsistence farmer."

Bolton looked perplexed. It was a look that Patrick had seen often. Here it comes – The Question: "What do you do for money?" asked Bolton.

"I don't use it much," said Patrick. "I have plenty to eat, and I'm happier not worrying about money." This answer, too, had been distilled from many longer answers in prior years.

"Do you own your property?" asked Bolton.

"I live in a cabin, about a mile from here," replied Patrick. "My animal pens and gardens are around the cabin. I found out about a year and a half ago that the land actually belongs to my church. They were as surprised as I was. They're happy to let me stay."

Bolton wanted to tread carefully. He nodded appreciatively, as if he were contemplating the generosity of the church. "Nice that the owner turned out to be your church, and not somebody else."

"Yeah, so the church is now basically my landlord. In return, I need to remember, you know, when I work on my cabin, that I'm maintaining it, in part, for the Parish."

When Bolton heard the words, "in return," he relaxed. He had what he needed. He excused himself again, explaining that he had to make a call, and stepped out through the front door to write down what he'd just heard.

CHAPTER 31

Returning to the seat beside Patrick a couple of minutes later, Bolton played a hunch. "Do you have some meals over at the church? Pot luck suppers, holiday things?"

"As often as I can," said Patrick. "We have a weekly Hospitality Supper after Saturday Mass. The advantage for me is that I can eat different foods that wouldn't be in my diet otherwise. Green vegetables, especially. And beef, chicken and pork."

"Do you volunteer any of your time to the church -- holidays, activities, whatever?" asked Bolton.

Patrick thought the question was a little odd, but didn't hesitate to answer it. "Well, I do handyman work at the church and at the rectory. You have to give back. It's part of the deal."

Marty Brace appeared over Bolton's left shoulder. "Hey Pat, great music, as always. Want a beer?"

"Sure, thanks. Marty, this is Art, from Cheyenne."

"Cool, great town," said Marty, while he bought a wooden nickel from Clem. "What brings you all the way up here?"

"Visiting my brother and his wife in Lovell," replied Bolton. He smiled. "We don't like taxes down in Cheyenne, either."

"Aw, don't listen to me," replied Marty. "No filter. I never know what I'm going to say. Paying taxes means you're still above ground. I'll take that deal." Marty turned to Patrick. "Can you use a couple of rolls of R-14 insulation? We left 'em out in the rain. It's no good to us, but you could dry it out and use it."

"Aw man, I just closed up the last part of the interior wall. But thanks for thinking of me. Coming over here for the Broncos on Sunday?"

"Absolutely, I'll be here," said Marty. "I may even come over to work the early games at 11:00."

Patrick turned to Bolton to explain, while Marty listened. "Starting at about 10:30 a.m. on Sunday, this bar is laptops from end to end. Clem turns on the NFL Network, and the wifi is running at capacity. The games in the East start at 11:00 Mountain Time. At any given time, half the patrons are happy, half are sad. And those categories change every five minutes, every time somebody in Buffalo or Baltimore scores a touchdown. Clem just wishes he were getting five percent, instead of Draft Kings."

"He speaks the truth," said Marty. He clasped Patrick on the shoulder, and headed outside for a cigarette.

"I used to work for Marty," said Patrick to Bolton. "Great guy, great boss, great contractor."

"Are there a lot of contractors in town?" asked Bolton.

"Not so many," said Patrick. "It's a small town. Marty has been here for years. Harry Detmer is probably the biggest. There are a couple of others. That's good for me in my situation, because all contractors generate excess materials, whether it's scraps or they just ordered too much for a job. I've been able to use a lot of that stuff for my cabin. It's win-win, in a sense. If I don't use it, they have to figure out what to do with it. With Harry, in particular, I have an arrangement where I'll drive his debris to the dump, every Friday at noon. And in exchange, I get to see what he has that might be excess."

"So, do you barter for everything that you can't make or create for yourself?" asked Bolton. Patrick had raised the subject of not working for money, so Bolton was no longer greatly concerned about raising suspicions. His questions, he hoped, would seem like polite follow-up.

"I actually don't barter that much," said Patrick. "I'm to the point now where most of what I need, I already have, and most of what I consume, I gather myself. But people help. Bobby Bays," – he nodded to his left – "he's sitting three seats down. He owns a feed store. He lets me know when he's got broken or expired feed bags, which I really need for my animals."

Bolton thought it odd that Patrick had mentioned animal feed in response to a question about bartering, but he hadn't described any services that he provided in return. Bolton was tempted to press him on it, but there is only so much you can expect to accomplish in a barstool conversation. He could interview Mr. Bays later.

Bolton shifted gears. "I'm an accountant, so I make a living keeping track of other people's money," said Bolton. "Accounting looks boring from the outside, but it's really pretty interesting." He took a sip of beer, glanced at the bar menu. "I've known a lot of my clients for a long time." Bolton had worked for the government for his entire career, and had no private clients. Telling lies was part of working undercover. "I've developed good relationships over time, and it's nice to save my clients some money on taxes here and there, and keep them out of trouble. I heard you say earlier that the IRS doesn't know you exist. Did you ever talk to an accountant about whether it's a good idea not to be filing returns?"

"I've always been told that if you don't make $600 in a year, you don't have to file," replied Patrick. "I certainly don't come close to that. As far as going to see an accountant – I don't know, I'd be afraid of what I might hear. Suppose I really did have enough income, so that I was supposed to be filing returns? I don't want to know."

"You must've filed a few returns while you were working. You seem like you know a little bit about taxes."

"The last time I filed a federal return was six years ago. It may be weird, but one of the reasons I don't want to make more than $600 is that I don't want to file a return, and then have the IRS show up to ask me where I've been for all these years. Probably not the most important reason, but still."

"I think you're right," said Bolton. "I've seen that happen."

"I have a friend who comes in here who skipped a few years, while he was drinking a lot, and then he filed when he sobered up," said Patrick. "He said the computers at the IRS spotted his failures to file right away, and they came after his bank account and God knows what else. He's still trying to pay off the back taxes. He's completely underwater. I don't owe any taxes, but I don't want to have to deal with that kind of scrutiny. Good way to ruin your day, having the IRS come to call. In all events, that's the least of my worries. A bear broke into my cabin a few nights ago. It scared the shit out of me."

Bolton cringed and laughed at the same time. "Did you talk to Game and Fish?" he asked.

"Yeah, they're looking into the problem," replied Patrick. "I hope they hurry up. I'm worried that the bear liked what he found in my refrigerator."

Bolton saw the patron from three seats down moving toward Patrick. He moved between Bolton and Patrick. "Hey Pat, can I interrupt?"

"Bobby, this is Art; Art, Bobby Bays," said Patrick, nodding toward each. "Sure, what's up?" he said to Bobby.

"Millie's going to the vet on Monday morning, and she's getting shots. Can you do Tuesday?"

"Sure, that's easy."

"OK, cool, see you on Tuesday morning, if for some reason I don't see you before." Bobby headed toward the dart board.

Patrick turned to Art. "I train his German Shorthaired Pointer. Great, great hunting dogs."

Bolton registered that information, and told Patrick he needed a bathroom break. "Too much beer, too quick," he explained. He made some more notes while he was in the men's room. He returned to the bar and decided he'd go with the chicken fingers. He gave Clem his order, and continued talking with Patrick while he ate. Football, hunting, country music, weather – Wyoming stuff. When he got up to leave, Bolton said he'd try to stop in again on some future Friday. He liked Patrick. Nice guy. It was too bad how it was likely to go from there.

CHAPTER 32

On Sunday afternoon, Bolton prepared his Preliminary Investigation Memo, describing the evidence against Patrick Flaherty, WM, hair -- dark, eyes -- BL, hgt. -- 6'1", weight -- approx. 185 lbs., age -- approx. 28 y.o. NCIC, Interpol, no prior arrests or convictions.

IRS procedures required Bolton to obtain permission from his SAC to open an investigation. He called Dan Price on Monday morning, and laid out what he had. Bolton didn't expect push-back or resistance, and he didn't get any.

"Go with it," said Price. "Put the case into CIMIS, and I'll upload an approval memo. Arthur, thanks for this. I got *two* calls from Washington while you were away asking about new bartering cases in the Field Office. They called me *directly* – it's unheard of for them to put pressure on a SAC without having the Area Chief on the line. And I got three other calls from Washington about charitable deduction fraud cases – different Assistant Chiefs for different crimes. Crazy. They want cases, yesterday. You're the first bartering case in the whole Western Area. Congrats on that. And . . ." He paused.

"You were about to say, 'Don't fuck it up,'" said Bolton.

Price laughed. "I was going to be more polite than that, but yeah."

"Dan, can you talk with the Criminal Tax Attorneys and get them to tee up some grand jury time with DOJ Tax Division? If the undercover goes as well as I hope it will, and if you and I can put the Centralized Case Review together in a hurry, I think we could be making our prosecution recommendation within two to three weeks. The people in the U.S. Attorney's Office in Wyoming are easy enough to get along with lately, but they're a bunch of pricks when it comes to getting grand jury time."

"I'll do better than that," said Price. "All these calls and memos said we'd get what we needed from DOJ to support the cases. If you get me the evidence, I'll put some pressure back up the pipeline. I'll tell them we need a lawyer from DOJ Tax Division in Washington to review the case and hop on a plane to – is the grand jury sitting in Casper or Cheyenne?"

"It's in Cheyenne right now. No excuses, they can fly into Denver if they can't find flights to Cheyenne," said Bolton.

"So they can come to Cheyenne. If DOJ Washington gets into an argument with DOJ Cheyenne about grand jury time, I know who's going to win."

"All right, that's good," said Bolton. "My plan is to head back to Sheridan on Thursday, and the undercover work should be done by early next week. Even if it's not, I'll just keep pushing. I'll check in with you on a daily basis."

"Excellent. Bye," said Price.

"Bye." Bolton hung up the phone and shook his head. He hadn't had a case move this fast since the Sinaloa Cartel thing ten years ago. "Karl, I need to talk to you." Bolton yelled to his subordinate in the next office. Special Agent Trainee Karl Lawless's face appeared in the doorway. "I'm looking for help with some UC work," said Bolton. "Sit."

Lawless sat in one of Bolton's visitor's chairs, coffee cup in hand. He hadn't had any undercover assignments, and was excited about the possibility. He offered, tentatively, "What's up?"

"Are you Catholic?" asked Bolton.

Lawless was surprised. "Well, two days a year. Christmas and Easter I go to Mass with my mom. I was raised Catholic, but I've drifted away from it."

"Do you think you can go to Mass, kneel at the right time, take communion, make it look natural?"

"Yeah, it's like riding a bicycle," said Lawless. "What case is this, and where's the church?"

"Actually, it's more than just a church, but a church is part of it. It's a case I'm developing up in Sheridan County," said Bolton. "I'll need backup when I do a couple of things wearing a wire, and we need to go into the church to identify some witnesses. I wouldn't be comfortable going into the church, one, because I'm not Catholic, and, two, the target will be there and would probably recognize me. Are you sure you'd be comfortable?"

"I can practice here in Cheyenne. They have daily Masses at the Cathedral of St. Mary, right across the street. I'll be ready. Am I going in wired when we get to Sheridan County?"

"I don't need you to wear a wire in the church. I'd be nervous about sending you into a church with a wire on. We'd be inviting pretrial motions to suppress the evidence. It's like mosques. Freedom of religion. All I really need are names and faces – I need to find out who's dealing with my target when he goes to something called the 'Hospitality Supper' after Saturday Mass. I also want to know who runs the parish day-to-day. We may need to call a witness or two before the grand jury. So it's just observe and identify."

Lawless could not imagine what a "Hospitality Supper" might have to do with criminal tax enforcement. But he assumed he probably ought to have known, and he didn't want to reveal his ignorance by asking his boss questions. "Sure, happy to help," he said. "Sounds interesting. Who's the target?"

Bolton began to read his trainee in on the case, and they planned their trip to the Wyoming/Montana border that coming Thursday. It would be 326 miles in a cramped, federal motor pool Malibu. Wyoming is a big place.

CHAPTER 33

Bolton and Lawless created a satellite headquarters on Thursday evening at the Best Western in Sheridan. They had brought along some extra body wire kits, a digital telephoto camera, disguises supplied by the FBI office in Cheyenne, secure walkie-talkies, and laptops. Their plan was to gather evidence on Friday and Saturday, take Sunday off, and gather evidence again on Monday. They would take it further into the following week if necessary.

Any investigation involved a lot of time spent on the internet. Both agents were on their computers until late at night on Thursday. They found the target's cabin on Google Earth, and found Bays Feeds, St. Ann's, Detmer Contracting, and Marty Brace's business in Google Street View. They established that the Sheridan City Landfill was the only landfill in Sheridan County that accepted contractors' debris, and they noted its hours and rates. They pulled ownership records for Cousin Clem's. Bolton explained the pros and cons of involving the Sheridan County Sheriff. On the one hand, it's nice to have armed back-up if things go sideways. On the other hand, local law enforcement is leaky, and the target might have friends among the local cops. Bolton decided that the risks of not having backup were more than justified on this job, and he decided not to tie in the Sheriff.

On Wednesday, Bolton had called Father Dave to set up a meeting to see the property on which the cabin was located, suggesting to Father Dave that he was interested in buying it. They had agreed to meet on Friday at the day camp in the lower southeastern corner of the property. At the Best Western on Thursday night, Bolton and Lawless brainstormed about how Bolton should handle the meeting, and what approaches might yield the most evidence of bartering.

During the morning on Friday, Bolton and Lawless drove around Coolidge learning where everything was. They spent some time finding Detmer Contracting, on Gillette Street; Bays Feeds on Route 14; Marty Brace's shop on Greene Street; and St. Ann's Church, on Baxter Street. They parked near Cousin Clem's, and Bolton explained to Lawless what he should expect when he walked in. They drove past the Town Hall; they noticed two shingles for accountants and tax preparers; and they drove up Side Road till it ended near a pond. They couldn't see Flaherty's cabin from the road.

In late morning, they drove a few miles into the Bighorn National Forest. Lawless had never been to the Bighorns, and Bolton wanted to show them off a little bit. The sun was bright, and the leaves on the few deciduous trees had begun to turn. They turned back to Coolidge for lunch, and stopped at The 14 Diner to eat.

CHAPTER 34

At 12:55, Bolton left Lawless at The 14, and at 1:00, he pulled up for his meeting with Father Hernandez at the property. Each parked at the edge of the road on Side Road, about a quarter mile from the turn-off from Route 14. Near the day camp. They shook hands, and Bolton presented a business card to Father Dave that said "Arthur Kramer – Wyoming Real Estate Strategies," with a phone number.

"Thanks for coming out to meet me," said Bolton. "When this parcel popped up on our radar, we got very excited about it. It's a great location, and we know a lot of churches are re-prioritizing their real estate holdings."

"Well, we haven't really thought about selling it, and it would possibly be up to the Diocese. But I'd like to be able to give them details if you're interested." They began walking toward the day camp.

"Is this a functioning camp?" asked Bolton. "Would you need to replace it somehow if you sold the property?"

"We haven't thought about it, truthfully. We might want to carve it out from the purchase – the camp itself only takes up about five acres. Or we could probably find another site for it."

"I'm sure we could work something out," said Bolton. He pointed to the prairie grass growing on the slope between the camp and the woods. "About how many acres are grassland?" he asked.

"It's about half, I think, which would mean it's about 125 acres of the 250 in the parcel, give or take."

"Who maintains the grassy part?"

"No one. It's just prairie. We allow hunters, because making it available for public use is one of the conditions for our tax exemption."

"I think it would be good ranch land," said Bolton. "That's our idea. Small ranches are hot right now. But what sets the entire parcel apart, we think, is that the wooded area is great for camping and hiking. We also think the wooded part would make a great spot for a 'Gateway to the Bighorns' kind of hotel."

"Interesting," said Father Dave. He scanned the grass as it moved in the breeze. "Well, you've seen what there is to see of the grassy area. Can I show you the upper part? I want to show you Water Creek, and we have a tenant living in a cabin on the property. I'll show you that too. We can drive."

As they drove separately up Side Road, Father Dave felt a stab of guilt. If the buyer was planning a hotel in the woods, Patrick's cabin was unlikely to be a part of the plan. The Diocese couldn't base a decision on whether the sale would affect Patrick, but maybe the buyer would see the benefits of a full-time human presence, at least until construction was finished. Father Dave pulled to the side near the path up to Patrick's cabin, and Bolton pulled in behind him. Father Dave got out and looked up the hill; with a wave, he invited Bolton to follow him up the path.

"This is called Hamm's Hill, the eastern half of which is part of our property," said Father Dave, over his shoulder as they walked. "The cabin is interesting. Apparently, it was once abandoned, but now it's really solidly put together. It doesn't look like much, but you'll appreciate the work that's gone into it."

"What can you tell me about the tenant?" asked Bolton.

"His name is Patrick Flaherty. He's a young guy, in his late twenties, a member of our Parish. Kind of interesting lifestyle – he feeds himself with hunting, fishing, chickens and goats."

"Does he have a lease?"

"No, he was here before we really even knew it's Parish land. So when we found out, of course we let him stay."

They had arrived in front of the cabin and were looking at the construction. They could hear chickens and goats in the side and back yard. Father Dave called out Patrick's name, but Patrick didn't seem to be around. Bolton was not in disguise. He had scheduled the meeting for when he expected Patrick to be driving Harry Detmer's trash to Sheridan, and he had Karl Lawless watching from the window of The 14 Diner to be sure that Patrick didn't return early. Lawless was instructed to watch for any truck with "Detmer Contracting" on the door, and to call Bolton on his cell if he saw one heading toward the property. There was a risk that Patrick would show up during Bolton's meeting with Father Dave, but it was a manageable risk.

Bolton and Father Dave drifted left toward the side yard between the cabin and the creek. Father Dave pointed to the two solar panels and the wind turbine as they came into view. "He has a low voltage set-up – 12 volts for all lights and electrical devices."

"Frankly, we'd need to pin down the nature of your arrangement with the tenant, before we get too deep into discussions," said Bolton. "The last thing we'd want would be to get tied up in litigation with a squatter."

Squatter? Father Dave jumped to reassure. "No, no, that doesn't describe Patrick at all. He's a bright guy. He's respectful of the rights of the Diocese, and a very law-abiding individual. He has every hunting license there is, he's careful about environmental laws. His cabin is completely green, he has a composting toilet, he gets all his energy from renewable sources."

"Well, again, what's your assurance that he'll take care of the place?" asked Bolton.

"If Patrick doesn't maintain the cabin, he won't be able to stay. And even though the vacant land isn't really a part of his tenancy, we ask him to maintain the stream and pond as well, making sure they don't clog, and making sure that beavers don't impede the flow. That's the deal, and he knows that. We can't have the place falling down, if for no other reason than somebody like you – some prospective buyer – might think we haven't been taking care of the parcel, at least to the limited extent it needs it. And I would like to think that your group will think as highly of Patrick as we do."

"That's a good deal for everybody," said Bolton. "I know you probably don't get involved in real estate deals very often, but property upkeep is important to any buyer. It's good to know that that's the deal." Bolton looked pleased, and Father Dave was reassured that his prospective buyer seemed happy.

Bolton had another thought. "Hopefully, the animal enclosures would be removed before a closing."

"No problem."

"OK, thanks, that's helpful," said Bolton.

Father Dave added, "Obviously, we would hope if we sold the property at some point, the buyer would consider letting Mr. Flaherty stay. It adds value to a property to have a full-time human presence. If we do get into discussions about a purchase and sale, I'm sure I'll be bringing that up again."

"Understood," said Bolton. "It looks like you believe he's earned your support. We get that."

"Let me show you the creek," said Father Dave. "It's a jewel." Pointing, he added: "You can see the wiring coming up out of the ground, connected to the car batteries under the house. Those wires run underground through PVC conduits to a hydraulic turbine where the stream narrows and falls. It's a really cool design."

The two men walked the fifty yards or so over to the stream and talked about possibilities for camping and recreation. Father Dave was interested; Bolton was now bored.

CHAPTER 35

After he ended his meeting with Father Dave, Bolton reconnoitered with Karl Lawless at The 14, and they drove back to Sheridan to spend a couple of hours at the Best Western. The task at hand was to organize the approach to Cousin Clem's. The kid was nervous, but plainly excited about his first opportunity to work undercover. They sipped on Diet Coke and nibbled potato chips from the vending machines down the hall. Most of the time was spent on "what if's."

What if someone asks for ID? Show him/her your Wyoming driver's license and claim that your undercover name is a nickname.

What if the owner isn't there? Stay, and see what else you can learn.

What if you bump into somebody who recognizes you from the real world? Not too damn likely; leave as fast as you can.

The plan was for Lawless to drop Bolton at The 14 at 5:55, and then drive over to Cousin Clem's. They rejected the idea of a body recorder – there would be too much noise in the bar for the recorder to hear any responses to Lawless's questions. Better to skip the wire altogether than to have questions with no answers.

The investigative objectives were limited. The point of the exercise was to get the owner to admit that the guitar player was paid for his services in food and beer. There was an easy way to do that.

An hour later, Lawless was standing at the bar, wedged between two stools. It was 6:00 on the dot. The customer on his left was talking to someone farther left; the guy on his right was talking to someone farther right. Good suggestion by Bolton to look for that geometry. Lawless had a good view of

Clem, Syrena and the guitar player on the stage. He waited for someone to take his beer order.

He had some luck. Clem was free before Syrena was, and asked him what he wanted to drink. "Hi, I'm Jake," Lawless said to Clem. Clem's bowling shirt, with "Clem" on the pocket, had simplified his job. He was talking to the owner. "Let me have a Coors Banquet, bottle please," said Lawless. He had seen a few bottles of Coors on the bar, and played it safe.

Clem turned and pulled a bottle of Coors out of the cooler and handed it to Lawless. He took the five dollar bill Lawless was handing him and started to make change. Lawless said, "Keep it, please." He began with the script he'd rehearsed with Bolton. "I really like the music. He's really good."

Clem smiled. He heard that a lot. "Yup, every Friday. We're never bored. He's a human jukebox."

"What's his name?" asked Lawless.

"Patrick Flaherty," replied Clem.

"Yeah, we don't have anyone doing this kind of music, at least not solo, down in Sheridan," said Lawless. "Do you think we could get him to come down for a private party we're having in a couple of weeks?"

"I don't know, you could ask him," replied Clem.

"OK, thanks." Lawless paused for a beat, just to show Clem that he was hesitating before asking his next question. "Ah, thing is, we have a limited budget. I don't mean to pry, but is he expensive?"

"That I can tell you, without asking," said Clem. "He won't accept money for playing music. It's more a question of whether he'd be interested in the gig, I think."

Lawless wanted to tread carefully. "Wow, OK. We would certainly give him all the food and drink he wanted. Do you comp him with food and beer, or guitar strings, or cigarettes, or whatever?"

Clem raised an eyebrow. Something about this guy said Wyoming Liquor Division. He wondered whether it was legal to offer drinks for services – he'd never asked himself the question. But if the guy really were WLD, Clem didn't suppose he was going to be able to hide what he was doing. "All our musicians eat and drink for free while they're playing."

"Oh, OK," said Lawless.

"Where do you like to go to listen to music in Sheridan?" asked Clem.

Bolton and Lawless had anticipated the question – it was one of the "what if's." "The Sheridan Inn on Broadway Street," replied Lawless.

"Nice place," said Clem. He found a glass farther down the bar that needed refilling, and ended the conversation.

Lawless held his beer and watched Patrick play for a few minutes. He had felt Clem's unease, and wondered if his questions had been awkward. He had to decide whether to wait until the suspect was done playing, to talk with him and see if he could gather any additional evidence. He knew the suspect would probably head for the kitchen after his set – Bolton had told him that – and he was concerned that if he tried to corner him before he got there, Clem might join the conversation. Too many risks and variables at that point.

He had what he needed. He had identified the suspect and the owner had admitted paying the suspect food and drink for music. It was time to go. He put his empty bottle on the bar, and headed for the front door.

Clem watched "Jake" leave. "Jake" hadn't talked to Patrick. He had only stayed for 10 minutes. WLD for sure. Clem resolved to find out whether offering beers to musicians was legal in Wyoming. Hard to believe it wasn't. If Google didn't know, maybe he'd ask Anita Boyle to find out for him.

CHAPTER 36

Mass was calming. Lawless was nervous about the Hospitality Supper to follow. He didn't feel he'd done well in Cousin Clem's, the evening before. Bolton, however, had been reassuring. "Don't worry, we got what we needed."

Father Hernandez was clear and competent. Every word of the Mass was familiar to Lawless, and he knew when to say, "And with your spirit," and when to say, "Amen." Like riding a bicycle. The suspect, sitting five or six rows in front of Lawless, was composed. He was in the seventh row, next to a developmentally disabled parishioner. They exchanged a word or two every so often. After the Lord's Prayer, the priest invited everyone to exchange a sign of peace, and the suspect shook hands with the parishioners around him. Lawless did the same.

During the announcements at the end of Mass, the reader invited everyone to Hospitality Supper in the Parish Hall. Lawless put on his fall jacket and made his way over to the pot luck dinner.

When he arrived, he approached one of the greeters. "Hi, I'm Jake Carlton. I'm up from Cheyenne for a week or two, and I wanted to buy a couple of Masses for my great aunt, who used to be a parishioner here. I was very close to her. Could you tell me who I should talk to?"

"Oh, you should talk to Mavis," replied Alice, the greeter that night. "She's over there in the purple dress, next to the American flag." Lawless turned to see "Mavis," talking to the suspect. He would have to wait a little.

"What was your great aunt's name?" asked Alice.

"Her name was Pauline Carlton," Lawless replied. "Do you remember her, by any chance?"

"No, I'm afraid I don't," said Alice.

"I would say she left Coolidge 20 years ago," said Lawless. "We took care of her in her last years down in Cheyenne." He was laying it on pretty thick.

"Oh, that's so nice," replied Alice, and she meant it. "Thank you for coming to Mass at St. Ann's. Please help yourself to all the food you can eat. We always have too much." She shook his hand warmly, again, and turned to the next person coming in.

Lawless headed over to the food line and began to fill a plate. Lasagna looked like the best bet – he liked Italian food. He chatted with the ladies who were serving the various dishes. Like a warm blanket on a cold morning. Food in the Parish Hall.

As he was getting to the end of the line, and the rolls, he saw the suspect head back toward the beginning of the food line. "Mavis" was checking a text on her phone, and was momentarily alone. Lawless crossed the room to talk to her, plate in hand.

"Hi I'm Jake Carlton," he said. He balanced his plate in one hand and shook hands with her with the other. Mavis smiled. Lawless continued, "I'm visiting from Cheyenne, and I'm told that you're the person to see about sponsoring a Mass or two for my great aunt."

"You have good information. I'm Mavis, I'm the Parish administrator. What was your great aunt's name?"

Lawless hesitated. All of a sudden, he'd forgotten his script, and the wheels inside his head were trying to catch up. "I'm sorry, uh, Mavis, what's your last name?"

Mavis was puzzled. Jake Carlton's generation didn't care about last names, and his question was completely unresponsive to her question about his great aunt. Social maladroits -- *sheesh*. "Mavis D'Antonio," she said, finally. "I'm sorry, what was your great aunt's name?"

"Her name was Pauline Carlton. She left Coolidge about 20 years ago."

"Mmmm," said Mavis. "I don't remember her, I'm sorry. When did she pass away? Was it recently?"

"About six months ago," replied Lawless. "She often talked about St. Ann's, and the family thought it would be nice to sponsor a Mass or two for her here. I'm the first family member to be coming north since she died, and they asked me to stop in. I really enjoyed the Mass, and the dinner is very nice."

"It was so nice of you to come by. If you're here on Monday, stop by the Parish office and I'll put your great aunt on the list. Otherwise, you can call, and we'll do it by credit card. I'll remember our conversation."

"That's very kind," said Lawless. He was almost there. He needed to establish that she knew the suspect, and maybe turn up some confirmation that he did work for the Parish. "By the way, I saw you talking with a tall guy a minute ago." He pointed across the room to the suspect. "What's his name?"

Mavis was mongrel Portuguese-Polish-Sicilian Catholic. Ten thousand years of evolution was at work in her head. When a stranger comes into your village and asks for somebody's name, the proper answer, as far as Mavis was concerned, was, "Why do you want to know?"

"Why do you want to know?" asked Mavis.

Lawless blushed. "Uh, I thought I might have recognized him." Clear lie.

"Probably not," she said. "I'm sure he's never spent any time in Cheyenne."

"Good, understood, I was probably mistaken," said Lawless. He knew the name and face of the Parish administrator, and knew that she was acquainted with the suspect. She could explain the suspect's work around the parish to the grand jury. "Thanks again, Mavis. I'll be in touch about those Masses."

Lawless needed to find someone he could talk with for as long as possible. He picked two older ladies who had just sat down with large plates of food, and he introduced himself. His skills as a conversationalist were marginal, but he needed to be there when the suspect loaded up on food.

Mavis didn't know what to make of Mr. Jake Carlton. It was probably nothing. No reason to talk to Patrick about it – yet. While Jake Carlton sat talking with Vera and Midge, Mavis kept an eye on him.

After 45 minutes or so, the crowd had dwindled to about eight people, including Lawless and the ladies at his table. Lawless watched out of the corner of his eye as the suspect filled a large knapsack with leftovers. There were at least five Styrofoam containers, some bread, and some desserts. After handshakes and kisses on the cheek, the suspect was out the door with his food. Mavis and three other ladies began to wrap and package the remaining leftovers. Lawless didn't see anyone else taking food home from the dinner.

IRS-CID Special Agent Trainee Karl Lawless had what he needed. Three minutes after the suspect left, Lawless said goodnight to the two ladies at his table and left the dinner, foam coffee cup still in hand.

Mavis watched him go. Her disquiet lasted for a full 10 minutes after the door closed behind him.

CHAPTER 37

"Overall, I thought it went pretty well," said Lawless the next morning. Bolton and Lawless were at the Best Western breakfast buffet, and Lawless was trying to work through his disappointment at the way his visits to Cousin Clem's and St. Ann's had gone. "But people can be really suspicious. I wanted to get to talk to the target, and I missed him at both places. I felt like people were protecting him."

"I think you're probably right," said Bolton, "but I doubt they had any idea he's a suspect in a criminal investigation. I think it's more the way people in a small town protect their own, when people they don't know are asking questions. Just human nature."

"I wish I had gotten more, that's all," said Lawless.

"We actually have a lot," replied Bolton. "We corroborated a lot of what the target told me. He gets free food when he plays music. And he gets free food when he goes to church. And you were eyes-on for that. If this thing ever goes to the grand jury, or to a plea or trial, the things you saw and heard are going to be important pieces of evidence. A case doesn't prove itself. You build the case with individual bricks, and you have to make sure that each one is as solid as possible. Otherwise, you're leaving room for reasonable doubt."

"I need to get going on my 302's" said Lawless. Lawless was fresh out of FLET-C, where most of the instructors referred to the report of a witness interview by its FBI designator, Form 302. "I'd like to go over those with you later, make sure I haven't left anything out that's supposed to be in there."

"That's fine," said Bolton, "but remember, the Broncos are the Sunday night game this week. I'm not interrupting that."

CHAPTER 38

That same Sunday, Patrick was in the downhill field cutting hay. Although the grass wasn't particularly tall at that time of year, he was able to cut about 150 pounds. He stacked it on his wheelbarrow and tied it on with an old cargo strap. Then he wheeled it down to Side Road, up the road to his path, and up the path to his hay bin. Although it was already the 11th of October, the main pasture down the hill from his cabin was still full of edible grasses. All four of his goats were grazing around him.

Patrick thought once again about the difficulties he was creating for himself by spending so much time hunting and working at the church. If he increased the size of his herd to fifteen goats, he could replace game meat with goat meat. He'd only have to cull about five or six males a year, and he would have at least five or six male kids to replace them. He could stop hunting, and he'd only have to cut hay for winter storage. He could easily do that while his goats were grazing.

As it was, the reason he could only manage five goats – thanks to the damn bear, he was down to four – was that he still needed to hunt on a lot of days, and he wanted to work at the church on the other days. And on Fridays, he drove to Sheridan and back. When he was hunting, or working at the church, he couldn't tend the goats while they grazed. If he didn't supervise the goats while they grazed, coyotes and the occasional cougar would be happy to help.

The result was that he had to spend more time than he wanted cutting hay, instead of letting his goats forage every day, because he had to confine his goats to their pen when he wasn't around. They needed to eat, and hay was their staple – fortunately, they liked it. The feed bags that Bobby Bays gave him were only a supplement.

If he were honest with himself – Patrick had plenty of time to be honest with himself – the key reason he wasn't tending goats full time was that he didn't want to think of himself as a "goatherd." A goatherd was some old fool who follows his herd around until a Predator drone blows him up by mistake. A goatherd is the guy who wanders into Seal Team Six's landing zone by accident, and then they have to decide whether they're going to kill him. A goatherd's lot is not a happy one.

The irony was not lost on him. One of the lesser reasons he chose the life he did was that he was put off by status-seeking. He believed that honest work was honest work, period. His friends from college, he recalled, would worry about whether they wanted to settle for pharmaceutical science when they had a shot at medical school, and that bothered him somehow. And here he was worrying about how he'd feel telling his friends he was a goatherd.

He had given some thought to getting a cow. Eric Dormer mentioned to him that he had a big, lactating Black Angus on his ranch that the other girls didn't like. She would easily have replaced all of his goat milk, and she could have handled a coyote, or even a cougar. She could have grazed on her own, and would probably have been findable every afternoon. But Patrick didn't know how he would have fed her in the winter. He didn't think he could gather that much hay. In all events, he was still thinking about it. He just didn't know enough yet to be comfortable with the idea.

With a jolt, Patrick realized he hadn't included bears on the list of predators that might be a threat to a cow. He never heard of a bear attacking a cow, but there were a lot of things about bears he once thought he knew that he didn't think he knew anymore.

Every once in a while, and that October afternoon in particular, Patrick thought about his future. He thought he'd like to get married and have kids. He was not unaware of the big problem -- he was not anyone's idea of an ideal husband. He figured he needed to find a farmer; a woman who had grown up on a farm, maybe, and would understand the life. With two people, they could manage cows, goats, and some crops, and do all sorts of things that one person couldn't do alone. Subsistence farming was brutal work, however, and he didn't know any 21st Century women who would be inclined to do it. Stacey was about as close as he'd come to finding her. Maybe he'd go down and hang around the Agriculture Department at Sheridan College, and strike up a conversation with the first co-ed in overalls who turned up. Thinking of his future made his brain hurt.

Scarlett O'Hara was right. I'll think about it tomorrow.

CHAPTER 39

Bolton had planned the visit meticulously. He wore a wig and false mustache, and thick horn-rimmed glasses. He had a five o'clock shadow. His clothes were polyester and a little loud. A body recorder was taped to the small of his back. He went into Bays Feeds on a Monday morning, when he expected Bobby Bays to be distracted with customers. He needed to be careful, because Bays had been introduced to him, briefly, and there was some risk that Bays would recognize him. He sought to minimize that risk.

Approaching the counter, he asked to speak to Bobby Bays.

"That's me," said Bobby, "how can I help you?"

"My name's Ed Keegan. I bumped into Patrick Flaherty while he was out exercising your dog" – he pointed to Millie, lying behind the counter – "and I asked him whether he knew any good German Shorthaired breeders. He said he didn't know any, but he was pretty sure you would. I'm hoping to find a good hunting dog."

"That's strange, I just reminded Patrick a couple of weeks ago how I got her. I don't see how . . ."

"No, it's been at least a month since I bumped into him. I live over in Ranchester, so it's taken me this long to get back to Coolidge. I'm gonna have lunch with a friend at The 14."

Bobby looked over Bolton's shoulder. "Hey Ann, I have your bison feed additive in. Do you still need it?"

"Absolutely," said Ann. "And do you have any senior horse? Silver just turned 20."

"Yeah, they're both over with the bulk feeds, I'll be over in a sec." He turned back to Bolton. "Yeah, I got her from a breeder down in Buffalo." He wrote down the name on a paper scrap. "Don't know the number, but they have a website. Tell them I sent you down. They'll know me, 'cause Millie is the second Shorthaired I've gotten from 'em."

"Thanks, really, I appreciate it," said Bolton. "I don't want to take any more of your time -- but do you think Patrick might agree to train the dog for me? And is he expensive?"

"I don't know, I guess you'd have to ask him. I can't tell you how much he would cost, because he doesn't charge me cash. I swap him feed for his chickens and goats. To tell you the truth, I don't think Patrick would accept cash, and he's also pretty busy keeping himself alive. He might do it in exchange for food or ammunition. I don't know, I have enough trouble getting him to accept feed for what he does. So I wouldn't be optimistic. Again, you'd need to ask him. If you wind up getting the dog, and if you have trouble finding Patrick again, let me know, and I'll give him a message."

"That's super, thanks," said Bolton. "I know you're busy, and I'm grateful for your time. I'll let you know if I wind up with one of Millie's cousins at some point. Have a good one."

"You do the same," said Bobby, as Bolton turned and headed back out. He didn't know why, but something struck him as odd about Mr. Ed Keegan. He made a mental note to ask Patrick about him; and because he didn't put the mental note on a scrap of paper, he promptly forgot it.

CHAPTER 40

After his meeting with Bobby Bays, Special Agent Bolton drove to meet Karl Lawless, who was waiting for him in The 14. Bolton had a big late breakfast, and they discussed strategy for the meeting with Harry Detmer. Both knew they couldn't count on being lucky – Detmer might be visiting his sister, or at the dentist, or anywhere but in his office. They were prepared to stay in Sheridan for up to a week, but they were hoping not to.

Finally, Bolton ambled out to the car – leaving Lawless to drink more coffee -- and headed out to Detmer Contracting. He didn't expect the visit to Detmer's office to be complicated. Bolton had never met Detmer. He had surveilled Detmer's home and business on Friday, recognized Detmer from his photo on his website, and was satisfied that they'd never seen each other at Cousin Clem's. So no disguises. He was wearing a wire under his jacket.

He walked up the driveway, past the residence, and to the door of the office in back. There were three workers in the lot to the right of the office, loading a van, but he didn't see Detmer in the group. He entered the office to find Detmer with a woman who looked to be in her 60's, both reading what looked like a print-out of a spreadsheet. It was 11:30 a.m.

"Good morning," said Bolton.

"Morning," said Harry and Nancy, at the same time.

"I don't want to take much of your time," said Bolton, "but I'm trying to talk with the contractors in town. My name is Paul Steinberger. I've been talking with Junk B Gone about a franchise opportunity that they're offering in Sheridan – the guy who's down there now wants to retire – and I'm trying to figure out whether there's a demand out in the county for a good disposal service, especially for old appliances, construction debris, residential junk, that sort of thing. I'm not looking for business at this point, or asking anyone for any kind of commitment. I'm just trying to assess demand before I make an offer on the franchise. So, with your permission, I have a one-question survey. Do you ever have need for junk or debris disposal?"

"Absolutely," replied Harry. "We send at least one stake-bed full of debris a week over to the Sheridan Landfill. We have a service that does it for us."

Bolton feigned surprise. "Ouch. Junk B Gone has been telling me there's no competition in the county right now. I hadn't heard of anyone else . . ."

"No, our guy is a one-man service. I don't think he does it for anyone else. So your information is probably good. Our guy collects our debris and takes it to the landfill, in exchange for cyclone fencing, and railroad ties, stuff for his animal enclosures. He also takes whatever materials in the debris might be usable for his purposes. The landfill has a rule that once it checks in, nothing checks out. The public can't scavenge at the dump. So it's a good deal for both of us. Anyway, our needs are met, but I honestly haven't heard of anyone else doing junk disposal in the county. It might be a good opportunity for you."

"I appreciate the encouragement," said Bolton. "And again, thanks for taking the time." He put his hand on the doorknob to leave. Then he turned back with a smile. "How's business? Good?"

"Business is good," said Harry. "Can't complain. Good luck with your due diligence, and don't hesitate to call if you have any other questions you think we might be able to answer."

As the door closed behind Bolton, Nancy said, "That was a generous offer. Do you really have time to hold his hand if he takes you up on it?"

"No, but I can remember when I opened this business. I didn't understand anything about how to run a business, and thank God for other people who were willing to answer my dumb questions. He seemed like a nice guy. I hope it works for him."

On the way back out the driveway, Bolton called his office to ask them to pull the last five tax returns from Detmer Contracting, Inc., to see if they'd been attributing too much business usage to a mixed use, business-residential property. Leverage was always good in dealing with potential witnesses.

When he got back to The 14, Bolton teed Karl Lawless up for a visit to Marty Brace. This time, Lawless would play the prospective "Junk B Gone" franchisee, and Bolton would wait at the diner.

Lawless caught Marty in the driveway of his business, and launched into the cover story. "I'm exploring demand for junk removal in Sheridan County . . ." he began. "I haven't got time to talk," replied Marty, while he was climbing into his pickup. And that was that.

Lawless returned to The 14 to talk with Bolton, expecting Bolton would want to stay another day in Coolidge to see if they could get Mr. Brace to talk on tape. But Bolton wanted to go home and write his investigative reports. "We'll send him a subpoena for records after we indict," he told Lawless, and the two headed back to Sheridan to check out of their hotel.

CHAPTER 41

SAC Price had put out feelers through an IRS Criminal Tax Attorney – Julia Peters, a friend of his in Washington – who identified a DOJ Tax Division lawyer who had been volunteered by his superiors to help with barter cases, as necessary. She warned Price that said DOJ attorney did not seem pleased by the assignment. Her boss in Washington was also speaking with DOJ about the case.

The conference call to talk about moving the *Flaherty* case forward was five-way. IRS-CID was represented by Dan Price, SAC Denver; Arthur Bolton, Acting ASAC Cheyenne; and Julia Peters, IRS Criminal Tax Attorney, Washington, D.C. Robert Cavelli, a young lawyer from the Chief Counsel's Office in the IRS, the office that handled civil cases in the U.S. Tax Court, was also on the call in case bartering issues came up. Arnold Renfro, a lawyer from the U.S. Department of Justice, Tax Division, Washington, D.C., was on the call for DOJ. The mood was low-key and collegial, until Renfro spoke his first words.

"I want to remind everyone that this prosecution goes nowhere, in fact, doesn't exist, unless DOJ decides to move it forward," said Renfro. "There are lawyers in the DOJ Tax Division who are all kinds of deferential toward the IRS and the IRS-CID. I'm not one of those guys. I've spent the last ten years hearing what great cases you have, and then I drill down into them, and we can't prove a thing. So I've stopped trying to win friends in the IRS. Let's reverse that. Why don't you convince me why your barter case should be the first one in the country to be taken to a grand jury."

There was silence among the other participants on the call. Julia Peters spoke first.

"The case has been through Centralized Case Review, and . . ."

"That's a given. A case doesn't reach my desk unless it's had CCR within the IRS," interrupted Renfro. "I read the file. Tell me why it's a good case."

Julia Peters began, "Well . . ."

"Julia, let me say something first," said Dan Price, "and I apologize for being the second person in a row to interrupt you. Mr. Renfro, I've been preparing criminal tax cases for 28 years. I've been IRS-CID Special Agent in Charge in Denver for 11 of those years. I know what a prosecutable case looks like. Washington has been all over me for more than a month insisting we develop a criminal barter case. It's not what we usually do, but we worked one up, it's been through CCR in record time, and you have the results in front of you."

Price paused briefly, and a couple of people coughed. "The impetus on this case came from Washington, not Wyoming or Colorado. It's a good case. I don't give a rat's ass whether DOJ likes the case or not, and I don't have to convince you of anything. I'll be retiring soon as a GS-15 equivalent, and whether this case gets pursued or not isn't going to make a dime's worth of difference to my retirement. So why don't you hand the case back to your boss, tell him you talked with the IRS SAC in Denver, and that you didn't like his attitude. Tell him I wasn't deferential enough to you. Ask him what he wants to do with the case. Tell him maybe DOJ should just move on to somebody else's barter case. And then maybe we'll reconvene this call after you've had that conversation. Or maybe not. I don't care which."

All five participants were silent. Special Agent Arthur Bolton was proud of his boss, but disappointed that his boss had invited DOJ to ditch his case.

Renfro had been in a lot of meetings lately where he'd pissed people off from the get-go. He wasn't sure why. He knew that what the Denver guy had said completely mooted any idea that IRS was highly motivated to keep DOJ happy on this one. So he fell back on the question he pulled out every time he felt himself losing an argument.

"What's your point?" he asked.

"I don't have one," replied SAC Price, immediately. There was silence again, as the two pugilists circled around the five-post electronic ring.

Renfro was not as close to retirement as Price was, and his boss, Kevin Paulson, Deputy Attorney General for Criminal Tax Enforcement, had made it very clear to him that he was to make the Wyoming case his top priority. That directive came straight from the Attorney General himself. The upshot was that Renfro was not in a position to go back to his boss and complain that he didn't like the IRS people in Colorado and Wyoming. But he didn't want to deal with Hicksville any more, or any longer, than he had to.

"I can see we're not going to get anywhere by telephone," said Renfro. "So let me tell you all how it's going to be. We'll draft an indictment here in Washington, based on the Centralized Case Review. I will talk with the U.S. Attorney's Office in Cheyenne and coordinate with them on grand jury time. A day or two before we present the case, Special Agent Bolton will meet with me in Cheyenne to prep his grand jury testimony. We'll just read the notes of his undercover conversations, and wire transcripts, into the record. If we need an expert witness, I'll find one. The grand jury will vote. We'll get the local U.S. Attorney to co-sign the indictment, we'll file it, and then we'll arrest the target. After the arraignment, we'll probably want to go back and bring witnesses from this little town before the grand jury – so we can use the testimony at trial if the witnesses go sideways on us – and then we'll get a superseding indictment. I will keep you all posted by email. Is there anything else?"

"I will brief the IRS side on this meeting," said Julia Peters. "We'll look forward to hearing from you."

CHAPTER 42

Patrick, his sister Annabelle, and their parents were sitting around the kitchen table at Ed and Dina's place in Adams Heights on Christmas Eve. Miriam Vogel was looking after Patrick's goats and chickens back in Coolidge. Annabelle was giving Patrick a hard time about his haircut. He was giving her a hard time about her third piercing in her left ear. When the conversation turned to tattoos, Dina said, "I'm sure I don't want to hear this," and got up to start a fresh pot of coffee.

All four were heading to Midnight Mass at St. Matthew's. Most of the Catholic churches in the Denver area had stopped having Midnight Mass on Christmas Eve, but St. Matthew's was keeping the tradition alive. Ed grumbled that he was going to be up until 1:30, and then awake again at 7:00, because he always woke up at 7:00, no matter what time he went to bed. "Wait until you're old, you'll understand." He wasn't really that old.

They still liked to exchange gifts on Christmas morning. It was easier now, because nobody made a big fuss, and some of the gifts had been standardized. Annabelle's gift for Patrick was always a full year of Wyoming resident hunting licenses. She created a "gift certificate" which promised that she would pay for whatever license he procured during the year, and she had been true to her word. Dina's gift for Patrick was always warm clothes. He needed them. She knew his sizes. And she knew where to find them at reasonable prices. Ed's gifts for Patrick were almost always (A) ammunition, and (B) tools.

Annabelle's gifts for her parents would vary; likewise, her parents' gifts for her. Books were always a good choice. Annabelle bought her parents "Alexa" one year, but they rarely talked to her. Something about feeling uncomfortable about bossing her around.

Patrick would build gifts, or carve gifts, or grow gifts, whatever it took. Some of his gifts, like the little table he built two years ago for Ed and Dina, were inspired. Others, not so much. Just like gifts that cost money.

In the afternoon, old friends would stop over, or the four Flaherty's would visit a neighbor or two. It was amazing to Patrick how quickly it all came back. Home. But Coolidge was home, too. Nice to have two.

Christmas dinner was the high point of Patrick's year, every year. Dina always found a big turkey, and they worked together to make the meal. At the table, they would talk about the past and the future.

Annabelle was a pediatrician in Chicago. She had joined a small group after her residency, and their practice had been absorbed by a big health chain. She was anxious about the pace of change, and dismayed that she spent more time dealing with recordkeeping than she did treating patients. But she loved what she was doing, and her career was on track. She had a new boyfriend -- a doctor -- and it seemed to be going well. The real challenge, as always, would be finding enough time to make a relationship work.

Ed and Dina had retired at the same time, two years earlier. They liked it so far. They were living on Social Security, their respective IRA's, and some cash savings. St. Ignatius High School, where Ed had taught biology for 35 years, didn't offer retirement benefits to faculty. Dina, a municipal librarian, had long ago rolled her small 401(a) – like a 401(k), but for municipal employees – into her even smaller IRA.

Patrick was the subject of most of his family's anxieties, a fact he regretted. But things had actually been getting better in the last couple of years. As Patrick proved that he was able to sustain himself in Coolidge, and even to thrive, his parents' worries lessened somewhat.

Two years before, when Ed and Dina announced that they were retiring, Annabelle convened a family conference call – Patrick borrowed a phone -- to talk about the monthly payment to Patrick. She wanted to persuade Ed, Dina and Patrick that the $100 would be an imperceptible part of her doctor's salary, but a noticeable slice of Ed and Dina's retirement income. She proposed taking over the payment. Ed and Dina reluctantly agreed, but provisionally. "OK, we'll probably give it a try," they said, "but before we change we need to talk about it again." Two weeks later, Dina sold her first painting, and the idea that Annabelle would take over the subsidy was tabled, *sine die*.

Of all the choices that Patrick had had to make to live as he was living, accepting $100 a month from his parents was by the far the most difficult for him. He couldn't rationalize it; he wouldn't lie to himself about it; and he couldn't pretend that there was anything noble about it. But looking at it clearly, he knew that if he gave up the $100, he would have to give up Cousin Clem's; and if he gave up Cousin Clem's he would be jeopardizing friendships, because that's where his friends were, night in and night out. He explained his feelings to his parents, and made clear that he was willing to get a job and open a checking account if they were uncomfortable about the subsidy. But he also had to be honest about the fact that his chrometophobia was real and not imagined, and he wasn't sure he could manage any wages he might earn.

Their response surprised him. "Listen, Pat, this is simple," said Ed. "Anyone who makes a major life decision on the basis of $100 a month is crazy. In the grand scheme of things, $100 a month is a rounding error. You're the only person I know for whom a hundred bucks is anything like sink or swim. So let's all just take a deep breath and figure that your being happy is worth way more than a hundred bucks a month, to all of us."

Annabelle was a tougher nut. When Patrick and Annabelle had some time alone, the discussion turned, as it did every year, to the life he was living. While she had been happy to offer to step in for Ed and Dina when it came to the $100, she was not shy about challenging his decisions otherwise. Couldn't you drive part time for Amazon? How are you ever going to put aside some money for when you're older? Do you realize you're not paying into Social Security, and when your body gives out, you're not going to be able to feed and clothe yourself?

On the last point, Patrick was in agreement. He was happy and living well now, but how was he going to survive when he got older? He could enter the priesthood – three squares and a cot for celebrating Masses, and the jobs were going begging, even for 70-somethings. But at least right now, he wasn't interested. Maybe he could find or create a lean-to within walking distance of a soup kitchen. Every town had one. That might work until he needed a hospital or a nursing home. He could find a caretaker's job, maybe in a private school.

Well, that was doubtful. He could get married and have children, which he'd like to do anyway. But that would mostly just transfer the problem from his shoulders to his family's shoulders. No good options.

One thing he knew. If you were persistent – as long as you didn't give up, or fall into drugs or alcohol -- it was difficult to starve to death or go entirely without health care in the United States of America. He would cross bridges as he came to them, and he would figure it out.

After Christmas dinner, Patrick played Ed's guitar, and they talked about people they all knew. They laughed often, and the memories were as fresh as always. As he was getting ready for bed, Patrick realized that he was just about as relaxed and happy as he had ever been. He thought about having leftover pumpkin pie for breakfast.

CHAPTER 43

Kathleen Patterson, Press Secretary, speechwriter, and spokesperson for the Attorney General of the United States, called Antoinette Aldridge at 9:30 a.m. sharp on Friday morning, January 15. Ms. Aldridge was the head producer for all courtroom, legal and criminal justice segments that aired on her cable network.

"Toni, listen, I have an arrest coming up that's, like, really interesting. It's breaking news, human interest, and drama, rolled into one. We're going to arrest a guy in Wyoming for cheating on his taxes, because he structured his life to avoid reporting his income. All of his principal means of support, I don't know, like, food, shelter, umm, food for his animals, he bartered for all of it. He traded his services for all of the things he needs to live, and avoided using cash. He tried to make it so the IRS couldn't track him. There are strict rules against bartering, but he ignored them. And the hook, I think, is that he's taking the old militia and tax resistance scam in a new direction – instead of being blatant about his opposition to the government, like a lot of these yo-yo's, he actually came up with a new scheme to try to get away with it. Stick it to Uncle Sugar, but stay under the radar. What do you think?"

Ms. Aldridge was not born yesterday. "Listen, Katy, I appreciate the head's up, but one guy living off the land in Wyoming isn't breaking news. Maybe it was in 1879, I don't know. I'd have to get a crew to Wyoming, and even then, I'd have to negotiate some air time with my boss." She paused, and thought. DOJ would not have called on this if it weren't important to them. "OK, if I can get this covered, can we have a one-hour head start on the AG's expected testimony on the Hill on prison reform?"

"Let me put you on hold."

She was gone for four minutes. The administration's evolving position on prison and sentencing reform was relatively big news, and promised to be one of the most important news stories for the month. Toni Aldridge figured that a one-hour head start might make them the go-to outlet on that story for most of a week. And maybe the Wyoming story wouldn't suck, you never knew.

Kathleen Patterson came back on the line. "OK, we can do that, provided you can get this on the air, and in rotation for at least a few hours," she said. "We would want chryons. Deal?"

"Deal."

"Cool. Now, the logistics might get tricky. I can't send you a pdf of the indictment yet, because it hasn't been filed. That's going to happen at about 4:00 this afternoon, and it won't be under seal. But you'll have at least three hours between the filing of the indictment, and the guy's perp walk. That's going to be in Casper, Wyoming, so you can pre-position your people during the day today. What I'll do is, I'll get you a pdf of the indictment just as he's being arrested. You can read it, and write the script for your people on the ground. You'll have at least two hours while he's being transported. If you want, I can stay late and help you understand what the allegations are about. I'll have a lawyer here with me. Just call me on my cell."

"I appreciate the offer, I really do," replied the producer. "I've got some ideas as well, and if I have any questions, I'll reach out. I'm looking at Google Maps; I'm guessing the crew's going to have to come from our Denver studio. We'll see. Anyway, I'll be in touch. Thanks Katy. Ciao."

"Bye."

CHAPTER 44

It was about 20 degrees outside, and wasn't supposed to get much colder, so Patrick was wearing his down jacket. Twenty degrees was comfortable for Coolidge in mid-January, and Patrick was happy to leave his big coat on the hook. It was Friday at 4:30, and the sun had not quite set. As always, he was revising his set list in his head as he walked. He wanted to try "Suite: Judy Blue Eyes" for the first time.

He turned left from his front path onto Side Road and walked downhill about fifty yards. Behind him, over his right shoulder, he heard footsteps coming out of the woods and onto the road behind him. Hunters, probably, but Friday afternoon was a weird time for them to be there. He had time to think that they were probably going to scout a tree stand for the following morning.

"Federal Agents! Get on the ground, now! Keep your hands raised and visible, and put them behind your head! You are under arrest! Get on the ground *now*, face down!"

The four shapes behind him were armed with M-4's, all pointed at his solar plexus. He was half way turned to face them when he saw four more black-clad figures in his peripheral vision, also armed, coming up the road from below. What the fuck? This had to be a mistake. Patrick slowly knelt, with his hands clasped behind his head, and then stretched on the pavement, face down. Whatever happened, he didn't want to give these lunatics any reason to shoot him. With his heart pounding, he waited for someone to approach him.

It didn't take long. Seconds after he hit the pavement, there was a knee at the bottom of his spine, and hands holding his shoulders down. More hands were gripping his wrists and moving them, one at a time, around to his lower back. He felt handcuffs click onto his wrists, and he was pulled up by his upper arms, to a standing position. An agent unzipped his coat and frisked him. They checked his pockets, and all were empty, except for his right front pants pocket. They took the ten dollar bill that was there.

A vaguely familiar face stepped in front of him and began to speak. "Patrick Flaherty, you are under arrest for federal tax evasion. You have the right to remain silent. If you choose to speak, anything you say can and will be used against you in a court of law. You have a right to a lawyer. If you cannot afford a lawyer, one will be appointed to represent you, at no cost to you. Do you understand these rights?"

What the *fuck*?

"Do you understand these rights?"

Patrick didn't understand anything. His mind was pin-balling from one thought to another. He had a gig at Cousin Clem's. His parents. His wrists hurt. "Can I give some more feed to my animals?"

"No, you can't. You can make a phone call when we get to Casper. Do you understand the rights that I just explained to you?"

"Uh . . . yes."

"Good. Sit down."

Casper? As he was lowered to a sitting position on the road, Patrick shook his head, involuntarily. His mind wouldn't clear. "Casper?" he asked. "What's in Casper?"

No one replied. In fact, no one said another word to Patrick for a long time. Everyone was in tactical gear, some "FBI," others "IRS-CID Police." All of the conversation was about the "wagon," phone calls the black-clad people needed to make, and who would drive which vehicle.

The sun had set. The agents talked about sealing up Patrick's cabin, and what, if anything, to do with his firearms. "Art, it looks like he has a lever-action, a shotgun, and a .357 revolver." One of them asked Patrick, "Is that right, just a rifle, a shotgun and a revolver?" Patrick nodded yes slowly, and then a dazed, "Ahhh, yeah."

After about five more minutes, Patrick spoke up. "The heat for my animals comes from the stove inside the cabin. Either somebody needs to keep the stove going, or the animals need to be moved somewhere else."

The agents didn't respond to Patrick, but they seemed to be huddling to discuss what he had said. Finally, one of the agents came back to him, and stood over him. "Your cabin is a crime scene, and will be locked until further notice. We have a warrant to search it, and we'll give you a copy in Casper. You can use your phone call to ask someone to come get your animals and take care of them, and we'll have an agent meet whoever that is. If you can't arrange for somebody to care for them, we'll take custody of them tomorrow, and see where it goes from there." Without waiting for a response from Patrick, the agent went back to what he was doing. A minute or two later, another agent said, "We have the firearms secured. There's meat in the refrigerator, it's still running. There's no running water to turn off. Lights are all off."

Eventually, a white van rolled slowly uphill, backwards. When it stopped, the agents opened the back door. Patrick saw that it was just benches, along the sides, and a series of handcuffs and leg manacles. They told him, "Climb up, watch your step." The minute he was seated, they manacled his ankles, and then uncuffed his hands, which were still behind his back. Handcuffs were then reattached in front of his body, and locked to another chain that extended up from his leg irons, through his legs, to his wrists. Finally, he was belted onto the bench. The last two agents jumped down from the back of the van and closed the back doors. A single dim light remained lit, and he could see the driver and a passenger through a narrow window, reinforced with a metal screen.

After a few minutes, the van started forward. Patrick felt, more than saw, the left turn onto Route 14, and he felt Coolidge falling away behind him. He knew they would get on the Interstate at Ranchester within about ten minutes, and then there would be a couple of hours of tire noise until Casper – assuming that was really where they were going.

CHAPTER 45

Patrick was used to being alone with his thoughts. He was afraid, but not terrified. He knew the government was not going to execute him for tax evasion. He assumed he was guilty – you don't send eight or nine armed federal agents to arrest somebody unless they've done something really, really wrong. He figured that not paying taxes for six years must have been too good to be legal. He should have known better. Shit, this sucks, really sucks. He should have known better.

He was embarrassed. His parents were going to find out he was a criminal, and it was going to break their hearts. And Clem, and his friends, and everyone at the church. And he had to assume he was going to jail for a few years. Humiliating.

Why did he think he recognized one of the agents? Where had he seen that guy before? If he was being investigated, somebody would have had to have shown up in Coolidge to investigate. Had he seen the guy in Coolidge?

He spent at least an hour worrying about his phone call. Suppose they only let him have one? Whom would he call? It couldn't be his parents, because they didn't know enough people in Coolidge to tie up loose ends. Who could arrange to get his animals fed, keep the stove lit, explain to Clem why he didn't show up for his gig?

He decided he'd call Clem. Clem would be there to take the call, and he knew Clem would help find someone to take care of the animals. And maybe Anita Boyle would be there, and Clem could hand the phone to her. Anita could probably tell him what kind of trouble he was in, and what was likely to happen next.

Patrick felt the van exit the Interstate, and make rolling stops at a couple of intersections. In a couple of minutes more, it stopped for good. The back doors opened, Patrick's manacles were unlocked from the floor and the bench, and he was led off the back.

He was assaulted by the glare. A huge light tree was illuminating Patrick, the van, and four or five agents. As the agents led Patrick around the corner of a large red brick building, the lights followed him, and he saw a camera following his steps. The lights and camera equipment moved up the sidewalk with him, and a young woman with a microphone shouted at him, in a more or less continuous loop, "Do you have any comment? Are you claiming innocence? Are you a member of a militia group? Are you resisting the federal government?"

Patrick was led through what seemed to be a side door, and into an office on the ground floor. The plaque on the door said "U.S. Marshals." He was photographed, fingerprinted, DNA sampled – cheek swab -- and escorted to a holding cell. They brought him a landline telephone with a long extension cord, and told him, "Call anyone you want. After three calls, if you make that many, come back and ask for permission if you want to make more. You only have ten minutes – the judge is waiting for us in the Magistrate's courtroom."

Patrick called his parents. His dad was quiet; his mother cried softly. No, coming up wouldn't help now, but he would call them later when he could, and try to explain what was going on. Something about tax evasion, they weren't real clear.

He called Clem at the bar. Arrested by federal agents. Sorry I missed the gig. Goats, chickens. There's no heat in their houses. Try calling Mrs. Vogel for the chickens, that's where they were from in the first place. Try calling Eric Dormer to help with the goats. Something about tax evasion.

"Is Anita there tonight?" asked Patrick.

"No, she hasn't been in. I can call her, I'll see if anyone has her cell number. Worst case, I'll go over to her house. How can she reach you?"

"I don't know," said Patrick. "All I know is that I'm in federal custody, I believe in Casper. They're taking me to see a judge. Hopefully that will be enough information for her to reach me."

CHAPTER 46

Ten minutes later, he was led down two hallways into a smallish courtroom, with eight or ten people milling about. He was still handcuffed, and a United States Marshal was at his elbow. As he was led to one of the tables, a bookish-looking man, probably of Middle Eastern or south-Asian descent, approached him and placed a hand on his shoulder. "Mr. Flaherty, my name is Khalil Omar. I'm with the Federal Defender's office. I'm here to represent you at your initial appearance."

No one else was listening in, or trying to. "Why was I arrested?" asked Patrick. "What taxes didn't I pay?"

Mr. Omar held up a thick-ish 8" x 11" document. "According to the indictment, you evaded taxes by entering into a series of bartering relationships – non-cash transactions – that you should have reported as income. They allege that you structured all this as a scam, to avoid paying taxes on self-employment income that you knew you owed."

"Fuck. OK." Patrick thought for a second. "If I'm found guilty, how much time would I spend in jail?"

"I'd have to look that up in the Federal Sentencing Guidelines. I'll be honest, my office doesn't handle many tax cases, because poor people don't get charged with a lot of tax crimes. So I don't want to guess. Is this your first offense?"

"Yeah, I've never been arrested before."

"Well, that's good," Omar replied. "There's reason for optimism. I seriously doubt you're facing a long, long sentence. But these are serious felonies. I don't want to kid you about that."

"Do I need to find a tax attorney?"

"Maybe. We can figure that out in the coming days. This is kind of an unusual case. I was called to come over tonight by the Magistrate Judge. A Magistrate Judge is like the Justice of the Peace in the federal system. He decides minor offenses, and advises people of their rights when they're arrested. You're going to see Magistrate Judge Dellarosa. His office told me that you have a complex case, and they suggested it needs to be handled by somebody with a lot of experience with federal criminal practice. That's me -- but I don't know anything about tax crimes." Patrick glanced up at him, and he continued. "Don't worry, you'll be fine having me represent you tonight. All you're going to do is plead not guilty, and they'll determine your conditions of release. I'm going to argue that the conditions should be as lenient as possible. I know the Magistrate Judge pretty well, and I think I can persuade him to be reasonable. The whole process will probably take less than ten minutes."

A figure in a black robe appeared in the courtroom and took the bench. Everyone remained standing until he was seated.

"Good evening, everyone. I see a couple of unfamiliar faces. I'm Magistrate Judge Peter Dellarosa. What do we have?"

A lawyer to Patrick's left spoke up. "Your Honor, this is *United States v. Patrick Michael Flaherty*. I understand you've been provided a copy of the indictment. The defendant is present for his initial appearance."

"Mr. Flaherty, I've been advised by the government that, as far as they are aware, you have no cash or substantial assets, in other words, no ability to retain private counsel. Is that correct?"

Mr. Omar nudged Patrick to his feet, and stood with him. "Yes, sir," replied Patrick. He was still wearing the clothes that he put on for his gig.

"You don't have any money to pay a lawyer?"

"No, sir."

"The Federal Public Defender in Casper, Mr. Omar, is present – Mr. Farragut, I took the liberty of giving Mr. Omar a head's up about the arrest. Unless Mr. Flaherty objects, and unless he desires to represent himself, I will appoint the Federal Defender as Mr. Flaherty's counsel. And of course, Mr. Flaherty, if you change your mind, or if you're later able to afford counsel, you can retain private counsel. But for now, Mr. Khalil Omar will represent you.

He's your lawyer, he doesn't work for the government. And I'll tell you, the Federal Defender's office is very good at what they do, and you're fortunate that Mr. Omar is available. For the record, do you consent to the appointment of the Federal Defender as your counsel?"

"Yes, sir."

"OK, let's proceed to the initial appearance, arraignment, and scheduling. Mr. Omar did you receive a copy of the indictment? Have you had a chance to read it, and talk with your client?"

"Yes, Your Honor, and we waive formal reading," replied Omar.

"How does the defendant plead?"

"Not guilty, Your Honor," replied Omar on Patrick's behalf.

Arnold Renfro jumped to his feet. He was tall, lean, black hair combed straight back, in a navy pinstriped suit, and somewhere between thirty-five and fifty. You couldn't tell. And he had decided he was going to make this his courtroom. "Your Honor, I object. Can we hear from the defendant? I don't want to have to respond to some sort of motion from a new lawyer to disqualify Mr. Omar because he wouldn't let the defendant speak for himself."

Magistrate Judge Dellarosa looked at Renfro. "Who are you?"

"Arnold Renfro, sir. I'm with the Tax Division of the United States Department of Justice in Washington. I co-signed the indictment. We want this case handled by the book."

"Well, first, Mr. Renfro, welcome to Wyoming. Because I'm feeling patient tonight, I will explain to you how it works here. In the District of Wyoming, when we hold a Rule 10 initial appearance, the 'not guilty' plea is essentially written down in the paperwork before the defendant ever arrives. Based on my conversations every year at the Tenth Circuit Judicial Conference, I suspect that every other district in this circuit does the same thing." The Magistrate Judge pinched the bridge of his nose; Renfro made his head hurt, and he'd only known him for twenty seconds. "Over the years, I've had maybe one or two initial appearances involving relatively minor charges where the government and the defense worked out a guilty plea in advance. Otherwise, I don't think I've ever accepted a guilty plea at this stage. If Mr. Flaherty, bless his heart, tried to plead guilty at his initial appearance, I wouldn't let him. I'd tell him, 'thanks for the input,' and then I'd strike his comments from the record, and I'd enter a plea of not guilty on his behalf. So, no – I don't need to hear from Mr. Flaherty himself. Mr. Omar's representation of his intentions is fine with me."

The Magistrate Judge checked his watch. "I note for the record that AUSA Jack Farragut is also present for the government. It's certainly the first time I've seen two senior federal prosecutors show up at a defendant's initial appearance. Especially at this time of the evening, we usually get the junior person in the office. Jack, will you be speaking for the government, or should I continue to deal with Mr. Renfro?"

"I'll speak for the government, Your Honor," replied Farragut. Farragut was Patrick's height – a little over six feet – with sandy hair and chiseled features. He looked like a TV lawyer, which may have partly explained why he decided to go to law school.

"OK, good," replied the Magistrate Judge. "Mr. Omar, do you request all discovery to which your client is entitled?"

"Yes, Your Honor," replied Omar.

"Does the government agree to disclose all Jencks Act material, and all other criminal discovery under Rule 16 not less than fourteen days before trial?"

"Yes, Your Honor," replied Farragut.

"OK, I'll put this case on the criminal docket, and I'll enter a scheduling order," said Magistrate Judge Dellarosa. He turned to his clerk to whisper some instructions. The room grew quiet, and Patrick realized how tired he was.

CHAPTER 47

"OK, let's talk about conditions of release," continued the Magistrate Judge. "Does the government have a position on bail or other conditions of release?"

"Yes, Your Honor, the government opposes the release of the defendant," said Farragut. "We have submitted a barebones written Motion for Detention – I doubt that you've seen it, I just handed it to your law clerk a minute ago – and our idea is to offer testimony from the case agent now, in open court, so that there will be a record to support whatever determination Your Honor makes on our motion."

"Your Honor, may I be heard?" asked Omar.

"Sure."

"I haven't seen the written motion -- I'll take Mr. Farragut's word for the fact that it's barebones," said Omar. "But it's clear from the face of the indictment that the defendant has strong roots in his community -- he's obviously 307 to the bone. The crimes alleged . . ."

Magistrate Judge Dellarossa saw Renfro urgently rising to talk again, and he thought he knew why. "Relax, Mr. Renfro. Three-o-seven refers to the telephone Area Code for Wyoming. It's one of the ways we say that someone is from here." And then to Omar, "Sorry, Khalil, go ahead," as Renfro sat back down.

"The crimes alleged are, to say the least, non-violent; and the government has already agreed – indeed alleges – that he has no money. He's not a flight risk, because if he tried, he'd run out of money before he reached the Montana border. Given the very strong presumption in federal proceedings that a defendant is entitled to pretrial release, I request that Your Honor deny the Motion for Detention summarily, and then we'll all have a real conversation about conditions for release."

The Magistrate Judge scratched his cheek, and thought. "Jack, Khalil, let's do it this way. I agree with Khalil that I could probably deny the motion without taking evidence, but I want to be fair to the government. Jack, let's hear from your agent for a couple of minutes. If he surprises me with facts that aren't apparent so far, I'll maybe take additional evidence. Otherwise, we'll just proceed to conditions for release. Jack, who's your case agent?"

"Your Honor, Special Agent Arthur Bolton of the Criminal Investigation Division of the Internal Revenue Service has worked on the case since its inception," said Farragut. "He's here this evening," he said, turning to Bolton. "We'll present his testimony on the Motion for Detention. Would you want him to go over to the witness stand, or would you prefer that he come up to the bar of the court?"

"Just have him stand beside you at counsel table," said the Magistrate Judge.

Bolton took his place next to AUSA Farragut. Patrick was still trying to remember where he'd seen the guy before. The Magistrate Judge addressed Bolton directly: "Agent Bolton, welcome to Night Court." It wasn't really called that, but Magistrate Judge Dellarosa was a fan of the old television show. "Where are you based? Cheyenne? Denver?"

"Our main office for the region is in Denver, Your Honor, but we have a satellite office in Cheyenne. I'm Acting Assistant Special Agent in Charge in Cheyenne. We only do criminal tax cases."

"Jack, can I keep going?" said the Magistrate Judge. "I'll let you fill in whatever I miss."

"Sure," replied AUSA Farragut, after a second or two of hesitation. He had to get along with Magistrate Judge Dellarosa on the next case, and the one after that, and the right to conduct his own questioning at a bail hearing was not a hill to die on. Renfro squirmed beside him, and Farragut surmised that he was not happy.

"Agent Bolton, do you swear to tell the truth, the whole truth, and nothing but the truth?" asked the Magistrate Judge.

"Yes, Your Honor."

"OK, I can't imagine we're talking about anything besides danger to the community or flight risk," said the Magistrate Judge to Special Agent Bolton. "What's your theory? Both? One or the other?"

Bolton had testified often enough that he was comfortable dealing with lawyers and judges in open court. He looked the judge in the eye, and tried to match the conversational tone he was hearing from the bench.

"Flight risk, Your Honor," Bolton replied. "I've searched the defendant's home. I've talked to his friends and neighbors. And, as you can tell from the indictment, the defendant has become an expert in self-sufficiency. He literally lives off the land. When we went into his home, his refrigerator was full of fish and game. He has wild onions and other edible plants in his kitchen area, so he knows how to feed himself in the woods. If he were released tonight, he could go home, and begin to prepare a flight into the Bighorn Mountains. We secured his guns, but he could borrow or steal a firearm and ammunition from someone in town. He has a net and fishing tackle. He has all the warm clothing he needs. He has unique skills, and because we believe there's a zero percent chance he's going to be able to pay his back taxes right after a conviction, and because the Sentencing Guidelines call for imprisonment, he has every reason to leave now. It wouldn't even change his life that much. He'd go on living off the land, anywhere in the mountains of Wyoming, Montana or Colorado. We might never find him. We're concerned that he has a serious grudge against government in all its forms, and he could escape from prosecution just to spite us. If he flees, we simply don't have the resources to find him again."

The Magistrate Judge was silent for a moment. "Not what I was expecting to hear," he said. "I think you make a serious case." He turned to Patrick's lawyer. "Khalil?"

"Your Honor, where does it say in the Bail Act that self-sufficient people are less entitled to pretrial release? That would be a seriously perverse presumption. Almost all of us have the *ability* to flee; what counts is an unusually strong *motivation* to flee. That isn't present here. Mr. Flaherty lives in his own house, he cares for his animals, and he has close connections with his church and community. If anyone deserves the presumption in favor of pretrial release, he does."

"All right," said the Magistrate Judge, "I'm going to deny the Motion for Detention. But I think Agent Bolton's point is a good one, and I think it should rightly influence my determinations concerning conditions of release. In addition to the conditions in the standing order – no firearms, no drugs, no passport, et cetera – I'm going to require a bond in the amount of $500,000, co-signed by one or more financially responsible individuals. Mr. Flaherty, you need to be aware that if you flee, you will be creating serious hardship for the people who trusted you enough to co-sign for your release. Five hundred thousand dollars is a lot of money. Remember that if you're tempted to take off for the hills."

The Magistrate Judge looked at Khalil Omar. "Khalil, if he can't find anyone to sign within a week, I'll consider a motion to reduce to $250,000. My objective is to see him released, not spend months in jail. But I'm not promising to reduce. And I'm not going below $250,000 – anything below that, you'll have to go to Judge Martin. And no promises on how I'm going to rule on your motion. So try to find somebody to co-sign at $500,000."

"For the record, Your Honor, the defendant's position is that the bond is far too high, and we'll have a motion for reduction," said Omar. "And yes, Your Honor, we'll see if we can find somebody who will sign at $500,000."

The Magistrate Judge looked at all of the lawyers. "Is there anything else we need to cover?" No one spoke. "OK, we're adjourned."

Patrick had no idea what had just happened. They led him back to the same van, and then to another building most of the way out of town. It was a jail; he wasn't sure which one. They took away his clothes and gave him an orange jumpsuit. It was past lights-out. They led him to a cell. He was instructed to lie down and go to sleep.

CHAPTER 48

The reporter stood silently, waiting for police vehicles and checking her watch. She wanted to get back to the hotel bar before it closed. She had never had reason to come to Wyoming before, and she didn't see much reason to stay. Her cameraman, Sonny, was a good guy, but very religious, and no fun to be with on the road. The IT and comms guy was new; Derek or something. Her twenty-seventh birthday was the next day, and she was disappointed she was going to be spending most of it in a news van heading back to Denver on Interstate 25.

The script that Toni Aldridge had sent her was short and simple. She would describe the charges, which they would probably run as a voice-over for the perp-walk. Then they would cut to her head shot, with mic, in front of the federal courthouse. She would describe the larger meaning of the case in that shot. Probably ninety seconds of air-time, altogether.

The caravan came down the one-way on Wolcott with roof lights flashing. There were five vehicles in all, with a big white van in the center of the convoy. Other than the reporter and her crew, there were no media present, and no other onlookers. There were three U.S. Marshals, waiting on the sidewalk, and a Casper police cruiser a few yards down the block, probably there more out of curiosity than anything else.

The light tree was set up. Sonny began to film as the vehicles were slowing, and pulling over to the curb on their left. He recorded black-uniformed agents hopping out of their sedans and SUV's and moving to the rear of the van. One of them opened the back doors, and Sonny was able to catch a view of the perp, sitting on a bench in manacles. After some fussing with keys, they led him out of the van, and onto the sidewalk.

The perp looked bewildered, and didn't try to hide his face. Great close-up! The agents succeeded in looking – confident. They knew they were doing important work. The perp, meanwhile, was dressed in camouflage pants. His down jacket was open in front, and he was wearing a kind of Hawaiian shirt without the flowers. Nikes. At least he was wearing socks. No baseball hat or Army beret, but maybe the agents took it. The reporter followed the procession up the sidewalk, shouting her questions: "Do you have any comment? Are you claiming innocence? Are you a member of a militia group? Are you resisting the federal government?" Sonny handled the camera, and Derek, or whatever his name was, carried and aimed the portable lights, until the crowd of agents turned right onto First Street, and reached a side door. The film, from getting out of the van to entry into the building, would time out to a minute-eight, which was just about perfect. Long enough to talk over, perfect length for looping, in whole or in part, if the story expanded.

They re-positioned the light tree on the front walk of the courthouse, to do the main shot. The night was clear and cold, so the reporter's breath made for great atmosphere. We Go Where the Stories Are. She looked directly into the camera and spoke with authority.

"Federal agents from the FBI and the Internal Revenue Service arrested a Wyoming man tonight on charges that he willfully evaded federal income taxes for five years using an ingenious scheme to barter his services for food and shelter. The suspect, Patrick Michael Flaherty, allegedly structured all of his commercial transactions as non-cash exchanges so that he could avoid detection by federal tax collectors. The officials we spoke to, who requested anonymity to be able to speak candidly, acknowledged that the prosecution is intended, in part, to send a warning to others who might be inclined to use bartering to avoid federal income taxes. Additionally, the defendant has allegedly expressed hostility to the federal government; he lives secluded in a cabin in the Bighorn Mountains in Wyoming; and there are indications that he is connected with, or at least sympathetic to, fringe militant groups who dress in camouflage and other military gear, and express similar hostility to federal authority. Trial of this case is expected in late spring. This is Tania Teagarden reporting from Casper, Wyoming."

The report was edited at headquarters, and first aired as a seventy-five second spot at 11:30 p.m. in the East. Quick turnaround – this was the big leagues. The chryon said, "Bartering to Evade Federal Tax." Patrick's face was shown in close-up. The story was aired through 9:30 a.m., EST, on Saturday morning. Millions of Americans saw it; few took much interest. Toni Aldridge was satisfied that she'd upheld her end of the bargain with Katy Patterson, and could now look forward to first dibs on prison and sentencing reform.

Patrick's parents, Ed and Dina, did not see the report when it was first aired. Patrick had already called them, and they were busy letting Annabelle and some of their close friends know. But then at 9:35 the phone started to ring, and friends and neighbors called to tell them how sorry they were, and was there anything they could do? They unplugged their phone a half hour later. Dina couldn't stop crying. Ed just shook his head in bewilderment. Neither was able to sleep that night, so they eventually gave up and made coffee at 4:00 a.m. They made a contingency plan to drive up to Casper, but they weren't sure whether they needed to stay close to home to help arrange for bail, or whatever.

The New York Times, the Washington Post, USA Today and the Associated Press ran short stories, based on the indictment. The indictment itself didn't mention militias or camouflage clothing, but all of the outlets except USA Today worked that possibility into their stories. Katy Patterson had done her work well. They weren't saying that Patrick was a member of a militia; they were simply reporting that his views about the federal government, as alleged in the indictment, aligned with the views of militia groups who were known to exist in the area where he lived. That was a fair take, based on reasonable inferences from the facts alleged.

Patrick had no idea that his face had been broadcast across the country. He had no idea he was in the New York Times. He slept fitfully, because the jail was noisy – at least compared to what he was used to. Saturday morning, well, that would be another day.

CHAPTER 49

Clem saw Anita come through the front door, just before 10 o'clock. She looked different, and good, that night – dressed well, make up, her hair was done. Anita was about five-four with dark hair. Not slender, or super-curvy, but in good shape, and her face was a New York neighborhood kind of pretty. She was from North Jersey, originally.

That night, she was with a guy. Clem didn't think she'd brought a date in for three or four years; heck of a night to start dating again. Clem circled the end of the bar and intercepted Anita before she could sit down. "Anita, I have to talk to you, alone, please. I'm sorry, it's important." He looked worried.

Anita turned to her companion. "I'm sorry Rick, give me a minute. Grab that table right over there, I'll be with you in a second."

Clem and Anita huddled in the back corner of the room, as far from the sound of the band as they could be, without being outside. Anita took off her coat and held it over her arm.

"It's Patrick," Clem began. "He never showed up to play music. Turns out, he was arrested this afternoon. He called from jail to ask me to find somebody to take care of his animals, and he asked to talk to you. You weren't here, and I don't have your cell number. I went around to your place, and it was dark. I'm sorry."

"OK, tell me what you know. Who arrested him?"

"He said it was federal agents," replied Clem.

"What was he charged with?"

"Not paying taxes, I think."

"Where did they take him?"

"All he knew was that he was somewhere in Casper."

"Do you know if they gave him a lawyer?"

"He didn't say. He said he was going to go see a judge."

"All right," said Anita, "I think I probably have enough to get started. I'll go online and find out where they hold federal prisoners. I doubt there's a federal jail in Casper, so they've probably got him at Natrona County, but we'll see. I'll call around till I find him. I'll talk to the people at the jail, and let them know I'm a lawyer, he's my client, and that I'll be stopping by in the morning."

"When do you need to go? Do you need anything else that we can help with?"

"I can't help him now. They wouldn't let me see him now. I'll head out from Coolidge at about 4:00 a.m. I'd like to get there before he's tied up in breakfast or something, and before the Saturday inmate visits heat up. I'll give you my cell phone number, and let me get yours. Let me know if you hear anything, and we'll coordinate."

"All right," said Clem. "Sorry to lay all this on you all at once, but he needs help. He sounds scared."

Anita couldn't help thinking – he should be scared. A federal prosecution was about the worst thing she could imagine happening to any friend of hers. She gave Clem a hug, and they exchanged cell numbers. "Thanks," she said. She turned and walked over to the table where her new friend Rick was sitting. She told him, simply, that the evening was over. "A client was arrested. I'll call you as soon as I can, really. It was fun."

Rick was disappointed, but kind of impressed as well. There seemed to be a lot to Anita Boyle. He drove her home.

CHAPTER 50

Anita was wearing a dark pantsuit and carrying a briefcase. She was led into the small meeting room by a young guard. There was a metal table and two metal chairs in the meeting room, surrounded by glass walls and bright lights overhead. The table and chairs were bolted to the floor. Every time she entered a jail she was struck by the same incongruity. Ordinary people – inmates, Corrections Officers, lawyers, ministers – were walking and talking like the ordinary people they were, even smiling occasionally. But the ones in the jumpsuits couldn't leave. They were trapped. The pleasant people in uniforms made sure they remained trapped.

The federal government had a contract with Natrona County, Wyoming, to hold federal pretrial detainees (don't call them inmates) in the Natrona County Detention Center. In a few large cities, detention facilities near federal courthouses had been built by the U.S. Department of Justice. In most parts of the country, however, the feds rent space from the locals. The arrangement works out fine for everyone involved. Anita had never been to the Natrona County jail, but nothing about it was surprising. Jails all looked the same to her.

Two Corrections Officers led Patrick up the hallway toward the meeting room. His hands were cuffed and secured to a chain around his waist, and his feet were manacled. He had to shuffle to move. His jumpsuit was orange, and "Natrona County Detention Center" was stenciled on the back. As he entered the room, Anita stood and took a half step toward giving him a hug – when she remembered why she was there, and stopped. She had a fleeting thought that a hug would probably have been more useful to him than anything else she was going to do for him that morning. It was 7:15 a.m. – attorney visits were permitted any time during the 7:00 to 3:00 and 3:00 to 11:00 shifts.

Patrick sat. The taller CO told Anita to push the call button by the door when she was ready to leave. He locked Patrick and Anita in the room, and both CO's left.

"You must've gotten up really early," said Patrick. "Thank you, I don't know what to say."

"I slept for a couple of hours. I'll have plenty of time to sleep later today. Have they assigned you a lawyer?"

"They did. He's a good guy, from the public defender. His name is Khalil Omar. Do you know him?"

"No, I haven't met him," replied Anita. "I know a couple of lawyers down here, but nobody who does criminal work."

Patrick winced at the word "criminal."

"We have two priorities right now," Anita continued. "We have to get you out of jail, and we need to figure out who can do the best job representing you. I don't know much about the Federal Defender in Wyoming, but when I dealt with them back in Virginia they were very good, very competent. So I'm glad they were assigned."

"The judge told me they were good."

"What is your bail situation? Did they tell you how much your bond is going to be?"

"Five hundred thousand dollars." Anita's jaw fell open slightly. Patrick continued, "The judge said something about reducing it to $250,000 after a week, but I wasn't following that part."

Anita nodded. "All right, we'll deal with it. Did you talk with your parents?"

"I did, but that was before they set bail. My parents can't afford anything like that."

"The feds don't use bail bondsmen, and they don't have cash bail," said Anita. "You just have people co-sign a bond, which is due and owing if you don't show up for trial. I expect Ed and Dina could sign for you, but there may be some net worth requirements, or that kind of thing. We might need more people to sign."

She took a note pad out of her briefcase. "I think I can be helpful rounding up co-signers, and hopefully we can get you out of here quickly. First, phone numbers: did you get a phone number from Mr. Omar, and can I have your parents' numbers?"

"Yeah, he asked me to memorize his cell phone number," said Patrick, "and my parents still answer their landline when you call." He gave her the numbers, and she wrote them on her pad.

"I need a cup of coffee," she said. "I'm going to see if I can ask Mr. Omar to meet me at Starbucks just after I leave here. I think together we can figure out how to get you out."

"OK," he said. "Thanks, that's great."

"Let me shift gears," she said. "I was able to do some research about tax evasion. I haven't seen the indictment yet, but if they're charging you with simple tax evasion – failure to declare income and pay taxes – they have to prove you did it 'willfully.'" Patrick nodded.

"Did the IRS communicate with you to let you know that you owed back taxes?" she continued. "Did they send you notices? Did you have problems with them years ago? What are they saying you did?"

"Mr. Omar said it has something to do with bartering. Apparently it's illegal to support yourself through bartering and not report it as income. He said they're saying I should have been filing tax returns for the last five years."

Anita made a couple more notes.

"Why five years?" asked Patrick. "Why not six or four or three?"

"The statute of limitations for tax evasion is six years. I'm not sure why they charged five years, but they probably have a good reason," responded Anita. "My guess is that it had something to do with the dates that tax returns were due, and that you only owed them five years of returns during the six years preceding the indictment."

"I think I filed a tax return, or maybe two, when I was working for Marty," said Patrick. "I sent my W-2 and stuff to my dad, and I'm pretty sure he filed for me. He uses TurboTax."

"OK, that's helpful," said Anita. "It means the indictment is probably talking only about things in Coolidge, and only for the past few years."

"Anita, how serious is this?" asked Patrick, quietly.

"Oh, it's serious. I don't know what else to say."

"I'm sorry, wrong question, I think." Patrick looked straight into her eyes. "What I meant was, if I'm found guilty, how much time in jail am I looking at?"

She thought for a second. "The worst thing about lawyers – and I really hate this about us – is that we want to answer every question with, 'It depends.' I won't do that to you – you already understand it depends on a lot of 'ifs.' Here's all I have at the moment: Mr. Google told me at 2:00 a.m. this morning that the average convicted tax evader is a first offender, and the average sentence is three to five years."

Patrick nodded. "That's helpful. Thanks for anticipating the question."

"Do you mind if I talk to you about possibly representing you?"

"I would like you to do it, but I can't ask you to work for free. The public defender's gotta be the guy."

"Not really; not necessarily," she said. "It's possible they've never handled a tax case . . ."

"Yeah, that's what he told me last night," said Patrick.

"It may be you'll be assigned somebody on what's called the CJA Panel," continued Anita. "Those are private lawyers who are paid by the federal government, under the Criminal Justice Act, to represent indigent defendants in federal criminal cases. Problem is, the pay sucks, and a lot of the people who are willing to do CJA cases are squeezing them in while they're trying to make a living with other things. So there are a lot of guilty pleas."

"Then why wouldn't I just stick with Mr. Omar?"

"I'll know more after I've met with him, but I think there's a risk they're going to ask the court to refer the case out to the CJA Panel."

Anita looked at Patrick and pursed her lips. "What I want you to know is that I'm not going to let you fall through the cracks. I'm not trying to sell you on hiring me; I just want to give you some reassurance if you wound up working with me. I think I could help. I majored in accounting as an undergrad, and

I'm comfortable dealing with the tax code. I went to law school at William & Mary, in Virginia, and worked for a summer interning with a federal magistrate. I'm still familiar with at least the basics in the Federal Rules of Criminal Procedure. I spent my first two years out of law school as an Assistant District Attorney in Fairfax County, Virginia, and I tried lots of cases – small ones, mostly, and only a couple of jury trials, but a trial is a trial. You don't forget how to do it. So even though it's been a long time since I handled a criminal case, I know enough to help. The most important thing is, I'll devote whatever time it takes to help you beat this. If I didn't, I'd never be welcome again at Cousin Clem's, and we can't have that."

She smiled, and Patrick tried to smile back. Without much success.

"Here's what I'm going to do," she said. "I'm going to meet with Mr. Omar and figure out where he's coming from. I'll get things moving on bail. I'm going to talk to Martina D'Antonio about helping us start a GoFundMe page. If it works, I'll get paid enough to be able to put other things aside for a while, and we can pay expert witnesses and investigators if we need them. You're going to be OK."

She stood, stuffed her briefcase, and crossed over to the call button. "We've got you, Patrick. We all do. Try not to worry."

CHAPTER 51

Anita clicked the "off" button on her phone with a good feeling. Khalil Omar had volunteered to drop what he was doing, and to come over to meet her at the Starbucks near the Eastridge Mall. She found a table and started on her third cup of coffee since 4:00 a.m. It was 8:15; Omar promised to be there by 9:00, wearing a red down parka. It was 10 degrees outside.

At 8:55, a compact, bearded, owlish-looking man came through the front door in a red parka, eyes up. Anita stood and gestured to him, inviting him over to the table she'd been saving. They shook hands. "Coffee?" she asked.

He smiled, and shook his head. "Yes, but no. By the time I finished explaining to you how I drink it, they'd have my order ready. It'll just take a minute. Can I get you a refill?"

"No, thanks. I've got plenty."

Anita reviewed her list of questions and tried to organize what she needed to cover with him. Khalil came back with his Vente and sat facing her across the small table. They exchanged business cards.

"Thanks for meeting me on such short notice," said Anita. "Everybody in Coolidge is worried. Let me jump into the deep end – what can we do to help get him released?"

"In a nutshell, we need to get somebody to sign an unsecured appearance bond for $500,000. I couldn't believe my ears when I heard Magistrate Dellarosa say it. If we appeal, I think we could get it lowered a lot, and even Dellarosa said he'd lower it to $250,000 if we couldn't find a co-signer within a week. The problem is, Dellarosa was spooked about the possibility that Mr. Flaherty could disappear into the mountains and never be heard from again."

Anita digested that information, and nodded. "I actually think we can probably find co-signers," said Anita. "But everybody is 180 miles away, and it's Saturday. What would be the logistics for getting everything signed, and getting him released?"

"There is an emergency judge and an emergency magistrate assigned every weekend, in rotation," said Khalil. "I'm not sure who it is this weekend, but I can find out. Hopefully, the emergency magistrate will be Dellarosa, and hopefully I can persuade him to reduce the amount down into five figures. It's right in the bail statute that he can't impose financial conditions that result in continued detention. I don't know what he's thinking, but he does this sometimes – makes up his own rules. Frontier justice, or something."

"Well maybe we can tag-team this," said Anita. "I'll round up co-signers, and get you names and amounts. What do you need in terms of information about the guarantors?"

"Usually Pretrial Services gets involved, but they were very quiet last night at the hearing. My inclination would be to just take a proposed Order to the emergency judge, with information about the co-signers, see if I can get the number reduced. And if we have somebody who will sign his name for 500k, I don't think Dellarosa could say no. I'll try to persuade him to order Patrick's immediate release. We can promise to provide all the financial paperwork for the co-signer later."

"All right, I can work on that," said Anita. "Can you email me some language for guaranteeing an appearance bond?"

"I think I have something, somewhere," said Khalil. "If not, I'll just say it in plain English. This is all kind of uncharted territory, and hopefully Dellarosa will realize he needs to pull in his horns."

Anita took a long sip of coffee. It helped. "Let's talk about the case a little bit," she said. "What are your initial thoughts?"

"My initial thought is that my boss is not going to let us keep it. We're down one lawyer as it is, and we're already shuffling between Casper and Cheyenne more than we'd like to. I think she's going to take one look at the indictment and turn it over for assignment to the CJA Panel. Otherwise, somebody – me – is going to have to learn up some tax law, and invent a lot of wheels. It'll crowd out other stuff, and we're already overextended."

"I'm prepared to handle the case," said Anita. "Patrick is important to the people in our town, and I think we can pass the hat. Well, we can pass the GoFundMe hat. I have the time, and the focus, and I had some trial experience early in my career. I think I can help. My problem, I think, will be federal criminal procedure. I've never handled a federal criminal case all the way through. I couldn't figure out the Sentencing Guidelines, or at least figure them out quickly, if my life depended on it. And I might be at a real disadvantage in plea negotiations. Hard work will overcome some of those problems, but I don't know what I don't know. I know it's a lot to ask, but would I be able to lean on you as a resource?"

Khalil smiled. "What I'm about to say might surprise you. Every lawyer in our office spends two or three hours a week on the phone with lawyers on the CJA Panel, giving them free advice. It's part of what we do for our client base. I can keep you pointed in the right direction, and I'll answer any question you have, on a 'no question is a stupid question' basis."

Anita exhaled. "Oh my goodness, that's good to hear."

"And this case is going to be very, very basic in some ways," added Khalil. "I don't see any documents as being important. The bartering agreements they describe in the indictment were all verbal. Mr. Flaherty didn't file tax returns, and he presumably didn't keep any records. There's nothing to read. I'm not too deep into the facts, but my impression is that the case is going to be about state of mind – did he willfully evade taxes? Hell, it's a fair question as to whether he ever gave taxes any thought at all."

"Is the indictment online yet?" asked Anita.

"Oh, I forgot! I have a copy of the indictment with me. I had my daughter copy it for you while I was finding my coat." He handed her a forty page document. "We ran out of copy paper three pages before the end. She used three sheets of her loose-leaf paper to finish the job." He thumbed those pages and smiled. "She's 12, going on 27."

"Does she want to be a lawyer?" asked Anita.

"Maybe. I tell her that ours is the only profession other than psychology where practitioners voluntarily immerse themselves in other people's conflicts. I suggest to her that she might like long-haul trucking if she tried it. She's withholding judgment until she's 13. Then she'll decide."

Anita stood and extended her hand. "Khalil, thank you. I'll call you this afternoon when I have the signatures lined up, as early in the afternoon as possible. I'll send you a withdrawal and entry of appearance early next week. For now, I'm going to see if they'll let me check into the Courtyard early, and start using the wifi. I can change and get cleaned up, so let me know if you need some support when you talk with the court, or if you're going to appear in person. As I gather signatures, I'll probably send some stuff over to you by email, with pdfs attached. Can I use the email address on your business card?"

"That works," he said. "We'll get this done."

CHAPTER 52

Clem hung up his call with Anita on the landline and thought for a couple of minutes. He checked the contacts on his cell phone and punched Eric Dormer's number. Eric answered on the second ring. It was 10:05 in the morning.

"Eric, it's Clem. Am I catching you at a good time?"

"I'm in the main barn trying to fix a track on the Snow Cat. Good time, no problem. What's up?"

"They set Patrick's bail at $500,000."

"That's insane," replied Eric.

"I guess the judge wants to keep him in jail."

"How does it work?" asked Eric. "Are there bail bondsmen, or whatever?"

"Anita says the usual deal is for somebody to co-sign a note. If Patrick doesn't show up for trial, the co-signer has to pay the money. Unfortunately, his parents don't have much. She says she already talked to Father Dave at St. Ann's, and he'll agree that if a co-signer ever has to pay money, he'll sell acreage from the church's property up on Side Road to give to the co-signer. And I've got fifteen or twenty people who will guarantee parts of it. Anita says she'll use GoFundMe money, if necessary, whatever that is. So he's getting a lot of support."

"OK, what can I do?" asked Eric.

"I'm calling you because – well, herding cats takes time, and Patrick is sitting in jail. I think you're the only person in Coolidge who could really afford to take the hit up front, if it ever came to that. I think we both know Patrick, and we know he wouldn't harm his friends. I'd like you to think about being the signer on the note, because Anita says we have to persuade – the prosecutor, or the judge, or somebody, I'm not sure – persuade them that the co-signer is solvent. It's a hassle. Could you maybe see your way clear to co-signing for him?"

"Clem, listen. When I signed the mortgage on this place 35 years ago, I felt like there were co-signers lining up on the street to co-sign for me. The mayor back then – Paul Orland, do you remember him, or was he before your time? He shook my hand and told me if I ever ran into trouble, he would personally pass the hat around town to help me out. Two years later, when we had the winter storm that killed all that livestock, I had people giving me steers, sheep, feed, hay. I don't think I would have made it without that help. So, yeah, this one is easy. Can you put me in touch with Anita?"

Clem gave him Anita's cell phone number. "Thanks, Eric. Your first beer is on me tonight."

Eric replied, "Let's see if we can get him sprung. Talk to you when I know something more."

CHAPTER 53

The conference call convened at 3:00 p.m. Khalil Omar, Jack Farragut and Magistrate Judge Dellarosa were on the line. Khalil was talking from his couch at home.

"Your Honor, thanks for taking our call on a Saturday," said Khalil. "This is the *Flaherty* case, again. We have a rancher up in Coolidge who will co-sign the appearance bond for the defendant. The rancher's name is Eric Dormer. He has signed a document that states, and I'm reading now, 'I hereby guarantee the payment of $500,000 to the United States Government in the event that Patrick Flaherty defaults on the terms and conditions of his appearance bond and/or the conditions of his pretrial release by failing to appear for trial in the matter of *United States v. Patrick Michael Flaherty.*' I have confirmed, and can represent to the Court, that Mr. Dormer is the record owner of the Bar-Twelve Ranch near Coolidge, which consists of a home, several barns and out-buildings, and 2,700 acres of grazing land. He has more than two thousand head of cattle. Mr. Dormer and the defendant will commit to executing any additional paperwork that Pretrial Services may require to document the appearance bond."

"Why can't this wait until Monday – I guess Tuesday, because Monday's a holiday -- when we can get some input from Pretrial Services?" asked the Magistrate Judge.

"Judge, we've worked together many times before, and you know I'm not going to be coy. We've met the court more than half way. Under Section 3142(c) of the Bail Act, the court is prohibited from imposing any financial condition that results in continued detention. This defendant doesn't have a dime, yet he's facing a five hundred thousand dollar appearance bond, and he's in jail, he's being detained. I'm willing to spend the rest of the weekend and most of next week appealing; I honestly don't think Your Honor's order would survive review. But we don't need to do that. In a little over twelve hours, this defendant found someone – not even a relative -- who will back him to the extent of a half a million dollars, and his guarantor put that commitment in writing. I would ask you, respectfully, to order his immediate release. We'll follow through on our commitment to dot the i's and cross the t's on the paperwork. And if we don't, you can revoke his release. But you won't need to do that."

"Jack, what's the government's position?" asked Magistrate Judge Dellarosa.

"Your Honor, Khalil sent me a pdf copy of Mr. Dormer's guarantee," said Farragut. "If we needed to, I think we could enforce it in its current form. Given the court's earlier denial of our Motion for Detention, the government has no objection to the release of the defendant on the terms Khalil just described." It was the weekend, and Monday was Martin Luther King Day. He didn't want to spend his time off answering a bail appeal, especially given that he was holding a written guarantee from a solvent guarantor.

"All right, I'm glad everybody agrees," said the Magistrate Judge. "I'll enter an order releasing the defendant. Look for it on PACER within the next half hour or so. I'll let the Marshal and Natrona County know as well. Thanks to both of you. Stay warm."

Khalil clicked off his cell phone, put on his coat, and drove over to Starbucks, where Anita was waiting. As he came through the front door, he saw Anita sitting in back, and he flashed her a thumb's up. Anita was finishing her fourth coffee since 4:00 a.m. Khalil filled her in on the Magistrate Judge's decision.

"I'll go see if I can still get him out this afternoon," said Anita. "I guess it'll depend on whether the staff at the jail have the documents they need from the Court."

"Do you know how to find your way back out to the jail?" asked Khalil.

"No problem," replied Anita. "I'll just re-trace my route from this morning." She extended her hand. "Thanks for everything, Khalil. You'll never have to pay for a meal in Coolidge, Wyoming."

Khalil shook her hand, and settled a baseball cap onto his head. "He's a good guy, and he doesn't deserve what's happening to him," he said. "But it's hard to win a case against these people – the United States Government has the resources to grind you down. All I can say is 'good luck.'"

"Thanks," she said, as she stepped into the cold to find her car. She hoped she would be driving her client home.

Patrick Flaherty was released from the Natrona County Detention Center at 5:55 on Saturday evening. He met Anita Boyle in the lobby in the clothes he had worn out of his house on Friday afternoon. His ten dollar bill was back in his pocket. Patrick and Anita called Patrick's parents on Anita's phone. They then walked together to the visitors' parking lot. Anita's Audi SUV was covered with a fresh dusting of snow.

"Can you drive?" asked Anita. "I'd fall asleep at the wheel within five miles of here."

"Sure," replied Patrick. She clicked the door-unlock and tossed him the keys. While she settled into the passenger seat, Patrick brushed the snow off the windows. He moved the driver's seat back, and climbed in to drive.

"Which way to I-25?" he asked.

"Right out of the parking lot, and then a left," she replied, pointing. "Go all the way down the hill to the stop sign, and take another left. Then take a left at the light, and you'll see signs for the northbound entrance. It's a left up the ramp."

"Will you want to stop to eat, or for a bathroom break, or should I just try to push through to Coolidge?"

"Honestly – wake me up when we're in front of your place."

Patrick started the engine. "Anita – thank you," he said, looking across at her.

"You're welcome," she said, as she reclined her seat.

CHAPTER 54

Patrick woke up on Sunday morning not knowing how he was going to collect his chickens and his goats. There was a note pinned to his door telling him that Mrs. Vogel and Eric Dormer had stopped by, and took the animals with them, to make sure they didn't freeze. He didn't know anyone who had an empty van or a covered truck that he could use to go get them. He could probably walk the goats from Eric's place, but you can't walk chickens. He was too embarrassed to go to Mass. He decided he would make his weekly pot of coffee – he only made coffee on Sundays -- and think about things.

Mrs. Vogel called from outside the cabin while Patrick was pouring his first cup. Word must have traveled fast that he was back from Casper. He stuck his head out the door and saw the same smile she always gave him. Eighty years old and always happy. He had to fight back tears for a moment.

"Hi Mrs. Vogel."

"Hi Hon. I have your birds."

"Mrs. Vogel, I need to thank you, I'm so sorry that this . . ."

"You don't need to thank me, and you don't need to apologize. Just stop it. You do need to help me get these birds up the hill."

Patrick walked down with her to her Ford Ranger with chicken wire across the bed in back. She had transported birds before. Patrick carried two birds, and Mrs. Vogel carried one, all the way up the 200 yards of the snow-covered pathway. They talked about feed, and egg quality, and lighting intensity, the kind of stuff that chicken people talk about. She fussed with the nests and the feeders while Patrick finished bringing up the chickens.

Just as they were latching the coop, they heard Eric Dormer come around the corner of the house leading four goats. Patrick knew that Eric had ten or fifteen employees at the ranch. He didn't have to come himself.

"Hi Miriam," said Eric. "Patrick, welcome home."

They exchanged handshakes and hugs, and led the goats toward their pen. Something reminded Mrs. Vogel and Eric about someone they knew years ago, and they laughed about something he had done. Patrick began, haltingly, to thank Eric for his help. Eric cut him off.

"You don't need to thank us. What you do need to do is get ready to fight this thing. It's going to take all of the energy you have, and there are going to be some really dark moments."

Mrs. Vogel nodded. "That's exactly right."

Eric continued. "One other thing. I didn't build my business by making bad investments. I'm counting on you to fight this thing, and counting on you to show up for your trial. Don't disappoint me, son."

Patrick saw not a trace of unseriousness in Eric's expression. He knew that Eric trusted him -- but Eric had a right to demand Patrick's cooperation up front, and out loud.

"I won't," said Patrick. He hoped that Eric believed him.

CHAPTER 55

When they left, Patrick was again alone with his thoughts. His firearms had been confiscated, and he wondered if he could learn how to trap in a hurry. Truthfully, newly-hunted game was not a major part of his diet in winter – he'd be OK. He gathered some wood, and restarted the fire in the stove. He turned all of his 12v heaters all the way up. He melted some snow for water, and cleaned himself up and made some food. He took twenty minutes to walk down to The 14, called his parents collect, and came back up the hill. He read an old paperback until the light faded, and then he turned on the radio. He picked his guitar, and tried to think about what would come next. He didn't know, and he slept fitfully.

Patrick ate some eggs for breakfast on Monday morning, and walked into town. He knocked on the door of Anita's office at 10:00 a.m. Priscilla Bates, Anita's part-time secretary/paralegal/administrative assistant, opened the door and offered him a cup of hot coffee. It was -3 degrees Fahrenheit outside.

Anita stuck her head out of her tiny office, and invited Patrick to come in and have a seat. She was in jeans, as was Patrick.

"Have you talked to your parents again?" she asked.

"Yeah, I called from The 14 last night. They're taking it pretty well, I think. My mom's biggest disappointment is that I can't come home. I can't leave Wyoming, according to the paper the Marshals gave me."

"Have them come up here. We can find a place for them to stay."

"I may do that."

"We made a copy of the indictment for you. I want you to read it and let me have your thoughts. I think we should meet at least twice a week for the next month or so. We have a lot of work to do."

"OK, I'll do that."

"I talked to Martina about the GoFundMe page. She's starting that process. We're looking to raise $75,000 for your defense. I don't see why we won't be able to do that."

"Suppose we can't?"

"Then I'll handle the case for free, or for whatever is left over after we've paid for things like expert witnesses or investigators," she said.

"Serious question – is that money taxable?" he asked.

"I checked, it's not. It's all small gifts, which aren't taxable to anyone."

She thumbed the indictment. "By my count, they're alleging five bartering relationships in the indictment. Bobby Bays, feed in exchange for dog training. Clem, food and drink for music. Harry Detmer, construction materials for driving. St. Ann's, free rent for maintenance and improvements to the cabin. And St. Ann's again, food for handyman work."

"All of that sounds true," said Patrick.

"Don't say that again, goddammit!"

She said it with a vehemence that Patrick had never seen from her. He just blinked.

"I'm sorry," she said. "From here on out, you need to think about your life and your relationships with people in a different way. You don't have any *written* barter agreements, and I'm guessing you don't have any handshake agreements either. So you don't have barter agreements or barter income, period. What you've been doing for the past five years is the simple informal exchange of favors that civilized people practice on a daily basis. By the time I'm done with you, you won't be able to think about any of this in any other way."

"OK." He didn't want to say more.

"Did I ever tell you the story of how I came to Coolidge?" she asked.

"I don't think so."

"I told you I was working in Northern Virginia. I had left the DA's office, and was working for EPA. My ex-husband worked for Exxon-Mobil, and when they moved his job to Houston, he took a job with Shell Oil in South Dakota. We lived near Spearfish, and used to come over here to camp. I loved it here. When we split up, I decided to move here – I needed a place with some pleasant associations.

"I wanted to be *here*, in Coolidge. I moved over and got admitted to the bar. I had one big client, in oil and gas. They didn't care where I worked from as long as their spill reports went out to administrators on time. And after I got here I took a couple of online seminars about how to write a will, and how to prepare a deed. Name changes, adoptions, stuff that people need. I love it here, and I love the people here.

"Patrick, this isn't Northern Virginia. It isn't New York City, and it isn't Newark. I'm sure there are decent people in all those places, and I've lived in all of them, but people don't *do* for each other there, the way they do here. That's all this indictment talks about – things you did for other people."

"This says I've been committing crimes," he said, lifting the indictment from her desk. "I was introduced to some serious people this weekend. I'd like to believe they're just making this up, but . . . jeez, I don't know."

"I think what this is, is culture," Anita replied. "The indictment is signed by some guy in Washington, D.C. He has no idea about Coolidge. He couldn't possibly. In his world, people are always jockeying for advantage, and wheeling and dealing for money, and he assumes that Coolidge operates by the same rules. But we don't, we really don't. Whoever thought of bringing this case has never lived anywhere near Coolidge, Wyoming."

"I think you're right," said Patrick. "But I don't understand their world, either."

CHAPTER 56

Farragut and Renfro knew their evidence on bartering was a little thin. Not thin in the sense that it made them question whether bartering had been going on, but thin in the sense it all came from Special Agent Bolton's undercover work, and was based on jotted notes and short snippets from recordings. As Renfro had predicted months before, they were going to need to bring witnesses in from Coolidge.

Grand jury subpoenas went out from the U.S. Attorney's Office in Casper to Bobby Bays, Harry Detmer, Clem Labrecque, Mavis D'Antonio, and Father Hernandez, compelling their attendance in the federal courthouse in Cheyenne, Wyoming, on Wednesday, February 3, and February 4 if necessary. A uniformed United States Marshal driving a marked vehicle served the subpoenas in Coolidge, in person, late in the week of January 17. The calls began to come into Anita's office immediately.

Anita tried to keep everyone calm, but it wasn't easy. Every witness had a job and responsibilities, and it wasn't easy to pack up and travel 300 miles to Cheyenne in the middle of the winter. Every one of the five had been unnerved and embarrassed that a uniformed officer had shown up at their work addresses to thrust a subpoena into their respective chests. They had no clear idea why the government wanted their testimony. And they were – anxious was probably the best word.

Worse, Anita felt she couldn't really talk to any of them. This was an unusual case where the defense attorney was closer to the government's witnesses than the government attorneys were. She knew that if she began to "coach" the witnesses she would create a conflict of interest, and the government would move to disqualify her from further participation as Patrick's lawyer. She might win that motion, she might lose. But she didn't want to take the chance. She thought back to her days on the sidewalks of Elizabeth, New Jersey. If somebody was getting in your face, the best response was to push back hard, and publicly.

"Patrick," said Anita, at their bi-weekly meeting, "we've been taking some punches, and we need to start throwing a few. My idea is to address the witnesses semi-publicly, with the message that you're innocent, without crossing the line into undue influence. Take a look at this letter, tell me whether it works for you. This one's addressed to Bobby, but all five witnesses are going to get a version of the same letter."

Patrick read:

> Dear Bobby,
>
> I'm writing to you in my role as counsel to Patrick Flaherty in the case of *United States vs. Patrick Michael Flaherty.*
>
> Patrick and I were dismayed to hear that you have been subpoenaed to appear this week before the federal grand jury in Cheyenne. Patrick, in particular, feels terrible about it – you are his friend, and he very much regrets that you are being inconvenienced by, and having to undergo the anxiety associated with, your subpoena.
>
> Please understand that neither Patrick nor I will be speaking to you about the case before you testify before the grand jury. We do not want there to be any opening for the government to claim that we have attempted to influence your grand jury testimony in any way. We urge you to appear before the grand jury as requested, and to testify completely and truthfully. And, of course, talk with a lawyer if you feel you should.
>
> I ask you to understand one other thing. This prosecution is not Patrick's fault. He did not intend for his friends to be embroiled in this, and, indeed, he had no idea that anything like this was remotely possible. We believe this prosecution exists because a few overzealous investigators and prosecutors have decided they needed to make an example of someone, and Patrick seems to be that someone.

> Finally, I want to say something else, as clearly as I can. Patrick Flaherty is not a criminal. He is, rather, the same decent, generous, hard-working person you and I have known since he arrived in Coolidge seven years ago. Trust your gut on that point. He will still be a valued member of our community when this prosecution has become a distant, and perhaps somewhat bizarre, memory.
>
> I have copied John Farragut, Assistant United States Attorney, on this letter, so that the government will be fully aware of the substance of my communication with you.
>
> Very truly yours,
> Anita C. Boyle

"Looks good to me," said Patrick. "Why would they think you're trying to influence anyone's testimony?"

"Because that's the way all prosecutors think," she said. "They think all defense attorneys lie, cheat and suborn perjury, all the time." She stopped. "Some do, I guess. No group of people are ever all one thing, are they?"

Patrick shrugged. "Maybe the Rockettes."

Anita smiled. She appreciated the New York reference. "Yeah, maybe the Rockettes."

Forty-eight hours later, Anita received the call she was expecting. "Ms. Boyle, this is Arnold Renfro, from the United States Department of Justice. What do you think you're doing?"

Because she had been expecting it, she knew what she was going to say. "Are you calling about my letter?"

"Yes, and you need to understand . . ."

"And are you calling to tell me that my letter violates attorney disciplinary rules, and that you're going to call the attention of the court and all relevant authorities to my misconduct?"

"That's only the beginning. By the time we're done with this, you're going to . . ."

"Mr. Renfro, wait, wait, just stop. I'll make this short. I'm going to say one thing to you, and then I'm going to hang up." She paused, to be sure he was listening. "When you file your complaints, spell my name right." She hung up.

When the phone rang again, she told Priscilla to let it go to voicemail. She knew her letters to witnesses had been proper. As expected, apart from one apoplectic voicemail, she never heard from the prosecutors about her letters again.

CHAPTER 57

It was already late March, and the Superseding Indictment had just been made available on PACER, the online service that made all duly-filed federal court documents available for inspection and download. It was near the end of the day. Anita downloaded the document, printed a copy, walked back to her place, hopped in her car, and drove over to Patrick's cabin. Patrick wasn't in, so she left him a copy of the new indictment, with a note asking him to stop by her office.

In the morning, Patrick walked down to town to meet Anita in 40 degree weather. At 4,000 feet, spring usually came to Coolidge a little later than it did in say, Augusta, Maine, which was on the same latitude. But this was a warm and early spring.

When Patrick sat down in her client chair, Anita poured them both a cup of coffee. That morning, Patrick had a larger concern than his impending trial.

"I saw the bear again last night," he said. "I was walking up the path to my place, and when I got near the top, he was standing near the corner of the cabin, just looking at me. I guess he's out of hibernation and looking for breakfast."

"When was this?" asked Anita.

"It was right around 6:00. It was starting to be dark."

"Oh my God, I must have just missed him," said Anita. She shuddered, involuntarily. "What did you do?"

"I sprayed bear spray. It was ridiculous. I was too far away from him to come anywhere close, but I was hoping the smell would bother him. He looked at me like I was an idiot, and turned and walked up the hill, into the woods."

"Did he take anything, any of your animals?"

"No, and I don't really have any idea what he wanted. Maybe he just wanted to let me know it's his space, and I'm only living in it because he's letting me."

"Should we be thinking about petitioning the court to get your guns back?" asked Anita.

"I don't know. Supposedly, bear spray is better protection anyway. Let's talk about it at some point." Patrick took a sip of coffee. "The indictment looked pretty much the same to me. I didn't read it carefully. What was new?"

"They just included some bits and pieces of grand jury testimony, mostly relating to the alleged bartering deals. Somebody, probably Mavis, said it would have been 'morally wrong' for the church not to feed you, because of the work you do there. Somebody else, probably Harry, said that you get fencing 'in exchange' for services."

"But we kind of knew all that," said Patrick.

"Yeah, but the purpose of bringing the witnesses to the grand jury wasn't to improve the indictment, and the Superseding Indictment doesn't really say anything new," replied Anita. "What they really wanted to do was use the questioning during the grand jury to extract statements that they could use at trial. If you give a good prosecutor an hour with a witness, without a judge or opposing counsel present, the witness can be made to say almost anything. And that's what they do at the grand jury. They filed the Superseding Indictment just to justify having pulled the witnesses in."

"I keep thinking about all this," said Patrick. "You tell me I wasn't bartering, I believe you. But the prosecutors are going to have lots of evidence that I accepted food and property, and that I was performing services. If that's what the evidence looks like at the end of the day, what's our defense?"

"It's simple," said Anita. "Let's assume you really were exchanging services for property. I don't think you were, but let's assume. Did you know that any of those transactions were taxable?"

"No."

"Did anyone ever tell you they were taxable?"

"No. At least until I was arrested."

"But when you were arrested, you learned something new, didn't you? You didn't know before?"

"That's right, yeah."

"Our defense is *Cheek vs. United States*, a U.S. Supreme Court case from 1991. You've probably heard the saying, 'Ignorance of the law is no excuse.' For example, you might not have known you were hunting out of season, but that's not going to help you if you were hunting out of season. You're still going to be guilty."

"I'm with you so far," said Patrick. "But that hurts us, it doesn't help."

"OK, you're right, stay with me," said Anita. "To prove tax evasion under Section 7201, the government has to prove that you 'willfully' evaded taxes. That you really, really did it on purpose. Otherwise, it's just a civil penalty. But a bunch of federal courts, back in the 1980's, I guess, said, 'Hey, wait a minute, you can't willfully evade taxes unless you knew something was taxable in the first place. And the tax code is just so complicated that nobody can be expected to know all the rules. Even lawyers and accountants have trouble keeping up.' So the courts started to say, 'If you didn't know what you were doing was taxable, you can't be convicted of tax evasion.' They were saying, in this circumstance, ignorance of the law really is an excuse. And in *Cheek v. United States*, the issue reached the Supreme Court, and the Court agreed. They said, 'Yup, that's right, ignorance of the *tax* laws is an excuse.'"

"So should I take the witness stand and say that I didn't know bartering was taxable?" asked Patrick.

"That's where I am right now," said Anita. "I'm lousy at reading minds, and I can't tell you why this case was brought. So take what I'm about to say with a grain of salt. I don't think they really care if they get a conviction. I think they're making an example of you because they want to get more money out of people who barter a lot, and who fail to pay taxes on the bartering income. With 12 people on the jury who probably never heard of bartering income, I can't imagine they're not going to believe you when you say that you didn't know you owed taxes. I don't see a jury finding you guilty. But I don't know. I really don't know."

CHAPTER 58

Anita called Clem's at 3:00 in the afternoon on Wednesday, April 14, to see if Patrick was there. He wasn't, so she asked Clem to ask him to stop by the office when he came in. She decided she'd drive to find Patrick if she hadn't heard from him by about 5:30.

It was Anita's experience that thoughts about a case came to her only when they came to her, even when she was trying to think of everything. She couldn't think of something if she didn't think of it. While she was in the shower that morning, the "diminished capacity" defense occurred to her.

She hadn't thought about it since law school, but it held some promise. The defense was available in cases where the charges required proof of specific intent, like attempted murder. You can't be convicted of attempted murder unless the jury concludes, unanimously, that you intended to kill someone.

Most often, the diminished capacity defense was essayed by drunks. The theory was that if you were so drunk that you didn't know where you were, or how you got there, you weren't lucid enough to form an intention to kill someone. Sometimes it worked. If it did, you could still be convicted of reckless endangerment – which required proof of reckless conduct – but you would skate on attempted murder.

That was the big difference between an insanity defense – where you had to be incapable of distinguishing right from wrong – and diminished capacity. With insanity, you got off Scot free. With diminished capacity, you could often still be convicted of a lesser offense if one were charged.

Tax evasion was a specific intent crime to the *n*th degree – the government had to prove that you willfully evaded taxes, knowing you were evading taxes.

Moreover, there were no lesser offenses alleged in Patrick's indictment. Every one of the 20 counts required proof of willfulness. Anita figured that if Patrick's chrometophobia were severe enough that it made him psychologically incapable of, say, selling eggs to generate cash to pay his taxes, she might be able to establish diminished capacity on every count. Not guilty, if it worked.

While she was researching the issue, Judge Thomas Martin's Deputy Clerk called to let her know that there would be a pretrial conference on April 26; that jury selection would begin on Monday, May 10; and that opening statements and witness testimony would begin on Tuesday, May 11. Anita's stomach flipped over a couple of times. Shit. Where was Patrick?

At 5:15, Patrick came into her office.

"Tell me what you know about your chrometophobia," she said without preamble. "How crazy are you?"

Patrick was neither surprised nor offended by the question.

"Hard to say. I looked it up once or twice. They define chrometophobia as an 'irrational fear of money.' The 'irrational' part certainly fits. But I wouldn't call what I have a 'fear,' exactly. It's more like the anxiety that everybody gets when you think you don't have enough money for the month. But in my case, I deal with it by avoiding money to the extent I can. It's just some sort of avoidance mechanism, I don't know. I don't like using money."

"Did you ever see a shrink about it?" she asked.

"Nah. It's never made me unhappy. I think most people who go to shrinks go because they're unhappy."

"When did you first realize you had it?"

"In high school, I think," he replied. "My first job was bagging groceries. I liked the work, and the people. When I got my first paycheck, my dad bought it from me for cash, and I put the cash in my sock drawer. Same thing week two. And week three. When I had six weeks' pay sitting in my drawer, my parents told me to think of things I wanted to do with it. I couldn't think of anything. They said, 'how about books?' I said no, I can get those at the library for free. 'How about video games?' No. So my dad said, 'How about drugs then?' He was very straight-faced, and I didn't realize he was kidding until he and my mom started laughing. And then we dropped the subject. I guess we all figured there were bigger problems in the world."

"Why did you work at all?"

"I liked the work. I just didn't like dealing with the money that came with it."

"When you started working for Marty Brace, did you spend what you made on yourself?"

"Yes and no. I saved most of it for the water turbine in the creek, my 12v refrigerator, and my toilet. Those were the big ticket items for my cabin, that I needed if I was going to live in it. After that, I started living mostly without cash."

Patrick interrupted himself. "I don't mind telling you about this stuff. But why are you asking? Does this have something to do with tax evasion?"

Anita explained the rudiments of the diminished capacity defense, and how it was different from an insanity defense. Patrick seemed to understand the concepts involved.

"Tell me more about the anxiety," said Anita. "Would you be able to tell a psychiatrist, if I found one to be a witness, that your chrometophobia would have prevented you from paying taxes, if you knew you owed taxes?"

Patrick tilted his head slightly and looked through the window of Anita's office into the middle distance. "Maybe, I don't know. Let me try to explain a little, I'll give you an example. Just before I came to Coolidge from Denver, I had lunch with a friend from high school. Nate. He was out of college, and had just started work with an investment bank in Denver. He was working long hours, and didn't seem to mind the work. I remember him saying, 'I'm getting a hundred and twenty six thousand a year, but I can't really make ends meet. The condo, the Land Rover, my girlfriend. It's not bad for a 23 year-old, but it's not enough.' When I heard that, I was just kind of speechless."

Anita nodded.

"It wasn't revulsion, exactly. Nate wasn't, and isn't, a bad guy. But we all have to decide who we want to be. I decided, at that moment, I didn't want to be Nate. I didn't want to *appear* to be Nate. I didn't want other people thinking of me whatever it was that I was thinking about Nate. I came to Coolidge a month later. And I mostly stopped using money a year after that."

"It sounds to me like whatever you're dealing with is pretty deep-seated," said Anita. "There's a pretty good way of telling whether the defense makes any sense at all. One question, and I know I'm kind of looping back to where we started: If you had known that you owed, say, a thousand dollars a year in self-employment tax, would you have sold eggs to be able to pay it?"

Patrick looked at his lawyer. "I'm facing the same question later if I'm acquitted, aren't I?"

"Maybe not. If you're not guilty, you're not guilty. You can decide which way you want to go with taxes after you beat this." She looked him in the eyes. "Again, if a shrink, or the prosecutor, or the judge, or somebody, asks you, 'Would you have sold eggs for cash if you knew you needed the cash to pay the tax?' What would your answer be?"

"My answer would be that I would have sold eggs to avoid all of this, if I had known."

Anita half-smiled. "Well, that takes care of the diminished capacity defense. The reason you weren't paying taxes is that you didn't know you owed them. Chrometophobia wasn't keeping you from paying them."

For the next three hours, Anita and Patrick went through the discovery materials again, and tried to formulate solutions to problems. The grand jury transcripts had been produced by the government. Globally, Patrick was hampered by the fact that he tended to agree with Harry, Bobby, Clem, Mavis and Father Dave whenever they were asked to describe the details of their arrangements with Patrick. Not exactly bartering agreements, but not exactly *not* bartering agreements. Anita began thinking harder about whether she should call Patrick as a witness in his own defense -- she was beginning to fear that Patrick would not make a very good witness on his own behalf.

Part of the decision would be based on whether the jury would like Patrick, and understand his story. Pretty much all Anita knew about Patrick's life before he came to Coolidge was that he was originally from Colorado, and that he'd had some college. She closed a file, tossed it on the stack, and got up to find a pop in the mini-fridge. "Where did you go to college?" she asked him, over her shoulder.

"Penn."

She turned around, startled. "Say again?"

"The University of Pennsylvania."

"You went to *Penn*? How did you find your way to Penn?"

"Oh boy, that's a story. I was down in Arizona with my high school baseball team for our spring trip, and Penn's baseball coach was there looking at prospects. He had family in Scottsdale and would go down every year for a week to scout for players from the western U.S. He saw me play for a couple of at-bats; I was having a good day. After the game, he started up a conversation. He asked if I had any interest in going to college in the East. I told him my parents didn't have a lot of money, and that I'd be looking at the University of Colorado. He told me Penn didn't have athletic scholarships, but they had need-blind admissions and lots of aid, and if I got in, I wouldn't have to worry about not having enough money. It looked like a good place to go to school. I applied, I got in – I think with Coach Kraft's help, although he never said. I played shortstop for them for four years."

"What was your major?"

"American History."

"Where did you learn how to hunt, fish and build a cabin? Certainly not at college."

"My dad was a handyman and a hunter, and taught me a lot growing up. And the rest I learned working for Marty and just doing it."

"But back to college. Did you win any awards at school, anything like that?"

"Yeah, Bachelor of Arts."

"No, seriously," said Anita.

"This is stupid," said Patrick.

In response, Anita gave him her best 'I'm not kidding around' look.

Patrick blew out some air. "OK. I was MVP of the baseball team in my junior and senior years. I did a project for Departmental Honors, but so did almost everyone else. Dean's List a couple of semesters. I was an RA in one of the dorms." He scratched his ear, and looked up at her. "We're not going to tell this stuff to the jury, are we? I don't want the jury to hate me before they've even met me."

"Why do you think they'd hate you?"

"Because if I were on the jury, and the defendant started talking about what a swell guy he was in college, I'd want to send him to jail. Let him experience some real life for a change – he could probably use it. Penn wasn't real life."

"The problem is, Patrick, I need the jury to understand that you're just a regular guy, and not a cave man. The prosecution is going to paint you as a social outcast, somebody who hates government, and therefore hates taxes. I can get Mavis and Father Dave and Clem to say you're really a very nice guy, and that you like people, you interact with lots of people, and you get along with people. But the jury will want to meet you in person. We have to weigh the benefits and possible costs of putting you on the witness stand."

"That's your call. Just don't make me testify about stuff from college."

Anita looked at him again, and pondered her response. "All right. For now, consider it off the table. But if I bring it up again, it will be because I've thought about it seriously, and I think you should reconsider. Fair enough?"

"OK."

She thought for a second. "American History, huh? Did Henry David Thoreau contribute in any way to the predicament in which you find yourself?"

Patrick shook his head. "No. He didn't really like the people of Concord very much. I actually liked them a lot better than I liked him."

CHAPTER 59

Judge Martin called a pretrial conference in the *Flaherty* case, mostly to see how long the trial would take – he liked to keep his courtroom filled with trials, one after another -- and partly because he was curious about the details of the case he had read about in the papers. There wasn't as much case management for the court to do in a criminal case as there was in a civil case, but he thought he might as well get everybody in and see what the case was looking like. He had the Deputy Clerk schedule the conference for 1:00 p.m. in the courtroom rather than in chambers, in case they needed to put something on the record, or in case the lawyers wanted to review how evidence was going to look on the screens.

It's hard to get anywhere in Wyoming right on time. Because of the distances involved, people are usually early or late. On this April 26, Farragut and Renfro came into the courtroom 15 minutes early. Anita and Patrick walked in 13 minutes early, and settled into their seats at counsel table. When he saw Anita and Patrick, Renfro had something to say. He stood up, crossed over to their table, and looked down at them.

"Ms. Boyle and Mr. Flaherty, I just want you both to know something," he began. "You may think you have a home court advantage, and you may think that all of the witnesses are going to protect you, but I want you to know – you're wrong. We are going to come at you like junkyard dogs, and you won't know what hit you. If I were you, son, I would plead guilty to the whole indictment without a deal, because the judge is going to treat you way better than I ever would. And if . . ."

"Arnold," interrupted Farragut, rising. "Would you excuse us, can I talk for a minute with these folks without you here?"

Renfro looked at Farragut as if Farragut had just swallowed a slug. "No, I'm not going anywhere. This is a team prosecution, and I'm the senior prosecutor."

"Well, if you don't step outside, then the three of us will step outside without you. And if you follow us, we'll go farther still, and eventually we'll get to my office, and I'll tell my secretary not to let you in. And that would be ridiculous. So, yes, please, go."

Renfro looked at all three, and then turned and walked out of the courtroom.

"Mr. Flaherty," Farragut began, "I want to apologize for the behavior of my colleague. We don't practice law that way in Wyoming, and I'm sorry about what he said." Patrick nodded, and Farragut continued. "I don't want to give you the wrong impression. I believe in our case, and my job is to convict you of tax evasion. I'm going to do the best I can to accomplish that. And you are going to hate my guts before this is over, just because. But the office of the United States Attorney for the District of Wyoming is going to play by the rules, and the rules don't include trying to coerce guilty pleas during pretrial conferences."

Anita and Patrick both nodded. There wasn't much to say. Farragut left the courtroom to go find his partner.

All of the lawyers were in place when the judge appeared on the bench. Judge Thomas Martin was about five feet eight, in his late 50's, with shortish red hair, a perceptible wine or beer belly that made him look portly but not fat, and reading glasses perched near the end of his nose. He smiled in greeting – he liked his job -- and installed himself in his big leather swivel chair behind the bench. Anita had never appeared before him, but he had a reputation for fairness. It was also said that he let lawyers try their cases without undue interference from the bench.

The conference went smoothly. Jury selection would start on Monday, May 10. Opening statements and evidence would begin on Tuesday, May 11. The prosecutors estimated that their case would take a week to a week and a half. AUSA Farragut noted that they would probably need to call up to four expert witnesses to testify about the value of the food, animal feed, fencing, and lumber transferred to the defendant. After talking it through with counsel, the court saw some possible bases for stipulations about value, and encouraged the lawyers to explore that possibility. If they could stipulate, they wouldn't need to bore the jury with expert testimony.

Judge Martin spent a few minutes on his rules of thumb for conducting trials. "I don't mind your stating the basis of an objection in front of the jury, but if it looks like the objection will require argument, or if you don't want the jury to hear it for some reason, I'll call you to sidebar."

"Do I need to object to proposed exhibits before trial?" asked Anita.

"You can," replied the judge, "but you don't have to. And if you object on the record when it's first offered, you don't have to renew the objection when the government moves all of its unadmitted exhibits at the end of its case. Make sure we have digital copies of all of your documentary exhibits, in pdf format, so that we can get them up on the screens."

"Will you explain to the jury that we're not permitted to say hello to them if we see them in the hallway or on the street?" asked Renfro.

"You bet," said the judge. "Just remind me."

After 20 minutes, the conference wrapped up. Anita and Patrick had traveled 185 miles for 20 minutes of courtroom time. They were looking at another 185 miles on the way back.

CHAPTER 60

Patrick and Anita were going over the government's exhibit list in Anita's office, on the Thursday before the Monday that trial was to start. The exhibit list was growing. The government had just sent over copies of Government Exhibit 14A-Z and 14 AA-TT, consisting of 46 photographs taken by the entrance security camera at the Sheridan City Landfill during the last tax year at issue, referred to as Year 5 in the Superseding Indictment.

Each of the 46 photos showed Patrick's face in grainy black and white, sitting in the driver's seat of a truck, usually the Detmer Contracting Silverado, but occasionally the Detmer Contracting stake body. Anita had to hand it to Jack Farragut (she doubted that Renfro would have thought of it). Showing 46 different photos of Patrick in grainy black and white was a good way to suggest to the jury that they were watching an episode of "Cold Case" or "Cops," and that the suspect had tripped up by forgetting there might be a camera at the scene of the crime. Also, 46 trips to the landfill was *a lot* of trips – would the defendant have made that many trips just to exchange favors? Anita realized, for the hundredth time, that the United States Government was sparing no expense in this case.

Priscilla stuck her head in the door, urgently, and said, "It's the governor's office. They want to talk to Patrick, and they want to know if we can find him."

"Put it in here," said Anita. Anita and Patrick exchanged puzzled looks. The extension phone rang on the sideboard table, and Anita gestured for Patrick to pick it up.

"Hello, this is Patrick Flaherty."

"Hold for Governor Watkins, please." About thirty seconds went by, and a mildly raspy voice came on the line.

"Patrick, this is Bill Watkins. I'm glad I found you this quickly. How are you holding up?"

"I'm fine, sir, thank you."

"I'm sure you're busy, so I won't keep you long. I'm calling, really, for two reasons. First, I bumped into Mayor Banner at an event we were having, and he let me know the Town of Coolidge is supporting you, and that's good news. But he also said that some of the same people who might be taking care of your animals also want to be there in Casper for your trial. So, I talked to Eleanor Sprague, our Secretary of Agriculture, to see how maybe we could help. She told me she'd be happy to detail some of her people to Coolidge for a week to take care of your animals while you're away, and, if you're OK with it, maybe help you make some improvements in their enclosures. And they'll tie in the UW Extension people too, from their Agriculture Department. Whatever they're thinking about goat and chicken enclosures is probably going to be state of the art. Is that all OK with you?"

"Ah, yes sir, I don't know what to say. Thank you."

"And the second thing is, I want you to know that my administration is behind you. I won't speak for the State of Wyoming, because I don't think that's a good thing to do when I'm weighing in on something that might have partisan implications. But we've been reading the news, especially the Wyoming papers. There are a lot of people, here in Cheyenne and across the state, who are hoping you win this thing."

"Thank you, sir." Patrick hesitated. "Governor, I may have voted in the last election, I'm not sure. And I'm not really sure which party you're in. If my case is getting to be political, then I'm not sure I understand the politics involved. I'm very, very grateful that you're sending help for my animals, but I just wanted to be sure that I'm not getting caught on one side or the other of a political fight. I would need to say 'no' to your offer, if saying 'yes' commits me to one side or another in that fight."

"Well said, and I get your concern. I don't need to publicize the fact that we're helping you out, and I don't plan to pick any fights with Uncle Sam. But you're one of ours, Patrick, and you're living the way a lot of us have lived here for a long time -- even if you do it with less cash than most other people. You know, if you should have been paying federal taxes, fine, then you owe them. But that's not the point. To charge you criminally for this was an outrage, in my opinion. So I wanted to call and let you know that."

"Thank you, sir, and thanks again for the help with my animals."

"It's our privilege. Good luck next week. Bye."

"Bye," said Patrick. The line was dead, and, presumably, the governor was on to his next call.

"Wow," said Anita. "Didn't see that one coming."

"Me neither," said Patrick. "But it's really going to help."

Anita was thinking about the remaining "preps" she needed to do with the Coolidge witnesses. Now that the grand jury investigation was concluded, there was no ethical prohibition on her meeting with witnesses to go over their anticipated testimony. She had set dates and times with Mavis, Clem, Bobby, Harry and Father Dave. There was a lot of work to do, and never enough time.

PART III

CHAPTER 61

It was 3:30 in the afternoon on Monday, May 10. Jury selection was over. The jury would be five men and seven women, with two alternates, both men. Anita had been looking to keep wage earners, farmers and hunters on the jury, and wanted to avoid government employees, teachers, and retirees. She wasn't sure about small business owners. On the one hand, it was possible they'd resent Patrick's not having paid the taxes they were paying. On the other hand, they were likely to resent the IRS because they were paying the taxes they were paying. She sized them up one at a time, and trusted her instincts.

Of the five men who made it onto the jury, one was a coal miner, two were in sales, one was a delivery driver, and one was a retired contractor. Of the seven women, two were raising kids, one was a gymnastics coach in a private gym, one was a medical secretary, one was an unemployed cook, one was a physician's assistant, and one – the one Anita was worried about – was a social worker. On the one hand, social workers could be amazingly clear-eyed about people and life. On the other hand, most social workers believed that taxes were the solution, not the problem, and they needed to be levied and paid. Anita was not pleased that a social worker made it to the final twelve – Anita had used up her challenges on people who were even more questionable -- but you could never tell anyway. She seemed like a nice lady.

The jury included one African American, one Native American, and one Latino. Anita was hoping the group would be less white than it turned out to be, but that wasn't easy in Wyoming, and the government used three of its six peremptory challenges on one African American male, and two Latinas. Anita had used her 10 on retirees, other people who made her nervous, a high school teacher, a college professor, and an auto mechanic. The mechanic just looked – hostile. Hard to say why.

Patrick and Anita checked into rooms at the Courtyard by Marriott, east of town. Patrick's room and Anita's room were being paid for by GoFundMe. Patrick's parents and a lot of the other people from Coolidge were on the same floor. Dinner was downstairs in the little restaurant, and the atmosphere was tense, and quiet. Anita excused herself early to work on her opening statement. She was going to say that Patrick had no idea he was breaking the law -- if in fact he was – and the government couldn't prove the contrary. Nobody else knew that bartering had to be reported, either, and you can't convict someone for something nobody knows is a crime.

"I'll be ready," said Anita. "See you at breakfast."

CHAPTER 62

The courtroom was crowded, but not overflowing, for the first real day of trial on Tuesday. Patrick was pleased to see his parents, his sister Annabelle, his friend Stanley Bartram, a lot of people from Clem's, Lloyd Grant, two or three guys from his softball team, and Ray, Ray and Toby from Four Toe Joe. Kahlil Omar, from the Federal Defender's Office, was sitting two rows back, which gave Patrick a boost. There was one row of seats, on the left side of the spectators' section, for media. The reporters, if that's who they were, looked young and prosperous.

Anita wondered how the print reporters, especially, could afford expensive clothes on the salaries they were likely being paid. Maybe they were rich kids when they started. How do you make a small fortune in the newspaper business? Start with a large fortune.

The judge greeted the jurors and described what to expect from the lawyers' opening statements. Each side was going to comment on what they thought the evidence would show, but their opening statements were not evidence, and couldn't be considered as evidence later, during jury deliberations.

From the defense table on the right side of the courtroom, Patrick looked at the judge, the jury, and the prosecution. The judge's bench was probably twelve feet long, and the judge's large leather chair swiveled and moved on castors. He moved side-to-side a lot. To the judge's right, and a little farther to Patrick's left, was the witness stand. There was a chair, a ledge for documents, and a good view of the jury and the two counsel tables. The jury box was set against the left-hand wall of the courtroom, extending between the witness stand and the prosecutors' table. There were 14 chairs, in two rows, for the jurors and the two alternates, and eight computer screens. In front of the jury box stood a small, portable lectern that the lawyers would use when they made their opening and closing arguments to the jury.

The two counsel tables were placed with their narrow ends toward the front and back of the courtroom – perpendicular to the judge's bench rather than parallel to it. Patrick was seated with his back to the right wall, facing the jury, all the way across the room. Between the two counsel tables, there was a large lectern, wired for sound. The lawyers would be standing behind that lectern when they questioned witnesses.

Finally, the prosecution table, to Anita's left, was filled with papers, binders and photos. Three people were sitting there, now all familiar to Patrick – Farragut, Renfro and the IRS agent.

Everything was heavy, dark wood, and there was a microphone at each counsel table, at the witness stand, and in front of the judge. There was a Great Seal of the United States on the wall above the judge's head, with an eagle holding arrows and olive branches, and a raised inscription, "United States District Court – District of Wyoming." There were large windows on every wall except the wall behind the spectator area, and plenty of light.

Judge Thomas Martin looked over the bench at the lawyers and spectators. "Mr. Farragut, Mr. Renfro, the government may proceed with its opening statement." AUSA Jack Farragut made his way to the lectern and looked at the jury.

"Ladies and gentlemen of the jury, my name is John Farragut, and I represent the United States of America. With me serving as attorney for the United States is Arnold Renfro, from the Division of Taxation of the United States Department of Justice. And sitting with us at counsel table is Special Agent Arthur Bolton of the Criminal Investigation Division of the Internal Revenue Service. First, I want to thank you in advance, on behalf of the government, for the time you will be spending on this case. We know that jury service is a sacrifice on your part, and we very much appreciate your willingness to serve.

Farragut paused for a moment. "The evidence in this case will show that the defendant, Patrick Michael Flaherty, intentionally and willfully evaded his obligations to pay federal taxes for five years in a row.

"The government will call at least eight witnesses to prove its case against Mr. Flaherty. The first witness who will testify is Special Agent Bolton." He gestured toward Bolton at counsel table. "As you all know, the Internal Revenue Service is the federal agency that oversees the collection of federal taxes, and in some cases, the payment of funds to poor Americans by way of the Earned Income Tax Credit. The IRS operates the Criminal Investigation Division to investigate instances of tax evasion and tax fraud, and it is Special Agent Bolton's job to gather evidence in those cases.

"Special Agent Bolton will testify that he met defendant Flaherty by chance, while he was off duty, at a restaurant and bar called 'Cousin Clem's' in Coolidge, Wyoming. Coolidge is a town of about 2,800 people just south of the Montana border, and Special Agent Bolton was on his way home to Cheyenne from the Bighorn Mountains when he stopped into Cousin Clem's for dinner.

"While he was sitting beside the defendant at the bar, Special Agent Bolton heard another patron, farther up the bar, complain about his taxes and the IRS. That patron kidded the defendant about not knowing what money is. The defendant responded to that statement, saying, 'I don't have any problems with the IRS. They don't know I exist – I'd like to keep it that way. Fuck the IRS.'

Both Anita and Patrick turned pale, and both looked ill. Anita knew that under federal criminal discovery rules, if a defendant makes a statement to someone without knowing that the listener is a government agent – usually, an undercover cop – the government isn't obliged to disclose the statement, or its intention to use that statement, before trial. "Fuck the IRS" was – unhelpful.

Farragut continued, "Please think about that, ladies and gentlemen, as you listen to the evidence. 'Fuck the IRS' was the defendant's reason for, and part of the proof of, his tax evasion. He was proud that the IRS didn't know that he existed, and he said so publicly.

"After he heard the 'fuck the IRS' statement, Special Agent Bolton struck up a conversation with the defendant. He initiated that conversation as an undercover agent – in other words, he didn't disclose to the defendant that he worked for the IRS. As Special Agent Bolton will explain to you during his testimony, undercover investigations are an important part of his job. Obviously, he doesn't expect tax evaders to admit what they're up to if he's already identified himself as a law enforcement officer. Like every other law enforcement agency, the Criminal Investigation Division of the IRS encourages its agents to use whatever legal tools are available, and, as you'll hear, those tools include undercover work.

"While he was talking to the defendant at the bar, Special Agent Bolton quickly learned how the defendant had contrived to stay under the IRS's radar. First, he moved into an old hunting cabin without asking anyone's permission, and continued living there for free even after he learned that the cabin and the land around it belong to his church. He raised chickens and goats on the land. He told Special Agent Bolton that he had a 'deal' – Farragut provided the quotation marks with his fingers – with the church to live there in exchange for fixing up the cabin.

"The defendant told Special Agent Bolton that he did handyman work at his church and the rectory in town. He would work at the church during the week, and then he would appear at pot luck dinners sponsored by the church after Saturday services, and he would go home with a knapsack full of leftovers – usually four meals' worth, not counting the meal he had just eaten. That food was important to him, because if you're going to stay off the IRS's radar, you still need to eat. And he told Special Agent Bolton that he accepted the food from his church as part of the deal. You have to give back, he said, and he worked for the church as part of the deal by which he received food.

"In fact, Special Agent Bolton saw an example of the defendant's bartering strategy – his strategy to stay under the IRS's radar – while he was in Cousin Clem's. When Special Agent Bolton arrived, the defendant was playing a guitar and singing on a stage near the bar. When he finished playing, the defendant accepted a beer without paying for it, and then Special Agent Bolton saw the defendant eating food from the kitchen. While he was talking with the defendant, Special Agent Bolton was able to confirm that the owners of Cousin Clem's gave the defendant free food and beer in exchange for playing two hours of music on Friday nights. So, in that way, the defendant met another day of his weekly dietary requirements.

"You will hear directly from witnesses who were on the other side of each of the bartering transactions in which the defendant was involved. We won't be hiding the ball, as the saying goes. You'll hear the facts directly from the people involved.

"Agent Bolton will also explain how the defendant intentionally avoided talking to an accountant, because the defendant plainly suspected that he owed taxes on his bartering income, and he didn't want to hear that he was breaking the law. He told agent Bolton, 'I don't want to talk to an accountant, because I'd be afraid of what I might hear. Suppose I was making enough income, that I should be paying taxes? I don't want to know.'"

This time, Anita went rigid, and the color drained from her face. The people behind her in the spectator benches couldn't see her, but Patrick could. It was primordial. The lookout at the mouth of the cave had just turned white, and the tribesman watching her knew it was bad. The sabre tooth tiger was close. Patrick felt the fear creeping up from his brain stem.

"Ladies and gentlemen, what will become apparent to you as the evidence develops is that the defendant has had a calculated plan over the last five years to avoid using money, so that he could avoid paying taxes. The evidence will show that he was running at least four business ventures – handyman services, driver, dog trainer, and musical performances – in which he accepted food, construction materials, and animal feed as a substitute for cash. He was avoiding the use of cash and bank accounts, because those can be more easily traced. Judge Martin will explain, during his instructions to you later in the case, that, under federal law, the value of property you accept in payment for your services has to be declared as income. With that in mind, the government will introduce expert testimony that the defendant accepted so much property in exchange for services that he was obliged to file a tax form, and federal self-employment taxes, for each of those four businesses. He didn't do that; his failure to do it was calculated and intentional; and that's why we're here.

"Failure to pay self-employment tax is a very serious matter. As our expert witness, Dr. Morris Tindle, will tell you, those taxes help support Social Security benefits for all of us. When they're not paid, we all suffer. You'll hear that the defendant admitted to Special Agent Bolton that evening in Cousin Clem's that he didn't want to file a tax return, because if he did, the IRS would show up and ask him where he's been for the past five years. He was right about that – his failure to file tax returns for the past five years was going to get him in trouble sooner or later."

Another statement that hadn't been disclosed in discovery. Anita knew she was trying a new and different case. The one she prepared was just a memory.

Farragut continued. "The defendant has now been charged with tax evasion as a result of that intentional refusal to file returns, and we believe that, at the conclusion of the evidence, you will agree that the defendant is guilty of criminal tax evasion beyond any reasonable doubt.

"We will do our best to present the government's case clearly and efficiently, and we'll be respectful of your time and the sacrifices you're making to be here. Mr. Renfro, Special Agent Bolton, and I would like to thank you, in advance, for your careful attention throughout the case."

Farragut nodded to the jury, and slowly returned to his seat at counsel table.

CHAPTER 63

Judge Martin looked over his glasses. "Ms. Boyle, you may address the jury on behalf of the defendant."

Anita rose. "Your Honor, I understand that the request I'm about to make is unusual. I listened to Mr. Farragut suggest a theory of his case that was not at all obvious from pretrial discovery. To respond properly, I need a moment to consult with my client. May I have a five minute recess to do that?"

The judge was clearly bothered by the request. "You're right, Ms. Boyle – your request *is* unusual, and I'm not inclined to grant it. The jury has waited a long time for the trial to begin, and now you're stopping the case in its tracks. But I'll give you three minutes to consult with your client, at counsel table. In the meantime, the jury and I will wait for you."

"Thank you, Your Honor."

Anita sat down and put her right arm across Patrick's shoulder. "Do you remember ever having talked to anyone about consulting with an accountant?" she whispered.

Patrick thought hard. "Not really. I might have said it to Bolton, I don't know."

"Our problem is the *Fingado* case," Anita replied. "*United States v. Fingado*. It's a case from the Tenth Circuit – our circuit – that says if you deliberately keep yourself ignorant about the tax laws, you can be convicted of tax evasion even if you were ignorant of the law. You can still be convicted of willful evasion. I kept seeing references to the case in my research, but I didn't have any reason to think it would apply to our facts. Now they're kicking the legs out from under our best defense. And they weren't obliged to tell us about the conversation in discovery."

"I thought *Cheek* says that we can always prove ignorance of the law," said Patrick.

"Oh, it does – but once we've shown ignorance of the law, the government comes back and says that you were deliberately ignorant, and they win anyway."

Anita thought for a second. "Move your lips, describe the menu at Clem's, say anything. Show the jury you're telling me some new facts."

Patrick began to describe, in a whisper, the wings, burgers and fries at Cousin Clem's. Anita nodded along absently, thinking and planning how she was going to modify her opening statement to the jury. The statement about the accountant sounded like something Patrick might have said. She made an on-the-spot calculation that, at the end of the day, the jury would probably find deliberate ignorance. It was still the first inning, and her opening statement didn't need to be the Gettysburg Address. All she needed to do was give the back half of the speech that she'd planned – there were no bartering agreements, just favors between friends – and then deal head on, somehow, with the evidence of willfulness. She smiled at Patrick, nodded confidently as if he'd just given her the facts that she needed, and stood to address the court.

"Your Honor, thank you for your patience," said Anita. "The defense is ready to proceed."

"You may address the jury."

CHAPTER 64

Anita hoped her panic was not obvious to the jury. She knew her case was in deep trouble. But that's the way trials go sometimes. She walked toward the jury box and stood before the jurors, without notes.

"Members of the jury, my name is Anita Boyle, and I represent the defendant in this case, Patrick Flaherty.

"Because the government can't prove what it needs to prove, you will hear lots of evidence about other things. You'll hear from witnesses about self-employment taxes, as if they have something to do with a man who doesn't have any employment. You'll hear about accountants, as if they have something to do with a man who doesn't have an accountant. You'll hear about cash equivalents, as if they have something to do with a man who uses almost no cash. Their whole case is based on make-believe facts – 'Let's make believe that giving somebody some meat loaf at a pot luck dinner is the same as giving someone cash.'

"The government's proof is directed toward a single objective. They want you to say to yourselves, 'I pay taxes and I file tax returns -- why shouldn't Patrick Flaherty do the same? Who does he think he is?' The fair answer to that question – and one that will be clear as you hear the evidence – is that Patrick Flaherty is just a guy who chooses to live a life that, a hundred and fifty years ago, was probably very typical in Wyoming. He chooses to live off the land, supplemented by food that's cooked by little old ladies who are very happy to feed him. He isn't evading income taxes – he doesn't have any income, and he doesn't owe any taxes.

"Listen for some key facts as I'm questioning witnesses that Mr. Farragut or Mr. Renfro will be calling for the government. You'll hear, first of all, that you can have income without being obliged to file a tax return or pay federal taxes. In fact, if you make $11,999 in a year in hourly wages or salary, you can spend it or save it without worrying about filing a tax return. It's yours. You'll hear that if you make $399 as an independent contractor, you don't have to file a tax return or pay any self-employment taxes. It's yours. So what you've always assumed -- that if you don't make any money, you don't have to pay taxes – is actually correct. Lots of people don't pay federal income tax, and lots of people don't need to file tax returns. If you live off of savings, and you don't have more than $600 in interest to report, you don't need to pay taxes or file a return.

"So don't let the government suggest to you that Patrick Flaherty is the only person in America not paying income tax or not filing tax returns. He's not.

"You'll also hear from the government's witnesses that you don't have taxable income when you receive a gift. Patrick's need for cash is very, very limited, but he receives $100 in cash each month from his parents to pay for necessities like soap and toothpaste, and an occasional beer at Cousin Clem's, the local bar and grill. The money that Patrick receives from his parents is not counted as income; it's not taxable; and he isn't obliged to declare it on any tax return.

Anita turned and crossed back to the small lectern. She took a sip of water from a glass she had placed on it. She collected her thoughts, and gave the jurors a moment to collect theirs.

"Patrick Flaherty moved to Coolidge, Wyoming, seven years ago, from the Denver area. He found work with a contractor in Coolidge, doing mostly carpentry. While he was working, he and a friend found an abandoned hunting cabin well outside of town, on what they thought was public land. As you may know, more than half of all of the land in Wyoming is public land, so their assumption was pretty reasonable. Patrick immediately saw possibilities. He began to renovate the cabin with materials he found around Coolidge, and in less than a year it kept out the weather, and he found he could live there.

"It was at that point, about six and a half years ago, that Patrick came up with the idea of living off the land. It was a gutsy idea, but he was determined, and it began to happen. He began to raise chickens and goats; he planted vegetables; he hunted for meat; and he wired his cabin to run on twelve volt power, supplied by renewable sources – wind, solar, and water. He decided to quit his job, and he began to live in his cabin. He didn't use much money, and he didn't need it.

"And now, this is the important part: Patrick Flaherty is not a hermit, he's not a cave man, and he's not antisocial. From the very beginning, he wanted to be a member of the Coolidge community, and he has never stopped being a member of that community. He has many friends, some of whom you'll meet; he is a parishioner at the local Catholic church; he participates in community events; and he plays music on Friday nights, actually pretty well.

"When it comes down to it, it is Patrick's connection with the Coolidge community that the government is trying to criminalize in this case. If only he had stayed shut up in his cabin, maybe he wouldn't be facing this trial. But what the government is calling 'barter transactions' are just the ordinary back and forth with favors that civilized people do in Coolidge, and certainly in your town as well.

"The evidence of 'barter transactions' in this case – food, feed bags, dog training -- will look a lot like when you borrow a cup of sugar from your neighbor, and then three days later you lend her a cup of milk. The government will make a big deal out of the fact that the people doing the favors in this case felt a sort of obligation to do so – and when your neighbor comes back for a cup of milk, *of course* you feel obliged to give it to her. And one of the reasons that you feel obliged to give it to her is that she gave you a cup of sugar three days before.

"What that is, ladies and gentlemen, is simple kindness. It's the social compact. It's the kindnesses that good people extend to each other every day. It's not a crime, as the government will try to paint it. When we extend kindness, do we expect kindness in return? Well, yes, because we know, or at least hope, that our neighbors are good people, and most of the time they are. Most of the time, our kindnesses are returned. But by and large, that isn't why we do them. The evidence will show that Patrick Flaherty was kind to his neighbors because he wanted to be, and *certainly* not because he had a grand plan to willfully hide his income.

Anita knew she had to spend at least a little time on the *Fingado* issue. She decided to thread the needle.

"Finally, don't abandon your common sense. The reason you have probably never heard that barter transactions are taxable is that almost nobody else has heard that barter transactions are taxable. The government has to prove beyond a reasonable doubt that Patrick Flaherty knew that he was failing to report income, and was willfully evading taxes. This notion that Mr. Flaherty didn't talk to an accountant because he didn't want to hear that he owed taxes is a stretch, to say the least. There is no reason on earth that a man who didn't make any money should have expected that he owed taxes; and if he didn't want to talk with an accountant he had a good reason. Accountants are expensive, and why should he pay good money, only to find out that he didn't owe any taxes? The government's so-called 'evidence' of intent will not withstand your scrutiny. There was no willful evasion of taxes, as the evidence in this case will make abundantly clear.

"Please listen carefully to all of the evidence, from both sides, and keep an open mind as the case goes along. Remember that the government must prove its case beyond a reasonable doubt. That's a very high standard of proof. We hope and expect that, after you've heard all of the evidence, you will conclude that the government hasn't come close to meeting that burden. At the end of the case, I will be asking you to return a verdict of not guilty."

CHAPTER 65

"Mr. Farragut, you may call your first witness," said Judge Martin.

"Your Honor, the government calls Special Agent Arthur Bolton."

Bolton made his way from counsel table to the witness stand. When he reached the witness stand, he stood and waited for the Deputy Clerk to appear with the Bible. "Do you swear or affirm that the testimony you are about to give in this matter will be the truth, the whole truth, and nothing but the truth, so help you God?"

"Yes," said Bolton, and he sat down. AUSA Farragut waited for his witness to get settled.

"Special Agent Bolton, please state your full name, your position with the United States Government, and your present duty assignment," said Farragut.

"My name is Arthur Bolton. I am a Special Agent with the Criminal Investigation Division of the United States Internal Revenue Service. 'IRS-CID' for short. I'm currently assigned as the Acting Assistant Special Agent in Charge of the IRS-CID office in Cheyenne, Wyoming."

"What are the job duties of an IRS-CID Special Agent?" continued Farragut.

"Our job is criminal enforcement of those parts of the Internal Revenue Code, and Title 18 of the United States Code, that provide for criminal penalties for failure to comply with the federal tax laws. As a practical matter, most of our cases involve either tax evasion or tax fraud."

"What is the difference between tax evasion and tax fraud?"

"There's a lot of overlap. In general terms, however, we usually charge tax evasion where someone has earned income, but no tax return was filed to report that income. And we typically charge tax fraud where a return was filed, but there were false statements in that return."

"Is the defendant in this case, Patrick Michael Flaherty, charged with tax evasion or tax fraud?"

"All of the charges in this case are for tax evasion, Title 26 of the United States Code, Section 7201, based on the defendant's failure to file tax returns reporting income that we allege he received."

"How long have you worked as an IRS-CID Special Agent?" asked Farragut.

"I've been a Special Agent for 19 years."

"What was your educational background before you came to work for the IRS?"

"I graduated from Kelly Walsh High School here in Casper, Wyoming, and then I attended, and graduated from, the University of Wyoming in Laramie, Wyoming. I double-majored in Economics and Criminal Justice at UW. After college, I went to work for the Wyoming Department of Revenue. I was helping with sales and use tax investigations, civil and criminal. But Wyoming doesn't have a personal income tax or a corporate income tax, so I was not learning as much as I wanted. I also took some accounting and tax courses during that period. After three years, I applied for and accepted a job with the IRS Criminal Investigation Division."

"What training did you receive to become a Special Agent?" asked Farragut.

"Our initial training is the same as for any other federal law enforcement officers, whether you're talking about the FBI, or the Drug Enforcement Administration, or Alcohol, Tobacco and Firearms. Almost all federal agents take their initial training at the Federal Law Enforcement Training Center, known as FLET-C. I was assigned to the FLET-C school in Glynco, Georgia. After FLET-C, I took a series of IRS-CID courses in federal tax law and enforcement, and then I was assigned as a Special Agent Trainee in Chicago. A year later, I was promoted to Special Agent, and learned the ropes, if you will, in Chicago."

"Are IRS-CID Special Agents authorized to carry weapons?"

"Yes, we are."

"Do you have arrest powers?"

"Yes, we do."

"Are you authorized to apply for arrest warrants, search warrants, and warrants to intercept electronic communications?"

"Yes, we are. We're authorized to use any investigative or enforcement tools that, say, an FBI Special Agent might use. The key difference is that an FBI agent is responsible for enforcing almost the entire federal criminal code, while our focus is limited to tax crimes."

"How did you find your way to the Cheyenne office?" asked Farragut.

"I worked in Chicago for about three years, and then I was assigned, at my request, to the Cheyenne office. I wanted to come home to Wyoming. I've worked in Cheyenne for almost 15 years. And as I said, for the past two years I've been Acting Assistant Special Agent in Charge in Cheyenne. We're a satellite of the Denver Field Office, which is part of the Western Area of IRS-CID."

Farragut had introduced his investigator. Now it was time to start presenting his investigator's case.

"Special Agent Bolton, I'd like to call your attention to October 2nd of last year," said Farragut. "Do you recall what you were doing on that date?"

"I do. I was finishing up some personal vacation time in the Bighorn Mountains, in Wyoming. I had been visiting my brother and his wife, who live in Lovell, Wyoming. I started my trip home to Cheyenne, by car, late in the day, and my plan was to stop in Sheridan for the night. Before I reached Sheridan, I stopped at a restaurant and bar in Coolidge, for some dinner. The bar is called 'Cousin Clem's.' It sits right on U.S. Route 14 in Coolidge."

"What time of day was it?"

"It was just before 7:00 when I went in."

"Was Cousin Clem's busy when you entered?" asked Farragut.

"It was. But I found a seat near the middle of the bar."

"Was there music playing when you went in?"

"There was. I saw the defendant, whom I later identified as Patrick Michael Flaherty, playing guitar and singing on a small stage in the right hand back corner of the room." Bolton pointed at Patrick.

"Your Honor, indicating, for the record, defendant Patrick Michael Flaherty," said Farragut.

"What happened next?" asked Farragut.

"As I was ordering a beer, it looked like the singer, Mr. Flaherty, was completing his set. I saw him accept a draft beer from the owner, whom I later identified as Clement Labrecque. I noticed that Mr. Flaherty didn't appear to have paid for the beer; at first, I didn't think much of that fact. I assumed that free drinks were part of his compensation."

Anita could have objected about the admissibility of Bolton's assumptions. But Farragut would have figured out some other way to get the evidence in, and it wasn't worth it. Fundamentally, jurors don't like objections, and Anita believed it's best to save them for when she wanted to keep the jury from hearing something that would really hurt her case – or when she needed to make an objection to preserve a claim of error for appeal.

"What did Mr. Flaherty do after he left the stage?"

"He went around the bar and passed behind me heading to my left, and into the kitchen. He came out a few minutes later, still eating a French fry. That made me wonder whether Cousin Clem's provided food as part of his compensation. After that, he sat in the seat next to me, which I think had just opened up."

"What happened next?" asked Farragut.

"At that point a gentleman farther up the bar began to complain about his taxes, and everybody was kind of chiming in. A woman nearby threw out a riddle – where is money printed in the United States? A lot of people made guesses, and then the man farther up the bar yelled to the guitar player sitting beside me, 'I knew you weren't going to get that one, because you don't use money.' And then the person next to me – the defendant, Mr. Flaherty – says 'I don't have any problems with the IRS. They don't know I exist – I'd like to keep it that way. Fuck the IRS.'"

"How are you able to remember the details of what the defendant said?" continued Farragut.

"After the defendant said 'Fuck the IRS,' I excused myself and jotted down some notes in the men's room while his words were still fresh in my memory."

"All right, continue. What happened next?"

"I came back to the bar and sat in my seat again. The defendant was still sitting to my left. I began to engage the defendant in conversation. Because it's my job, I wanted to explore a little whether the 'Fuck the IRS' comment maybe indicated evidence of tax evasion. So, I introduced myself as Art Smalls, and told him that I was on the way from Lovell to Cheyenne. He told me his name was Patrick Flaherty. I told him I enjoyed the music – which was actually true, he's a pretty good musician – and told him I hoped he received free beer and food in exchange for his musical services. He confirmed that he did, which was consistent with what I'd seen when I came in."

"What else did you talk about?" asked Farragut.

"At that point I asked him what he did for his day job. He told me that he's a farmer in Coolidge, and that he grows vegetables and raises chickens and goats. When I asked him if he sold eggs and milk, he told me 'no,' and explained that he didn't use money very much. I asked him, just in a conversational way, whether he owned his own land, or rented from someone else. He responded that he lived on land owned by his church, and that his church was letting him live there. He said that, in return, he was maintaining the cabin for the Parish. I pretended I needed to go outside to make a call, and I went outside and wrote down what the defendant had just said."

"Were you fully off vacation, and back on duty, so to speak, at that point?"

"Yes. At that point, I had concluded that the defendant had shown hostility to the IRS and the whole idea of money and taxation. He had implied that he wasn't filing tax returns, or at least that's what I presumed he meant when he said the IRS didn't know that he existed. He admitted that he was bartering his musical services. And he had admitted that he was bartering maintenance services for rent."

"Objection, Your Honor," said Anita, "to the witness's conclusions about 'admitted' and 'bartering.' In the context of this case, both of those are legal conclusions, not testimony about facts."

"I'll allow the testimony," said Judge Martin. "But I caution the jury that the witness is giving his conclusion that bartering was taking place. It will be up to you to decide, on the basis of all of the evidence in the case, whether the defendant was involved in bartering, and whether he admitted as much to Agent Bolton." And then to Farragut: "Proceed."

"OK," said Farragut, "we're at the point where you had just completed taking a note or two outside the bar. What did you do next?"

"I went back into the bar and sat back down in my seat next to the defendant. I was essentially undercover, and my objective was just to keep him talking. I told him I was an accountant, and I referred to the earlier conversation at the bar about taxes. I wanted to get him talking about his finances, and taxes generally, and I figured that holding myself out as an accountant would explain my interest in his situation."

"Did he seem suspicious or hesitant to talk to you?"

"No. He was open about his life choices, I would say. I asked him how he procured the materials for maintaining and improving the cabin and the property around it. He explained to me that he worked with one of the contractors in town, Detmer Contracting. They let him take whatever excess material he needed for his property. In exchange, he drove one of their trucks to a landfill, on a regular basis, to dispose of construction debris. The way the defendant explained it to me, he took the useful materials from the back lot, and then he would provide driving services in exchange. He also said he would comb through the construction debris, and pulled out things he needed to maintain or improve his cabin. That trip back and forth to the dump consumed at least a couple of hours a week, and I concluded that Mr. Detmer freed up productive time for people in his crew, by not having to send an employee to the dump on a weekly basis."

"Did the defendant talk about any other similar arrangements he had?" asked Farragut.

"At that point, we had talked enough about bartering that I was comfortable asking him if he had any other bartering deals. In response, he told me that he obtained bags of animal feed for his animals for a Mr. Bays, who owns a feed store in Coolidge. The defendant apparently needs commercial feeds for his chickens and goats, to supplement their diets. He didn't describe what, if anything, he did for Mr. Bays in exchange. But as it happened, a man whom the defendant identified as Mr. Bays came over to where we were seated, and he told the defendant that his dog was going to the veterinarian on Monday, and could the defendant train her on Tuesday? The defendant agreed. It was a short interaction between Mr. Bays and the defendant. After Mr. Bays moved away, the defendant told me that Mr. Bays's dog was a German Shorthaired Pointer."

"Was there anything else that you talked with the defendant about?"

"Because I was curious about the defendant's diet, I asked him if he ate other meals in town, and he confirmed that he usually has his dinner on Saturdays at St. Ann's Catholic Church in Coolidge. I don't recall whether I asked him about it specifically, or whether he volunteered, that he did a lot of handyman work at his Parish. He told me that he did that work, quote, 'to give back, it's part of the deal,' close quote.

"Toward the end of the conversation, we talked about the fact that I was an accountant. It was at that point I mentioned that I'd heard him say that the IRS didn't know that he existed, and I asked him whether he had ever talked to an accountant about whether it's wise not to be filing tax returns. He said, 'I don't know, I'd be afraid of what I might hear. What if I have enough income, so that I'm supposed to be filing returns? I don't want to know.'"

"Did he say anything else about taxes or tax returns?" prompted Farragut.

"Yes," replied Bolton. "He said one of the reasons he structured his affairs the way he did was that he didn't want to have to file a tax return, and then have the IRS show up to ask him where he'd been for all those years. In fact, he gave an example of a friend of his who got into trouble with the IRS because he filed a tax return after skipping a few years. At that point, I excused myself again and went to take a few more notes. When I came back again, I placed a food order and shifted our conversation to other topics. I didn't want to dwell too much on tax issues, because I didn't want to make him nervous, or have him suspect in any way that he was under investigation. Eventually, I said goodnight, and left the bar about an hour and a half after I'd gone in."

"Your Honor, would this be a good point to take our morning break?" asked Farragut.

"Members of the jury, we're going to take a 15 minute break," responded Judge Martin. "Remember: Don't discuss the case with each other, or with anyone else, until you've heard all the evidence. If you hear one of your members starting to discuss the case, remind him or her of what I've told you. We'll see you in 15 minutes."

CHAPTER 66

Anita and Patrick made their way out through the back of the courtroom, toward the Attorneys' Conference Room off of the outer corridor. Patrick had time to nod hello to his family, but his family and friends had been cautioned by Anita that she would need his full attention during breaks. Anita opened the door of the conference room, flipped on the light, and sat at the end of the table. Patrick sat to her left.

"Do you remember the conversation at Cousin Clem's?" she asked.

"Not at all," he said. "I would have told you about it if I remembered it. I have a really vague recollection that I talked to somebody who was just visiting, but that's about all."

"I think it's one of the most screwed-up aspects of federal criminal practice," she said. "They have to give us tapes and transcripts if you've given a statement while you're in custody, or even if you're not in custody but you're being interviewed by a uniformed officer. But if you said something to an agent who's acting undercover, they don't have to tell you about it before trial. So we'll just have to deal with it."

"It felt strange listening to a description of me saying things I don't remember saying."

"Do you think you said them?"

"Yeah, I mean, it sounded like stuff I would have said. Most of it was true – I mean, if I said those things to a stranger, they would have been accurate descriptions of my life. So I could have said them."

"I have to tell you, 'Fuck the IRS' doesn't sound, to me, like something you would say."

"Yeah, me too. Until all this happened, I just never thought about the IRS. I didn't have any reason to." He had another thought. "What were you saying about that Tenth Circuit case?"

"It was just something that kept coming up in my research. As I said, criminal tax law is about the only place you can claim ignorance of the law, and it will be a defense if the jury believes you. The theory is – and I think this was a judicially-created doctrine -- the tax laws are so complex that you can't prove willful tax evasion without also proving that the defendant knows he's breaking the law. That's the *Cheek* case I told you about. But I kept seeing this case where the Tenth Circuit distinguished *Cheek* by saying that ignorance of the law shouldn't be a defense if you kept yourself deliberately ignorant. That's the *Fingado* case. And the judge has to follow it, because we're in the Tenth Circuit. This is really going to change our strategy. We were going to argue that you had no reason to know that bartering creates income – no one else knows that either, practically speaking. But now the government is going to keep pointing to their evidence that you were deliberately ignorant. They'll say that you could have talked to an accountant, but you didn't want to know. Our fallback defense is now going to be our first line of defense. We'll try to show that there were no bartering agreements – just people doing favors for each other. I still think we win on that."

"What did you think of Bolton?" asked Patrick.

"He knows the jury isn't going to like him, so I think he's just shooting for having the jury believe him." She smiled, weakly. "Given that *you* believed him, I expect he will achieve that limited objective."

Anita closed her notebook. "Let me visit the ladies' room. I'll meet you back inside."

CHAPTER 67

A few minutes later, Judge Martin tapped his gavel and said, "We're back in session."

Farragut went back to the lectern; Bolton was already sitting in the witness chair.

"Special Agent Bolton, what actions did you take with respect to defendant Flaherty after you left Cousin Clem's that evening?"

"I got back to my office in Cheyenne by mid-day the next day, which was Saturday, the 3rd. The first step I took was to run a search in our database to confirm the defendant's statement that he had not been filing tax returns. I found a return from a Patrick Flaherty living in Coolidge, Wyoming, from seven years ago. I noted his Social Security number, and was able to locate some earlier returns from when he was in college. But the system showed that he hadn't filed any federal tax returns during the previous five years.

"I checked the tax law, which is something I always do early in a case. I confirmed that when a bartering transaction results in the receipt of valuable property in exchange for services, the regulations require that the fair market value of the property be reported as income. But Mr. Flaherty hadn't reported any income.

"At that point, I felt I had a reasonable suspicion that a crime had been committed, and so I opened an investigative file and did all the paperwork associated with that.

"My next step was to plan our investigation. I had the defendant's statements, but I felt I needed to gather some evidence from the other people who had been involved in what looked to me like bartering transactions. So I spent some time online to find Mr. Detmer's company, and Mr. Bays' company, and St. Ann's Church. I established that the Mr. Detmer mentioned by the defendant was Harry Detmer, the owner of Detmer Contracting, Inc. I found a Robert Bays, who was the owner of Bays Feeds, a feed store in Coolidge. I identified the head priest of St. Ann's as Father David Hernandez, and their Parish Administrator as Mavis D'Antonio. I checked land records, and confirmed that a trust with the same name as the church owned a sizable piece of property just outside of Coolidge. And I established that Cousin Clem's is owned by Clement Labrecque and his wife, Claire Laperriere. I noted all the addresses, and learned what I could about their respective businesses.

"I also did a series of internet searches to see what else I could learn about the defendant, Mr. Flaherty. I learned that he grew up in the Denver suburb of Adams Heights, and graduated from high school there. He has a bachelor's degree from the University of Pennsylvania. And he finished third and got a bronze medal in a taco-eating contest in Coolidge a few years ago, on the 4th of July." Bolton paused briefly to collect his thoughts.

"What did you do next?" asked Farragut.

"Early in the following week, the week of October 5, I worked with Karl Lawless, who was then a Special Agent Trainee in our office, to develop an investigation plan. My idea was to approach the church and each of the businesses in an undercover capacity to see what information I could obtain."

"Was Special Agent Trainee Lawless ultimately promoted to Special Agent?" asked Farragut.

"Yes, recently."

"I'll refer to him as Agent Lawless during the period during which he was a trainee, and that way we'll both save some time. Did you, in fact, approach the church and each of the businesses?" asked Farragut.

"Yes. We began with Father Hernandez, from the church. I called him and told him that I worked for an entity called 'Wyoming Real Estate Strategies.' I said my name was Arthur Kramer, and that we were interested in perhaps purchasing the 250 acre parcel owned by the church. I made an appointment to see the property on Friday, October 9th. In the meantime, Agent Lawless and I planned visits to Cousin Clem's, Bays Feeds, Detmer Contracting, and the Hospitality Supper at St. Ann's."

"Let's talk about each of those, one at a time," said Farragut. "Describe your meeting with Father Hernandez on Friday, October 9th."

Bolton recounted his walk with Father Hernandez on the lower part of the property, and their hike up the hill to look at Patrick's cabin. He explained that he had scheduled the visit for when he believed Patrick would be driving to Sheridan for Harry Detmer. Farragut prompted him with questions here and there, but when a good case agent and an experienced AUSA are describing events, not too many questions are needed. They fall into a rhythm like a good off-Broadway play -- smooth dialogue, conversational, relaxed, just get a good story told for a small audience. The jurors knew, or sensed, that they were hearing the basic facts of the case from Agent Bolton -- from the get-go -- and they were paying close attention.

"Did you say anything to Father Hernandez about the tenant?" asked Farragut.

"I told him that we would need information about the arrangement between the Parish and the tenant, so that we – meaning Wyoming Real Estate Strategies – wouldn't find ourselves tied up in litigation with a squatter if we bought the land."

"What did Father Hernandez say in response to that?"

"He said that Mr. Flaherty was there with the permission of the Parish. He also said that if Mr. Flaherty didn't maintain the property, he wouldn't be able to stay. As Father Hernandez put it, 'That's the deal.' Father Hernandez stressed that the Parish needed to keep the cabin well maintained, to appeal to any prospective buyer."

"Did Father Hernandez point out any of the improvements that Mr. Flaherty had made to the property?"

"I recall that he pointed out the 12 volt electrical system that the defendant had installed. It had a windmill, two solar panels, and a water-driven generator in the stream. And I could see that the roof had been recently shingled, and the exterior stucco seemed relatively fresh and well-maintained. I could see that the defendant was recognizing enough income to maintain the place pretty well, even if that income was coming from bartering."

"Objection, Your Honor," said Anita, standing.

"Sustained," said Judge Martin. "The jury will disregard the witness's conclusion about bartering income. That will be up for you to decide."

"Did you leave a business card with Father Hernandez?" asked Farragut.

"Yes, we had it printed for purposes of our undercover operation. It identified me as 'Arthur Kramer,' with 'Wyoming Real Estate Strategies.' The telephone number rings to a line that we keep in service in Cheyenne that we answer with, 'Cheyenne Business Services – Your party is unavailable right now. May we forward your message?' That way we can use it in various undercover operations. If we're pretending to be a larger organization, we'll create a dedicated line with a different number."

"What did you and Agent Lawless do after your meeting with Father Hernandez?"

"At that point, we needed to prepare for Agent Lawless's visit to Cousin Clem's – and I understand that Agent Lawless will be testifying, so he can describe that for you – and we needed to prepare for Agent Lawless's visit to St. Ann's Church the next evening. I returned to our hotel in Sheridan – which we had kind of set up as a field headquarters – and helped Agent Lawless plan his strategy. We talked some more about the mission. I jotted down some notes about my meeting with Father Hernandez. And finally we hopped back in our car and headed back to Coolidge, at about 5:00 in the afternoon. The idea was for us to get back to Cousin Clem's while the defendant was playing music there. I didn't want to go into Cousin Clem's with Agent Lawless, because I didn't want to be recognized. Agent Lawless dropped me at the diner in town at 5:45. I ate a slow dinner, and then Agent Lawless picked me back up at 6:45. We headed back to Sheridan for the evening."

Farragut asked Bolton to describe the preparations for Lawless's visit to St. Ann's on October 10th. They had prepped the issue without being certain whether the testimony they had prepped would be used. They opted to go with it, in case it was a subject of concern to the jurors.

"Special Agent Bolton, why did you decide not to have Agent Lawless wear a concealed sound recording device during his visit to St. Ann's Church, and to the St. Ann's Parish Hall?" asked Farragut.

"Well, we thought about it, and we talked about it. There is no rule against using standard undercover techniques in a place of worship, or at least none I'm aware of. But we're not robots. It just seemed to us that secretly recording people's conversations in a place of worship – whether it's a mosque, or a synagogue, or a church – is a really intrusive step, and we didn't want to do it. So Agent Lawless and I agreed that he would just observe and listen to interactions involving the defendant, and limit the facts he gathered to those relating to this defendant, and other people's interactions with him. And that's what we did."

Farragut picked up a new folder. "Special Agent Bolton, let me jump ahead to Monday, October 12," said Farragut. "What did you have planned for that day?"

"Our plan for Monday included undercover visits to two local businesses, Bays Feeds and Detmer Contracting. We planned to record any conversations that took place during those visits."

"Did you do that?"

"Yes."

"Which was first. Please describe that visit."

"We began early on Monday, October 12, with a visit to Bays Feeds, on Route 14 in Coolidge, owned by Robert Bays. I went in alone, wearing a body recorder. I was in disguise, because Mr. Bays had been in Cousin Clem's the night I was there, and I didn't want to take a chance that he would recognize me. It was basically a wig, glasses and a mustache, from the FBI office in Cheyenne. Good quality. So I got into the store, and I asked for Mr. Bays. He said, 'That's me.' I introduced myself as 'Ed Keegan,' and I told him I was from Ranchester, Wyoming, which is about eight miles from Coolidge. I noticed a German Shorthaired Pointer in the corner behind the counter, which made the visit a little easier."

"Why?" asked Farragut.

"I told Mr. Bays that, last time I was in Coolidge, I had seen a German Shorthaired Pointer that was being trained by a young man. I pointed to the dog behind the counter and said, 'I think that's her.' He replied, "Yeah, that's my Millie.' So I explained that I talked to the trainer, who introduced himself as Patrick Flaherty. I told Mr. Bays that I had told Mr. Flaherty I was interested in owning a German Shorthair, and asked him if he knew where her breeder was located. Mr. Flaherty didn't know the answer to my question, but suggested that I go see the dog's owner, Bobby Bays at Bays Feeds."

"How did Mr. Bays respond?"

"I had a kind of nervous moment, because Mr. Bays found it odd that Mr. Flaherty didn't know who or where Millie's breeder was, because Mr. Bays and Mr. Flaherty had just had a conversation about it a couple of weeks before. I covered up as best I could, explaining that my conversation with Mr. Flaherty had taken place a month earlier, and this was the first time I'd been over to Coolidge from Ranchester since that conversation. Mr. Bays seemed satisfied with that explanation."

"What else did Mr. Bays say?"

"He told me that he bought his dog, and an earlier dog, from a breeder in Buffalo, Wyoming, and he suggested that I look at their website."

"What did you say in response," asked Farragut.

"I thanked him for the information, and then immediately posed a question. I asked him if he thought Patrick Flaherty might be willing to train a dog for me if I bought one, and if his services would be expensive."

"How did Mr. Bays respond to that question?"

"He replied, and I'm reading from my notes now: 'I don't know, I guess you'd have to ask him. I can't tell you how much he would cost, because he doesn't charge me cash. I swap him feed for his chickens and goats. To tell you the truth, I don't think Patrick would accept cash, and he's also pretty busy keeping himself alive. He might do it in exchange for food or ammunition.'"

Anita knew that Bolton was reading from the transcript of the recording that was made on his body recorder – she had been provided a copy of the transcript during discovery. She might have objected to Bolton's reading notes, instead of playing the tape, but she was happy that the tape was not being played for the jury – at least not yet. She stayed seated.

"How did you respond to Mr. Bays's statements?" asked Farragut.

"At that point, I had confirmed what I needed to confirm, so I thanked him for his time, and told him I would let him know if I wound up owning one of Millie's cousins. I left the store."

"Let me take you to a point later in the day on Monday, October 12th. Do you recall where you went after you left Bays Feeds?"

"Yes, I do. First, I met with Agent Lawless at the diner, and we talked about the conversation I'd had with Mr. Bays. We also talked about the encounter I was planning on having with Mr. Detmer. We went back to the car and I made sure there was enough space in the memory of the digital recorder to handle another interview. There was, so we were OK on that. And I took off the disguise I was wearing when I talked to Mr. Bays, because I had never met Mr. Detmer, and I didn't need it. After that, I left Agent Lawless at the diner again, and drove over to Detmer Contracting."

"Where is Detmer Contracting located?" asked Farragut.

"The company's office and yard are at 17 Gillette Street in Coolidge," replied Bolton.

"How big a company is it?"

"I believe they have about 10 employees."

"What time was it when you arrived at Detmer Contracting?"

"About 11:30 in the morning."

"Did you enter the company's office?"

"Yes. I went in through the main office door. There was a counter, and I guess you would call it a small reception area."

"Who was there?"

"There was a woman sitting at a desk behind the counter, later identified as Nancy McDermott. Standing next to the desk I saw Harry Detmer. I recognized Mr. Detmer from his picture on their website."

"What did you say to them?"

"I introduced myself as Paul Steinberger – again, I was undercover. I told them I was considering purchasing a Junk-B-Gone franchise that I said was available in Sheridan County. I said I was doing some research to determine what the demand for junk disposal services was in the county, and told them that I was visiting contractors and construction companies. That was basically it."

"How did they respond?" asked Farragut.

"Both were very pleasant. They responded pretty much as I expected. Mr. Detmer said, 'We send at least one truckload of debris to the landfill every week. But we already have a service that does it for us.' Because Mr. Flaherty had already told me about the arrangement he had with Detmer Contracting, I expected that answer from Mr. Detmer. So I pretended to be surprised. I said, 'Junk B Gone has been telling me that there's no competition in the county right now. This is disappointing news.' Mr. Detmer then explained that he thought the information I was getting from the franchisor, that is, from Junk B Gone, was probably good. He said, 'Our guy is a one-man service. I don't think he does it for anyone else.'"

"What else did Mr. Detmer say?"

"I'd like to refer to my notes, if I may," replied Bolton. "Mr. Detmer said, quote, 'Our guy collects our debris and takes it to the landfill, in exchange for cyclone fencing, and railroad ties, stuff for his animal enclosures. He also takes whatever materials in the debris might be usable for his purposes.' I understood him to be referring to the defendant, and to the Sheridan City Landfill. At that point, I thanked both of them, and I turned to leave. Mr. Detmer told me that he thought the Junk B Gone franchise I had described might be a good opportunity, and wished me luck with it."

"Is there such a thing as 'Junk B Gone'?" asked Farragut.

"As far as I know, there isn't," replied Bolton. "But there are junk removal services with similar names, and some of them offer franchise opportunities to people who want to own their own business. I thought it was a plausible cover story."

"Your Honor, I have no further questions for Special Agent Bolton." Farragut returned to his seat.

CHAPTER 68

Anita rose from her chair and straightened her skirt. She arrived at the lectern, and let a long moment pass, just staring at Special Agent Bolton. She had decided she wasn't going to address him as "Special Agent." "Mister" was too civilian -- he was a cop, not a storekeeper. She settled on "sir" – a sobriquet to which he couldn't object, but a signal to the jury that she didn't like him, and didn't like the case he had brought.

"Good morning, sir. My name is Anita Boyle, and I represent the defendant, Patrick Flaherty."

"Good morning, Counsel," replied Bolton.

"Sir, my notes of your testimony on direct examination indicate that you had concluded by October 3rd of last year that there was a reasonable suspicion that a crime had been committed by Mr. Flaherty. Did I get that right, was that your suspicion at that time?"

"Yes."

"Do you rely on your experience as a criminal tax investigator in deciding whether you have a reasonable suspicion of criminal conduct?" asked Anita.

"It depends, I think. Generally, yes."

"And, of course, you consider the applicable law and the facts in deciding whether you have a reasonable suspicion of criminal conduct?"

"Yes."

"OK, let's talk about the law, and the facts, and your experience," said Anita. She picked up a folder.

"Law first. Had you read IRS Publication 525 on the subject of bartering transactions when you formed your reasonable suspicion of criminal conduct?" she asked.

"Yes."

"And some Treasury regulations?"

"Yes."

"OK, facts. The facts entering into your reasonable suspicion were, one, the statements you claim Mr. Flaherty made in Cousin Clem's; two, your observations of Mr. Flaherty's conduct in Cousin Clem's; three, your check of the database to see whether Mr. Flaherty had filed recent returns. Is that all correct?"

"Yes."

"OK, your experience. Other than Patrick Flaherty, have you ever arrested anyone for a tax crime that included unreported income from bartering?"

"Objection, Your Honor," said Farragut. "Relevance."

"Your Honor, may we see you at sidebar," replied Anita.

The lawyers gathered with the court reporter at the far end of the bench, and Judge Martin turned their way in his swivel chair. "Ms. Boyle," he said.

"Your Honor, the government opened this door. They made it relevant. When you have a witness testify on direct that he had a 'reasonable suspicion' of criminal conduct, you're using testimonial evidence to prove, 'Hey, we're just being reasonable, this is a perfectly respectable case we've got here.' They are inviting the jury to reach that conclusion with them. I didn't bring up the subject of probable cause or reasonable suspicion. They didn't need to prove it – the only standard at trial is beyond a reasonable doubt. But they introduced the evidence anyway. And so I asked the witness whether he considers the law, the facts, and his own experience in determining reasonable suspicion, and he said 'yes' to all three. My question about prior arrests is perfectly appropriate, given what the government has presented."

"Your Honor, the government didn't open any doors," responded Farragut. "The question of whether Special Agent Bolton has ever arrested anyone else for this crime is utterly irrelevant to Mr. Flaherty's guilt or innocence. Mr. Bolton's passing reference to the reasons that he did what he did in pursuing his investigation were not an attempt by the government to prove anything. It was a momentary reference to provide some context to the investigative steps he was taking."

The judge took a sip of water from a glass on his bench. "I think the jury needs to hear the answer to Ms. Boyle's question. The agent described his actions as reasonable, partly based on his experience. This is not a case of obvious criminality. That doesn't mean there weren't any crimes committed. But the jury should understand that they're being presented a complex picture, as to law and facts. We won't pretend that this is a case like an illegal gun sale, or something where the only question is, 'Did he do it.' Jurors aren't dumb, and the context will be helpful for them. And the government opened the door. Objection overruled."

Anita returned to the lectern. "Sir," she said to Bolton, "again, other than Patrick Flaherty, have you ever arrested anyone for a tax crime that included unreported income from bartering?"

"No."

"What prompted you to think of Publication 525?" she asked.

"I don't recall," he lied. Although his answer was, in a sense, literally true. He didn't remember whether the memo from Washington mentioned Publication 525, or whether he ran across it in his research after he read the memo.

"Did anyone in Washington, D.C., send you a memo encouraging you to work up a bartering case?" Anita was just fishing. She looked over at Renfro for effect.

"No." Bolton was not an addressee of the memo, and he received his copy from Denver, not Washington.

"Did you receive any policy guidance from anyone within the IRS to be on the lookout for a possible bartering case?"

"Objection, Your Honor," said Farragut. "These questions are way beyond the issue of reasonable suspicion we discussed at sidebar, and they're irrelevant to the case before this jury."

"Sustained," said Judge Martin. "Ms. Boyle, let's move on."

"Very well, Your Honor." Anita gathered her thoughts and moved to the next topic she had for Bolton. "Sir, it's possible, is it not, for a full-time resident of the United States to have income but not be obliged to file a tax return?"

Bolton had heard Anita's opening statement to the jury, and knew where she was going. But he wasn't going to make it easy for her. "Generally speaking, you have to declare all your taxable income, and pay the appropriate tax on it."

"Sir, I don't think you answered my question. Is it possible for a U.S. person to have income but not be obliged to file a tax return?"

"Well if you earn less than $12,000 in a year, you don't need to file a return. Unless you're self-employed."

"Exactly. But let's set self-employment to one side for a moment. If you made, say, $10,000 in wages from W-2 employment last year, and you didn't have any self-employment or other income, would you have needed to file a federal tax return?"

"No. That's the law," responded Bolton.

"During the past five tax years, did Patrick Flaherty earn enough cash wages in any of those years that he would have been obliged to file a federal tax return to declare those wages as income?"

"I have no evidence that he earned wages. I don't know. But this case isn't about wages. It's about a self-employed person engaging in bartering." Bolton was an experienced trial witness, and he explained his answers whenever he felt he needed to.

Anita wanted her point to be clear, so she repeated her question. "Sir, to your knowledge, during the past five tax years, did Patrick Flaherty earn enough cash wages in any of those years that he would have been obliged to file a federal tax return declaring those wages as income?"

"Not to my knowledge, but this case isn't about wages."

"Just to be clear, your answer to my question is 'No'?"

"My answer was my answer."

"Well, sir, you seem very insistent that this is a case of a failure to report self-employment income. So, by all means, let's talk about that. Isn't it possible for a self-employed U.S. person to earn self-employment income, but not be obliged to report that income on a tax return, and not be obliged to pay tax on it?"

"Only if the self-employment income involved is less than $400 during the year," Bolton replied.

"*Exactly.* Consider, for example, college students who mow a few lawns in the summer, retired accountants who prepare tax returns for a few friends, musicians who play only a few times a year. Would you agree with me that there may be, let's say, thousands of people, at least, across the United States who earned self-employment income, but aren't required to pay self-employment tax because they didn't earn $400?"

"That's possible," conceded Bolton. She had asked him at least three questions in one, but he wasn't going to quibble. He found himself wishing that Farragut had objected to more of her questions.

Anita checked her notes and crossed off a couple of topics she had covered. On to the next. She wasn't afraid of a few moments of silence in the courtroom. She was examining a witness, so it was her courtroom. She understood the value of giving the jurors some time to let their thoughts wander.

"Sir, do you still have your notes of your undercover conversation with Mr. Bays on October 12, one of the conversations that you taped?"

"Let me dig them out," he said, shuffling through his file folder. "OK, got 'em."

"When you were asking Mr. Bays about the possibility of Mr. Flaherty's accepting goods in exchange for training services for your hypothetical dog, did Mr. Bays say to you, quote 'I wouldn't be optimistic,' close quote."

"Let me look at the full context," responded Bolton. He checked his transcript. "He did use the words, 'I wouldn't be optimistic.' In context, he was talking about the possibility of Mr. Flaherty's exchanging services for food, ammunition, or animal feed."

"Were you here for Mr. Farragut's opening statement?" Anita asked.

"Yes."

"Did you hear Mr. Farragut talk about Mr. Flaherty's 'calculated plan' to operate 'four business ventures' based on bartering?"

"Yes, and that's what Mr. Flaherty was doing," responded Bolton.

"Don't you find it odd, sir, that one of Mr. Flaherty's close friends, someone who knew him well, wasn't optimistic that Mr. Flaherty would enter into a bartering arrangement with you, if bartering was the basis of Mr. Flaherty's calculated business plan?"

"No, not necessarily. Maybe he had all the work he could handle, or maybe Mr. Bays's supposition was wrong."

"Why didn't you investigate further? Where was the rush?"

"In any investigation, I have to decide what leads to follow. I can't follow them all," replied Bolton.

"So when you heard evidence that was favorable to Mr. Flaherty – Mr. Bays's saying that he wasn't optimistic that Mr. Flaherty would do business with you – you declined to investigate further, but when you heard something you could construe as incriminating, like in Cousin Clem's, you immediately wrote it down, correct?" The point Anita was making was contained within the question, so Anita didn't care what answer he gave. She should have.

"Counsel, we're going to give you, and the jury, several days' worth of evidence of your client's guilt. Every investigation has facts or statements that don't quite fit. You weigh them, and you decide whether they undermine other conclusions you're reaching. I don't think Mr. Bays's opinion about what Mr. Flaherty was likely to do, or not do, if I had tried to hire him to train a dog, is an important fact in light of all of the other evidence in the case."

Anita was a little nonplussed, but determined to have the last word. "Did you go to the source while you were carefully planning your undercover effort? In other words, did you devise a business offer that you could make directly to Mr. Flaherty to see whether he'd barter with you?"

"No."

"So you had a 'suspect' – I'll call him that to be generous to you – and this suspect had a 'calculated plan' to run 'four business ventures' – again, I'm quoting Mr. Farragut – but you never tried to do some bartering business with this suspect who was supposedly running this big tax scam?"

"No."

"So what you bring this jury is evidence about my client's exchanging favors with friends, but it didn't occur to you that maybe the jurors would want to hear about what would have happened if you had tried to deal with Mr. Flaherty directly?"

"Objection, Your Honor," interjected Farragut. "If there were any facts being sought by that question, I can't find them. It's argument."

"Let me re-phrase, Your Honor. Mr. Bolton, didn't you want to know what would have happened if you had tried to do a bartering deal with Mr. Flaherty directly?"

"Same objection, Your Honor," said Farragut.

"Overruled," said Judge Martin. "The witness will answer the question."

"Well," said Bolton, "dealing directly with a suspect is always a last resort. We were able to build our case with other evidence."

"Who says dealing with the suspect is always a last resort?" Anita shot back, reasonably confident that there wasn't some relevant bullet point in an investigative field manual somewhere.

"Well, that's been my experience," replied Bolton.

"Oh, we're back to your experience," said Anita. "Is it your experience that the IRS Criminal Investigation Division refrains from dealing directly with suspects in most of its investigations that involve bartering?" She knew she had him, finally.

The same realization dawned slowly on Bolton. He thought for almost 20 seconds, an eternity in a courtroom. If he answered any form of "yes," she would ask him what those investigations were, and he wouldn't be able to name any. He gave the only answer he could, and he would let the chips fall where they would.

"This is the first IRS-CID case of which I'm aware that involves bartering."

Not a perfect answer, but an answer Anita thought was good enough. Now the jurors, like everyone else involved in this shabby excuse for a federal criminal case, knew – or at least suspected -- that Patrick Flaherty was just about the unluckiest son of a bitch who was ever hauled into a federal courtroom.

"Thank you, sir," said Anita. "Was Detmer Contracting letting Patrick Flaherty take whatever he wanted from the construction debris he was driving to the Sheridan City Landfill?"

"Yes, I believe so."

"Detmer Contracting was throwing the materials away?"

"Yes," replied Bolton, not knowing where the questioning was going.

"Wouldn't you agree with me then, that Detmer Contracting had already concluded, and declared, that the debris had no value to Detmer Contracting?"

"Yes."

"But, if I understand you correctly, you're also saying the construction debris was *a part* of this supposed bartering deal, correct?"

"Yes."

"But doesn't the regulation on which you're relying – and that, I believe, would be Section 1.62-2 of the Treasury regulations – only apply to exchanges of labor for property that has a fair market value?"

"Yes, I believe that's correct."

"So which is it, sir? Are you making the debris a part of your case, or not?"

"I think it is. It was part of the agreement, I believe."

Anita wanted there to be as much confusion as possible about where the construction debris fit into the case as a whole. Confusion was doubt, and lots of confusion was, perhaps, reasonable doubt. The prosecution's principal witness had just mixed up property that has a fair market value – like fencing – with property that has no market value at all. It wasn't her job to help the prosecution clarify things for the jury. She pressed on.

"Do you have trash collection where you live in Cheyenne?"

"Yes."

"Objection, Your Honor," said Farragut.

"The witness has already answered the question," said the judge.

"Do you have trash pickers in Cheyenne?"

"Objection, Your Honor," said Farragut.

"I'll connect, Your Honor. The relevance will be clear," replied Anita.

"All right, but get to the point," said the judge.

"Do you have trash pickers in Cheyenne?"

"Yes, we do," replied Bolton.

"When trash pickers take things out of your trash, do you let them?"

The judge started to smile, but stifled it.

"Yes."

"Then, by your standards, you've entered into a bartering exchange with your trash pickers, have you not?"

Bolton hesitated. Finally, he said, "No, I've never talked to them."

"You haven't reached a meeting of the minds, correct?"

"No, we haven't."

That was a good answer for the defense.

"Why did you pretend to be an accountant when you were talking to Patrick Flaherty at Cousin Clem's?"

"Because I find that people want to talk to an accountant about their taxes. It's an effective undercover identity."

"What is the average hourly billing rate for a Certified Public Accountant in Wyoming?"

"I don't know," said Bolton.

"Well, that's pretty astonishing, because what do you do when a suspect, or a target, or whatever you call them, asks you, in your role as an accountant, how much do you charge?"

"That's never happened."

"It's happening now. If you were undercover, and I told you I was interested in hiring you and asked for your hourly rate, what would you tell me?"

"Objection, Your Honor, can we see you at sidebar?" said Farragut.

"Your Honor, respectfully, we don't need a sidebar," replied Anita. "I am gathering facts about the witness's claim to have been posing as an accountant."

"I'll see counsel at sidebar," said the judge.

When counsel arrived at the bench, Farragut came to the point. "Your Honor, it's a hypothetical question, with no relationship to the facts of this case. The witness didn't claim that he discussed fees with the defendant."

"Your Honor," replied Anita, "I'm not obliged to accept the witness's statement that he posed as an accountant when he spoke with Mr. Flaherty. His credibility is always at issue. If he can't tell me how he would have answered a question about his rates, then I will argue to the jury that he wouldn't have dared to pose as an accountant in his dealings with Mr. Flaherty."

"The objection is overruled," said the judge.

Farragut and Renfro returned to their counsel table, and Anita walked back to the lectern. "Sir, if you were undercover, and I told you I was interested in hiring you as an accountant, and asked for your hourly rate, what would you tell me?" continued Anita.

"I would tell you $100 per hour."

"In your undercover role, did you suggest to the defendant that he could pay you to research whether he was obliged to file a tax return?"

"No, I wouldn't have done that," replied Bolton.

"Did you tell him he should strongly consider filing a tax return?"

"No."

Anita took a breath, and stared at Bolton. Suddenly, she was seething. "Just so we're clear, sir," Anita began. "Just so we're clear. You didn't feel any need to advise this young man that you thought he should file a tax return, but you had no compunction about arresting him four months later for *not* filing a tax return, is that correct?"

Bolton didn't know what to say. Farragut hadn't objected. The jury and the judge were waiting for his answer. "That's correct," he said. The kid was guilty, he thought. There was no reason to apologize for locking him up.

"No further questions, Your Honor." Anita returned to her seat. She had done the best she could.

Farragut went back to the lectern for re-direct. "Special Agent Bolton, do you normally advise the targets of your undercover investigations, before you arrest them, that they're breaking the law?"

"No, of course not. My job is to investigate the possibility of illegal conduct, and to bring charges where they're appropriate. It's not my job to give a suspect the chance to cover up incriminating evidence before my investigation is done."

"Counsel suggested that you should have told the defendant about his obligation to file tax returns. Hadn't the defendant already told you that he didn't want to know whether he owed taxes?"

Bolton said, "Yes." Anita said, "Objection." "Overruled," said Judge Martin.

"I have no further questions of this witness, Your Honor," said Farragut.

"We'll take our lunch break," said the judge. "Members of the jury, be back in the jury room by 2:00, and we'll work for just a while this afternoon. Don't discuss the case with each other. See you at 2:00."

CHAPTER 69

"Your Honor," said Farragut, "the government calls Special Agent Karl Lawless."

Lawless made his way to the witness stand and was sworn in by the Deputy Clerk. Farragut tended to schedule his less important witnesses for the 2:00 hour. The jurors were typically subject to post-prandial narcolepsy, and everyone else in the courtroom was a little tired. Farragut used the 2:00 witness to check some boxes, *i.e.*, prove some facts he had to prove that weren't controverted very much by the defense.

"Special Agent Lawless, please state your full name, your position with the United States Government, and your present duty assignment," said Farragut.

"My name is Karl Lawless. I am a Special Agent with the Criminal Investigation Division of the Internal Revenue Service, assigned to the field office in Cheyenne, Wyoming."

Farragut went quickly through Lawless's education and training, and then led his witness through the preparations he had made with Bolton to work undercover in Coolidge, including the plans to go to Cousin Clem's and St. Ann's. Lawless had never testified in a jury trial before, but he had done well in prep sessions, and Farragut wasn't worried about how he would hold up. The facts about which he would testify just weren't that complicated. Farragut took his witness to Cousin Clem's on Friday, October 9.

"Special Agent Lawless, what time was it when you arrived in Cousin Clem's?"

"It was 6:00 in the evening."

"What did you observe when you entered the establishment?"

"It's a big room, with a full bar at the back and a lot of room for tables. There was a small stage in the back right corner as you come in the door, and there was a musician playing as I entered."

"Do you see that musician in court today?" asked Farragut.

"That was the defendant, Patrick Michael Flaherty," responded Lawless, pointing at Patrick.

"Let the record reflect that the witness has identified the defendant," said Farragut. "Was the room crowded, noisy that night?"

"It was," replied Lawless. "I stood and listened to the music for a minute, and then I found a place to stand at the bar, between two barstools."

"What happened next?"

"I was waited on by a gentleman wearing a shirt that said 'Clem' on it, C-L-E-M, who I had been told was the owner, Clement Labrecque. I ordered a beer, and told Mr. Labrecque that I liked the music. I asked him what the singer's name was, and he told me Patrick Flaherty. I also recall that he called Mr. Flaherty a 'human jukebox.' At that point, I told Mr. Labrecque that I was from Sheridan, and that my friends and I might be interested in hiring Mr. Flaherty for a private party; did he think Mr. Flaherty might be interested? He said he didn't know. I asked him whether he thought Mr. Flaherty would be expensive." Lawless paused there, per his prep.

"How did Mr. Labrecque respond to that question?" asked Farragut.

"He said that he was certain that the defendant, uh, Mr. Flaherty, wouldn't accept money for playing music."

"What did you say in response to that?"

"I told Mr. Labrecque that my friend and I would be happy to provide food and drinks in exchange for Mr. Flaherty playing music at our party. I then asked Mr. Labrecque whether Cousin Clem's provided Mr. Flaherty with food and drinks in exchange for music. The way I put it, I said, 'Do you comp him with food or beer when he plays?" Lawless paused again.

"How did Mr. Labrecque respond to your question?"

"He said, 'All our musicians eat and drink for free while they're playing.'"

"Did you leave the bar at that point?" asked Farragut.

"Not long after, yes."

"Special Agent Lawless, I'd like to turn your attention to Saturday evening, October 10 of last year. Did you go to Mass at St. Ann's Catholic Church in Coolidge, and then to the Hospitality Supper afterwards?" The question, technically, was leading – presenting facts not yet in the record, and suggesting the answer – but most judges will permit leading questions to facilitate the presentation of non-controversial parts of a party's narrative.

"Yes, I did."

"Describe, please, what you did and what you observed at St. Ann's that evening?"

"I'm a Catholic, so I went to Mass at 5:00. At the end of Mass, there was an announcement that everyone was invited to go over to St. Ann's Parish Hall for Hospitality Supper. The Parish Hall is very close to the church itself. I entered the Parish Hall and I asked the greeter if I could speak to the person who arranged and accepted sponsorships for Masses. In the Catholic tradition, you can pay a fairly nominal amount as a contribution to the Church, and a Mass will be celebrated in the name of someone who has died, usually a family member or a loved one. The greeter told me that I should speak with Mavis D'Antonio, and pointed Ms. D'Antonio out to me. Coincidentally, she was talking to the defendant at that time. I waited until that conversation was over, and then I had a brief conversation with Ms. D'Antonio and confirmed that she was the person identified as the Parish administrator on St. Ann's website."

"What happened after that?" asked Farragut.

"I had some dinner, and I chatted with a couple of parishioners while I ate. At the end of the dinner, I observed the defendant, Patrick Michael Flaherty, place four or five Styrofoam containers of cooked food in a knapsack that he was carrying, as well as bread and desserts. Mr. Flaherty left the Parish Hall with the knapsack just after he did that."

"Your witness," said Farragut to Anita, and he sat down.

CHAPTER 70

There was not much Anita was going to be able to do to challenge the witness's testimony. The facts were probably as he described them. But criminal defense is about giving the jurors opportunities to find reasonable doubt if they otherwise like your client and his case.

"Sir, before you left Cousin Clem's, did you write down the statement that Mr. Labrecque supposedly made to you about giving food and drink to musicians?"

"No, I wrote it down in the parking lot afterward," replied Lawless.

"May I see your handwritten notes?"

"No, it's our practice to destroy those notes when we prepare our typed contact summary."

"You destroyed your original notes? Did I hear that correctly?"

"Yes."

Anita knew what the practice was in IRS-CID, not to mention the FBI. But the jurors presumably did not. She had made her point.

"During your *numerous* criminal investigations of bartering transactions, did you ever run across a bar or a restaurant that did *not* provide its musicians with free food and drinks on the evenings they were playing?"

Farragut thought about objecting – Lawless hadn't testified that he'd been involved in numerous bartering investigations.

Lawless didn't know where this was going. He gave the safest answer he could. "No."

"Maybe my question shouldn't have assumed that you've been involved in numerous criminal investigations of bartering investigations. I apologize. How many criminal investigations involving bartering have you been involved in, other than this one?"

"Objection, Your Honor," said Farragut. "Relevance."

"I allowed Agent Bolton to testify on this subject," said Judge Martin. "I think the door's been opened, at least a little bit. Overruled."

"Again, sir, how many criminal investigations involving bartering have you been involved in, other than this one?"

"None," replied Lawless.

"Did you hear anyone at St. Ann's Parish talking to Patrick Flaherty about the work he supposedly would be required to do at the Parish in exchange for free food from Hospitality Supper?"

"No."

"The IRS-CID can issue subpoenas compelling the production of documents, can it not?"

"Yes."

"Well, did you subpoena any written agreements between Patrick Flaherty and St. Ann's memorializing their supposed understanding that Patrick would do work in exchange for food?"

"No."

"Why not?"

"Well, we didn't have any reason to believe there was a written agreement."

"Why not?"

"I don't know. I guess because there would have been no reason to put it in writing."

"Don't guess. Why did you believe there was no written bartering agreement?"

"Because there was no reason to put it in writing."

"Do you usually stop your tax investigations when you have some evidence of an unlawful agreement, but before you've subpoenaed documents that might be helpful?"

"I don't know, I can't generalize. Every case is different."

"Do you know what an IRS Form 990 is?" asked Anita.

"I'm not sure," said Lawless, "but I believe it's the annual tax return that a church files, even though they usually don't have any taxable income. That's outside of what we usually do in CID."

"Right, that's what a Form 990 is. Didn't it occur to you to obtain St. Ann's Form 990's for the years at issue, and the ledgers and worksheets supporting them, to see whether they had reported the value of the food they transferred to Mr. Flaherty as an organizational expense?"

"No."

"I take it that you didn't believe St. Ann's thought the food being transferred was an expense, correct? Otherwise you would obviously have obtained their records?"

"I don't know what officials at St. Ann's believed. We were focused on the bartering scheme being operated by the defendant," replied Lawless.

"You were investigating a supposed two-sided bartering agreement and *you didn't care* how one of the parties to the supposed agreement viewed it?"

"Correct," replied Lawless.

"You didn't care whether St. Ann's believed the food was payment for services?"

"I didn't personally, no."

Farragut and Renfro sat stone-faced. Each of them was thinking that it's never a good idea to call a young agent as a witness before he's ready to handle it.

"I have no further questions for this witness," said Anita.

"Redirect?" inquired Judge Martin.

"No, Your Honor," replied AUSA Farragut. Get Special Agent Lawless off the witness stand as quickly as possible.

"Members of the jury," said Judge Martin, "we will conclude testimony for the day. Please don't discuss the case among yourselves, either this afternoon or tomorrow morning when you arrive. If you see any mention of this case in the newspaper, or online, or on TV or radio, please put down the paper or turn off your computer, or your TV, or your radio. We want everything that you hear about the facts of this case to be presented here in court. That's very important. Thanks for your attention today. We'll see you tomorrow."

As the jury filed out, Judge Martin said, "Counsel, wait for a minute." When the door to the jury room closed, he said, "I thought it made sense to wrap up a little early today. The jurors seemed a little tired. Who do we have tomorrow?"

"Your Honor," replied Farragut, "our first witness tomorrow will be Ms. Mavis D'Antonio, Parish administrator at St. Ann's. She'll be followed by Clement Labrecque, the owner of Cousin Clem's. After that, we'll have Father David Hernandez from St. Ann's Parish. Maybe a witness from the landfill, if we have time. And we may get to Harry Detmer of Detmer Contracting; maybe Robert Bays of Bays Feeds.

"After the fact witnesses, we'll hear from Dr. Morris Tindle," he continued. "Dr. Tindle will testify as the government's tax consequences expert. He'll talk about a taxpayer's filing obligations, the thresholds for when a return has to be filed, the effect of the regulations governing bartering, the fair market value of certain property, and some related matters, as detailed in his expert report. You have a copy of his report in your evidence binder."

"Have all the grand jury materials for all grand jury witnesses been provided, or will we need to do that after direct examination for each witness?" asked the judge.

"The defense has everything, Your Honor," replied Farragut.

"OK, we'll see you tomorrow morning at 9:30."

CHAPTER 71

Tania Teagarden was standing in front of the courthouse on Wolcott Street, looking confidently into the camera. "Today, in a federal courtroom in Casper, Wyoming, the federal government began its case against Patrick Michael Flaherty, a resident of Wyoming, and the alleged architect of an ingenious tax scam. The prosecution has set out to prove that the defendant was engaged in a calculated plan to operate four business ventures, avoiding the use of cash and bank accounts that could be traced by the government. His technique? Elaborate and continuous bartering. Witnesses for the government described how the defendant entered into a series of bartering arrangements by which he obtained food, free rent, construction materials, and food for his farm animals, all in exchange for services provided by the defendant. Here's the rub, according to the government. Unlike you and me, the defendant didn't pay a dime in taxes, and did not even file tax returns, even though, according to the government, he should have been paying substantial amounts into the Social Security system, so-called self-employment taxes. The government also presented evidence that the defendant harbors a deep-seated resentment for agencies of the federal government, and, as we previously reported, the defendant seems to have adopted the dress and attitudes of various anti-governmental private militia groups who have been active recently in Wyoming. The defendant has pleaded 'not guilty.' Testimony will continue tomorrow. This is Tania Teagarden, reporting."

CHAPTER 72

"Good morning, Your Honor. At this time, the government calls Ms. Mavis D'Antonio."

Mavis was standing in the hallway outside the courtroom when the Deputy Clerk came to summon her. She stepped into a silent and packed courtroom, with every eye in the room on her as she made her way up the side aisle toward the witness stand. The jurors, seated to her left in the jury box as she walked past them, stared at her as she stepped up to the witness stand. She turned into the box and began to sit, with the jurors, all twelve of them, now to her right.

"Please remain standing," said the Deputy Clerk, sternly and abruptly.

Mavis was startled, and locked her knees upright. Like a Methodist in a Catholic church for the first time, she was oblivious to the rules governing standing and sitting. All of a sudden, she knew how they felt.

"Administer the oath, please," said the judge.

The Deputy Clerk looked at Mavis. "Raise your right hand. Do you swear or affirm that the testimony you are about to give in this matter will be the truth, the whole truth, and nothing but the truth, so help you God?"

"Yes."

"You may be seated."

"Your Honor, may we see you at sidebar?" asked AUSA Farragut.

The judge threw him a puzzled look. "I'll see counsel."

Anita and the prosecutors made their way around their respective tables, across the well of the courtroom, and over to the side of the judge's bench facing away from the jury.

Farragut explained what he wanted. "Your Honor, each of the government's next five witnesses is a friend of the defendant, Mr. Flaherty. As the discovery provided to the defendant makes clear, each of the five witnesses hesitated, in the grand jury, to provide any information helpful to the government. We elicited enough testimony to support the Superseding Indictment, but it was like pulling teeth. In addition, every one of the five witnesses refused to participate in a witness prep session with us immediately before trial. I assume they have prepared with Ms. Boyle. I've asked for a sidebar before any of the five witnesses begins to testify, to make a global request to treat each of the five witnesses as hostile under Rule 611(c)(2), so that I can question them as of cross-examination, and ask leading questions. I thought this procedure -- asking for a sidebar once, in advance -- would make more sense than repeating the application five times."

"Ms. Boyle?" asked the judge, turning to Anita.

"Your Honor, the defendant opposes the application. It was the government's decision to build its case on the testimony of these five witnesses, and . . ."

"But that's often true in federal trials," said the judge, interrupting. "You have possible co-conspirators, you have relatives of the defendant, you have current prisoners, all kinds of people who would rather not cooperate with the government, and it's almost more common than not for the government to have to present most of its case 'as of cross.' Why should I treat this circumstance differently?"

"Because these witnesses cooperated fully, Your Honor," replied Anita. "Every one appeared voluntarily at the grand jury, and the government must have liked what it heard from them about bartering transactions, because it has built its case on their anticipated testimony. The government hasn't given you enough reason at this point to invoke Rule 611(c)(2). They don't know that the witnesses are hostile, or that they're identified with the defendant. And, more important, the jury needs to hear about these bartering '*agreements*'" – she provided the quotation marks with her inflection – "in the witnesses' own words. Mr. Farragut isn't here to testify; but if he's permitted, in essence, to restrict the witnesses to 'yes' and 'no,' we're going to hear the government's theories about barter transactions, and not the witnesses' descriptions of what they believed they were doing."

Judge Martin adjusted his glasses. "I'm going to permit Mr. Farragut to proceed by way of leading questions under Rule 611(c)(2), with each of the next five witnesses. I've reviewed a lot of the grand jury testimony, or at least the parts included in the government's evidence binder, and I agree with Mr. Farragut's characterizations of the difficulties he had before the grand jury in eliciting relevant testimony. Also, I think it's noteworthy that he hasn't been able to interview most of his own witnesses. So I'm going to allow questioning under Rule 611(c)(2) as to all five witnesses, but with a word of caution. Mr. Farragut, if I get the sense that we're hearing too much from you, and not enough from the witnesses, I'm going to make you do it the hard way. I don't want to hear any speeches in the guise of questions. Also, while we're on the subject of grand jury testimony, it's my practice – Ms. Boyle, I know you haven't appeared before me before, so I'm letting you know, as well – to refer to the grand jury as a 'pretrial proceeding.' That's easier than explaining the entire grand jury process to the jury. OK, I've ruled. Mr. Farragut, you may proceed." He turned his chair back to the center of the bench as Anita returned to explain the ruling to Patrick. AUSA Farragut walked over to stand at the lectern, beside his counsel table.

"Ms. D'Antonio, thank you for coming today. My name is Jack Farragut, and I represent the United States of America."

Mavis nodded slightly. The jurors watched her with interest.

"Ms. D'Antonio, where do you live?"

"Coolidge, Wyoming."

"Where do you work, ma'am?"

"At St. Ann's Roman Catholic Church in Coolidge."

"What is your job at St. Ann's?"

"I'm the Parish Administrator. I keep the books and run the business of the church, so to speak."

"How long have you worked in that job?"

"Twenty years. Twenty-one years in September."

"Is Father David Hernandez currently the pastor at St. Ann's?"

"Yes, Father Hernandez is our Parish priest."

"Do you know the defendant, Patrick Flaherty?"

Mavis's eyes welled up. "Yes, I do."

"For how long?"

"For seven years."

"Would you look around the courtroom please, and tell the jury whether you see him here."

"Objection, Your Honor." Anita was on her feet, clearly angry. "Identification is not an issue in this case. Both case agents have already identified the defendant. And the defendant will stipulate that Ms. D'Antonio knows Mr. Flaherty and would identify him."

"Your Honor, the government always has the right to prove identity in a criminal case, and we want to do that through a witness who has known the defendant for several years."

Patrick felt himself blush with shame, and hoped neither the jurors nor his parents saw it.

"Overruled. The witness will answer the question."

An angry tear fell out of Mavis's left eye. "Mr. Flaherty is sitting at the table over there with Ms. Boyle," she said.

"Your Honor, let the record reflect that the witness has identified the defendant, Patrick Michael Flaherty," said Farragut. There he is, members of the jury, that's the thug who shot up the bank.

"So noted," said the judge.

"Ms. D'Antonio, did you meet with Ms. Boyle, counsel for the defendant, to discuss the fact that your testimony was going to be required at this trial, and to prepare for what to expect?"

"Yes."

"Was I present at that meeting?"

"No."

"Did I invite you to meet with me before trial, to talk informally about your testimony?"

"Yes, you did."

"Now, I understand you had a perfect right to refuse that invitation" – Farragut was forestalling an objection – "but did you refuse to meet with me?"

"Yes."

The jurors probably didn't blame her, but they understood that Farragut would have to be more aggressive with his questioning than would otherwise have been necessary.

"Ms. D'Antonio, does St. Ann's hold what it calls a 'Hospitality Supper' after most Saturday evening Masses?" asked Farragut.

"Yes."

"The Hospitality Supper is normally held in the Parish Hall, correct?"

"Yes."

"All members of the parish are welcome to attend the Hospitality Supper, correct?"

"Yes."

"But it's not open to the public, is that right?"

"We don't advertise it as open to the public, so I suppose that's right. But occasionally non-parishioners drop by, and no one would ever say anything about it."

"When you have left-over food after a Hospitality Supper, do you store some of it in a big refrigerator, and then later take it over to the food kitchen at Sunrise Evangelical Church?" he asked.

"Yes."

"So if there are left-overs, they belong to St. Ann's, and St. Ann's decides what happens to them, correct?"

"Yes, I guess you could say that, but if somebody made something for the supper and wanted their leftover back, we'd give it to them. That happens every once in a while."

"But isn't it true that the food prepared by parishioners is treated as being donated to St. Ann's? Don't you often initial their Albertson's receipts to acknowledge you received the items shown on the receipt, so that the parishioners can then deduct the amount from their taxes?"

"Yes."

"And you often give some of the leftover food to the defendant, Patrick Michael Flaherty, correct?

"Yes."

"So when St. Ann's gives food to Patrick Flaherty, that food is St. Ann's to give, is it not?

"Yes."

"You don't consider it as belonging to the person who made it?"

"I guess not, no."

Farragut turned away from his lectern to pick up a piece of paper from his counsel table. "Ms. D'Antonio, I'll get back to the food in a moment, but first I want to explore another subject with you." He cleared his throat. "Does Patrick Michael Flaherty perform maintenance work on church property?"

"Yes, sometimes."

"Would you say he comes over to do work at St. Ann's most weeks?"

"Yes."

"Has Mr. Flaherty done painting for St. Ann's?"

"Yes."

"Floor cleaning and polishing?"

"Yes."

"Light carpentry – hammers, nails, drills and saws?"

"Yes."

"Landscaping and tree work?"

"Yes."

"How many hours is he usually there when he works?"

"I'm not sure."

"Do you recall testifying at a pretrial proceeding that it was usually two and half, to three and a half hours at a time, and usually twice a week?"

"Yes."

"Do you stand by that testimony?"

"Yes."

Farragut picked up another file. "Let's go back to the Hospitality Suppers. Were there usually leftovers after a Hospitality Supper?"

"Yes, almost always."

"Why?"

"Well, because most of the prepared food – the main dishes and the vegetables – are made by parishioners, and I think everybody who makes food figures their dish might be the most popular that week, and they keep in mind there will usually be about forty people there. So people make large dishes, and a lot is usually left over."

"How do you decide who makes what?"

"There's an app called 'pot-luck-hub' that we use – it's at potluckhub.com. There's a lot of that kind of app out there, that's just the one we use. The app has a list of what's needed that week, and people sign up to provide it, and that lets everyone else know what they're going to bring. We usually like to have three main courses with meat, and at least one vegetarian dish. And then we have vegetables, salads and desserts. The Parish provides the refrigerators, a couple of microwaves and warming trays, and the drinks. But the app doesn't really control portions, or the size of the dishes involved, so we always have too much food."

"You testified earlier that the Sunrise Evangelical Church food kitchen gets a lot of the leftovers, correct?"

"Yes."

"How does Sunrise handle that food?"

"They serve it to poor families on site, or by a meals-on-wheels arrangement. Our poor families in Coolidge are not very visible, but they're there, and Sunrise does a very good job of getting food to them quietly and confidentially."

"Does the defendant, Mr. Flaherty, usually take leftovers home with him?"

"Yes."

"Does Mr. Flaherty get 'first cut,' or 'first dibs,' as it were, of the leftovers, and then what remains goes to Sunrise?"

"Yes, I guess you could say that. But I think more goes to Sunrise than to Patrick. It depends on how much food is left."

"Is Mr. Flaherty usually at Saturday evening Mass?"

"Yes, pretty much always. Attendance at a weekly Mass is a holy obligation for Roman Catholics. Patrick usually comes on Saturday evening."

"Is there any individual, other than Mr. Flaherty, who consistently takes leftovers home from Hospitality Supper?"

Mavis thought for a minute. "No, not really. We don't usually advertise the leftovers at the end of the supper, because we know we're going to be delivering food to the food kitchen at Sunrise. I guess every once in a while someone will pack a doggy bag -- it seems to me I've probably seen that from time to time in twenty years – but if so, I couldn't tell you who it was."

"How much food does Mr. Flaherty ordinarily take home with him?"

"Usually three or four meals, I would say. Meat from each of the meat dishes, some vegetables, some bread. And then some dessert, if it's cake or cookies, and readily transportable. We put it in Styrofoam containers for him, like you get at restaurants, and he'll usually put five or six of those containers, and maybe some bread in a plastic bag. It all goes into his knapsack."

"Your Honor, will you see counsel at sidebar?" requested Farragut.

"Sure, I'll see counsel."

Farragut and Anita traveled back to the bench. "Your Honor, Ms. Boyle and I have agreed to a stipulation that will shorten the trial a little bit. The government was going to call Edward Catton, a micro-economist specializing in the food industry. Professor Catton was going to provide expert testimony concerning the value of food that Mr. Flaherty took home from his church in each of the years in the indictment. Ms. Boyle has a copy of his expert report, and it's in the Court's evidence binder as well. The parties were going to argue about whether to use a restaurant metric, or a cooked-at-home metric, and about some other food-related valuation issues. Finally, Ms. Boyle and I agreed that neither side is going to benefit, particularly, from forcing the jury to listen to that testimony for half a day. So, we've reached a stipulation, subject to the Court's approval, that the fair market value of the food that Mr. Flaherty took home from St. Ann's in each of the years in question was $1,500."

"Ms. Boyle?" asked the judge.

"So stipulated, Your Honor," said Anita

"OK, I'll advise the jury of the stipulation," said the judge. Farragut and Anita went back to their seats, and the judge turned toward the jury.

"Members of the jury, the prosecution and the defense have reached a stipulation, that is, an agreement, that the value of the food that the defendant took home from his church in each of the years covered by the indictment was one thousand five hundred dollars. I want to commend counsel for reaching that stipulation, because it will save us all from listening to half a day of expert testimony that, frankly, would have been pretty dull. A stipulation is an agreement between the parties that a certain fact will be deemed proven and established – in this circumstance, the value of the food at issue -- and you won't have to determine that fact later when you go out to deliberate. You'll just take it as a given, so to speak, that the food in question was worth $1,500 per year. Mr. Farragut, you may proceed."

"Ms. D'Antonio, was St. Ann's obliged to give food to the defendant?" asked Farragut.

"I don't think so, no."

"Do you recall testifying under oath at a pretrial proceeding in this case, and I'm quoting, 'With all the work that Patrick did for St. Ann's in the last five years, it would have been morally wrong not to share the Hospitality Dinner leftovers with him,' close quote?"

"I'm surprised, in retrospect, that I said it that way, but yes, I recall saying it."

"Was there any other *particular* individual that had earned that status? That is, was there anyone else who, if you hadn't provided food to him or her, you would have been doing them wrong?"

"No, no one in particular."

"Was St. Ann's providing food to Patrick Flaherty in significant part because he provided labor to help maintain the parish property?"

Mavis hesitated. "Could you repeat the question, please?"

"Was St. Ann's providing food to Patrick Flaherty in significant part because he provided labor to help maintain the parish property?"

"Yes, but I think we would have given him the food anyway, even if he hadn't done all that work. He needed the nourishment, and giving him food would have been the Christian thing to do."

"You've already told us that no individuals other than Mr. Flaherty routinely took food home; and that leftovers were basically earmarked for the food kitchen in town; and that the Hospitality Supper wasn't open to the public, correct?"

"Yes."

"Isn't it possible that if Mr. Flaherty had appeared at Hospitality Supper but was otherwise uninvolved in Parish life, and if he had repeatedly asked to take food home with him, that you might have said, 'If we do it for you, we'd have to do it for everyone, so we can't; but it's going to be available down at the food kitchen at Sunrise Evangelical, and you can get it there?"

Almost despite herself, Mavis saw the force of the argument, and didn't like where the questioning was going. "I don't know what we would have said – I can't put myself in that place five years ago and try to tell you what we might have said to a different Patrick Flaherty."

"Exactly," he said. "Your understanding with Mr. Flaherty was unique, wouldn't you say?"

Mavis was trying to listen carefully, but this was all hard. She missed the word "understanding." "Yes, unique is probably the best word," she replied.

"Ms. D'Antonio," Farragut continued, "the defendant has agreed, through his counsel, that the annual value of the food he took home from Hospitality Supper was $1,500. Would you agree that Mr. Flaherty was providing handyman services to the Parish throughout the five-year period that were worth at least $1,500 per year to the Parish?"

"Mr. Farragut, if we could have purchased what Patrick gave us in each of the last five years for only $1,500 per year, the Bishop would have given us a medal."

The witness hadn't answered the question directly, but it was time to shift gears. "Aren't there members of the parish who are very poor, with few or almost no means?"

"Yes."

"Do you give them a special invitation to Hospitality Supper, so that you can send them home with leftovers when it's over?"

Mavis gulped. During the prep sessions with Anita, no one had seen that question coming. "No, we don't," she conceded.

"That's all I have for this witness Your Honor." AUSA Farragut sat down.

"Ms. Boyle, you may inquire," said the judge.

CHAPTER 73

Anita rose from her chair briskly, signaling to the jury that she was eager to hear what Mavis had to say. She put her notes on the lectern and rested her eyes on Mavis.

"Ms. D'Antonio, you told Mr. Farragut that you met with me before trial to talk about your testimony. When did I meet with you?"

"Wednesday, last week."

"Did I tell you what to say when you took the witness stand?"

"Yes, you did."

Anita paused, and raised an eyebrow, showing mild surprise.

"What did I tell you to say?"

The jury was all ears.

"The truth," said Mavis.

The jury relaxed. It was an old trick, designed to defuse a suggestion that the party with sole access to a witness was using that access to fabricate testimony. It was an old trick because it usually worked.

"Ms. D'Antonio, did St. Ann's enter into a written barter agreement with Mr. Flaherty that St. Ann's would give him food in exchange for work around the parish?"

"No."

"Did you shake hands with Mr. Flaherty, on behalf of St. Ann's, to confirm to him that St. Ann's would give him food in exchange for work around the parish?"

"No."

"Did you and Mr. Flaherty reach a verbal agreement with each other that St. Ann's would give him food in exchange for work around the parish?"

"Objection!" The prosecutor was on his feet. "Your Honor, the question asks the witness for a legal conclusion."

"A verbal exchange about an agreement -- or the lack of one -- is just a fact, Your Honor, like any other fact," responded Anita.

"I'll sustain the objection."

Anita thought the ruling was wrong. Every judge makes some mistakes during a trial, and the bad ones make a lot of mistakes. Judge Martin was better than most. She tried another tack.

"Ms. D'Antonio, did you say to Mr. Flaherty, in words or substance, 'Patrick, St. Ann's will give you food if you work around the parish?'"

"Same objection Your Honor."

"Overruled," said the judge. "The witness may answer."

"No."

"Did Patrick Flaherty say to you, in words or substance, 'I'll do work around the parish if you give me food from Hospitality Supper?'"

"No."

"You testified in a pretrial proceeding that it would have been wrong not to give food to Mr. Flaherty, considering all the work he did for the Parish. Why do you believe that?"

"I'm not sure I do believe it."

The answer caught Anita by surprise. Mavis was "her" witness, and you never wanted your witness to disavow earlier testimony unless it was absolutely necessary. Disavowal requires a lot of explaining, and when you're explaining, you're losing. Not to mention the risk of a perjury charge. Anita had to trust that Mavis was not digging a hole for herself, and for Patrick. "Why do you say that?"

Mavis was emotional. "Because lots of parishioners contribute extraordinary amounts of time to the church, and we don't give them rewards for it. God does. So when I said it would have been morally wrong, I'm not even sure what I meant. The first time, before trial, I was responding to a question from Mr. Farragut, and -- it's really hard to do this. You lawyers want 'yeses' and 'noes,' and you can seize on any little word." She paused, and thought. "I can tell you what I think I meant to say. Patrick isn't a saint, but he was living *like* a saint, in voluntary poverty, however he managed to get to that point. He was poor. He still is. And I just meant that a church, as a community, is morally obligated to help those who need it, *and* those who are deserving of help because of their good works. Patrick deserved the help for both reasons."

Anita realized that she had stumbled into the best testimony that Mavis could possibly have offered. "I have no further questions, Your Honor."

"Any redirect, Mr. Farragut?" asked the judge.

"Yes, Your Honor." Farragut resumed the lectern.

"Ms. D'Antonio, were you aware that Mr. Flaherty told Special Agent Bolton, 'I do handyman work at the church and at the rectory. You have to give back. It's part of the deal.'"

"I'm not sure whether I heard about that statement; I might have, I just don't recall."

"Do you believe that Mr. Flaherty intended to help the church when he was doing maintenance work?"

"Yes, I do."

"And did St. Ann's intend to help Mr. Flaherty when it gave him food?"

"Yes."

"And you said, just a minute ago, that he was deserving of the help because of his good works, correct?"

"Well . . ." Mavis wondered whether she had said it that way.

"Would you like me to have the court reporter read back your testimony? My recollection, and the jury and the judge will have their own, was that you testified that he was 'deserving of help because of his good works.' That was your testimony, was it not?"

"Well, yes."

"No further questions, Your Honor," said Farragut, and Mavis was excused.

CHAPTER 74

"Mr. Farragut, call your next witness," said the judge.

"Your Honor, the government calls Mr. Clement Labrecque."

Clem was escorted in from the hallway, and stood by the witness box. "Do you swear or affirm that the testimony you are about to give in this matter will be the truth, the whole truth, and nothing but the truth, so help you God?"

"I do," said Clem.

"You may be seated," said the Deputy Clerk.

"Mr. Labrecque, my name is Jack Farragut, and I represent the United States of America in this case. Thank you for coming down to Casper to testify. Let me begin by asking you for some background information. Where do you live?"

"In Coolidge, Wyoming," replied Clem.

"How long have you lived there?"

"For thirty years, now."

"Do you own a bar and restaurant in Coolidge called 'Cousin Clem's?'"

"Yes, with my wife, Claire. We're co-owners."

"How long have you owned Cousin Clem's?"

"Same length of time, thirty years."

"Do you know the defendant, Patrick Flaherty?" Farragut asked, pointing at Patrick.

"Yes, very well."

"How do you know him?"

"Patrick is a regular customer at Cousin Clem's."

"How long have you known him?"

"About seven years I think; since he started living in Coolidge."

"You said that Mr. Flaherty is a customer. Isn't it true he's also a part of the entertainment at Cousin Clem's? Doesn't he perform music on Friday nights?"

Clem could have quibbled with half the words in the question. What do you mean by "entertainment?" What do you mean by "part of?" Do you mean *every* Friday night? But Clem made his living as a bartender; it wasn't his job, or in his nature, to split hairs. "Yes, that's true," he replied.

Then, Farragut, almost casually: "Just to be clear, your entertainers don't work as employees of the bar; they're independent contractors, correct?"

"Yes, that's right."

Anita had always admired Clem for his candor. But *come on*, man, don't make it so easy for them. Fight back a little! You just admitted that Patrick was working for the bar! Anita knew that Clem loved Patrick like a son, but he lacked a gene for deviousness, and he was about to hurt Patrick's cause badly, without realizing it. Anita knew she was going to have a lot of repair work to do when it was her turn. Clem was a disaster for Patrick's case, so far.

Farragut sized Clem up like an elephant poacher hungry for ivory. Clem, in turn, could see that Anita was upset, but he had no idea why. He couldn't fix what he couldn't understand.

"Mr. Labrecque, Mr. Flaherty would usually play on Fridays from 5:00 to 7:00, is that correct, during Happy Hour, in other words?

"Yes."

"He sang and played guitar?"

"Yes."

"What kind of music did he play, if you know?"

"Usually classic country, some acoustic rock, an occasional Beatles or Elton John song, that kind of thing. Music you can play with one guitar and one voice, if you adapt it. I think he tried to pick music that worked well when he was singing solo." Clem hesitated, thinking he was giving too much detail.

Farragut gave him a "you can continue" gesture. Clem felt the need to explain: "I was in bands when I was younger, so Pat and I would talk about music, and how to pick music that a bar crowd will like."

"Do you have other bands come in?" asked Farragut.

"We have a small stage, so we can't fit a big band. We have a three-piece band that plays country and southern rock, with some originals, on Friday night. They start at about 9:00 and play till quitting time. And we have a Saturday night band."

"How much do you pay a band for an evening of work?"

"We started at $225 a few years ago. Now it's $270."

"Did you normally give Mr. Flaherty dinner and free beer on Friday nights?"

"Yes. I'd serve him a cheeseburger with tomatoes, pickles and ketchup, or I'd tell him to pick something from the menu, and I'd refill his beer when it was empty."

"Why?"

"Because I didn't think it was fair to pay the band, while Patrick was doing the same work for free."

Farragut was not expecting that answer, and didn't quite know quite what to do with it. So he took the simple approach – he told Clem the answer he wanted.

"During testimony you gave before trial at a pretrial proceeding, do you remember my asking you why you gave free food and beer to Mr. Flaherty on Fridays, and do you remember telling me, quote 'because he earned it,' close quote?"

"Yes."

Clem gave Farragut a "what's your point?" face; not belligerently, but genuinely puzzled. Farragut had extracted what he wanted, and was happy to move on.

"Did Mr. Flaherty understand that you were giving him free food and beer because he was playing music?"

"Objection, Your Honor." Anita knew she'd win this one. "Counsel is asking the witness to read someone else's mind. Lack of personal knowledge."

"Sustained."

Farragut tried a different tack. "Did Mr. Flaherty ever ask you, on Friday, 'Why is the food free tonight?'"

"I don't think so."

"Did he ever ask you why his beers on Friday night were free?"

"No, I don't think so."

Farragut paused. Then: "Did you let Mr. Flaherty know that his food and beers were free on Friday because he played music for Happy Hour?"

Clem thought for a second, and tried to answer as honestly as he could. "I think I would have had to, or else he would have been trying to pay me. That's the way Pat was. But I don't know."

Farragut turned to valuation. "Mr. Labrecque, if you can recall, how much did Cousin Clem's charge for a cheeseburger with tomatoes, pickles and ketchup five years ago?"

Certainly Clem recalled. That was his business. "Seven dollars and fifty cents."

Farragut walked Clem through the prices for cheeseburgers and draft beers over the previous five years, and asked him to provide his best estimate of how many weeks a year the defendant played for Friday Happy Hour in each of those years. He provided Clem with paper, pen and pocket calculator. Meanwhile, the jurors looked around the courtroom trying to decide who was with whom, and who was with the media. After too long, Farragut wrapped it up with Clem.

"So would you agree with me, Mr. Labrecque, that your best estimate of the aggregate menu price for the food and beer you provided to Mr. Flaherty on Friday nights during each of the five years in issue was $650 per year?"

"Yes, that's the closest I can come at this point."

Farragut turned to the judge: "No further questions, Your Honor."

CHAPTER 75

"Ms. Boyle, you may inquire."

Anita replaced Farragut at the lectern. "Good morning, Mr. Labrecque, I just have a few questions. Did Cousin Clem's enter into a written barter agreement with Mr. Flaherty that Cousin Clem's would give him food and drink in exchange for musical services?"

"No."

"Did you shake hands with Mr. Flaherty, on behalf of Cousin Clem's, to confirm to him that Cousin Clem's would give him food and drink in exchange for musical services?"

"No."

"Did you say to Mr. Flaherty, in words or substance, 'Patrick, we'll give you food and drink on the condition that you provide music services on Friday nights?"

"No, nothing like that."

"Did Patrick Flaherty say to you, in words or substance, 'I'll provide musical services on Friday evenings on the condition that you give me food and drink?"

"No."

The preliminaries out of the way, Anita began to work on the other issues on which they had focused during prep. "Mr. Labrecque, did I ask you to go back through your records and calendars to determine whether you were working behind the bar of Cousin Clem's on Friday, October 2 of last year?"

"Yes, you did."

"What did you find out?"

"I was 'dere working the bar that night, from 5:00 to closing."

"Do you recall hearing Patrick Flaherty say, 'Fuck the IRS' on that night, or on any other night?"

"No, I don't. I never heard him say anything like that."

"Did you ever hear Patrick Flaherty complain about, or even mention, the IRS on any other occasion before he was arrested?"

"No."

"Mr. Labrecque, did Mr. Flaherty put out a tip jar when he sang on Fridays?"

"No, he doesn't like money."

Farragut began to rise to object to the witness's mind-reading, but thought better of it and sat back down. You need to pick your battles.

"Did Mr. Flaherty bring his own guitar to Cousin Clem's on Friday nights?"

"No, I lent him mine."

"You told Mr. Farragut that Mr. Flaherty never asked why his food and beers were free on Friday nights. Isn't it true that Mr. Flaherty seldom paid for beers on any of the other nights, either?"

Clem smiled, picturing himself behind his bar, which was where he really wanted to be right then. "That's true. He would usually pay cash for his first beer of the night, and then people would buy rounds, and he would be able to have a couple more beers for free."

"Did Mr. Flaherty say where his cash came from?"

Farragut thought about objecting, but decided that the answer wouldn't hurt his case.

"He told me once that he receives $100 a month as a gift from his parents."

"Was Mr. Flaherty a big drinker, compared to other patrons of Cousin Clem's?"

The judge interrupted. "Mr. Labrecque, counsel hasn't told you what she means by 'big drinker,' and she hasn't told you which other patrons of Cousin Clem's she means. But I'll let you answer the question if you understand it."

"I think I do, sir. Most of our regulars will drink, say, four or five beers and a couple of shots of whiskey during the night. Patrick -- Mr. Flaherty – would drink three beers, tops."

"So, from Mr. Flaherty's side of the bar, is it accurate to say that his cash expenditures for beers would not have looked much different on a Friday night than on any other night?"

"Yes, I think that's right."

"Let's talk about food. Did you occasionally feed Patrick for free on days other than Fridays?"

"Yes."

"How often?"

Clem thought for a second. "Actually, fairly often. Probably two or three times a month. Often when it was slow, and he and I were just talking."

"Do you remember the time two years ago when Patrick's parents came up from Denver, and a big group celebrated his birthday?" Anita knew to ask the question because she had been there.

Clem smiled again, recalling. "Yeah, that was a great evening. We had a good time."

"How many people were part of that group?"

"About a dozen, I think."

"Who paid for dinner and drinks that night, for about a dozen people?"

Clem was surprised by the question. He reddened slightly, a little embarrassed. "Claire and I did. It was on the house."

Anita was wrapping up. "Do you recall making any *clear* statement to Patrick that his obligations to pay for food and beer were different on Friday nights than on any other nights?"

"No."

"No further questions, Your Honor."

The judge looked at Farragut. "Mr. Farragut, any re-direct?"

"No, Your Honor. Well, actually, one question." Farragut posed the question from his counsel table. "Mr. Labrecque, when you fed Mr. Flaherty on a Friday night after he had played music, in your mind was that food provided to him for free because he had played music?"

Clem thought for a second. "Yes," he said.

"No further questions, Your Honor."

Judge Martin turned to the jury. "Ladies and gentlemen, we'll take our lunch break at this point. You can go out for lunch, but please be back in your jury room at 1:45. We'll start testimony at around 2:00. As before, don't discuss the case among yourselves, and don't talk to anyone else about the case. We'll see you after lunch."

CHAPTER 76

"Your Honor, the government calls Father David Hernandez," announced Farragut.

Father Dave made his way from the back door of the courtroom to the witness stand, while Farragut and Renfro consulted, and Anita was saying something to Patrick. The jury watched Father Dave carefully, sensing that a Catholic priest's testifying in a criminal case was likely a rare event. Father Dave was dressed in his black suit, with black shirt and white clerical collar. He was wearing black shoes and a gold crucifix. Plainly nervous, he was wringing his hands unconsciously, and seemed shorter than his 5'9".

"Do you swear or affirm that the testimony you are about to give in this matter will be the truth, the whole truth, and nothing but the truth, so help you God?"

"Yes." Father Dave sat, and took a breath. Farragut was in no hurry to begin the examination. When the Lord is on your side in a trial, you want to prolong the moment.

"Father Hernandez, good morning, and thank you for coming to testify today. Before we begin, I want to emphasize to you that I'm not going to be asking you any questions that pertain to anything you might have heard in a confessional setting, with any person. If I or Ms. Boyle asks you a question that causes you to believe that you're being asked to divulge privileged or confidential information, please let us know, and we'll address the problem with the court." Farragut wasn't worried about infringing on the confessional privilege, but he wanted to be sure that he addressed the concerns of any juror who might have believed that a priest couldn't be forced to testify about anything. Now, instead of being the guy who was invading the privilege, he was the one who was protecting it.

"All right," said Father Dave. Farragut had told him something similar during the grand jury.

"Father Hernandez, are you currently serving as pastor of St. Ann's Roman Catholic Church in Coolidge, Wyoming?"

"Yes, I am."

"How long have you served in that position?"

"About two and half years."

"Where were you assigned before you came to St. Ann's?"

"I was an assistant parish priest, that is, a parochial vicar, at St. Bartholomew's Parish in northern New Jersey."

"How long were you assigned there?"

"For two years."

"Were you in seminary before that?"

"Yes, I studied at St. Joseph's Seminary and College in Yonkers, New York."

"How did you find your way to Coolidge and St. Ann's?"

"Normally, parish assignments are pretty strictly controlled, and we normally don't have much choice in deciding where we're going to go. But the U.S. Church has a small program for recruiting parish priests for underserved areas. Right now, the entire Diocese of Wyoming only has, I think, 35 priests. I always loved the West, and wanted to be out here if I could. When the spot at St. Ann's came open, I applied through the program and got the job."

"Does St. Ann's Parish own any real estate?" asked Farragut, beginning his questioning concerning the matter at hand.

"Yes, we do."

"How is title held for that property? And do you know what I mean by that question?"

"I think I do. Under Church Law, well, Canon Law, the parish can form a Parish Corporation to hold title to property. So, St. Ann's has a Parish

Corporation, and under Wyoming law, the Parish Corporation takes title to church property."

"What property does the parish own in the name of that Parish Corporation?"

"We own our church building, our Rectory, and the Parish Hall, where we have social events. And, I guess you would say, the land that all of that sits on. That's on Baxter Street in Coolidge."

"Please take a look at Government Exhibit 1 on the big screen to your right. Do you recognize what's in that picture?"

"Yes, that's an aerial view of St. Ann's."

"I'll represent to you and to members of the jury that Government Exhibit 1 is a screen-capture from Google Earth."

Farragut shuffled folders. "Does the parish own additional property outside of Coolidge?"

"Well, indirectly. Years ago, the Parish Corporation established a trust that took title to land that had been given to the parish as a gift. The pastor of the Parish – in this case, me, right now – is designated as the trustee of the trust. We operate a small summer day camp on the property. I believe the ownership is structured that way to comply with Wyoming law, to make sure that we're eligible for the exemption from real property tax. Like most churches, we're tax exempt for pretty much everything."

"How big is the property that's owned by the trust?"

"You mean, in terms of acreage?"

"Yes."

"It's about 250 acres."

"I would like you to take a look at Government Exhibit 2." Farragut clicked up another aerial photograph. "This is another picture from Google Earth; the red lines were added by technical personnel in my office. Do you recognize that picture?"

"Yes. That looks like the property we were just describing."

"Your Honor, the government moves for the admission of Government Exhibit 2," said Farragut.

"No objection, Your Honor," said Anita, rising to her feet and sitting back down. Anita followed the rule of thumb that she had learned as a young D.A. – if you're talking in a courtroom, however briefly, you're on your feet. Too many lawyers ignored that rule. But judges notice, and so do jurors.

"Government Exhibit 2 is admitted," said Judge Martin.

"Were you serving as pastor at St. Ann's during October of last year?"

"Yes, I was."

"Do you recall receiving a telephone call from someone who identified himself as Arthur Kramer of Wyoming Real Estate Strategies?"

"Yes."

"Did you meet with a person identifying himself as Arthur Kramer after that phone call?"

"Yes."

"Did you later learn that Arthur Kramer was, in fact, Special Agent Arthur Bolton, working undercover?"

"Yes."

"But when you met with him, you believed him to be Arthur Kramer, a real estate person, correct?"

"Yes."

"Did he give you a business card that said "Arthur Kramer, Wyoming Real Estate Strategies, with his phone number on it?"

"Yes, he did. I kept the card."

"OK, just to avoid confusion, I'm going to refer to Arthur Kramer as Special Agent Bolton as I'm asking you questions about your meeting. When Special Agent Bolton first talked with you on the telephone, did he tell you why he wanted to meet with you."

"Yes, he said his company, or maybe a client of his company, might be interested in purchasing our property off of Side Road. That's the 250 acre property we were just talking about."

"Did he ask to meet with you at the property to look at it?"

"Yes, he did, and we set up a time to meet."

"How soon after your phone call did the meeting take place?"

"I forget, at this point. It was within a day or two after the phone call."

"Special Agent Bolton has testified that he met with you on October 9th of last year. Does that sound about right to you?"

"I don't know. We met. I have no recollection of the date."

"Did you show him the property during your meeting?"

"Yes."

"Would you recount, please, in your own words, where the two of you went, and what you described to him about the property?"

Father Dave thought for a moment, trying to access the memory. "We met on Side Road, just outside of Coolidge. I think he arrived first. We introduced ourselves, and we started walking toward the day camp. I showed him the camp, and then we walked out onto the prairie above the camp. I explained that we let hunters use the open area, because it was part of our tax exemption, to make the property available for public use. After that, I believe we went back to our cars, and we both drove up Side Road to the upper part of the property. We walked up the pathway to the cabin; I showed him the cabin from the outside, and explained that it was inhabited by a tenant, Mr. Flaherty" – Father Dave nodded toward Patrick – "who was there before we realized, or at least before I realized, that the Parish owned the property. I pointed out the 12 volt electrical system that the cabin had, what we could see of it from the outside. And finally, we went over to look at Water Creek, which flows through a corner of the property. That's what I remember."

"While the two of you were looking at the cabin on the property, did Special Agent Bolton describe Patrick Flaherty as a squatter?"

"He did."

"Did you agree with that characterization?"

"No, I told him that Mr. Flaherty was living there with the permission of the Parish."

"Why did the Parish give permission to Mr. Flaherty to live on its land?"

"Because Mr. Flaherty was living there before we realized the Parish owned the property."

"So you felt an obligation to let him stay?"

"Yes."

"Why?"

Father Dave knew this question was probably going to be asked, and had talked with Anita before trial to discuss how he would answer it, truthfully. "Because he had spent a lot of time fixing the place up, and we didn't think it would be fair to toss him out of his home when we hadn't warned him that the cabin was on Parish land."

"Well, OK, but why didn't you charge him rent when you realized he was living on Parish property?" continued Farragut.

"Because we knew he didn't have any money," responded Father Dave.

Farragut had anticipated the answer, and proceeded to the heart of his questioning: "But he had the ability to work, did he not?"

"Yes."

"And he was investing time and labor into continuously improving the cabin, was he not?"

"Yes."

"Did the improvements to the cabin benefit the Parish, the owner of the cabin?" It didn't matter how Father Dave answered the question; the jury knew that the answer had to be "yes."

"I suppose there was some small benefit, but not in proportion to the time he spent," replied Father Dave. "And his work on the animal enclosures wasn't benefiting the Parish at all. In fact, Agent Bolton made it clear that any prospective buyer would want them removed. At the end of the day, it was still a one-room hunting cabin without running water, a heating system, or 120 volt electricity. The only person who really benefited from the work was Patrick." Father Dave had paid attention during his prep session with Anita.

"Well, and I don't want to misquote you, you said the Parish enjoyed a small benefit from Mr. Flaherty's work to make the cabin livable, correct?"

"Yes."

"And in fact, not so small a benefit; Mr. Flaherty's work made the cabin livable, and if you wanted to sell the property, having the cabin occupied was a selling point, was it not?"

"I don't know."

"And Mr. Flaherty also maintained the part of Water Creek that flows through the property, did he not? For example, dismantling beaver dams?"

"Yes."

"Didn't you tell Special Agent Bolton that having a human presence on the land added value to the property?"

"I honestly don't recall. I know that he said that I said it."

"Do you have reason to doubt Special Agent Bolton's recollection, especially if it's written down in his notes about your meeting?"

"No. But again, I don't remember saying it."

"Do you recall saying to Special Agent Bolton, quote, 'If Patrick doesn't maintain the place, he won't be able to stay. That's the deal, and he knows that,' close quote?"

"I'm not going to answer that question," replied Father Dave.

CHAPTER 77

The courtroom was quiet.

After a moment, Farragut asked, "Why not?"

"Because if I said that, I shouldn't have, and I'm not going to compound the sin by repeating it."

"Your Honor, I would ask the Court to please instruct the witness to answer the question," said Farragut to Judge Martin.

"Father Hernandez, under the rules of this court, you are obliged to answer Mr. Flaherty's question," said Judge Martin. "Did you make the statement to Special Agent Bolton that Mr. Farragut described in his question to you?"

"Your Honor, again, I decline to answer that question."

Judge Martin thought for a second. "Father Hernandez, I've instructed you to answer the question, and if you don't, I can hold you in contempt of court, and there could be serious consequences for you if I were to do that. You can have the question read back to you, if you'd like. I'm instructing you, again, to answer the question that was posed to you."

"I can't, in good conscience, answer that question," replied Father Dave.

The judge thought for a moment. "Let me see counsel at sidebar," he said.

The lawyers made their way to the far end of the judge's bench, and huddled with the judge, the judge's law clerk, and the court reporter. The judge began the discussion.

"Jack, did you know he was going to refuse to answer the question?"

"He refused to answer it before the grand jury, Your Honor, but I honestly expected he'd change his mind if he received an instruction from the Court."

"You should have given me a heads up this was coming."

"I should have, Your Honor," said Farragut. "I apologize."

"All right," said Judge Martin, "I have to figure out what to do. One thing I'm not going to do is hold the witness in contempt. The evidence just isn't that important, because it's cumulative to what Agent Bolton already testified. The judiciary has enough problems, without picking an unnecessary fight with the clergy. Try putting on this robe for a day, and let me know whether you disagree. So what's the remedy if he won't answer? Mr. Farragut, what's the government's position?"

"Well, obviously our position is that he should be required to answer the question. Failing that, I think we're entitled to an instruction to the jury to the effect that they must assume that the answer would have been unfavorable to the defendant."

"Ms. Boyle?" asked Judge Martin.

"Your Honor, you can't possibly instruct the jury to draw an unfavorable inference against the defendant, based on a refusal of a *prosecution* witness to answer," replied Anita. "As far as I'm aware, unfavorable inference rules are only triggered when a *party* refuses to provide discovery or other information in its possession, and you hold the failure to disclose against the party that engaged in the misconduct. The defense didn't call this witness, and doesn't control his decisions about whether to testify. Also, if you instructed the jury to draw an inference adverse to the defendant in this circumstance, you're creating a huge problem under the Confrontation Clause of the Sixth Amendment. I can't cross-examine a required inference. The evidence, as you said, is cumulative. The best solution to this problem is just to move on. Let's go to the next question."

Judge Martin thought quietly for at least 30 seconds. "I'm going to split the difference." He motioned to indicate that the sidebar was concluded, and the lawyers returned to their seats. The judge made a note or two and turned to address the jury.

"Members of the jury, after consultation with counsel, I have decided not to require the witness to answer the pending question. However, I instruct you that you *may* draw, but are not *obliged* to draw, whatever inference from that refusal to answer that you believe is supported by all of the evidence in the case. You may consider the substance of the statements the witness made in declining to answer the question. If you believe, based on what you've heard, that the witness made the statement to Agent Bolton that was recited in the question, then you can infer that the witness would have testified to that effect if he had followed the Court's instruction to answer the question. But you're not required to reach that conclusion, and if you conclude, based on all of the evidence in the case, that the witness made some other statement, or that the conversation was not as described in Mr. Farragut's question, then you are permitted to ignore the question and the witness's refusal to answer, altogether. How you decide those issues are for you, the jury, to determine."

Anita considered objecting, but realized that the instruction to the jury was reasonably favorable to the defense.

Farragut checked his notes, and continued his questioning. "Father Hernandez, does St. Ann's have any other landlord-tenant arrangements in which St. Ann's is the landlord?"

"No, we don't," replied Father Dave.

"As a matter of Parish policy, if a homeless person set up a tent blocking the main entrance to your church, would you require that person to re-locate?"

"Objection, Your Honor," said Anita, standing, "the question is hypothetical."

"Your Honor," replied Farragut, "I'm merely exploring the Parish's policies concerning squatters, to determine whether Mr. Flaherty was treated in accordance with that policy, and, if not, why not."

"The objection is overruled. The witness will answer."

"I suppose that we would find shelter for that homeless person, and ask him or her to move after we found that shelter," replied Father Dave.

"Why didn't you ask Mr. Flaherty to find shelter elsewhere when you realized that he was living on Parish land?" asked Farragut.

"Objection, Your Honor, asked and answered," interjected Anita.

"Overruled," replied the judge. "The witness will answer."

Father Dave thought for a second. "Because, as I said, Patrick had spent time fixing the place up, and it wouldn't have been fair to evict him under those circumstances. He wasn't hurting anyone, and he wasn't hurting the property."

Farragut was ready for the question that litigators dream about -- whatever answer he got would help his case. "Father Hernandez, let me boil your previous answer down to its essence, and you tell me whether my statement is accurate: 'Patrick Flaherty had worked on the cabin; therefore, he was permitted to occupy it.' Is that an accurate statement?"

If Father Dave answered "yes," the government had established its *quid pro quo* from the Parish's perspective, which would be 80% of the way toward proving a bartering agreement. If Father Dave answered "no," he would undermine two explanations he'd already given, and would be left trying to find another reason that Patrick had been permitted to stay. There wasn't any, and he would look ridiculous.

"Yes, that's true," replied Father Dave.

"Your Honor, I have no further questions," said Farragut, and he returned to his seat.

"Ms. Boyle, you may inquire," said Judge Martin.

CHAPTER 78

Anita took her time moving to the lectern. She wanted to begin in the same way with Father Dave as she had with the other Coolidge witnesses. Some things couldn't be repeated too often.

"Father Hernandez, did St. Ann's enter into a written barter agreement with Mr. Flaherty that St. Ann's would permit him to occupy the cabin on its property in exchange for maintenance and improvement work that he had performed or would perform on that property?"

"No."

"Did you shake hands with Mr. Flaherty, on behalf of St. Ann's, to confirm to him that St. Ann's would permit him to occupy the cabin on its property in exchange for maintenance and improvement work that he had performed or would perform on that property?"

"No."

"Did Patrick Flaherty say to you, in words or substance, 'I'll do work on the cabin and the property if you let me occupy the cabin?"

"No."

"Did you, on behalf of St. Ann's, say to Patrick Flaherty, in words or substance, 'We will let you occupy the cabin if you do work on the cabin and the surrounding property?"

"No."

"Did you have a written lease with Patrick Flaherty?"

"No."

"Did you inspect the cabin at any point?"

"Yes, once or twice I went in when I was dropping Patrick off from some event."

"Was it well-maintained?"

"Yes."

"Did you ever tell Patrick, in words or substance, that the Parish expected him to maintain his cabin?"

"No. He did that on his own."

"Was the cabin environmentally compliant?" Anita had a reason for the question – she was setting up a point for her closing argument, later in the trial.

"Yes, in fact, he has a composting toilet, which is required by Wyoming DEQ regulations. And the electricity is from 100 percent renewables."

"Did you know Patrick Flaherty as a member of your Parish before you learned that he was living on Parish land?"

"Yes, for a little while."

"Did you know that he was living his life almost without any money at all?"

"Yes, I did. Patrick doesn't really talk about it, but I knew it, and it's common knowledge among the staff and many parishioners."

"When you discovered that Patrick's cabin was on Parish land, did it ever occur to you to ask him to move for *any* reason, whether money, or labor, or just because?"

"No, of course not. That cabin is his home."

"Father Hernandez, please describe for the jury some of the good works that members of St. Ann's perform during the course of a year."

"The list is long, but I can give you some examples," replied Father Dave. "Our congregation tends to be older, so we try to meet the needs of our older parishioners. We prepare and deliver Meals on Wheels. We make sure that consecrated Host is taken to the nursing home in Coolidge, and to any of our folks who are shut-ins. As far as general community outreach goes, our people solicit for Catholic Charities Appeal. We participate as a group in Habitat for Humanity, where we help build housing for people in need. We operate a turkey drive at Thanksgiving, and a canned food drive at Christmas. We solicit for Toys for Tots, and work with the Marine Corps Reserve to do that. We help find shelter and food for refugees from war-torn or crime-ridden countries, we have a committee for that."

"Do persons other than Patrick Flaherty donate time and effort, rather than just cash, to maintain the Parish properties?"

"Yes. We often have what we call 'Saturday Task Forces' to do big projects that require a lot of people. Within the last year we painted the inside of the Parish Hall. We re-did every flower bed around the property. We, aah, we cleaned the stained-glass windows. Things that are labor-intensive, and give us an opportunity for fellowship."

"Did parishioners prepare food for the Saturday Task Forces?" asked Anita.

"Yes, in fact, that tends to be the best part of the day. We'll eat sandwiches, with cookies or brownies and ice cream, cold drinks from coolers."

"Does the Parish pay for some of the food out of its budget?"

"Yeah, uh, yes, fairly often. Not all of the food, but we always pay for some."

"Do you tell the participants in your Saturday Task Forces that the food is being made available in exchange for their labor?"

"No, of course not," replied Father Dave.

"Then why do you provide food?"

"Well, because it's nice to have food."

Anita turned to Judge Martin. "No further questions, Your Honor."

"Mr. Farragut, any re-direct?" asked the judge.

"Just a few questions, Your Honor," replied the prosecutor. He stepped up to the lectern.

"Father Hernandez, when you said earlier that you didn't want to compound the sin by answering the question that I posed to you, what sin were you talking about."

Father Dave looked uncomfortable. "I suppose I meant the sin of saying something to Agent Bolton that I wasn't sure was true when I said it."

"Did you feel bad about what you said immediately after you said it?"

Father Dave hesitated. "No, that was later."

"You mean, after you found out that what you said was harmful to Mr. Flaherty?"

"Yes."

The courtroom was quiet. Farragut had made his point. "No further questions, Your Honor," said Farragut, and he sat down.

"The witness is dismissed," said Judge Martin. He could have thanked Father Dave for coming, or he could have been more polite generally. He was still annoyed, however, with Father Dave's having refused to follow his instruction to answer a proper question.

CHAPTER 79

When Father Dave was gone, Judge Martin said, "Mr. Farragut, call your next witness please."

"Your Honor, the government calls Mr. Ezekiel Evans."

A tall, thin, bald man made his way across the courtroom to the witness stand. He was about 60 years old, at least partly Native American, and dressed in well-worn Dickies work clothes. He was plainly nervous. Anita found herself marveling that the United States Government was willing to spend hundreds of thousands of dollars on this trial, but couldn't find $150 to buy a sports jacket and slacks for a witness with not much money, who was probably feeling like a fish out of water already.

After the witness was sworn, and seated, Farragut placed his notebook on the lectern and held his clicker for the computer screens in the courtroom.

"Mr. Evans, thank you for coming. Where do you work?"

"I work at the Sheridan City Landfill," replied the witness.

"What's your job title, and what are your responsibilities?"

"I'm the Assistant Superintendent, and I'm responsible for overseeing operations during the daytime hours when the landfill is open for business."

"I'm showing you what has been marked as Government Exhibit 3. I'll represent to the Court, Your Honor, that Exhibit 3 is a grand jury subpoena for CCTV recordings for the year before last, Tax Year 5 as described in the Superseding Indictment. I'm putting a copy on the screens. Mr. Evans, did your employer ask you to help retrieve the recordings identified in the subpoena?"

"Yes."

Farragut asked a series of questions about how the system operated, how pictures were stored, how long they were kept, and how they were retrieved. He then turned to the evidence at issue, the reason Mr. Evans had been called.

"Were you able to retrieve all of the CCTV footage from the entrance cameras for the year before last, from January 2 through December 31?"

"Yeah, it was simple. I just downloaded all available footage, from the entrance cameras, onto a solid state drive, and held onto the drive. It was basically two commands. All I had to specify was the cameras and the dates."

"Did all of that film fit on one drive?"

"Yeah, because the system isn't video-based. At the entrance, it's motion-activated, and once it's activated, it only records still photos, in eight second intervals, for two minutes, or longer if the motion continues. And it's low-resolution black and white. But it's pretty reliable. We get time-stamped pictures of everybody who comes in and out through the main entrance."

"Did Special Agent Bolton" – Farragut pointed to Bolton behind him at counsel table – "and a computer technician visit you in late January of this year to look at the materials on the disc?"

"Yes."

"Did Special Agent Bolton and the computer tech spend some time with the disc and a laptop, in your office trailer?"

"Yes, they did."

"And at the conclusion of their day there, did they give you a list of the photographs that they wanted you to copy separately?"

"Yes."

"And did you do that, and give it to them on a separate drive, a so-called flash drive or thumb drive?"

"Yes."

"Did they ask you to look at the photos on your computer, and did you do that?"

"Yes."

Farragut handed the witness a three-ring binder full of large photographs. "Are these the photographs the agents asked you to print out?"

Mr. Evans looked them over carefully. While he was doing that, Anita was huddling with Patrick. Finally, the witness said, "Yes, these appear to be the photographs I separated for them."

"Your Honor, I move for the admission of Government Exhibit 14 A-Z and 14 AA-TT, representing 46 photographs from the Sheridan City Landfill. In support of admissibility and relevance, I would note that each photo is dated and time-stamped on a Friday of Tax Year 5, most between 12:00 and 1:00 p.m. The pictures show trucks in which the lettering 'Detmer Contracting' is visible on the door. We've established chain of custody. We would leave it to the jury, of course, to decide whether it is, in fact, Mr. Flaherty shown in the pictures."

Judge Martin looked across the well of the courtroom at Anita. "Ms. Boyle, any objection?"

"No, Your Honor."

Farragut turned to Anita. "Your witness."

Anita exchanged a final word or two with Patrick, and then walked over to the big lectern, without notes. She wanted to turn the tables a little. "Mr. Evans, do you know Patrick Flaherty?"

"Yes."

"How long have you known him?"

"Probably five or six years."

"Is he the person depicted in these pictures, collected as Government Exhibit 14?"

"Yes."

"Why do you know Patrick Flaherty well enough to identify him from pictures?"

"Because I work with him pretty much every week – or at least I did until recently – to get his debris weighed, so we can price his load. And then he'll fill out the check from Detmer Contracting for the right amount. Oft times, he'll sit down with me for a quick cup of coffee in the office trailer, and we'll talk and catch up. So, yeah, we know each other pretty well."

"Did Special Agent Bolton tell you not to tell Patrick that the government had taken copies of pictures of him?" Anita surmised that he had, because word never got back to Patrick that the feds had visited the landfill.

"Yes."

"What do you and Patrick talk about, usually, when you sit down for coffee?"

"Lots of stuff. He'll ask about my family. We talk about hunting. The Broncos. Sometimes we'll talk about Coolidge, because I have a cousin up there, and we know a couple of the same places and people. As long as the entrance to the landfill isn't jammed, we usually have time to catch up."

"Have you ever heard Patrick complain about the federal government?"

Ezekiel smiled. "No."

"Have you ever heard Patrick complain about the Internal Revenue Service, the IRS?"

"No."

"Have you ever heard Patrick complain about anything?"

The witness thought for a moment. "Not really. Maybe the weather."

"No further questions, Your Honor."

Farragut had just seen his witness turned into a witness for the defense. If this trial had proved anything, it was that Anita Boyle could think on her feet. "No redirect, Your Honor," said Farragut.

"At this point, ladies and gentlemen of the jury, we're going to recess for the day and let you start your evening," said Judge Martin. "As before, don't discuss the case with each other, or with anyone else." The jury stood, a couple of members stretched, and all 12 began to file out through the jury door to their left.

"Counsel, thank you for your work today. Mr. Farragut, how much more time for the prosecution's case?"

"We'll finish tomorrow, I think, Your Honor."

"OK, we'll see everyone tomorrow morning at 9:30."

CHAPTER 80

Anita and Patrick were sitting at the desk in Anita's hotel room, planning for the next day of testimony. It was almost 10:00, and both were exhausted. Patrick opened one of the cold beers his parents had brought over a few minutes before.

"I can't put you on the witness stand," said Anita, finally. "The more we talk about it, the more convinced I am it just isn't necessary."

"OK," said Patrick. "Your call."

"I can't fix the fundamental problem we have, which is all about how cross examination works in the real world. It isn't like on 'Law and Order.' I'm not worried he's going to get you to confess on the witness stand. But the real way cross-examination works is he can ask you a long list of 'yes or no' questions. He already knows the answers, and they will be questions you can only answer one way."

"Not a hundred percent sure I know what you're saying."

"I'll give you examples. 'Did you train Bobby Bays's dogs?' 'Did you accept free feed bags?' 'Did you sing almost every Friday night at Cousin Clem's?' 'Did you know you weren't being charged for your beers when you sang?'"

"Well, yeah, from Day One we've agreed with most of the facts," said Patrick.

"Exactly. And then after he's done getting you to admit the basic facts, he'd ask you a series of questions that he doesn't care how you answer, because the jury will know what the real answer is. He could ask, 'On a day where you'd just selected $200 of fencing to take from the back lot at Detmer's, would you have been willing to say you weren't going to drive to the landfill that day?' If you say, 'No, I wouldn't have been willing to say that,' he'll argue that you acknowledged the basics of a bartering agreement. If you say 'I could have said no, I was under no obligation,' the jury will think you're a jerk. And worse, they might not believe you. He can pose that question 50 different ways, and you have no good answers."

"What happens, finally, if I don't testify?" asked Patrick.

"The judge will explain to the jury that you have no obligation to testify, and that they shouldn't hold it against you. Some probably *will* hold it against you, but they likely won't feel free to say that to the other jurors during deliberations. And the fact is, in most criminal cases the defendant doesn't testify, and a lot of those cases result in acquittals."

"OK," said Patrick.

"And you know," said Anita, "the more I think about it, the more I think this is one of those cases where the jury really will be holding the government to its burden of proof. The government has turned your life upside down, and they want to put you in jail, over a few thousand dollars. Every one of the jurors can picture himself or herself in the same spot. I think the jury will want to be 100% convinced that you're guilty before they'll vote to convict. Or at least I hope so."

CHAPTER 81

"Good morning, Your Honor," said Farragut. "At this time, the government calls Mr. Robert Bays."

The Deputy Clerk followed the ritual, and administered the oath. For the first one or two witnesses, the jurors had observed the ritual carefully. By the fifth or sixth witness, they were editing their grocery lists in their heads, waiting for the actual testimony to start.

Bobby was nervous, but he'd been through worse – Desert Storm in 1991. He was sad for Patrick. At least in a war, you can fight back. In this case, they were trying to capture and imprison him, and all Patrick could do was sit and watch.

"Mr. Bays, thank you for coming," Farragut began. "Where do you live?"

"Coolidge, Wyoming," replied Bobby.

"What is your occupation?"

"I own and operate an animal feed store in Coolidge."

Farragut spent some time developing how Bobby got into the business, what kinds of feeds he sold, and who his customers were. After a few minutes, he reached the point of the exercise.

"Do you know Patrick Michael Flaherty?" asked Farragut.

"Yes."

"How long have you known him?"

"For about seven years."

"Mr. Bays, are you a small game hunter, and in particular, game birds?" asked Farragut.

"Yes, I am."

"During the past six years, have you owned German Shorthaired Pointer dogs?"

"Yes, three over that period," replied Bobby.

"Am I correct that you owned a German Shorthaired by the name of Mollie, beginning about six years ago?"

"Yes."

"And then Mollie died suddenly about four years ago, and you acquired Millie soon after, also a German Shorthaired Pointer?"

"Yes."

"You still have Millie, and then early this year you acquired another German Shorthaired by the name of Misty, correct?"

"Yes."

"Did Patrick Flaherty train Mollie to point, retrieve and track?"

"Yes."

"Did Patrick Flaherty train Millie to point, retrieve and track?"

"Yes."

"Is Patrick Flaherty now training Misty to point, retrieve and track?"

"Yes."

"And is Patrick Flaherty also continuing to do refresher training with Millie?"

"Yes, he is."

"If you know, what are some of the training objectives when a trainer is training a hunting dog?" asked Farragut.

"There's a lot to it," Bobby began. "A German Shorthaired has an instinct for pointing and retrieving, but you have to reinforce and control those instincts with training. You have to get the dog used to the sound of a shotgun – if they cringe or cower, they're no help in the field. You have to discourage crouching or lying down on point. A big challenge is to teach the dog not to range too far, or stay too close. You have to teach a dog to use a soft mouth, so as not to crush a bird. And to do all of that, you have to start with basic obedience training, using rewards to motivate the dog to follow commands. German Shorthaireds are very smart, and like to train, but, as I said, there's a lot to do."

"Would it be fair to summarize the objectives of the training as teaching the dogs to find game, retrieve game after it's been shot, and track game if it's been wounded and is still moving?"

"Yeah. Yes, that's fair."

"Do you train only during hunting season?"

"No, training is year-round, weather permitting," replied Bobby. "There are always commands that you can reinforce. Also, you can do shed-hunting, which is training the dog to find antlers that have been shed by deer or elk. That helps keep the dogs in shape, and lets you practice commands that are going to be important during bird hunting season."

"Do you recall testifying at a pretrial proceeding in this case?" asked Farragut.

"Yes, I do," replied Bobby. How could he forget being hauled before a grand jury in a place three hundred miles from home, to testify against a friend? When Bobby appeared as a witness before the grand jury, Farragut used Bolton's tape of his visit to Bays Feed to paint Bobby into a corner. Bobby listened to his own words, telling Bolton that it was his practice to "swap" with Patrick – chicken and goat feed for dog training. Farragut re-stated that idea in six different forms, and asked Bobby to agree or disagree. Eventually, he got Bobby to say it the way Farragut wanted the trial jury to hear it.

"Do you recall telling me during that pretrial proceeding, and I quote, 'I give Patrick bags of chicken and goat feed for training my dog,' close quote?"

"Yes." Bobby couldn't look at Patrick.

"And was that statement true when you made it?"

Bobby hesitated. Finally, "Yes."

"Have you been giving the defendant bags of chicken and goat feed for training your dogs since you obtained Mollie, six years ago?"

"Yes."

"And each year since?" Farragut was making sure he covered all of the Counts in the indictment.

"Yes. But I should add that I only give him bags that are torn, or close to their sell-by dates."

Farragut went back to his counsel table and picked up three four-inch-thick binders. "Your Honor, may I approach the witness?"

"Yes," replied the judge.

Farragut stood at the witness stand, binders in hand. "Mr. Bays, I'm showing you what has previously been marked for identification as Government Exhibit 4." The witness stand had a shelf in front of the witness that would hold elbows or documents. Farragut placed the binder on that shelf. "Mr. Bays, is Government Exhibit 4 a compilation of inventory records from Bays Feeds for the past six years?"

"Yes."

"Did you produce those documents for the government in response to a subpoena?"

"Yes."

"Do those documents truly and accurately account for the transactions reflected in them?"

"Well, those are our records," replied Bobby.

"As those records were compiled, you were doing your best to track your inventory properly, were you not?"

"Yes."

"And those records were the result of those efforts, correct?"

"Yes."

"To the best of your recollection, was every feed bag you gave to Patrick Flaherty over the past six years on your sales floor, and available for purchase by customers, at the time you gave it to him?" asked Farragut.

"Yes. But, as I told you, most of those were almost expired, and some were a little torn."

"Cross examine," said Farragut.

CHAPTER 82

Anita had met with Bobby Bays for four hours in Coolidge, the week before. Bobby was a quick study. He understood the issues in the case, and he knew the points Anita wanted to make. Anita rose to question him.

"Mr. Bays, did you have a written agreement with Patrick Flaherty that you would give him bags of feed in exchange for dog-training services?"

"No."

"Did you shake hands with Patrick Flaherty to confirm an agreement that you would give him bags of feed in exchange for dog-training services?"

"No."

"Did you ever say to Patrick Flaherty, in words or substance, 'If you'll train my dogs, I'll give you bags of goat and chicken feed?'"

"No."

"Did Patrick Flaherty ever say to you, in words or substance, 'I'll train your dogs, but only if you give me goats and chicken feed?'"

"No, he loves those dogs like his own."

"Mr. Bays, did you tell Patrick Flaherty last year, before he was arrested or charged, that you would give him the animal feed for free, whether he trained your dogs or not?"

"Yes, I did," replied Bobby.

"Where did that conversation take place?"

"We were in my store."

"Why did you feel it was necessary to make that statement to him?"

"Well, I just felt that the effort he was making to train my dogs – which he'd do roughly three times a week -- was a very large interruption in his typical day. He had to spend a great deal of time every day just keeping himself alive, you know, gathering wood, hunting, tending his vegetables, tending his chickens and goats, keeping water heated and ready for use, you name it. He was living at a subsistence level, if you could say it like that. On the other hand, I felt the dollar value of the feed bags I was giving him had basically no effect on my bottom line. I knew he didn't have any money. I was happy to give them to him, just because he's a friend, and an important part of our community."

"When did you first feel that way?" asked Anita.

"From the get-go, when Patrick started training Mollie. Years ago."

"You described Patrick Flaherty's home. Did you visit his cabin from time to time?" asked Anita.

"Oh yeah, fairly often, because I would pick him up when we were going hunting together."

"What did you see during those visits about the things that Patrick was doing to support himself?"

"He grows his own vegetables in a vegetable garden out in back of the cabin. He raises goats for milk and meat, and he raises chickens for eggs and meat."

"After he hunts, do you know whether he eats game for food?"

"Oh, yes, he eats what he kills."

"Have you ever hunted with Patrick out of season?"

"No, definitely not. Patrick is careful about hunting seasons. He won't take any animal out of season, at least when he's with me, and we hunt together a lot."

Anita shifted gears. "Have you ever bought Patrick a drink at Cousin Clem's?"

Farragut thought about objecting, but he didn't know where the questioning was going, and wouldn't have been able to articulate a basis for an objection.

"I have, often," responded Bobby. "There've been times when I've bought a round for everyone at the bar, just because I wanted to be sure that Patrick would have his next beer paid for, without being singled out as a charity case. He just doesn't have much money."

Patrick was pained when he heard Bobby's statement. He had suspected as much.

"Thank you, Mr. Bays, no further questions," said Anita.

Farragut wanted bartering to be the only thing the jury would associate with Bobby Bays. He arrived back at the lectern for re-direct, replacing Anita. "Mr. Bays, I assume that one of the reasons you felt the need to make a statement to the defendant that he could have feed bags whether or not he trained your dog, was that he might not have known that fact, correct?"

"I don't know, I suppose so."

"You made the statement because you wanted to impart information to the defendant, correct?"

"Yes, I wanted him to know."

Farragut had just teed up an important argument to the jury: the only reason to tell Patrick he could have the bags without training the dogs, was that he wasn't already aware of that fact. Farragut would argue, in his closing argument, that it was necessary for Bobby Bays to let him know that the deal had changed, because Patrick would otherwise have believed that the "swap" was still in place.

"No further questions, Your Honor," said Farragut.

"The witness is excused," said the judge. "We'll take a fifteen minute break."

CHAPTER 83

"Your Honor, the government calls Mr. Harold Detmer," said Farragut.

Harry Detmer entered through the back door of the courtroom and made his way forward to the witness stand. The jurors tracked his progress. Harry carried himself with pride, and a certain ferocity. He looked at Farragut, Renfro, and Judge Martin without fear or uncertainty. He clearly didn't want to be in this courtroom, for this trial. But if he had to be there, he would be there on his terms.

The Deputy Clerk administered the oath, and Harry sat. Farragut had not yet looked up to see Harry's face, and missed the new mood in the room.

"Good morning, Mr. Detmer," said Farragut, raising his eyes.

Harry did not respond. Not a word, not a blink. A few of the jurors thought, 'this could get interesting.'

"Mr. Detmer, where do you live?" asked Farragut.

"Coolidge, Wyoming," replied Harry.

"What is your occupation?"

"Contractor," replied Harry.

"Where do you work?"

"Mostly in Coolidge," replied Harry.

"I meant, for what company do you work?"

"My own."

"What is the name of that company?"

"Detmer Contracting, Inc."

"What does Detmer Contracting, Inc., do?"

"General contracting."

Obviously, Harry Detmer wasn't in a volunteering mood. Which, as Farragut understood, was a mark of a well-coached witness. Anita had apparently prepped him well. "Do you know Patrick Michael Flaherty?" asked Farragut.

"I know a Patrick Flaherty. If Patrick Michael Flaherty is the same person, then the federal government seems to have given him a middle name when they brought this case."

True, thought Farragut, we did -- and on purpose. All the really bad criminals have three names. "How long have you known Mr. Flaherty?"

"For six or seven years."

"Does Patrick Flaherty drive construction debris to the Sheridan City Landfill in a Detmer Contracting truck on most Fridays?"

"Yes."

"Is that construction debris generated by Detmer Contracting, Inc., in the course of its contracting activities?"

"Yes."

"Does Detmer Contracting compensate Patrick Flaherty in cash for his driving services?"

"No."

"Do you recall testifying at a pretrial proceeding in this case?" asked Farragut.

"Yes."

"Do you recall testifying about a conversation you had with Special Agent Arthur Bolton when he visited the office of Detmer Contracting, Inc.?"

"No, I don't."

Farragut wasn't expecting that answer, but given Harry's demeanor, he wasn't surprised, either. He grabbed a three-ring binder from his counsel table. "Mr. Detmer, I'm going to read from the transcript of that pretrial proceeding, and then I'll be asking you a few questions about it. I'll remind you that I was present at that proceeding, and asking questions on behalf of the government." He found the right page. "I asked you, quote, 'Is that your voice on the tape recording I just played, saying: "Our guy collects our debris and takes it to the landfill, in exchange for cyclone fencing, and railroad ties, stuff for his animal enclosures. He also takes whatever materials in the debris might be usable for his purposes.'" Close quote. And you responded, quote, 'Yes,' close quote."

Harry looked at Farragut, and said nothing. But that was because there was no question pending.

"Does my reading from the transcript refresh your recollection of my having asked you that question at the pretrial proceeding, as well as the answer that you gave?"

"No. I testified months ago. I don't remember the details."

Farragut wasn't flustered, exactly, but he had lost his rhythm and lost control of the narrative. "Your Honor, we will move the admission of the transcript of the relevant question and answer from the pretrial proceeding as past recollection recorded. The government will excerpt the relevant verbiage and will create a Government Exhibit . . . I'm sorry, what's our next exhibit number?"

"That would be Government Exhibit 15" said the Deputy Clerk.

"We'll create a Government Exhibit 15," responded Farragut.

"Very well," said Judge Martin.

AUSA Jack Farragut knew that his first and most important job was to get evidence admitted. It wasn't always pretty, or smooth. But Harry Detmer's admission at the grand jury that he gave the defendant fencing and other materials "in exchange for" driving services was now before the trial jury. Arthur Bolton's description of the conversation in the Detmer Contracting office had been corroborated. On to the next fact.

Farragut picked up another binder full of accounting records from the prosecution's counsel table. "Your Honor, may I approach the witness?"

"Yes," replied Judge Martin.

"Mr. Detmer, I'm showing you what I have marked for identification as Government Exhibit 5," said Farragut. After a moment or two, he added the formulaic "Have you looked at it?"

"No."

Farragut had forgotten to instruct the witness to examine the document. "Please look at the document, sir, and tell the jury whether this document binder includes inventory records from Detmer Contracting, Inc., for the past six years?"

Harry took his time. He wasn't afraid of silence, and he didn't like Jack Farragut at all. Finally, "Yes, those are copies of our inventory runs."

"Did you produce those documents for the government in response to a subpoena?"

"I didn't, no."

"Did Detmer Contracting, Inc. produce those documents for the government in response to a subpoena?"

"Yes."

"Do those documents truly and accurately account for the transactions reflected in them?"

"I have no idea. I didn't compile the documents that we sent in response to your subpoena, and I didn't read them."

Farragut tried another tack. "Were those inventory records maintained in the ordinary course of the business of Detmer Contracting, Inc.?"

Harry looked again at the inventory run. "Yes," he replied.

"Was it also Detmer Contracting, Inc.'s practice to maintain these records during the past six years, at or about the dates reflected in the records?"

"Yes."

"Were these records kept in conformity with those practices?"

"Well, they haven't changed," replied Harry. "Yes."

"No further questions of this witness, Your Honor," said Farragut. He sat down, happy to be through, or mostly through, with Harry Detmer.

CHAPTER 84

Anita placed her notebook on the lectern. Harry didn't relax, exactly, but his expression had softened.

"Mr. Detmer, do you recall a conversation in your office last year during which you said to Patrick Flaherty, in words or substance, that he was welcome to anything he needed from your slow-moving inventory?"

"Yes."

"Did you say to Patrick Flaherty, in words or substance, that he could have the materials he was taking from inventory, whether he drove debris to the dump, or not?"

"Yes, that's what I told him," said Harry.

"And did Patrick Flaherty also continue to use materials from your construction debris for his cabin?"

"Yes, although that stuff has no value, it's no longer part of our inventory."

Anita wasn't really asking Harry to comment on valuation – that was the prosecution's issue – but the remark hadn't hurt her case, and she moved along to the next subject.

"Have you trusted Patrick Flaherty with the keys to your trucks during the past six years?"

"Yes, of course."

"Have you trusted Patrick Flaherty with blank checks for supplies and landfill fees?"

"Yes, all the time."

"Have you trusted Patrick Flaherty to load and drive materials to your crews, without worrying about whether he would skim off materials for himself?"

"Yes. He's never touched even a screw or nail that we didn't give him."

"Mr. Detmer, did you have a written agreement with Patrick Flaherty that you would give him fencing, lumber and construction debris in exchange for his driving to the landfill?"

"No."

"Did you shake hands with Patrick Flaherty to confirm an agreement that you would give him fencing, lumber and construction debris is exchange for his driving to the landfill?"

"No."

"Did Patrick Flaherty ever say to you, in words or substance, 'I'll drive to the landfill with your debris, but only if you give me fencing and lumber out of usable inventory'?"

"No, he never said anything like that."

"Did you or anyone on behalf of Detmer Contracting ever say to Patrick Flaherty, in words or substance, 'We'll give you fencing and lumber out of usable inventory, but only if you drive to the landfill with our debris'?"

"No, we never said anything like that."

"No further questions, Your Honor. Thank you, Mr. Detmer," concluded Anita.

"Mr. Farragut, any redirect?" asked Judge Martin.

"Briefly, Your Honor." He arrived at the lectern. "Mr. Detmer, I would like to ask you about the conversation you told Ms. Boyle you had with Mr. Flaherty, in your office. When did that conversation take place?"

"I'm not sure. I would say sometime in August or September of last year. It was still fairly warm."

"Only about eight or nine months ago, in other words?"

"Yes, approximately."

"Would you agree with me that you didn't tell me about that conversation during the pretrial proceeding?" asked Farragut.

"Well, if I didn't, that could only be because you didn't ask me about it," replied Harry.

Farragut decided to quit while he was behind. "No further questions, Your Honor."

CHAPTER 85

For the first time during the trial of Patrick Michael Flaherty, Arnold Renfro stood and addressed the Court on the record. "Your Honor, the government calls Dr. Morris Tindle."

The Deputy Clerk opened the rear door of the courtroom for a very short man in a grey pinstriped suit. Dr. Tindle was fire-pluggish, with broad shoulders and a thick neck. He looked like he might once have been a boxing referee. But maybe just for short guys, like bantamweights or welterweights. As he reached the witness stand, the Deputy Clerk arrived with her Bible.

"Do you swear or affirm that the testimony you are about to give in this matter will be the truth, the whole truth, and nothing but the truth, so help you God?"

"Yes," replied Dr. Tindle.

"Dr. Tindle, please state your full name for the record," Renfro began.

"Morris R. Tindle."

"Dr. Tindle, thank you for coming today. Would you please summarize your educational and work background for the members of the jury, please?"

Thus began the "qualification" of Dr. Morris Tindle as an expert witness. He had studied Economics at the University of Rhode Island (B.Sc.); law and tax law at New York University (J.D. and LL.M); and Economics again at Columbia (Ph.D.). He worked as a tax lawyer in New York City before joining a professional tax and economics consulting firm that specialized in providing expert testimony in federal tax, tort and employment cases – the Institute for Taxation and Economic Analysis. If you wanted to know how much tax somebody owed, you called Dr. Tindle. If you wanted to know how much they lost in future wages from an auto accident, you called Dr. Tindle. If you wanted to know the value of fencing materials or feed bags, you called Dr. Tindle, who would work up a regression analysis on his computer.

Renfro was surprised at how easy it had been to obtain permission to hire Dr. Tindle for the *Flaherty* case. Tindle charged $600 per hour, and would spend more than 120 hours working on the case. Ordinarily, the Tax Division used IRS employees as experts on "tax consequences," and approval to hire a firm like ITEA was infrequent. Because Dr. Tindle was a "two-fer" – he could testify about tax consequences and market valuations – he was an easy choice for *Flaherty*. The big budget approved for this case reflected its importance to DOJ.

"Dr. Tindle, please look at the evidence screen in front of you," said Renfro. "I am showing you what has been marked as Government Exhibits 6 and 7, for identification." He paused. "Have you looked at Government Exhibits 6 and 7?"

"Yes," replied Tindle.

"What are they?" continued Renfro.

"Exhibit 6 is my current curriculum vitae, my CV" replied Tindle. "Exhibit 7 is my expert report for this case."

"Your Honor, I offer Dr. Tindle's curriculum vitae as Government Exhibit 6 and his expert report as Exhibit 7," said Renfro.

"No objection, Your Honor," said Anita, standing and sitting down again.

"Your Honor, the government offers Dr. Tindle as an expert in the areas of tax consequences of various services provided by the defendant, as well as on the valuation of certain goods received in return." Renfro turned to Anita. "Voir dire?"

Renfro was offering Anita the opportunity to question Dr. Tindle about Tindle's qualifications as an expert.

Anita rose. "Your Honor, the defendant will stipulate to the witness's qualifications. Of course, we reserve the right to oppose any opinions he may offer from the witness stand that are not included within the four corners of his expert report." With that, Anita sat down again.

"The Court rules that Dr. Tindle is qualified to testify as an expert as to the opinions set forth in his expert report, which is Government Exhibit 7," said Judge Martin. "Members of the jury, you will not be reviewing Dr. Tindle's expert report, because his testimony at trial supersedes, or replaces, that report. Now, normally, witnesses must testify only as to facts. When a witness has been qualified by the Court as an expert, as Dr. Tindle now has been, that expert witness is entitled to express opinions on matters within his or her area of expertise. I expect that Dr. Tindle will do so. Mr. Renfro, you may continue."

Renfro turned toward his witness. "Dr. Tindle, in simple terms, what is the federal Self-Employment Tax?"

"The Self-Employment Tax," Tindle began, "is designed to collect Social Security and Medicare taxes from people who aren't subject to wage withholding. To make sense of Self-Employment Tax, I need to begin with how employees are taxed. Most of us are familiar with the line on our paystub that describes 'FICA' withholding. It also shows up on our W-2 form at the end of the year, when we do our taxes. About seven and a half percent of a worker's wages are deducted from his or her pay, and applied toward social security benefits later in life, or at least that's the theory. The employer of that person pays another seven and a half percent or so, and the employee gets credit from the Social Security Administration for that amount as well. FICA is the biggest tax for many hourly workers. It exceeds federal income tax for any workers making under $33,000 per year, and also exceeds most state income taxes. And there's also a line in a W-2 for Medicare Tax withholding.

"Now, self-employed people, like Mr. Flaherty, don't receive wages, and they're not subject to wage withholding. Self-employed people make profits rather than wages. To make sure that self-employed individuals make the same contributions to Social Security and Medicare, self-employed people are required, in a sense, to pay both halves of the FICA tax. They pay the employee's half, and the employer's half, and the result is a tax of about 15% on their profits. A self-employed individual has to pay the Self-Employment Tax in quarterly installments, that is, every three months throughout the tax year."

Renfro waited for his witness to pause, and offered the next question. "At what level of income does the obligation to pay Self-Employment Tax kick in?"

"The Internal Revenue Code sets that number at a very low threshold," replied Tindle. "If you earn self-employment income of $400 or more in a year, you have to declare that income in a tax return, typically on Schedule C to your Form 1040, and pay Self-Employment Tax on it."

"Currently, what is the threshold for when a W-2 wage earner must file a federal tax return?" asked Renfro.

"That number is at about $12,000 at the moment," replied Tindle. "At first blush that sounds like wage earners are getting a big advantage, but not really. When you receive wages, FICA tax is being withheld from your paycheck as you go along, and it goes to the government while you're earning it. Your employer sends in your half and its own half of the FICA tax at intervals during the year. So the tax is being paid. If you're only making $11,000 per year in wages, and you don't have other income, the government doesn't really need to hear from you, I mean, ah, the government doesn't need a tax return from you. You don't owe any federal *income* tax on your wages – with the standard deduction, income tax starts at about $12,200 of earnings. And, as I said, at that level, the government already has your FICA payments."

"Why is the threshold so much lower for self-employed persons, that is, why is it only $400?" asked Renfro.

"Because there hasn't been any employer withholding," replied Tindle. "The government wants to be paid Social Security and Medicare taxes almost from the first dollar you earn, whether you're a wage-earner or self-employed. Because there has been no withholding of Social Security or Medicare tax on behalf of a self-employed person – if you're self-employed, there's no paycheck to withhold from -- the self-employed person is obliged to pay it himself or herself, and the filing and payment obligation starts at $400."

"What if a self-employed person is engaged in more than one trade, let's say, a landscaper during the day, and a baker at night?" asked Renfro.

"Then there would be two $400 thresholds," replied Tindle. "The businesses are treated separately, because they report two different profit numbers. In your example, if the baking business is new, and losing money, those losses would not offset profits from the landscaping business, for purposes of Self Employment Tax. Even if the losses from baking were equal to all of the profits from landscaping, the self-employed person would still have to pay Self Employment Tax on the full profit from the landscaping business."

"Dr. Tindle, as you know, the defendant did not file federal tax returns for the past five years. As part of your expert analysis, did you calculate the Self Employment Taxes that the defendant would have been obliged to pay if he had been declaring his self-employment income on tax returns, and paying the required taxes?"

"I did," replied Tindle. "I prepared what are called 'pro forma' tax returns. You could also call them hypothetical returns. The idea is to calculate unpaid tax by seeing what would have been declared as income if the defendant had filed a properly prepared return in each of the last five years. And then the same tax returns show the calculations of the Self Employment Tax that was due."

"Let's start with the year before last year," said Renfro, "what I'll call Year 5. Dr. Tindle, take a look at Government Exhibit 8 on your screen. Is that the most recent of the pro forma tax returns that you prepared for Mr. Flaherty?"

"Yes, it is," replied Tindle.

"How does this tax return describe the defendant's businesses?"

"I used four businesses. Those were the defendant's activities as a handyman at the church and at the cabin; as a driver; as a musician; and as a dog trainer."

"What income streams did you use for your calculations?" asked Renfro.

"Well, there were five," replied Tindle. "First, there was food that he received from St. Ann's. There was a stipulation between the government and the defendant that the value of that food was $1,500 each year, including last year. Second, there was $650 in food and drink from Cousin Clem's, each year. That number was from testimony by Mr. Clement Labrecque in a pretrial proceeding, which, I understand, he has reaffirmed here at trial. Third, there was free rent in the amount of $6,000 per year, for the last two years. That number, again, was by stipulation between the prosecution and the defense. The other two numbers are expert opinions, so I would like to describe those separately, and how we came to them."

Tindle proceeded to describe accounting conventions for the valuation of construction inventory, and his regression analysis for the values he ascribed to feed bags. The jury lost interest until he reached his bottom line numbers. "I determined that last year, Tax Year 5, the inventory transferred to the defendant from Detmer Contracting had a fair market value of $1,099.60, or $1,100 as reported on a tax return," said Tindle. "The 40 fifty-pound bags of goat feed, and 22 fifty-pound bags of chicken feed had a total fair market value of $1,175 last year." He provided similar numbers for Tax Year 1 through Tax Year 4.

On the subject of animal feed, it occurred to Anita that Tindle had mathematized what every grocery store in America determines by trial, error, observation and experience – what price do we set for this item if we're going to have to throw it away in a week, or two weeks, or a month? The government had probably spent fifteen or twenty thousand dollars to induce Dr. Tindle to calculate the value of $5,000 worth of feed bags, received by Patrick over five years. *United States of America vs. Patrick Michael Flaherty* was not about the U.S. Government's need for the tax revenues that Patrick Flahery had allegedly failed to pay. What it *was* about – Anita wasn't quite sure.

"Dr. Tindle, I wanted to clarify one point about the value of free rent that the parties have stipulated," continued Renfro. "You'll recall that amount was $6,000 per year. But there was also testimony that the defendant used materials from Detmer Contracting to improve his animal enclosures. When you were calculating his total income, why didn't you subtract the amount of the property improvements from the free rent the defendant received?" asked Farragut.

"Because, in accounting terms, those were leasehold improvements, not permanent improvements to real property. The landlord wasn't interested in keeping the animal enclosures, and wasn't benefited by them. They only benefited the defendant. Hence, the materials were income to the defendant, but not property that was transferred to the Parish in lieu of rent."

"Dr. Tindle, what did you calculate as the defendant's total income from self-employment in Year 5?"

"We calculated that amount as $10,425. But, of course, that figure is only the income we knew about, or had evidence of, I should say."

"Dr. Tindle, what does your Year 5 tax return for the defendant show for total tax due?" continued Renfro.

"The tax due for Year 5 was $1,053."

"Dr. Tindle, what were your calculations for total income, and total tax due, for Year 4? Please refer to the pro forma tax return you prepared for that year, Government Exhibit 9."

"The numbers were a little different because the defendant received more fencing material in Year 4, at different values, and feed prices were a little different. We calculated his total income as $11,620, and the tax due at $1,232."

Renfro shifted screens with his mouse. "Dr. Tindle, please take a look at Government Exhibit 10 in your monitor. Is that the pro forma tax return you prepared for Year 3?"

"Yes, it is," replied Tindle.

"Doctor, I noticed that the income and tax due are a lot lower for this year. Why is that?"

"The big difference was the value of rent. We were advised that the defendant and his church did not learn that his cabin was on Parish land until Year 4. So there couldn't have been bartering income in the form of rent for Years 3, 2 and 1. Free rent was $500 per month, by stipulation of the parties, so subtracting that amount from the defendant's income results in a reduction of income of $6,000 per year in Years 3, 2 and 1." Tindle looked at Renfro.

"Continue. You were explaining income and tax due for Year 3," said Renfro.

"Combining the food values I've already mentioned, plus the Detmer and Bays inventory records, and our analysis of feed prices, we calculated income as $4,495, and tax as $315, in Year 3."

"Please look at Government Exhibit 11, your pro forma tax return for Year 2. What were your income and tax numbers for that year?"

"Income of $4,401; tax due in the amount of $302."

"And finally, Government Exhibit 12, your pro forma tax return for Year 1?"

"Income of $4,550; tax due in the amount of $325."

"Did you factor the Earned Income Tax Credit into your calculations?" asked Renfro.

"No, because a taxpayer must file a return and then claim the credit as part of that return, before he or she is eligible for the credit. The defendant did not file tax returns, and therefore waived any right to claim the credit."

"Dr. Tindle, do you hold the opinions you have expressed today to a reasonable degree of professional certainty?"

"I do," replied Tindle.

"Cross-examine," said Renfro, and he sat down, very satisfied with himself, and with his witness -- in that order.

Anita walked to the lectern, without notes in her hand. She looked at Dr. Morris Tindle for a moment, and then said, "By my math, you're suggesting that there was $3,227 in tax due, over five years, is that right."

"Yes, that's correct," replied Tindle.

"About $650 a year on average?"

"Yes."

Anita shook her head slightly. "All of *this*" – she extended her arms, and turned slowly to both sides of the courtroom, the spectators, the judge, the jury, the Marshals – "over an amount less than the cost of a very used Honda, is that what you're saying?"

Tindle decided to play dumb. He hesitated. "I haven't looked into the cost of used Hondas," he replied, finally.

"While we're on the subject of what you've looked into, has the government paid your expert witness fee?" asked Anita.

"Yes."

"How much is that?"

"To date, about $75,000."

Anita had made her points. "Your Honor, I have no further questions of this witness."

"Dr. Tindle, you may step down," said Judge Martin, effectively ruling that there was no need for redirect. "The government will call its next witness."

CHAPTER 86

"Your Honor," said Renfro, "the government calls Ranger Lawrence Forstman."

The witness entered the courtroom in his Forest Service uniform. Anita was expecting him, because the government had been obliged to turn over information on any statements Patrick had made to government agents, knowing that they were government agents. Technically, Ranger Forstman was a government agent when he picked up Patrick's phone call to the Forest Service. But Anita was silently dreading the testimony.

Ranger Forstman was sworn, and Renfro began his questioning. "Ranger Forstman, please state your full name, your position with the United States Government, and your present duty assignment."

"My name is Lawrence Forstman. I am a District Ranger with the United States Forest Service. I am presently assigned to the Tongue Ranger District Office in Sheridan, Wyoming."

"Does the District Office get its name from the Tongue River that flows from the Bighorn Mountains through Sheridan County, Wyoming?"

"Yes, I believe so," answered Forstman.

"How long have you served in that position and in that office?" continued Renfro.

"I've been a District Ranger for 22 years," replied Forstman. "I've been posted to the Tongue Ranger District Office for the past five years."

"Were you assigned to the Tongue Ranger District Office in September of last year?"

"Yes, I was."

"Do you recall taking a telephone call at the Tongue Ranger District Office from an individual who identified himself as Patrick Flaherty?"

"Yes, I do."

"On what date did you field that telephone call?"

"That was September 29 of last year."

"How did you know the caller was named Patrick Flaherty?"

"Because he introduced himself by that name."

"Did he say where he was calling from?"

"He told me he lived on the edge of the Bighorn National Forest in Coolidge, Wyoming. Either he didn't say where he was calling from, or I didn't note that fact," said Forstman.

"Did you make notes of the conversation with Mr. Flaherty while you were talking with him?"

"I did."

"Would you look at your monitor please? Government Exhibit 13, for identification, is on the screen. Is that a copy of your handwritten notes of the conversation?"

"Yes, it is," replied Forstman.

"Are those notes kept in a phone log in your office?"

"Yes, they are."

"How did you happen to get involved in this case?" asked Renfro.

"When I heard about this case on television, the report mentioned that the defendant was living in a cabin near the Bighorn Mountains. That triggered a recollection of a phone call that I had, and the name Patrick Flaherty sounded familiar. I went back through our phone logs, and I found our record of the call. I called the U.S. Attorney's Office to tell them about the conversation."

"Would you please recount for the jury the substance of that conversation?" prompted Renfro.

"Mr. Flaherty called to report an encounter with a black bear, which he claimed had stolen one of his goats from his goat enclosure. I asked him, politely, whether the alleged incident had occurred in the Bighorn National Forest. He responded, very clearly and without any uncertainty, that the event had taken place at his cabin, which he said was outside of the National Forest. I explained, again very patiently and courteously, that the Forest Service didn't have jurisdiction to take any action on his complaint, because the alleged event didn't occur in the National Forest. I encouraged him to reach out to the Wyoming Fish and Game Department, which routinely responds to reports of bear incursions."

"How did he respond to your explanation?" asked Renfro.

"He said to me, 'You're a dick,' and hung up the phone."

"No further questions, Your Honor," said Renfro. He returned to his seat.

Anita knew, from Patrick, that the witness had mischaracterized the conversation, but the written notes didn't reflect any facts that weren't in his testimony about the call. In fact, the notes hardly said anything at all. She could only do what she could do. She stood behind the lectern, facing the witness.

"District Ranger Forstman, are you aware that about half of the land in the State of Wyoming is federally-owned?"

"Yes, I believe the figure is 48.1%," responded Forstman.

"And a lot of the land in Wyoming is owned by the state as well, correct?"

"Yes, I think about six percent."

"If somebody is having a problem with a bear, then, there's better than a 50/50 chance that the bear lives on public land, correct?"

"I suppose so."

"Did the caller explain that the bear tracks were headed toward the National Forest and that the bear almost certainly lived there?" she asked.

"I don't know about his saying where the bear lived. My notes say, quote, the tracks were headed toward the National Forest, close quote."

Anita picked up a copy of Government Exhibit 13, Forstman's notes of the phone call. "You put the quotation marks to indicate the actual words that the caller said, did you not?"

"Yes."

"Take a look at the bottom of your note. Do you see the words 'called dick'?"

"Yes."

"Would you agree with me that 'called dick' is not in quotation marks, it's just two words written on the page?"

"Yes."

"Did you note that the caller explained to you that Wyoming Game and Fish had suggested that he call the U.S. Forest Service?"

"I don't recall. That isn't in my notes."

"You spend most of your work day in an office, do you not?"

"I suppose that's true. I get into the forest a lot, however."

"The word 'bureau' is French for 'office,' and the word 'bureaucrat' comes from French as well. Are you a bureaucrat?"

"Objection, Your Honor," interjected Renfro. "That question . . ."

"I can't think of any reason she can't ask that," responded the judge. "Overruled."

"No, I don't think I'm a bureaucrat," responded Forstman.

"Does the United States Forest Service have jurisdiction over bears who live in a National Forest?" asked Anita.

"Yes, that's part of our wildlife habitat function."

"Does the Forest Service take action to deal with nuisance bears in National Forests?"

"Yes, we have a variety of tools available to deal with that situation."

"Would you expect that a person who just had a goat stolen out of his yard by a large black bear would be frightened by that event?"

Forstman hesitated. He wanted to say he didn't know, but of course he did know. "Yes, that could be frightening."

"Where does it say in Forest Service regulations that you can't accept a report about a nuisance bear that likely lives in the National Forest?"

"That's our practice, if the nuisance is outside the National Forest."

"District Ranger Forstman, I didn't ask you what your *practice* is. I asked you, where does it say in Forest Service regulations that you can't accept a report about a nuisance bear that likely lives in the National Forest?"

There was a long silence. "I don't know if I could cite a regulation that says that."

"Were you concerned that Mr. Flaherty might be injured or harmed if no governmental authority took action on his bear report, and the bear came back to Mr. Flaherty's home?"

"No, I wasn't." Forstman had told the truth before he realized what he was saying.

"No further questions, Your Honor."

"Redirect, Mr. Renfro?" asked the judge.

The defendant had said what he said, and even his lawyer didn't challenge that fact. Time to close it down. "No further questions, Your Honor."

CHAPTER 87

"Mr. Farragut, Mr. Renfro, does the government have any further witnesses?" asked Judge Martin.

"No, Your Honor," Farragut replied. "We move for the admission of Government Exhibits 1 through 15."

Anita made objections at sidebar to a few of the exhibits, but Judge Martin admitted them all, with the proviso that Dr. Tindle's expert report would not be sent out with the jury. The jurors would have to rely on their respective recollections of his testimony. After the lawyers had returned to their seats, Farragut stood and addressed the court.

"Your Honor, the government rests."

Judge Martin turned to the jurors. "Members of the jury, we're going to give you a 20 minute break while we take care of some legal matters. Don't discuss the case with each other."

The jurors filed out, and the judge began again when the door closed behind them.

"Counsel, let's proceed to the next step," said Judge Martin. "Ms. Boyle, do you have a motion?"

Anita rose. "Your Honor, the defendant moves for a judgment of acquittal on each charge, and on all of the charges, pursuant to Rule 29. No reasonable juror could conclude, beyond a reasonable doubt, that the defendant knew that he was violating the tax laws, and facts supporting the application of the *Fingado* exception, if it's still good law, have not been proved. Additionally, there is reasonable doubt as a matter of law about whether these were bartering transactions, and therefore reasonable doubt about whether any tax was due. Thus, that element of the crime of tax evasion has not been proved. The case fails for lack of proof on required elements of the crimes alleged."

"Mr. Farragut, I won't need to hear from the government on this one," replied Judge Martin. "The motion for judgment of acquittal is denied as to all counts. I'll see you all back here in 20 minutes."

Anita led Patrick back to the Attorney's Conference Room. He looked concerned as they sat down.

"Anita, why didn't he even think about your motion? How come he decided it without argument?"

"Not to worry. He knows he'll have plenty of other opportunities to throw out the verdict on technical grounds if he doesn't like it. Rule 29 motions are almost never granted, because they take the case away from the jury. Most judges figure they'll let the jury have their say, and then take it from there."

"Are we calling Sam Harrison next?" asked Patrick.

"Yup. He could be our game-changer."

Twenty minutes later, the judge, jury and lawyers were back in their seats. Judge Martin turned toward the defense table. "Ms. Boyle, will the defendant be presenting any evidence?"

"Your Honor, the defendant calls Samuel Harrison, CPA" replied Anita.

As Sam Harrison was making his way to the witness stand, Farragut was on his feet. "Your Honor, the government requests an offer of proof. May we see you at sidebar?"

"OK, Mr. Farragut, Mr. Renfro, Ms. Boyle, let's talk about it."

The lawyers made their way to sidebar, and the judge turned his chair to face them. "Ms. Boyle, I'm not going to ask you in any detail what the witness is going to say – the defense doesn't have any obligation to provide non-expert discovery in a criminal case – but I need to determine relevance. And given the fact that he's a Certified Public Accountant, I want to be sure that he's not being offered as a previously-undisclosed expert."

"Your Honor, Mr. Harrison will testify, as a fact witness, that in his forty years of preparing thousands of tax returns for residents and businesses in Coolidge, he has never prepared a tax return that has declared bartering income."

"He can't . . ." Farragut began.

"Oh boy," said the judge. "We should give the jury a break and talk about this in chambers." Turning to the jury: "Members of the jury, we're going to give you *another* break for twenty minutes or a half hour. Sometimes it just works that way. Please return to your jury room, and, as always, don't discuss the case." To the court reporter: "Sally, come on back to chambers with us." To Sam Harrison: "Mr. Harrison, if you wouldn't mind finding a bench out in the hallway, somebody will come find you after we've talked with counsel." To the lawyers: "Counsel, let's head back to my office."

Anita gestured to Patrick "see you in a bit," and the judge, the reporter, and the lawyers made their way through the back door of the courtroom to the judge's chambers.

CHAPTER 88

They gathered around Judge Martin's round conference table, and everybody was quiet, at first. The windows were letting in a lot of light.

The judge turned to his court reporter: "Is your portable recorder ready; are we all set to go back on the record?" She nodded yes.

"Oh, before we go back on -- Jack, Arnold, Anita, would any of you like a glass of water or some juice?" In Wyoming, judges call lawyers by their first names when their conversations are not on the record. Wyoming's lawyers are fine with that. "No thanks," they replied.

"All right, we're on the record. Let's talk about this," said the judge. "I want to skip past the question of whether the witness is effectively being offered as an expert, to get to what I think is the more important question: Ms. Boyle, why is this testimony relevant under Rule 401?"

"Your Honor, Rule 401 only requires that I demonstrate that the evidence has a tendency to make any fact I'm trying to prove a little more likely to be true than if the evidence weren't admitted. To get a conviction for tax evasion and criminal failure to file a return, the government has to show that my client intended to cheat the government out of tax revenue."

"OK, sure," said the judge.

Anita continued. "There are twenty eight hundred people in Coolidge, and let's say, a hundred or two hundred business returns filed from Coolidge every year, whether on Schedule C or on a partnership or corporate return. We have heard substantial testimony that my client was friends with, or acquainted with, many residents of the town who owned their own businesses. Mr. Harrison will testify that he prepares about two hundred individual returns a year, and at least thirty business returns. He will also testify that while practicing as a CPA in Coolidge for forty years, he has never -- *never* -- prepared a return that included barter income." She paused to let the point sink in.

"Your Honor, people talk about taxes and tax returns, and they gripe and compare notes. I will argue to the jury, on the basis of Mr. Harrison's testimony, that bartering income was just not on the radar, that there were no cues, or hints, or suggestions, or whatever you'd call them, that would have reached Mr. Flaherty's ears to the effect that bartering creates income. I think the inference will be persuasive, because I'm counting on the fact that jurors bring their life experiences to a trial with them; and I'm confident that not a single one of the twelve ever heard of bartering income before stepping foot in your courtroom. Mr. Harrison's testimony will tend to show – it won't prove it all by itself, but it will *tend* to show -- that my client had no earthly reason to believe he was cheating on his taxes by failing to declare bartering income, and that he therefore lacked criminal intent."

"Mr. Farragut?" said the judge.

"Your Honor, frankly that is the weakest argument for relevance I've ever heard."

Anita began to get angry. The stress of three days of trial was taking its toll.

He continued: "Through our evidence of the defendant's statements at Cousin Clem's, we have proved that the defendant is living the way he is living to avoid taxes. We have proved that he intentionally refrained from seeing an accountant to educate himself about what taxes he owed. We don't need to prove that he knew which taxes he was avoiding, as long as we can show, beyond a reasonable doubt, that he intended to evade paying tax. We've never suggested, and wouldn't suggest, that he would have heard about bartering income from friends. We don't know whether he did, and neither, I submit, does Ms. Boyle, really. And we don't care. I understand that Mr. Flaherty is not obliged to testify, but it's a remarkable stretch, to say the least, for Ms. Boyle to suggest that she can prove what the defendant was thinking, or not thinking, through the testimony of someone else, who, from what I can tell from Ms. Boyle's offer of proof, never seems to have talked to the defendant about his taxes. She hasn't suggested he was the defendant's CPA. If she wants the jury to hear Mr. Flaherty's thoughts about bartering, she's going to have to call him to the witness stand."

The judge scratched his chin. "Ms. Boyle, let me say, I think you're right that you don't have to demonstrate your evidence has a high level of probative value to show some relevance. Your hurdle isn't that high, and I'm fairly liberal about admissibility. But I've got to hear something that would suggest to me that some of the town's collective ignorance on the subject of bartering was somehow transferable or imputable to your client – otherwise, the evidence isn't even arguably relevant under Rule 401. I haven't heard that foundation evidence." He paused to let Anita respond.

Anita's frustrations from the past few months began to boil over. "Your Honor, I think even Mr. Farragut would agree that if the jury hears Mr. Harrison's testimony, and understands how unfairly selective this prosecution really is, his chances of obtaining a conviction will be just about zero. Why is this despicable prosecution even here?"

She raised her voice another notch. "Mr. Farragut can pretend that this case is just a dispassionate application of federal tax law, but he knows better. This case *stinks*, and when the jury hears from our CPA that virtually no one pays tax on bartering income, they'll agree. *That's* why he opposes the evidence, not because he doesn't think it's relevant. He thinks it's *too* relevant."

Judge Martin interrupted. "Ms. Boyle, take a deep breath. I don't need to hear about Mr. Farragut's motivations, and you don't need to resort to that kind of argument. OK, I've heard enough." He felt bad he had to chastise her. She'd tried a good case, and, as a rule, he liked lawyers who cared.

"Mr. Farragut, just to clarify, do you object to the evidence on the basis of a lack of relevance?"

"Yes, Your Honor."

The judge turned to his court reporter, to memorialize his ruling for any eventual appeal. "I'm going to exclude the testimony from Mr. Harrison as irrelevant under Rule 401; and I also want to make clear that I'm excluding it under Rule 403 as well, because even if it's marginally relevant, its tendency to confuse the issues, or invite the jury to decide the case on an improper basis, outweighs any probative value."

"Let's go off the record." To his reporter, "Sally, go grab a coffee if you'd like, thanks."

After the reporter had left, Judge Martin turned to the lawyers. "Counsel, we've now spent most of a week on this case, and I hope you won't mind if I vent a little, just because."

He addressed Farragut first. "Jack, just because I don't think you deserve the blame for this case being here, doesn't mean I like what I've heard. I think it's an egregious waste of judicial resources, and a waste of the jurors' time. I have no idea why DOJ thought this case is winning them any friends among the masses."

He continued, turning to Anita. "Having said that: Anita, I think you're looking at a guilty verdict. I think the government's case is a little weak on the whole Hospitality Supper thing – I don't see real solid evidence of an agreement or *quid pro quo*, although I will tell you I think there's enough to go to the jury. But on the other four charges . . ." He began to count them off on his fingers – "The construction materials in exchange for junkyard runs; the repairs in exchange for free rent; the feed bags in exchange for dog training; and, especially, the music in exchange for food and beer. For all those, I think your guy was bartering, and I think he owed self-employment tax on the income. And his statements in the bar are enough to support a conclusion that he was intentionally evading tax. I agree with Jack that the government doesn't need to prove that he knew which tax he was avoiding, so long as they can show that he was deliberately ignorant within the meaning of *Fingado*. So I think the government has proved what it needed to prove. Fortunately for you, I'm not the decision-maker in this case -- the jury is."

Anita was pained at the judge's words. She thought her case was going pretty well, and it hurt to hear a neutral party predicting the worst.

Judge Martin continued. "To be clear, I'm not telling you this to influence plea discussions in any way, assuming that plea negotiations have been occurring. I'm not allowed to get involved in plea discussions, and I wouldn't do that. I'm really only amplifying my reasons for denying your motion for acquittal, and giving you some idea of what my charge to the jury on intent is going to look like. Having said that, if you want me to recess for the day to give the parties time to talk about a plea, I'm happy to do that."

"I don't think we need more time Your Honor," said Farragut. "We're pretty much deadlocked on any kind of plea deal."

Anita felt that she had been placed on the spot to explain her client's decision to proceed to a verdict. "Judge, I appreciate that you can't be involved in plea discussions, but since your courtroom is now taken up with a case in which the defendant is insisting that the government bear its burden of proof, I want to explain to you why that is. And a lot of these issues might come up again at sentencing, when we address acceptance of responsibility, or a lack thereof."

She collected her thoughts, and continued. "I think the evidence has shown that Patrick Flaherty is a good man. He's generous, and he's built a good life for himself in the past seven years, even if it's a life that most of us wouldn't choose. If he pleaded guilty, he'd owe taxes and penalties and court costs that he doesn't have the cash to pay. More important – far more important – he'd lose everything he has, maybe not right away, but ultimately. As a felon, he wouldn't be able to keep his firearms, so he wouldn't be able to hunt for food. If he were a convicted criminal, a tax cheat, St. Ann's is not going to let him live on its land for free, and wouldn't be sending food home with him. Why should they? It just invites trouble. It's the same with Mr. Bays at the feed store. He would train his own dogs, and my client would have to find cash he doesn't have to feed his goats and chickens, if he still has them. Cousin Clem's would be sure to charge him for all his food and drink, because why wouldn't they?"

She took a breath, and looked at Judge Martin. "We like to think we know who people really are, and that we'll give them the benefit of the doubt, but how true is that, really? If he admits he's guilty as charged, would his neighbors in Coolidge ever feel the same way about him? He isn't sure. And that's why he doesn't want to plead guilty. Continuing on to a verdict is not a bad option for him. If he were convicted, he might do some extra time in jail that he could have avoided with a plea, but at least he would have three free meals a day, and, ironically, he wouldn't owe tax on them. And when he got out, he'd be facing the same challenges that he would if he'd pleaded guilty, no worse."

She looked at the prosecutors and the judge. "If he's acquitted, on the other hand, he can go back to his life and his community. He can keep what he's built for himself. That's the goal."

The room was quiet. Judge Martin tapped a pencil, and Jack Farragut looked at his legal pad. Arnold Renfro smirked at the ceiling.

"Makes sense," said the judge. "That's why we have juries."

CHAPTER 89

The lawyers filed back into the courtroom, while the judge handled a phone call in chambers. Anita explained to Patrick that Sam Harrison's testimony had been excluded. The jury came back into the jury box. Five minutes later, the judge reappeared on the bench.

"Members of the jury, for technical reasons, we have determined that Mr. Harrison's testimony would not be helpful to you in deciding the case. And that's no criticism of the defense – it was a close legal question, and the defense had every right to offer his testimony, subject to the court's ruling on its admissibility."

Turning to Anita, the judge asked, "Ms. Boyle, does the defendant wish to call any other witnesses or offer any additional evidence?"

Anita had considered calling character witnesses, but had decided that Harry, Clem, Bobby, Mavis and Father Dave had shown how Patrick was regarded in the community. She rose to respond to the judge: "No, Your Honor. The defense rests."

"Members of the jury," Judge Martin continued, "I want to emphasize to you, again, that the defendant never has any obligation to testify or present evidence in a criminal case. The burden of proof remains solely on the prosecution. I instruct you that you are to draw no adverse inferences against the defendant because he did not present any evidence in his own case – and, of course, as you'll recall, Ms. Boyle elicited a great deal of evidence on the defendant's behalf during the prosecution's case. The defendant is fully within his rights not to present additional evidence, and fully within his rights simply to require the government to prove its case."

The judge checked his notes and his watch. "Members of the jury, at this point I will dismiss you for the day. We've heard a lot of evidence, and I'm sure you're ready for your trip home, or to your lodging if you're staying in Casper. Again, if you see anything about this case in the newspaper, or on TV, or online, or hear anything on the radio, please turn it off or put down the paper. Everything you hear about the facts of this case will be, and should be, presented here, in court. Don't discuss the case among yourselves. Thanks for your attention today. We'll see you tomorrow."

When the jury was gone, the judge turned to the lawyers. "Counsel, my law clerk will give you a printout with our rulings on your respective points for charge. We'll see you tomorrow morning for closing arguments."

CHAPTER 90

Anita, Patrick, Patrick's family, and a few friends climbed into Ubers and headed back to their hotel for the evening. Dinner was pizzas and subs, delivered. It was staying light until almost 8:30, and a couple of the ladies from St. Ann's went for a late walk.

Anita was rehearsing her closing argument, and finding the process difficult. Not because she didn't know what she wanted to say – on the contrary, she had thought about her argument so much that it had begun to feel a little stale. She opted not to repeat Judge Martin's prediction – a guilty verdict – to Patrick or his family. There was no point.

Ed and Dina's room was serving as headquarters again. When Anita took a break from her rehearsal, she dropped in to see how everyone was doing. Patrick saw her come in, and rose to meet her. "Give me a minute in the hallway?"

"Sure," said Anita.

They both leaned against the wall, tired and subdued. "It's a shame neither of us smokes." said Anita. "This would be a perfect time to head outside and light up."

"Yeah. It's amazing how doing something like that let's you think, and not think, at the same time. I don't want to think." He sighed, and looked at Anita. "I wanted to hear *your* thoughts. Globally, how did we do?"

"We did fine. Better than fine. You need to believe that, and your parents need to believe it."

"That's what's killing me," Patrick replied. "If I were alone with all of this, I think I could block it out, even accept the possibility of a guilty verdict. Time in jail wouldn't be – won't be – the end of my life. But it's not fair to my parents. They have to go through all this pain because of my choices."

Anita considered her response. "I understand why you're saying that, but you're not the only one. It's true of everyone. We live our lives, and everything bad that happens to us – illnesses, accidents, divorces, unemployment, you name it – causes pain to our parents. And some of that pain can be the result of decisions we made that didn't work out. But that doesn't mean we can stop making choices for ourselves. Parents have to trust their children to live their own lives. It's just the way it is, and always will be."

"Sure. But that's one of those things that's easy in the abstract, and hard when you're living it. I wish I had somehow been traveling in New Zealand, and I could have called them and said, 'Miss you guys, by the way I'll be in jail for three or four years, see you when I get out.' They could have dealt more easily with the worst case if it had happened all at once. But this Chinese water torture is just awful."

"Patrick, listen to me. The best thing about you is that you care about other people. You're not some selfish bastard trying to game the system, the way they're portraying you in court. I believe in juries, and I believe this jury has figured out who you are. Trust that they'll get it right."

Patrick nodded. In that moment, at least, he believed her.

CHAPTER 91

"Members of the jury, good morning," Judge Martin began. "As you heard, the prosecution and defense have both rested. We are now going to be hearing the closing arguments of counsel for each side. We will begin with the defendant's argument. The prosecution will argue second, and last, because the government always has the burden of proof. Please remember that what the lawyers say in the next hour or so is not evidence. Their role, at this point, is to examine the evidence and tell you what they believe the evidence shows. Keep an open mind until you've heard all of the arguments. But if a lawyer says something about the evidence that doesn't conform to your recollection, remember that it's your recollection of the evidence that controls, not theirs. You are the final and only judges of the facts." Judge Martin looked across his bench and the well of the courtroom to Anita. "Ms. Boyle, you may present the closing argument for the defendant."

"Thank you, Your Honor," said Anita, as she took her place before the jury box. She knew what she wanted to say – she had known it for months – and she spoke without notes.

"Ladies and gentlemen, good morning.

"I served on a jury once, when I was in college. I remember I had already pretty much decided how I was going to vote on the case as I was headed into the courthouse on the morning for closing arguments. I wasn't much interested in what the lawyers were going to say about the evidence, because I had heard all of their evidence as it was presented.

"Technically, that was wrong of me. As Judge Martin just explained, you need to keep an open mind until you've heard all of the arguments from counsel, and, especially, the instructions on the law from the court.

"But we're all human, and you wouldn't be human if you didn't have some private views about the evidence that you'll want to share with other jurors, for the first time, when you begin to deliberate later on today. That's all been pent up for the last few days, so it will feel good, finally, to be able to talk with each other about the case. I'm not going to try to persuade you of anything you might not agree with, or talk you into something – I'm not going to insult your intelligence. My goal, now, is much more modest. If I'm able to remind you of a fact here and there, or cause you to see a particular piece of evidence in a new light, then I will have done my job. Your job is the one that's really important today. Patrick Flaherty's future is in your hands.

"As Judge Martin will explain in his instructions a little bit later, to find Patrick Flaherty guilty of tax evasion, the first thing you need to figure out is whether he owed taxes. Simple, right? And to find that he owed taxes, you would first have to conclude – beyond any reasonable doubt – that other people paid for his services by giving him valuable property, meals, or free rent. That's the operative phrase: 'paid for.'

"Now, the prosecution will tell you that Patrick had five different bartering transactions going on, all at once. Well, OK, let's look at that. First, ask yourself: What does it mean when someone 'pays for' something?

"For example. You put your bottle of vitamins on the counter at the drugstore. When does the clerk put them in the bag and give them back to you? When you've paid the money. Does she let you have them if you haven't paid money? No.

"Or in the context of bartering. I go to the car dealer. I have a big, expensive used car that I want to trade for a small new car. The dealer says 'OK, sure.' Does he give me the keys to the new car without my signing over the title to my used car? No, of course not. I don't get the new car until I give my car to the dealer.

"Or you want to take a trip. You go online to find a flight or a bus ticket. You tell the airline or the bus company what time you want to leave and where you want to go. They tell you sure, you can have a ticket – but first we need your credit card information. No credit card, no ticket. You have to pay for it.

"And then there's Amazon. If only I could get them to send me some of the ridiculous things I buy without giving them my credit card. But, as you know, it doesn't work that way. You have to pay for the things you want.

"We all accept it as a fact of life, and some of us" – Anita pointed to herself – "actually think shopping is fun. But that's the way it is with transactions – you have to pay for stuff, and you don't get until you give.

"With that in mind, let's look at the prosecution's evidence of five supposed bartering transactions. Let's begin with the dog training. Mr. Bays said, before this case was ever brought or even considered, that he would give the animal feed to Patrick whether Patrick trained his dogs or not. You could hear the affection he had for Patrick, and you could tell he was obviously telling the truth. And Patrick plainly loved the dogs, and he hunts with them. Nobody was saying, 'You don't get the dog training until you pay for it.' Patrick didn't say that, he wouldn't say that. Mr. Bays didn't say, 'you don't get the feed bags unless you train my dogs.' Why? Because neither would have said something like that, or meant it. Because there was no bartering agreement.

"Next up is fencing materials and lumber from Detmer Contracting. Mr. Detmer told Patrick that he could have the older inventory from the back lot whether he drove to the dump or not. And he said the debris had no value at all, and Patrick was happy to drive the truck just to get a chance to pick through it. Again, nobody was saying, 'I'm not driving unless you pay me for it.' Because there was no bartering agreement.

"The prosecution is O for 2. Batting third, Hospitality Supper for handyman work at the church. Come on, really? Picture Mavis D'Antonio and the nice ladies at the church who cook and serve food every Saturday night. Did they ever once say to Patrick, 'no food for you young man, unless you paint the storage closet in the Rectory'? Of course not.

"Do you recall the testimony by Agent Lawless? He testified that the IRS didn't care whether St. Ann's believed the food was payment for services. The IRS didn't care whether there was a real two-sided bargaining agreement. They were willing to prosecute Patrick Flaherty because he believed, however naively, that kindnesses should be returned.

"The only evidence of a deal that they have is Mavis D'Antonio saying 'it would be wrong' not to give Patrick food each week, given what he gave to the Parish. Well, she explained that statement: they would have given him the food no matter what. No one was saying, 'Unless you work around the Parish, we won't pay for your services with food.' No bartering agreement there.

"Fourth, music for food. Here, I think, the key is to look at Patrick Flaherty's conduct first. It's the dog that didn't bark, like in the Sherlock Holmes story. A nothing that proves something. What was that? Patrick didn't put out a tip jar. No tip jar. What that means, of course, is that he was happy to play music for free. His friends were all there, and he loved to play music. He went into Cousin Clem's four or five nights a week as it was, and often spent what little money he had to be with his friends. And Clem Labrecque – you remember him, the big guy. He gave Patrick a free meal every chance he got, just because. Patrick was playing his heart out every Friday night, for free. He never said to Clem, or thought to himself, 'Clem, you don't get any music until you pay for it.' Because they weren't bartering.

"Finally, number five. The big dollar item in this very no-dollar case. Free rent, says the prosecution, in exchange for maintenance and upkeep of the cabin. There was a *'deal'* they say. But they're grabbing one word that was maybe said by Father Hernandez to Agent Bolton, and taking it out of any reasonable context. Then they're trying to hang a criminal charge on it. The truth, the whole truth, and nothing but the truth was contained in one question and answer while Father Hernandez was testifying. It went by quickly, and it would have been entirely understandable if you missed it. I asked Father Hernandez, 'When you discovered that Patrick's cabin was on Parish land, did it ever occur to you to ask him to move?' And he replied, immediately, 'No, of course not, that cabin is his home.' There was no written lease, there was no handshake, there was no deal. In short, St. Ann's never said to Patrick, and was never going to say to Patrick, "we're giving you free rent to pay for your maintenance work on the cabin.' So there was no bartering agreement.

"As Judge Martin will explain, the operative phrase in all this is, 'pay for,' and you're going to decide whether anything was 'paid for' by looking at all of the facts and circumstances. The question is, did St. Ann's, Mr. Bays, Mr. Detmer, and Mr. Labrecque 'pay for' Patrick Flaherty's services with property, food and rent? Well, we know that some property and food were given, but the 'for' part, that's the real issue. It's not 'pay *to*.' The phrase 'pay for,' and the word 'for,' itself, describe a two-sided agreement, a genuine meeting of the minds on all of the terms of payment. You can't pay 'for' something unless the other side knows and agrees what you're paying 'for.' Otherwise, it's just a gratuitous transfer of possession, essentially, a gift. Without the bow and the card, of course, but still a gift.

"Now, Mr. Farragut is a very capable attorney, and I expect he is going to deal with these issues head on. I think you're going to hear some version of, 'Well, there's a lot of ways to express agreement on the terms of a deal, and one of those ways is to do the work, knowing that you're being compensated for it.' I will grant you, I really will, that that argument gets him into the ballpark, and maybe to first base. It makes it look like *maybe* there was some sort of meeting of the minds. But, despite my analogies, for which I apologize, this isn't baseball, it's a criminal trial, and Mr. Farragut and the United States Government must prove the existence of each of these bartering agreements *beyond a reasonable doubt*. And this is the most important thing I will be saying to you: You can never be sure that both sides were looking at an arrangement as a payment *for* something, rather than as a gift or a favor, unless somebody said, clearly and unmistakably, 'Pay me: You don't get until you give.' No party to any of these events ever said, 'I won't work unless I'm paid for it,' or 'I won't pay you unless you work.' Therefore, there *has to be* reasonable doubt. And where you have a reasonable doubt, you have a solemn obligation to vote not guilty.

Anita went back to counsel table for a sip of water, and gave the jurors a chance to think about what she had just said. She resumed her spot before the jury box.

"Now, one of my jobs right now is to answer the hard questions you would be asking me if you could. And you're probably concerned about two statements: 'Fuck the IRS,' and 'You're a dick.' The prosecution says those statements reflect my client's anger at the United States Government and show that he was motivated to cheat the government out of tax revenues.

"You heard Clem Labrecque testify that he was behind his bar on the night of October 2nd of last year, the night Agent Bolton came in, and he didn't hear Patrick shout 'Fuck the IRS' all the way down the bar to the gang at the other end. He never heard Patrick say anything like that at any other time, either. So I submit to you that there's reasonable doubt about whether Patrick said it, and whether Agent Bolton heard him correctly. And as for 'You're a dick,' you'll recall that, in his notes of the call with Patrick Flaherty, Ranger Forstman put quotation marks around actual quotes. But the words, 'called dick,' were not in quotes. I suggest to you, respectfully, that the actual words might have been, 'Please, sir, don't be a dick about this.' Not polite, to be sure, but something a frustrated 29-year old whose animal pen had just been destroyed by a bear might say when he was getting nowhere with his call for help from the Forest Service. Certainly reasonable doubt as to whether the words indicated some deep-seated resentment of the federal government.

"But I don't want to split hairs about these comments. Rather, I'd like to ask you to look at the bigger picture. You've gotten to know Patrick Flaherty during the trial. You've heard from his friends. He grows his own vegetables, he raises goats for milk and meat, and he raises chickens for eggs and meat. He hunts game for food, but only in season. He works hard, with pride, and he takes responsibility for himself and his choices. Apart from these two fragments of impolite language, does Patrick Flaherty sound to you like an angry person? Does the young man who talks with little old ladies after church sound like an angry person? Does the singer and guitar player who plays music for his friends sound like an angry person? Does the young man who invited his parents to celebrate his birthday with a dozen friends at Cousin Clem's sound like an angry person? For that matter, does the person who engaged a total stranger, Agent Arthur Bolton, in pleasant conversation on a Friday night sound like an angry person?

"What I'm about to say will maybe sound like I'm talking about religion, but I'm not. We all come from different traditions, and of course I respect that. But just about every religion, every culture has some version of the axiom, 'you know a person by his deeds.' Patrick Flaherty spends *a lot* of time doing for other people. There was a lot of evidence about that. What you didn't hear was any evidence, other than these two very random alleged comments, that Patrick had some sort of grudge against the federal government. If that were true, you would have seen a real pattern, not two isolated comments reported by federal employees who had a motive to read something sinister into them.

"Finally, let me talk about state of mind. Judge Martin will instruct you that, to find Patrick Flaherty guilty of tax evasion, you must find that he willfully attempted to evade or defeat tax. Normally, the government has to prove that the defendant understood that his transactions were taxable before they can convict him of tax evasion. There's a sort of exception to that rule, however, and the government is relying on the exception. They say that if the defendant was deliberately ignorant about his obligations under the tax laws, then the government doesn't have to prove that the defendant knew and understood that his transactions were taxable.

"What's the government's evidence that Patrick was 'deliberately ignorant' about his tax obligations? That would be Agent Bolton's testimony that Patrick said he never went to an accountant because he 'didn't want to know' if he owed taxes.

"Oh boy, if there were ever a danger that an agent were hearing what he wanted to hear, this is it. You heard Agents Bolton and Lawless admit that this was the first bartering case they'd ever been involved with. They had to be worried that Patrick could show that he had no idea that bartering was subject to federal tax, and that would be a good defense. So, how convenient – Bolton pretends he's an accountant, and he asks his target, Patrick Flaherty, why he didn't go see an accountant about his taxes. He's obviously maneuvering to get a statement that will help him prove that the target 'deliberately' avoided learning about his tax obligations. And so Patrick supposedly says – we don't know, because it wasn't on tape – but Patrick supposedly says something in response to 'Why don't you go see an accountant' that sounds to Agent Bolton like 'I don't want to know what he'd tell me,' and, all of a sudden, here we are in a federal courtroom.

"Respectfully, Agent Bolton, let me help you understand your notes." She turned to face Bolton sitting 15 feet to her left. "The target, Mr. Flaherty, doesn't have a dime, and couldn't afford an hour of an accountant's time if he scraped out every quarter or nickel from his couch cushions for the rest of his life. Additionally, Agent Bolton, there was a zero percent chance that Patrick Flaherty was ever going to hire a $100 per hour accountant to look at his taxes, whether he was concerned about what he would hear, or not. The fact that you could maneuver him into saying, half-jokingly it sounds like, that he didn't want to hear any bad news from an accountant proves that you have a talent for causing nice people to say things they don't really mean over a friendly beer on a Friday night. It doesn't prove, beyond a reasonable doubt, that Patrick

Flaherty was deliberately avoiding knowledge of his tax obligations." She turned back to the jury.

"Ladies and gentlemen, if there is one piece of evidence in this case that cries out for reasonable doubt on your part, it's this supposed 'I don't want to know' statement. It's the government's whole case. Unless you're 100% sure that Patrick Flaherty was really, really, really trying to avoid learning about federal tax laws, for fear that he owed money, then the government hasn't proved its exception, and ignorance of the tax laws is a complete defense.

"So let me help you evaluate the statement that Agent Bolton claims Patrick made. 'I don't want to know if I owe tax,' supposedly. It sounded to me like bar talk, but let's take it a step further. Suppose Agent Bolton had said, 'You know, I'm an accountant, and I can tell you that if you're bartering, you may have to pay income tax on it. Seriously. I think you should pay a quick visit to an accountant. You probably don't owe much – maybe six hundred dollars a year, maybe more – but you should check it out. It's serious business, and no joking matter.'

"What if he had said that? What do we know about Patrick Flaherty's state of mind? Well, on the subject of complying with laws, we know a lot about Patrick Flaherty. He won't hunt game out of season, even though game meat is an important part of what he lives on. Bobby Bays told you that. And he complies with environmental laws, even though he lives in an isolated cabin out in the woods. Father Hernandez told you that. Ask yourself: Does this sound like the kind of person who, if he had been told by a professional accountant that he really might owe taxes, he would have said, 'forget it, I don't want to know'? If you have any doubt about whether Patrick Flaherty was intentionally avoiding getting answers to those tax questions, there is reasonable doubt, and you have to vote to acquit. As Judge Martin will explain, the government can only prevail if you believe, beyond a reasonable doubt, that Patrick Flaherty was *deliberately ignorant* of the tax laws. If you think he might well have seen an accountant if Agent Bolton had talked to him about bartering in a helpful, respectful way, then you must vote to acquit.

"Was Agent Bolton helpful and respectful? Nope, not even a little. What a nice thing to do." She turned again to face Bolton. "Get your target talking about bartering, Agent Bolton, but don't let him know that bartering is subject to federal income tax. No, just arrest him for it four months later. What a travesty." She turned from Bolton back to the jury.

"Ladies and gentlemen, let me say it again, as clearly as I can. This case is a travesty. The United States Government has decided to try to criminalize our social compact. Some people call it the social contract, others the social compact, it's the same thing. It's a part of our language. 'One good turn deserves another,' or, 'Give, and you shall receive.'

"As I said to you at the beginning of the case, the social compact says that I borrow sugar from you on Tuesday, you borrow milk from me on Thursday. It's the glue that holds us all together. You take your elderly neighbor's trash cans to and from her side yard to the street on trash day; she bakes you cookies every so often to show she appreciates it. You watch your daughter's friend while her mom is still at work; her mom takes both of the girls out horseback riding on the weekend. You watch your neighbors' home while they're camping – they even give you a key. In turn, they make sure to let you know that there's a coyote in the neighborhood, so you can keep your cats safe. The list is endless.

"Patrick Flaherty will admit one thing, ladies and gentlemen, whether it helps his case or not. When Bobby Bays helped him feed his animals, and when Harry Detmer helped him build out his cabin, *of course* he wanted to do something for them in return. When Clem Labrecque showed him and his parents every kindness imaginable, and gave him a place to be with his friends, *of course* he was happy to play music for free. And when St. Ann's Church helped him in so many ways, *of course*, he wanted to give back. He wouldn't be who he is if he didn't. But those aren't bartering transactions. They weren't two-sided agreements, where each party conditions their performance of a contract on the other side's performance of the contract. On the contrary, they're perfect examples of simple mutual kindnesses. They're what the social compact is all about.

"Ladies and gentlemen of the jury, let me go back to where I began. You've learned a lot about Patrick Flaherty in the past three days, and nothing that I said is going to affect your judgment about him. Nor should it. That's your judgment to make. I will say this, on Patrick's behalf – he is very grateful, and thankful, that he has all of you standing between him and the immense power of the United States Government. He knows that, whatever your verdict, you have given him a fair hearing, and he deeply appreciates that. Thank you again for your time and your attention."

With that, Anita took a breath, and returned to her seat beside her client. Patrick squeezed the back of her hand without realizing he was doing it.

CHAPTER 92

Farragut put his notes on the small portable lectern, now positioned in front of the jury box. "Good morning, ladies and gentlemen. My name is John Farragut. With me, as you know, has been Arnold Renfro. It is my privilege to address you one last time on behalf of the United States.

"The defendant, Patrick Michael Flaherty, is charged with 20 counts of willful evasion of federal taxes. We submit to you that the government has proved each of those charges beyond a reasonable doubt.

"In our century, we've reached the point in our civil life where, at least when it comes to taxes, you don't get to say, 'Stop the world, I want to get off.' That may be a hard truth, and maybe some of us would wish it weren't so. But that's the truth. It's the real social compact, if you will. You can't just declare yourself an independent country and insist that everyone else pay your taxes.

"No one is telling Patrick Flaherty how to live his life. But there are simple rules about what he owes in taxes given the life he's chosen. I didn't make those rules, Judge Martin didn't make those rules. The people's democratically-elected representatives made those rules.

"The defendant, however, thinks he can make his own rules, and judge himself innocent. How did his lawyer put it? You have to give or get to give, or whatever. Judge Martin will explain the law governing this case, and I guarantee you that give, get, got will not be any part of what he tells you.

"It shows breathtaking arrogance that the defendant would make up his own standards and ask you to apply them. But that's how he has behaved all along. He thinks he makes his own rules.

"The defendant was engaged in five separate, continuous bartering transactions. Let's look at the evidence for each of those five, one at a time.

"First, musical performances, paid for by free food and drink. Here, the defendant earned one seventh of his weekly dinners for two hours of work. There was no question -- no question – about the terms of this arrangement. The defendant told Special Agent Bolton that he provided musical services to Cousin Clem's in exchange for free food and drink. It was one of the first things that Special Agent Bolton asked him about, and, in fact, it was the first bartering arrangement that the defendant disclosed. And, remember, Special Agent Bolton actually *saw* the defendant drink a beer he hadn't paid for, and saw him eating a French fry that he brought from back in the kitchen.

"Then, Agent Lawless went back to Cousin Clem's and asked the owner, Clement Labrecque, whether the defendant received free food and drink in exchange for musical services. Mr. Labrecque told him, 'All our musicians eat and drink for free while they're playing.' And when he testified here in court, Mr. Labrecque told you that he gave the defendant food on nights he was playing music because he had earned it. He had earned it.

"When you have both sides of a transaction admitting that it was food and drink to pay for musical services, there's not much more to say. The defendant was bartering. He received $650 per year in food and drink. The defense is just trying to confuse the issue. Don't be misled.

"Next up – free rent in exchange for maintenance services. Ladies and gentlemen, for the life of me, I can't even understand the defendant's argument on this one. St. Ann's Parish owned the cabin, through a trust. As the landlord, St. Ann's could decide what to do with it. Father Hernandez testified before you that Patrick Flaherty had worked on the cabin; therefore, he was permitted to occupy it. Father Hernandez also told Special Agent Bolton that the defendant was obligated to maintain the cabin to be permitted to stay in it. Father Hernandez described that understanding as, and I quote, 'the deal.' Which is an interesting choice of words, because it's exactly what the defendant said to Special Agent Bolton in Cousin Clem's: he was maintaining the cabin for the Parish as 'part of the deal.' And why wouldn't he be doing that? Can you actually envision the Parish letting him stay if he were letting the cabin fall into ruin, and diminishing the value of the whole property?

"Let's look at the third bartering deal. Driving services in exchange for fencing and building materials. The defendant tells Special Agent Bolton, in Cousin Clem's, that he took fencing and building materials from the back lot at Detmer Contracting, and in exchange, he drove one of Detmer Contracting's trucks to the landfill on a regular basis, to dispose of construction debris. Later, Special Agent Bolton goes into Detmer Contracting, in an undercover capacity, and asks about Detmer Contracting's trash disposal needs. They reply that they already have a guy doing it for them. Mr. Detmer says, 'Our guy collects our debris and takes it to the landfill, in exchange for cyclone fencing, and railroad ties, stuff for his animal enclosures. He also takes whatever materials in the debris might be usable for his purposes.' So, again, both parties to the bartering transaction describe it in similar terms. Fencing and lumber paid for driving services.

"Next deal: the defendant needs animal feeds for his goats and chickens, and animal feeds cost money. The defendant decides to barter instead. Mr. Bays says to Special Agent Bolton that he couldn't say how much the defendant would charge, in cash, for dog training, because the defendant doesn't charge cash. As Mr. Bays summed it up, in exchange for dog training services, 'I swap him feed for his chickens and goats.'

"Finally, the very substantial bartering deal that the defendant worked out with St. Ann's to obtain food on Saturday nights. He was eating his fill on Saturday, and then loading up a knapsack with four more nights' worth of food, which, when you combine it with his Friday dinner from Cousin Clem's, meant that the defendant was bartering for five of his seven weekly dinners. As you're listening to the arguments the defense is making about a vegetable garden, goat's milk, and eggs, remember that other people are cooking a substantial majority of the defendant's dinners. Is that important enough to barter for? You bet.

"You heard Ms. D'Antonio, the Parish administrator, say that St. Ann's was providing food to Patrick Flaherty in significant part because he provided labor to help maintain the Parish property. She testified that the Parish's, quote, 'understanding,' close quote, with Patrick Flaherty was unique. She said the Parish has a moral obligation to give him the food. And no one else, other than the defendant, regularly took food home from Hospitality Supper.

"The defendant confirmed that arrangement. He told Special Agent Bolton, in Cousin Clem's, that he did handyman work at the church and at the rectory. And about that work he said, 'You have to give back. It's part of the deal.'

"So there they are, five bartering transactions. All continued for the five years at issue, except the deal for free rent, which was in effect during the last two of the five years.

"The incredible thing is that the defense doesn't even argue about the basic facts – and by that I mean, the basic facts about the value the defendant received, and the labor that he provided in return. The defense is pushing this crazy notion that if you would have done something for nothing, then you can't have been 'paid for' your labor.

"But that doesn't make any sense. We have all known people who love their jobs, and they keep working long after they could have retired. And they don't need the money, and will tell you that. Is the United States Government supposed to say, 'Oh, well, that's all right, you don't have to pay tax on your income, because we know you'd probably work for free anyway.' Come on, that's not the way it works. If you accept pay – or, in this case, valuable property -- for what you do, you have to pay tax on it. Whether you would do it for free, or whether the other party would give it to you for free, is beside the point.

"And please pay particular attention to this evidence from Mr. Bays and Mr. Detmer about how they're now ready to give materials to the defendant for free. When did they say that? Both of them said it in September of last year, which was after the fifth tax year in issue. But go back, say, four years, when the defendant had only been in Coolidge for a year or two. Was Harry Detmer -- a hard-headed businessman if I've ever seen one -- was Harry Detmer going to say to a guy he'd only known for a year or two, 'that's OK, take more than a thousand dollars of inventory out of my lot each year, you can have it for free.' Why would he have said something like that? You know that he was giving the defendant the fencing materials and lumber because he was getting driving services in return. Don't believe the defendant's spin based on supposed conversations years later.

"Another thing. Why would Mr. Bays, or Mr. Detmer, feel a need to tell the defendant that he could have something for free, unless they believed the defendant understood, at that point, that the property he was getting was paying for his labor? There was no reason to tell him it would be free, except that both parties knew that they were exchanging property for labor, and the deal, maybe, was about to change.

"Let's talk about things the defendant said. The defense wants you to ignore 'Fuck the IRS' and 'you're a dick,' and look at other things the defendant has said or done. Well, I guess I don't blame them. When you've said something really incriminating, of course you want the jury to focus on something else.

"But this is where you can apply your knowledge of people, how they talk, how they think. Have you ever had the experience where you've known somebody for a year or two, and they're kind of a friend, or maybe halfway between an acquaintance and a friend? And then all of a sudden, one day, they blurt out something incredibly racist. It could be one word, or two or three. But you can't think of them the same way anymore. Only a real racist could say something like that, even if it's only once.

"Or maybe you have a close friend, and, for whatever reason, you didn't know her husband very well. But you're starting to get to know him, and he seems like a nice guy, but all of a sudden he says something incredibly cruel and demeaning about his wife, your close friend. It changes everything, in an instant, because a little window was opened, and you saw how the person really thinks.

"Now, of course I'm not saying that Mr. Flaherty is a racist or demeaning to women, and I'm not using those examples to suggest to you that he is. I'm not trying to get you to associate him with bad things. But I know you understand my point. Sometimes a person will say something that will tell you a lot about himself or herself, and you just can't un-hear what was said.

"That's what 'Fuck the IRS' does. It opens a window. If Patrick Flaherty were the person depicted by the defense – a brave and selfless woodsman who lives off the land, and never has the slightest reason to think of taxes or the tax collector – then it would be just about impossible for that person to have yelled 'Fuck the IRS' in a crowded bar. How do you never think about something or someone, but somehow you tell a crowd of people one night, 'Fuck them'?

"Well, you don't. There's a principle that's well known, I don't know, in college debating societies or somewhere – it was probably a big deal at the University of Pennsylvania -- called Occam's Razor. That principle says that if you're trying to explain a complex set of facts, the simplest explanation that accounts for all of the facts has got to be the right answer.

"So here you have a guy who barters for his livelihood, intentionally avoiding cash even where it would make his life easier. He will trade labor for things of value, but he's very selective about whom he'll deal with. He'll work for his church, in exchange for his living space and a lot of food, because he can try to disguise his labor as charitable work. He'll accept your building materials or animal feed if they're older inventory, and you can disguise the transfers of ownership as a write-off. He won't put a tip jar out at Cousin Clem's, obviously, because he doesn't want to be seen accepting money that he's not going to report on a tax return. But he'll accept a big meal and free beers.

"You look at all these facts, especially in light of 'Fuck the IRS,' and the simple explanation that ties them all together is obvious. The defendant was putting one over on all of us. He said to himself, 'I'm going to live a middle class sort of life, with all my friends at a bar that looks like 'Cheers.' And I'm going to eat food cooked by other people five nights a week. And I'm going to drive around in somebody else's truck with the radio on. And I'm going to hunt with other people's fancy hunting dogs. And, most important, I'm not going to pay a dime in taxes. I went to an Ivy League school, and I'm smarter than all of you, and I don't need to file tax returns. Taxes are for the little people.

"And where else do you see that attitude? I think you know what I'm going to say. When the defendant told a Wyoming forest ranger, who, like the rest of us, was just trying to make a living: 'You're a dick.' Why did he say that? Because he felt he was entitled to.

"And *that,* ladies and gentlemen, is why he said to Special Agent Bolton, 'I don't want to talk to an accountant about my tax situation.' He didn't want to talk to an accountant because he already knew he was cheating on his taxes. He didn't want to know the precise details. The government doesn't have to prove to you that he knew exactly which laws he was violating, as long as he was deliberately ignorant about those laws. That's what Judge Martin will explain to you, and I will leave that to him, very respectfully.

"The defendant didn't want to know which exact laws he was violating. But he certainly knew he was cheating on his taxes. He told Special Agent Bolton, 'I hope the IRS never finds me.'

"Finally, ladies and gentlemen, I want to address, head-on, that moment conjured up by defense counsel -- the 'used Honda' moment. It was dramatic, wasn't it? Ms. Boyle complains that the United States Government is making all this fuss about a thirty-three hundred dollar tax bill, and how ridiculous is that?

"Don't let the defense insult you like that. It's not the dollar amount, but the crime itself, that brings us here. We all say to each other, at one time or another, money isn't what's really important in life, and in this case, that expression actually applies. Imagine, if you will, that you could live in your home without a mortgage or a rental payment – just agree to look after it, and you can stay. Imagine that you could eat without paying cash for your food. Five nights a week, you eat meals that have been cooked for you by others . All the eggs and milk you could use, thanks to bags and bags of food for your chickens and goats. Game meat, a lot of it hunted with somebody else's fancy dogs. Your electricity is free, thanks to wind, solar and water, and you can pick through a friend's construction debris to upgrade your electrical system and weatherproof your home.

"And now imagine that you didn't have to pay a dime in taxes for all of that. What is all that worth? Just thirty-three hundred dollars? No. It's priceless, if you can get away with it. Just chuck all of the responsibilities you have as a citizen and a taxpayer. Travel roads your neighbors pay for. Hunt, fish and hike in the National Forest, right in your backyard, and other citizens will maintain it for you. Take advantage of the national defense that your neighbors provide with their taxes. Live the good life at your neighbors' expense. What would *that* be worth, if you were unprincipled enough to actually enjoy it? Thirty-three hundred dollars doesn't begin to describe it."

Farragut paused to collect his thoughts, and to let the jury collect theirs. He hoped he was combining the right doses of evidence and outrage, but he couldn't be sure. He wanted to come out of this miserable case with any kind of a conviction. That's all, just "guilty" on one count – it didn't matter which.

"Before I close, let me say a word about the indictment and your verdict sheet. The way it's organized, there are four business ventures unreported on Schedule C, based on bartering transactions that continued for five tax years apiece – a total of 20 charges. The four business ventures are: food for music; food and free rent for handyman work benefiting the Parish; building materials for driving; and animal feed for dog training; and each of those four ventures continued during five different tax years.

"The government contends that it has proved all 20 charges of tax evasion beyond a reasonable doubt. Beyond *any* reasonable doubt. But let me be candid with you. In any case where there are 20 charges, and of course 12 jurors, there may be some instances where some of you will say, 'the evidence on that charge just doesn't seem as convincing as on some of the others.' If that happens, it will still be your duty to agree on a verdict, if you can, on the other charges. If all of you are in agreement that the defendant is guilty of tax evasion beyond a reasonable doubt on even one charge, then, as Judge Martin will explain, you are still required to render a verdict of guilty on that single charge.

"Mr. Renfro and I want to thank you again for your close attention in this case. We are confident that you will reach a verdict that is fair and right. I am proud to practice law in Wyoming, in large part because we have jurors, like you, who take this process so seriously. We don't know what sacrifices you've had to make to participate as a juror in this case, but we know you've all made many. We want you to know: we do not take your service for granted."

Farragut returned to his seat, and the quiet in the courtroom was palpable. Dina cried softly.

"Ladies and gentlemen of the jury," said Judge Martin, "we will take a 15 minute break, after which I will give you my instructions on the law governing this case. Don't discuss the case among yourselves; we will see you in 15 minutes."

While the jury was out, Anita objected to "I'm smarter than all of you," and "Ivy League," and "Taxes are for the little people," on the basis that each was trying to demonize the defendant unfairly. She objected to "racist" and "cruel and demeaning" for the same reason. The judge ruled that each of the comments had been fair argument. Having ruled, he retired to his chambers for 15 minutes to tweak his jury instructions.

CHAPTER 93

Judge Martin turned toward the jury, with his reading glasses perched near the end of his nose. Every eye and ear in the jury box was on him.

His instructions began with some familiar points that the jurors had heard in the video welcoming them to jury service. They also echoed what Judge Martin had told them in the course of the trial. Jurors were the sole judges of the facts. They were obliged by their oaths to follow the instructions on the law that they would hear from the court. It was their job to determine the credibility of all witnesses, and they could believe or disbelieve any of the testimony they heard, even from expert witnesses. They could apply their common sense in deciding whether a witness was remembering something accurately. If the court had instructed them to disregard certain testimony, they were not to consider it in reaching their verdict.

The judge then turned to instructions that were unique to criminal cases. The prosecution had the burden of proof on every charge, and was obliged to prove the defendant's guilt beyond a reasonable doubt. The indictment was just an allegation – it had no value as evidence. The fact that there was a superseding indictment simply meant that the government had amended the original indictment, and the jurors did not need to concern themselves with how the indictment may have looked in its original form. The defendant had no obligation to testify or present evidence, and the jury was to draw no adverse inference from the fact that the defendant in this case chose to exercise that right. Police officers or federal agents bringing charges were neither more entitled than other witnesses to be believed, nor less; they were to be treated like any other witnesses.

After covering the basics about the jury's role, and the tools they should use to evaluate evidence, the judge turned to the elements of the offense charged: tax evasion. The parties had wrestled about what the court would say during pretrial motions and during trial, and had submitted written briefs arguing for their interpretations of the law governing the case. The court's instructions, finally, were its own. Judge Martin knew that virtually every criminal conviction resulting from a jury verdict is appealed by the unhappy defendant to a United States Court of Appeals. Almost all of those appeals claimed some error in the instructions given to the jury at the conclusion of the case. Judge Martin considered the input from counsel about what he should instruct the jury, but, in the end, his job was to get it right.

"Members of the jury," said the judge, "I'll turn now to the elements of the crimes with which the defendant has been charged. There are 20 counts in the Superseding Indictment, and each of those counts alleges a separate crime. Each count, however, has a common legal basis: each count alleges tax evasion.

"The defendant is charged under Section 7201 of Title 26 of the United States Code with evading the payment of federal income tax. To convict the defendant of tax evasion on any of the 20 counts, the government must prove each of the following three elements beyond a reasonable doubt:

- first, the existence of a tax deficiency, that is, the failure to pay tax that was due;
- second, an attempt by the defendant to evade or defeat tax; and,
- third, willfulness, that is, that the defendant's attempt to evade or defeat tax, if you find it to have occurred, was undertaken willfully.

I'll discuss each of these elements in more detail.

"Let me go back to the first element. As you are certainly aware from the evidence in this case, the parties spent a lot of time on the question of whether there was a tax deficiency at all. The government contends that the defendant was obliged to report income, and pay income tax, on the value of property, meals and accommodations that he allegedly received in exchange for labor.

"The government relies, first, on Section 1.61-2 of Title 26 of the Code of Federal Regulations, which provides, in relevant part, that if services are paid for in property, the fair market value of the property taken in payment must be included in income as compensation.

"The government also relies on Section 1.61-1 of Title 26 of the Code of Federal Regulations for the proposition that the defendant should have reported income for the value of free rent and meals that he allegedly received, and that he should have paid tax on that amount. In particular, Section 1.61-1 says that gross income means all income from whatever source derived, and income may be realized in the form of meals or accommodations.

"Now, you need to be aware that these regulations that I have just read you are not criminal laws, and the government could never convict the defendant of tax evasion just by showing that there was tax due under these regulations, and that the defendant failed to pay it. But to sustain or prove a charge of tax evasion, the government must *first* prove that there was tax due, and that is why I am calling your attention to these regulations.

"As you heard, the key language in these regulations, as applied to this case, is whether the defendant's services were '*paid for*' – the judge emphasized those two words – 'in property, meals, or accommodations.' To determine whether services were paid for in property, meals, or accommodations, you should consider all of the evidence presented by the parties, and all of the surrounding circumstances as reflected in that evidence, and you should apply your common sense in evaluating that evidence.

"Now I have some additional instructions about the second element of the charge of tax evasion: an attempt to evade or defeat tax. The government contends that the defendant attempted to evade or defeat tax in two respects. First, says the government, the defendant decided not to file tax returns. Second, says the government, the defendant structured certain transactions as bartering transactions to avoid discovery of the fact that he was not reporting income. The defendant denies that any of his conduct was undertaken in an attempt to evade or defeat tax.

"The third element that the government must prove to sustain a charge of tax evasion is willfulness. Willfulness is defined in federal law as a state of mind which is intentional, conscious and directed toward achieving a purpose.

"In this case, the defendant has raised, as a defense, a claim that he was ignorant of the tax laws that the government claims he evaded, and that he therefore could not have acted willfully. I instruct you, as a matter of law, that the government has neither proved, nor attempted to prove, that the defendant was aware that property he may have received in exchange for services was taxable income.

"But, in this case, that isn't the end of the inquiry, because the defense of ignorance of the law is not available if the government proves, beyond a reasonable doubt, that the defendant was deliberately ignorant of his obligations under the tax laws. If you find, beyond a reasonable doubt, that the defendant deliberately closed his eyes to facts that he would have discovered if he had tried to do so, with a conscious purpose to avoid enlightenment, then the defendant cannot rely on ignorance of the law as a defense. Stated another way, a defendant's knowledge of a fact may be inferred from willful blindness to the existence of that fact.

"If you find, beyond a reasonable doubt, that the defendant was deliberately ignorant of his obligations under the tax laws, then ignorance of the law is no excuse. And then you're back to the question of whether the defendant's attempt to avoid or evade tax, if any, was otherwise willful. You may consider all of the evidence in the case, including any statements that you may have found the defendant to have made, in deciding that question.

"I should note, here, that if an act is done negligently, or unintentionally, it cannot be willful. Also, if property is received as a gift, that property is not taxable income for the recipient." The judge was inserting points for charge that Anita had requested on behalf of the defense.

"I remind you," Judge Martin continued, "that you must find each of the three elements of the crime to find the defendant guilty of tax evasion. If you were to find, for example, that the defendant acted with willfulness, but you also find that there was no tax deficiency, then you must find the defendant not guilty. Or if you find that there was a tax deficiency, and an attempt to evade or avoid tax, but no willfulness, then, again, you must find the defendant not guilty. It is the government's burden to prove each of the three elements of the crime of tax evasion beyond a reasonable doubt.

"You will be considering 20 different charges of tax evasion. Your verdict must be unanimous – all 12 of you must agree on a verdict on each separate charge. And the requirement of unanimity applies both ways – you must be unanimous in finding the defendant guilty or not guilty of each charge. We understand that we are giving you a lot of work to do. But your job is to deliberate in good faith until you reach a unanimous verdict, guilty or not guilty, on each of the 20 charges.

"We will send a verdict sheet out with you to guide your deliberations, and to record your verdicts on the charges. You'll see that the charges relate to the four business ventures in which the defendant was allegedly involved – handyman, driver, musician, and dog trainer – over five separate years. Four times five equals 20, which is the number of crimes charged. You'll need to decide, separately, whether the defendant was engaged in each of the four business ventures, and if so, in which of the five years at issue. We'll also let you have a copy of the Superseding Indictment, but remember, the indictment is just a series of charges, it isn't evidence. You should elect a foreperson, whose job it will be to record the votes on the various charges, and, when you advise us of your decisions, we will record your verdict on each charge separately.

"Having said that, I have found over the years in these complex cases that juries occasionally reach the same verdict for all of the charges, either guilty or not guilty. If, for whatever reason, that happens to be the case here, when we ask you for your verdict on Count 1, you are permitted to let us know right away that you have found the defendant guilty on all counts, or not guilty on all counts. Similarly, if you were to find the defendant guilty on a few counts, but not all, you can tell us the numbers of the counts on which you have found the defendant guilty. We will follow up from there with appropriate questions for you about your verdicts on those counts, and on the other counts.

"If your verdict is guilty on any count, you may be polled individually, one at a time and in open court, to ensure that each of you concurs in the verdict. We won't know about that until it happens, but I wanted to let you know about that possibility.

"You are now ready to deliberate and to reach a verdict. Remember that you may only find the defendant guilty on a charge if you conclude, unanimously, that he is guilty of that charge beyond a reasonable doubt. If you conclude, unanimously, that there is reasonable doubt of the defendant's guilt on any charge, then you must find the defendant not guilty on that charge.

Judge Martin took off his reading glasses and turned toward the lawyers out front. "I'll see counsel at sidebar."

There began a long process – probably 15 minutes – during which Anita objected to parts of the charge to preserve her arguments for any potential appeal. The jury remained in the jury box. In particular, Anita objected to the "deliberate ignorance" instructions, arguing that the Tenth Circuit's decision in *United States vs, Fingado*, even though it had never been overruled, was inconsistent with the Supreme Court's decision in *Cheek vs. United States*. Judge Martin noted the objection, but Anita knew that, as a district court judge in the Tenth Circuit, Judge Martin was bound by decisions of the Tenth Circuit Court of Appeals, whether he agreed with them or not. While the argument among counsel was lengthy and she thought she made some good points, her objection was overruled. She also objected to the judge's having emphasized to the jurors that they could consider the defendant's "statements" – he was clearly referring to 'Fuck the IRS' -- in connection with their determination of willfulness. Judge Martin declined to modify the instruction on Patrick's behalf.

With all objections now of record, the judge turned back to the jury. "At this point, I will excuse the two alternate jurors, Jurors 13 and 14. As you know, the jury deliberates with only 12 members, which is a rule and a tradition which goes all the way back to English law. I want to thank the two of you for your service. We greatly appreciate it. Please leave your contact information with the Marshal, that's Marshal Engstrom in the back of the courtroom. Sometimes, if one of the first 12 jurors falls ill or has another sort of problem, we will ask an alternate juror to step in. Both sides, prosecution and defense, have to agree to taking that step, but it sometimes happens. And if so, the deliberations would start again from the beginning, and you would deliberate to verdict."

Judge Martin waited while the alternates left through the rear door of the courtroom, and then he turned to the remaining 12 jurors. "Ladies and gentlemen of the jury, you will now begin your deliberations in your jury room. Marshal Engstrom will take your lunch orders, and we will bring you lunch at about noon or 12:30. You can deliberate through lunch or take a break while you're eating. That will be up to you. Please agree on all counts before you let the Marshal know that you've reached a verdict on any particular count. When you have reached a verdict on all counts, whether today or tomorrow or whenever, let the Marshal know, and we'll take it from there."

The jurors stood and began to file out, using the door to the left of the jury box. When they were gone, and the door closed, Judge Martin said, "Counsel, don't go too far away. If the jury has questions, we'll need you to come back ASAP. If you leave the building, make sure my Deputy Clerk has your cell number."

With that, the waiting began. Patrick had been told to bring his toothbrush, in case the verdict was guilty. If so, he would be heading to jail directly from the courtroom. Release pending appeal, if any, would be days or weeks away. He patted his jacket pocket and felt the toothbrush still there.

CHAPTER 94

Patrick had mostly lost his appetite. Anita tried to take a sandwich order, but Patrick couldn't think of any sandwich he might want. They were in the Attorneys' Conference Room off of the main hallway outside the courtroom.

Ed and Dina were taking a short walk outside. Annabelle was making some calls to parents of her patients. At Anita's urging, most of the people from Coolidge who were able to stay in Casper were headquartered in one of the rooms they had rented at the Courtyard, on the east side of town. Anita knew that Patrick needed a break from people – it's hard to make small talk when you're scared – and she had promised them she would call over to the hotel if there were a verdict. You always had at least a half hour between the notification that there was a verdict, and the point at which the judge, his staff, the lawyers, the defendant, the press, and all of the spectators were gathered back in the courtroom to hear it.

There was a knock on the door. Patrick got up and opened it. When he saw the face and the uniform, it took a minute for him to put the two together. Alice Harmon, Wyoming Game and Fish Department.

"Patrick," she began, "I know this is a difficult time for you, but I was in touch with the WGFD unit that's been helping up at your cabin with the Ag Department people, and they all suggested that I reach out to you here. I'm thinking that good news never comes at a bad time, and since there's no verdict yet, I thought 'why not?'"

Patrick gave her a quizzical look. "OK."

"Why I'm here – we found your bear. He was roaming about a mile from your place, on the other side of the stream. He was huge, for Wyoming, almost

450 pounds. We darted him, we tagged him, we matched his paws to the prints we took at your place, and we transported him out past Burgess Junction in the Bighorns. He won't be coming back."

Patrick's grin was so wide it almost hurt. He had carried so much tension around because of that damned bear, for so long, that it felt like Christmas morning. "I'm really happy you came to tell me. This really helps right now. I don't know what to say."

"You don't need to say anything," she said. "We're all praying for you in our office. Just beat this, somehow." She offered her hand, shook his, and told him that she'd keep him updated on his bear. "I know I gave you my card a while ago, but here's another one. Call me if you have any questions."

As she turned and walked down the hallway, Patrick knew he'd call her. The question was whether he'd be calling her in three days, or three years.

The jury deliberations continued all afternoon. It was Friday, a fact of which Patrick was vaguely aware. At 4:00, the judge called everyone back into the courtroom, including the jury. He inquired whether they felt they were making progress, and whether they preferred to deliberate on Saturday, or take a break until Monday. They retired to their jury room for a minute, talked it over, and came back to advise the court that they were making progress, and that they'd like to come back on Saturday.

Ed, Dina, Annabelle, Anita and Patrick watched two movies that night from the hotel cable box before they turned in. Patrick didn't sleep well. When the alarm went off in the morning, he tried to remember the films they had watched the night before, and he couldn't.

Everyone made his or her way downstairs for breakfast. A breaker had tripped in the breakfast area, and the hot breakfast buffet was mostly cold. Patrick hoped that wasn't an omen. Friends from Coolidge stopped at their table, and clapped Patrick on the shoulder. They filed out to the lobby and, like everyone else in the hotel, started passing time on their phones.

Because it was Saturday, the courthouse was quiet when they got there at 8:45. The security line was quick and painless. Anita, Patrick and Patrick's family went back to the Attorneys' Conference Room to wait. At 10:55, there was a knock on the door, and Marshal Engstrom poked his head in. "We have a verdict," he said. Patrick felt like he wanted to throw up.

CHAPTER 95

"Ladies and gentlemen of the jury," Judge Martin began, "we understand that you have reached a verdict."

"Yes, Your Honor," replied Juror No. 1, the foreperson. She was the social worker.

"The Deputy Clerk will take the verdict," instructed the judge.

As the Deputy Clerk rose from her chair in front of the judge's bench, she opened a notebook and faced the jury box. The court reporter was poised to record the next words to be said. Patrick's heart was beating so hard it made him short of breath. He felt the toothbrush in his left breast pocket moving with his heartbeat.

"Ladies and gentlemen of the jury, please rise," instructed the Deputy Clerk. All 12 jurors rose and faced her. "The defendant will rise and face the jury." Patrick complied.

"In the matter of *United States of America versus Patrick Michael Flaherty*, what is your verdict on Count I of the Superseding Indictment?"

The foreperson looked up from the verdict sheet in her hands. "We find the defendant not guilty on all charges."

CHAPTER 96

Tania Teagarden taped her report on the verdict, with the front entrance of the courthouse as her backdrop. She asked the new IT guy to skylink it, and then called Toni Aldridge on her cell. Her boss answered on the second ring: "This is Toni."

"Toni, it's Tania. We have a verdict in the militia case out here in Wyoming, the tax evasion charges," Teagarden began. "I just taped a report, and you should have it in the skylink box."

"Cool," said Aldridge. "What'd the jury do?"

"They found him not guilty on all counts. Hard to believe. There weren't very many of us who were expecting it, and I was . . ."

"Did the U.S. Attorney make a statement?" asked the producer.

"No, they boogied home, I think. It's Saturday. Do you want me to tape another report with a script, or do you want to think about it? When do you think you'll air the piece with the not guilty?"

Aldridge thought for a second. "We're jammed tonight. There's just too much happening, with the thing in Berlin. I don't think the evening producers are going to want to spend any time on this story, and I don't want to use up any chits arguing for it. Send me a written blurb, maybe a hundred words, and I'll drop it into the 'Law and the Courts' section of the website." She added, "Travel safe," and hung up the call.

Tania Teagarden was a little disappointed, but it was hardly the first time she'd filmed a piece that wasn't going to make it onto the air. She closed her notebook, and opened her Starbucks app, in anticipation. She found her guys, and they headed toward the truck. She had a satellite modem, and she'd send the blurb from her laptop on the way back to Denver.

CHAPTER 97

Arnold Renfro made some calls to Washington. He had a few numbers in his phone, and finally reached Kevin Paulson, Deputy Attorney General for Criminal Tax Enforcement. Mr. Paulson was buying tomato vines at the garden center in Silver Spring.

"Kevin, it's Arnie Renfro. We have a verdict in our bartering case in Wyoming."

"Good news, I hope," said Paulson.

"Well, no. The jury found him not guilty."

Paulson blew out a breath. "That really sucks, Arnie. You told us at least three times this was going to be a guilty verdict, and everybody here believed you."

"There's nothing we could have done. I think the jurors out here all hate the government. They would have acquitted Ted Bundy, just to spite us."

"Suffice it to say, Arnie, you weren't telling us that yesterday. Did you talk to the jurors to find out why they voted the way they did?"

"No. The local AUSA just started packing his briefcase, and I followed his lead. Not my fault. The courtroom emptied pretty quickly."

"Well, look, come back and we'll triage the fallout. I'll explain to the AG that this was never about whether or not he was guilty. We wanted to send a message, and who knows, maybe a few people heard it. But we have more important things to worry about. Turn the page."

CHAPTER 98

Patrick hugged his parents, and said goodbye. They needed to check out of their hotel, and they wanted to reach out to their house-sitter. They were going to make their way to Coolidge separately. And, in all events, Patrick didn't want his lawyer to have to drive back to Coolidge alone.

He hugged and kissed his sister, and she smiled and cried. She was going to try to find a flight back to Denver, and then Chicago, but she'd call around and find him when she got home.

Patrick and Anita went back to the conference room to collect their trial bags. They piled them onto the carry-cart. Patrick collected his notes and his copies of documents. After the papers were all put away, he crossed the room to Anita and hugged her hard, for a long time. He couldn't say anything. Finally, he said, "Do you mind if I use your phone to call the people looking after my animals, let them know when we'll be getting to Coolidge?"

She handed him the phone. As he found the number on a paper in his pocket, and as his call was making it through cell towers, Patrick said to Anita, "A year from now, this will all be just a bad memory."

"No, you're wrong," she said. "This will be a great memory." She smiled. "Can we get to Cousin Clem's in time for Saturday Happy Hour?"

THE END

ABOUT THE AUTHOR

Richard G. Tuttle lives and writes in Philadelphia, Pennsylvania. *Wyoming* is his first novel.